The Drama Onstage Was Impossibly Romantic. . . . The Romance in the Audience Was Simply Impossible.

Catherine Cumfrit had a funny little coo of a voice, and she was altogether a bit more rounded than was fashionable, but still very pretty. Of course, Christopher had only seen her in the dimmed lights of the theater where they met, and she laughed at his eager pursuit of her. She laughed a great deal around Christopher, and even though widowhood had reduced her to a London flat, one servant, and just five hundred pounds a year, she was suddenly feeling very young indeed. . . .

Christopher Monckton thought Catherine had a perfect three-cornered face, like a kitten or a pansy. He believed she was somewhat older than he, but nothing at all to matter. A great, loosely built young man with flame-colored hair, only three years out of Balliol, he had never really been in love. Age, he insisted, was a foolish barrier to romance, and he was determined to win Catherine's heart. . . .

Rev. Stephen Colquhoun looked regrettably avian with his hawk-like nose, and he had never been a good preacher until he wed Catherine's daughter, Virginia. Now his sermons on "love" were deemed inspirational. He never let anyone forget that he was happily married and the master of Chickover, the Cumfrit mansion. Older than his mother-in-law, he found that taking a young bride had the most salutary effects on a man. . . .

Virginia Colquhoun believed that one should give up everything to follow love. Naturally, she meant the right love, like the one she had with Stephen. Tucked away in their country estate, Virginia enjoyed, she was sure, complete and private bliss. Public displays of affection were so unseemly. And now she was perplexed by how youthful her mother looked . . . and what she could possibly be doing with that alarming, red-haired boy. . . .

Books by Elizabeth von Arnim

The Enchanted April
Love
Vera

Available from WASHINGTON SQUARE PRESS

LOVE

ELIZABETH von ARNIM

With an Afterword by
Terence de Vere White

WASHINGTON SQUARE PRESS
PUBLISHED BY POCKET BOOKS
New York   London   Toronto   Sydney   Tokyo   Singapore

A Washington Square Press Publication of
POCKET BOOKS, a division of Simon & Schuster Inc.
1230 Avenue of the Americas, New York, NY 10020

Copyright 1925 by Elizabeth von Arnim
Afterword copyright © 1988 by Terence de Vere White

Published by arrangement with Virago Press Limited

ISBN: 0-671-88392-5

First Washington Square Press trade paperback printing
November 1995

10 9 8 7 6 5 4 3 2 1

WASHINGTON SQUARE PRESS and colophon are
registered trademarks of Simon & Schuster Inc.

Cover design and art by Marc Burckhardt

Printed in the U.S.A.

∾ PART I ∾

✑ I ✑

The first time they met, though they didn't know it, for they were unconscious of each other, was at *The Immortal Hour,* then playing to almost empty houses away at King's Cross; but they both went so often, and the audience at that time was so conspicuous because there was so little of it and so much room to put it in, that quite soon people who went frequently got to know each other by sight, and felt friendly and inclined to nod and smile, and this happened too to Christopher and Catherine.

She first became aware of him on the evening of her fifth visit, when she heard two people talking just behind her before the curtain went up, and one said, sounding proud, "This is my eleventh time"; and the other answered carelessly, "This is my thirty-secondth"—upon which the first one exclaimed, "Oh, I *say!*" with much the sound of a pricked balloon wailing itself flat, and she couldn't resist turning her face, lit up with interest and amusement, to look. Thus she saw Christopher consciously for the first time, and he saw her.

After that they noticed each other's presence for three more performances, and then, when it was her ninth and his thirty-sixth—for the enthusiasts of *The Immortal Hour* kept jealous count of their visits—and they found themselves sitting in the same row with only twelve empty seats between them, he moved up six nearer to her when the curtain went down between the two scenes of the first act, and when it went down at the end of the first act, after that love scene which invariably roused the small band of the faithful to a kind of mystic frenzy of delight, he moved up the other six and sat down boldly beside her.

She smiled at him, a friendly and welcoming smile.

"It's so beautiful," he said apologetically, as if this explained his coming over to her.

"Perfectly beautiful," she said; and added, "This is my ninth time."

And he said, "This is my thirty-sixth."

3

And she said, "I know."

And he said, "How do you know?"

And she said, "Because I heard you tell some one when it was your thirty-secondth, and I've been counting since."

So they made friends, and Christopher thought he had never seen anybody with such a sweet way of smiling, or heard anybody with such a funny little coo of a voice.

She was little altogether; a little thing, in a little hat which she never had to take off because hardly ever was there anybody behind her, and, anyhow, even in a big hat she was not of the size that obstructs views. Always the same hat; never a different one, or different clothes. Although the clothes were pretty, very pretty, he somehow felt, perhaps because they were never different, that she wasn't very well off; and he also somehow felt she was older than he was—just a little older, nothing at all to matter; and presently he began somehow also to feel that she was married.

The night he got this feeling he was surprised how much he disliked it. What was happening to him? Was he falling in love? And he didn't even know her name. It was the night of her fourteenth visit and his forty-eighth—for since they had made friends he went oftener than ever in the hope of seeing her, and the very programme young women looked at him as though they had known him all their lives—that this cold feeling first filtered into his warm and comfortable heart, and nipped its comfort; and it wasn't that he had seen a wedding ring, for she never took off her absurd, small gloves—it was something indescribably not a girl about her.

He tried to pin it down into words, but he couldn't; it remained indescribable. And whether it had to do with the lines of her figure, which were rounder than most girls' figures in these flat days, or with the things she said, for the life of him he couldn't tell. Perhaps it was her composure, her air of settled safety, of being able to make friends with any number of strange young men, pick them up and leave them, exactly when and how she chose.

Still, it might not be true. She was always alone. Sooner or later, if there were husbands they appeared. No husband of a wife so sweet would let her come out at night like this by herself, he thought. Yes, he probably was mistaken. He didn't know much about women. Up to this he had only had highly

4

unsatisfactory, rough and tumble relations with them, and he couldn't compare. And though he and she had now sat together several times, they had talked entirely about *The Immortal Hour*—they were both so very enthusiastic—and its music, and its singers, and Celtic legends generally, and at the end she always smiled the smile that enchanted him, and nodded and slipped away, so that they had never really got any further than the first night.

"Look here," he said, or rather blurted, the next time he saw her there—he now went as a matter of course to sit next to her—"you might tell me your name. Mine's Monckton. Christopher Monckton."

"But of course," she said. "Mine is Cumfrit."

Cumfrit? He thought it a funny little name; but somehow like her.

"Just"—he held his breath—"Cumfrit?"

She laughed. "Oh, there's Catherine as well," she said.

"I like that. It's pretty. They're sweet and pretty, said together. They're—well, extraordinarily like you."

She laughed again. "But they're not both like me," she said. "I owe the Cumfrit part to George."

"To George?" he faltered.

"He provided the Cumfrit. All I did was the Catherine bit."

"Then—you're married?"

"Isn't everybody?"

"Good God, no," he cried. "It's a disgusting thing to be. It's hateful. It's ridiculous. Tying oneself up to somebody for good and all. Everybody! I should think not. *I'm* not."

"Oh, but you're too young," she said, amused.

"Too young? And what about you?"

She looked at him quickly, a doubt on her face; but the doubt changed to real surprise when she saw how completely he had meant it. She had a three-cornered face, like a pansy, like a kitten, he thought. He wanted to stroke her. He was sure she was exquisitely smooth and soft. And now there was George.

"Does he—does your husband not like music?" he asked, saying the first thing that came into his head, not really wanting in the least to know what that damned George liked or didn't like.

She hesitated. "I—don't know," she said. "He—usedn't to."

5

"But he doesn't come here?"

"How can he?" She stopped, and then said softly, "The poor darling's dead."

His heart gave a bound. A widow. The beastly war had done one good thing, then—it had removed George.

"I say, I'm most frightfully sorry," he exclaimed with immense earnestness, and trying to look solemn.

"Oh, it's a long while ago," she said, bowing her head a little at the remembrance.

"It can't be so very long ago."

"Why can't it?"

"Because you haven't had time."

She again looked quickly at him, and again saw nothing but sincerity. Then she was silent a moment. She was thinking, "This is rather sweet"—and the ghost of a wistful little smile passed across her face. How old was he? Twenty-five or six; not more, she was sure. What a charming thing youth was—so headlong, so generous and whole-hearted in its admirations and beliefs. He was a great, loosely built young man, with flame-coloured hair, and freckles, and bony red wrists that came a long way out of his sleeves when he sat supporting his head in his hands during the love scene, clutching it tighter and tighter as there was more and more of love. He had deep-set eyes, and a beautifully shaped broad forehead, and a wide, kindly mouth, and he radiated youth, and the discontents and quick angers and quicker appreciations of youth.

She suppressed a small sigh, and laughed as she said, "You've only seen me at night. Wait till you see me in broad daylight."

"Am I ever to be allowed to?" he asked eagerly.

"Don't you ever come to the *matinées?*"

She knew he didn't.

"Oh—*matinées*. No, of course I can't come to *matinées*. I have to grind all the week in my beastly office, and on Saturdays I go and play golf with an uncle who is supposed to be going to leave me all his money."

"You should cherish him."

"I do. And I haven't minded till now. But it's an infernal tie-up directly one wants to do anything else."

He looked at her ruefully. Then his face lit up. "Sundays," he said eagerly. "Sundays I'm free. He's religious, and won't play on Sundays. Couldn't I—?"

6

"There aren't any *matinées* on Sunday," she said.

"No but couldn't I come and see you? Come and call?"

"Hush," she said, lifting her hand as the music of the second act began.

And at the end this time too, before he could say a word, while he was still struggling with his coat, she slipped away as usual after nodding good night.

The next time, however, he was more determined, and began at once. It seemed to him that he had been thinking of her without stopping, and it was absurd not to know anything at all about a person one thinks of as much as that, except her name and that her husband was dead. It was of course a great stride from blank knowing nothing; and that her husband should be dead was such a relief to him that he couldn't help thinking he must be falling in love. All husbands should be dead, he considered—nuisances, complicators. What would have happened if George had been alive? Why, he simply would have lost her, had to give up at once—before, almost, beginning. And he was so lonely, and she was—well, what wasn't she? She was so like what he had been dreaming of for years—a little ball of sweetness, and warmth, and comfort, and reassurance and love.

The next time she came, then, the minute she appeared he went over to where she sat and began. He was going to ask her straight out if he might come and see her, fix that up, get her address; but she chanced to be late that night, and hardly had he opened his mouth when the lights were lowered and she put up her hand and said "Hush."

It was no use trying to say what he wanted to say in a whisper, because the faithful, though few, were fierce, and would tolerate nothing but total silence. Also he was much afraid she herself preferred the music to anything he might have to say.

He sat with his arms folded and waited. He had to wait till the very end of the act, because though he tried again when the curtain went down between its two scenes, and only the orchestra was playing, he was shoo'd quiet at once by the outraged faithful.

She, too, said, putting up her hand, "Oh, hush."

He began to feel slightly off *The Immortal Hour.* But at last the whole act was over and the lights were up again. She turned her flushed face to him, the music still shining in her eyes. She was always flushed and her eyes always shone at the

7

end of the love scene; nor could he ever see that lovely headlong embrace of the lovers without feeling extraordinarily stirred up. God, to be embraced like that. . . . He was starving for love.

"Isn't it marvellous," she breathed.

"Are you ever going to let me come and see you?" he asked, without losing another second.

She looked at him a moment, collecting her thoughts, a little surprised. "Of course," she then said. "Do. Though—" She stopped.

"Go on," he said.

"I was going to say, Don't you see me as it is?"

"But what is this?"

"Well, it's two or three times every week," she said.

"Yes, but what is it? Just a casual picking up. You come—you happen to come—and then you disappear. At any time you might happen *not* to come, and then—"

"Why then," she finished for him as he paused, "you'd have all this beautiful stuff to yourself. I don't think they ever did that last bit *more* wonderfully, do you?" And off she went again, cooing on as usual about *The Immortal Hour,* and he hadn't a chance to get in another word before the confounded music began again and the faithful with one accord called out "Sh—sh."

Enthusiasm, thought Christopher, should have its bounds. He forgot that, to begin with, his enthusiasm had far outdone hers. He folded his arms once more, a sign with him of determined and grim patience, and when it was over and she bade him her smiling good night and hurried off without any more words, he lost no time bothering about putting on his coat but simply seized it and went after her.

It was difficult to keep her in sight. She could slip through gaps he couldn't, and he very nearly lost her at the turn of the stairs. He caught her up, however, on the steps outside, just as she was about to plunge out into the rain, and laid his hand on her arm.

She looked round surprised. In the glare of the peculiarly searching light theatres turn on to their departing and arriving patrons he was struck by the fatigue on her face. The music was too much for her—she looked worn out.

"Look here," he said, "don't run away like this. It's pouring. You wait here and I'll get you a taxi."

"Oh, but I always go by tube," she said, clutching at him a moment as some people pushing past threw her against him.

"You can't go by tube to-night. Not in this rain. And you look frightfully tired."

She glanced up at him oddly and laughed a little. "Do I?" she said. "Well, I'm not. Not a bit tired. And I can quite well go by tube. It's quite close."

"You can't do anything of the sort. Stand here out of the rain while I get a taxi." And off he ran.

For a moment she was on the verge of running off herself, going to the tube as usual and getting home her own way, for why should she be forced into an expensive taxi? Then she thought: "No—it would be low of me, simply low. I must try and behave like a little gentleman—" and waited.

"Where shall I tell him to go to?" asked Christopher, having got his taxi and put her inside it and simply not had the courage to declare it was his duty to see her safely home.

She told him the address—90A Hertford Street—and he wondered a moment why, living in such a street with the very air of Park Lane wafted down it from just round the corner, she should not only not have a car but want to go in tubes.

"Can I give you a lift?" she asked, leaning forward at the last moment.

He was in the taxi in a flash. "I was so hoping you'd say that," he said, pulling the door to with such vigour that a shower of raindrops jerked off the top of the window-frame on to her dress.

These he had to wipe off, which he did with immense care, and a handkerchief that deplorably was not one of his new ones. She sat passive while he did it, going over the evening's performance, pointing out, describing, reminding, and he, as he dried, told himself definitely that he had had enough of *The Immortal Hour*. She must stop, she must stop. He must talk to her, must find out more about her. He was burning to know more about her before the infernally fast taxi arrived at her home. And she would do nothing, as they bumped furiously along, but quote and ecstasise.

That was a good word, he thought, as it came into his head; and he was so much pleased with it that he said it out loud. "I wish you wouldn't *ecstasise*," he said. "Not now. Not for the next few minutes."

"Ecstasise?" she repeated, wondering.

"Aren't your shoes wet? Crossing that soaking pavement? I'm sure they must be wet—"

And he reached down and began to wipe their soles too with his handkerchief.

She watched him a little surprised, but still passive. This was what it was to be young. One squandered a beautiful clean handkerchief on a woman's dirty shoes without thinking twice. She observed the thickness of his hair as he bent over her shoes. She had forgotten how thick the hair of the young could be, having now for so long only contemplated heads that were elderly.

To him in the half darkness of the taxi she looked really exactly like the dream, the warm, round, cosy, delicious dream lonely devils like himself were always dreaming, forlornly hugging their pillows. And as for her feet—he abruptly left off drying them. The next thing he felt he would be doing would be kneeling down and kissing them, and he was afraid she mightn't like that, and be angry with him, and never let him see her again.

"You've spoilt your handkerchief," she remarked, as he put it, all muddy, into his pocket.

"I don't look at it like that," he said, staring straight out of the front windows, and sitting up very stiff and away in his corner because he didn't trust himself, and was mortally afraid of not behaving.

It was now quite evident to Christopher that he was in love, deeply in love. He felt very happy about it, because for the first time he was, as he put it, in love properly. All the other times had been so odious, leaving him making such wry faces. And he had longed and longed to be in love—properly, with somebody intelligent and educated as well as adorable. These three: but the greatest of these was the being adorable.

Out of the corners of his eyes he stole a glance at her. She didn't look tired any more. What ideal things these dark taxis were, if only the other person happened to be in love as well. Would she ever be? Would she ever be again, or was all that buried with that scoundrel George? She had been fond of George; she had called him poor darling; but then one easily called the dead poor darlings, and grew fond of them in proportion as the time grew long since they had left off being alive and obstructive.

"Where do you want me to drop you?" she asked.

"We've passed it," he said. "At least, he hasn't gone

anywhere near it. I live in Wyndham Place. I'll see you safely home and then take him on."

"It's very kind of you," she said, "but you'll have to let me pay my share."

"And I say," he went on quickly, waving whatever she was doing with her purse impatiently aside, for by now they were careering across Berkeley Square and he knew the time was short, "you haven't said if I may come and see you. I would like so frightfully to come and see you. There are such a lot of things I want to say—I mean, hear you say. And we do nothing but talk about that infernal *Immortal Hour.*"

"What? Why, I thought you loved it."

"Of course I love it, but it isn't everything. And we've given it a fairly good innings, haven't we. Do let me come and see you. I shall"—he was going to say "die if you don't," but he was afraid that might put her off, though he'd be hanged, he said to himself, if it wasn't very likely perfectly true, so he quickly substituted "I shall be in London all next Sunday."

They were at the bottom of Hertford Street. They were rushing along it. Even while he was speaking they were there at 90A. With a grinding of the brakes the taxi pulled up—a violent taxi, the most violent he had ever met; and he might just as easily have had the luck to get one of those slow, cautious ancient ones, driven by bearded patriarchs who always came to his call when he had to catch a train or was late for a dinner, and always at every cross street drew back with an old-world courtesy and encouraged even horse-traffic to pass along first.

"May I come next Sunday?" he asked, obliged to lean across her and open the door, because she was preparing, as he didn't move and merely sat there, to open it herself. "No—don't get out," he said quickly, as she showed signs of going to. "It's no use standing in the wet. Wait here while I go and ring—"

"But look—I have a latchkey," she said. "Besides, the night porter is there."

The night porter was; and hearing a taxi stop he opened the door at that moment.

"And about Sunday?" asked Christopher, with a desperate persistence, as he helped her out.

"Yes—do come and see me," she said, smiling up at him her friendly, her adorable smile; and his spirits leapt up to heaven. "Only not this Sunday," she added; and his spirits banged down to earth.

"Why not this Sunday?" he asked. "I shall be free the whole day."

"Yes, but I won't," she said, laughing, for he amused her. "At least, I feel sure there is something—"

She knitted her brows, trying to remember. "Oh yes," she said, "Stephen. I've promised to go out with him."

"Stephen?"

His heart stood still. George was settled, completely, felicitously, and now here was Stephen.

Then, just as the door was going to shut on her, leaving him out there alone, a warm and comforting light flooded his understanding: Stephen was her son; her little son, her only little son. Hateful as it was to reflect upon—really marriage was most horrible—George had perpetuated himself, and this delicate small thing, this exquisite soft little creature, had been the vehicle for his idiotic wish to carry on his silly name.

"I suppose," he said, detaining her, his hat still in his hand, the rain falling on his bare head, the porter holding the door open and looking on, "you're taking him to the Zoo?"

He could think of no place so likely as the Zoo on Sunday for Stephen, and to the Zoo he also would go, and have a look at those jolly little monkeys again.

"The Zoo?" she repeated, puzzled.

Then she began to laugh. "I wonder," she said, her face brimming over with laughter, "why you think Stephen wants to be taken to the Zoo. Poor darling"—another poor darling, and this time a live one—"why, he's as old as I am."

As old as she was. Stephen.

She waved her hand. "Come some other Sunday," she called out as the door shut.

He stood for a moment staring at it. Then he turned away slowly, putting his hat on as he went down the steps, and he was walking away through the rain lost in the most painful thought, mechanically heading for home, when the taxi-driver, realising with amazed indignation what his fare was doing, jerked him back to his obligations by vigorously and rudely shouting "Hi!"

◈ II ◈

Ten days to wait till the Sunday after. It was only Friday night. He would see her in between, of course, at *The Immortal Hour,* and might perhaps manage to take her home again, but would he be able in these snippets of time, these snatches, these beginnings interrupted by the curtain going up or the lights going down, to find out from her who and what was Stephen? It was intolerable to have at last come across her and instantly to find oneself up against Stephen.

Dismal were his conjectures as he was rattled home by the taxi so lately made sweet by her presence. Stephen couldn't be her brother, for nobody made appointments ahead and carried them out so conscientiously with brothers; and he couldn't be her uncle or her nephew, the only two remaining satisfactory relationships, because she had said he was as old as she was. Who, then, and what was Stephen?

A faint hope flickered for an instant in the darkness of his mind: sometimes uncles were young; sometimes nephews were old. But the thing was too feeble to give warmth, and almost immediately went out. All Stephens should be stoned, he thought. It was what was done with the first one he had ever heard of; pity the practice hadn't been kept up. How happy he now would have been except for Stephen. How happy, going to see her the next Sunday but one, going really to see her and sit down squarely with her by himself in a quiet room and look at her frontways instead of for ever only sideways, and she without the hat that extinguished such a lot of what anyhow was such a little. He might even, he thought, after a bit, after they had got really natural with each other—and he felt he could be more natural with her, more happily himself than with any one he had ever met—he might even after a bit have sat on the floor at her feet, as near as possible to her little shoes. And then he would have told her all about everything. God, how he wanted to tell somebody all about everything—somebody who understood. There wasn't anybody *really* for understanding except a woman. It didn't need brains to

13

understand; it didn't need learning, and a grind of education and logic and scientific detachment, and all the confounded rig-out Lewes, who shared his rooms with him, had. Such things were all right as part of a whole, and were more important, he was ready to admit, than any other part of it if one *had* the whole; but a man starved if that was all—just starved. Life without a woman in it, a woman of one's own, was intolerable.

His face as he opened the door with his latchkey was gloomy. Lewes would be sitting in there; Lewes with his brains. Brains, brains. . . .

Christopher had no mother or sister, and as long as he could remember seemed to have been by himself with males— uncles who brought him up, clerics who prepared him for school, again uncles with whom he played golf and spent the festivals of the year, Christmas, Easter, and Whitsuntide; and here in his rooms Lewes was waiting, always Lewes, making profound and idiotic comments on everything, and wanting to sit up half the night and reason. Reason! He was sick of reason. He wanted some one he could be romantic with, and sentimental with, and poetic, and—yes, religious with, if he felt like it, without having to feel ashamed. And how extraordinarily he wanted to touch—to touch lovely soft surfaces, to feel, to be warm and close up. He had had enough of this sterile, starved life with Lewes. Three years of it he had had, ever since he left Balliol—three years of coming back in the evenings and finding Lewes, who hardly ever went out at night, sunk deep in his chair, smoking in the same changeless position, his feet up on the chimney-piece, lean, dry, horribly intelligent; and they would talk and talk, and inquire and inquire, and when they talked of love and women—and of course they sometimes talked of love and women—Lewes would bring out views which Christopher, whose views they used to be too, only he had forgotten that, considered, now that he had come to know Catherine, as so much—the word was his—tripe.

He shut the door as quietly as possible, intending to go straight to bed and avoid Lewes for that evening at least. He had been injudicious enough after the first time he sat next to Catherine and made friends with her to tell Lewes about it when he got back, and to tell him with what he quickly realised was unnecessary warmth; and naturally after that

Lewes asked him from time to time how things were developing. Christopher almost immediately left off liking this, and liked it less and less as he liked Catherine more and more; and among many other things he afterwards regretted having told Lewes in the excitement of that first discovery, was that she was the woman one dreams of.

"No woman is ever the woman one dreams of," said Lewes, who was thirty, so knew.

"You wait till you've seen her, old man," Christopher said, nettled; though it was just the sort of thing he had freely said himself up to the day before.

"My dear chap—see her? I?"

Lewes made a fatigued gesture with his pipe. "I thought you long ago realised that I'm through with women," he said.

"That's because you don't know any," said Christopher, who wasn't liking Lewes at that moment.

Lewes gazed at him with mild surprise. "Not know any?" he repeated.

"Not intimately. Not any decent ones intimately."

Lewes continued to gaze.

"I thought," he said presently, with patient mildness, "you knew I have a mother and sisters."

"Mothers and sisters aren't women—they're merely relations," said Christopher; and from that time Lewes's inquiries were less frequent and more gingerly, and mixed with anxiety. He was fond of his friend. He disliked the idea of possibly losing him. He seemed to him to be well on the way to being in love seriously; and love, as he had observed it, was a great sunderer of friendships.

He heard him come in on the Friday night, and he heard him go, so unusually, into his room after that careful shutting of the front door, and he wondered. What was the woman doing to his friend? Making him unhappy already? She had made him more cautious already, and more silent; she had already come down between them like a deadening curtain.

Lewes moved slightly in his chair, and went on with Donne, whom he was reading just then with intelligent appreciation tinged with surprise at the lasting quality of his passion for his wife; but he couldn't, he found, attend to Donne as wholeheartedly as usual, for he was listening for any sounds from the next room, and his thoughts, even as his eyes read steadily down the page, were going round and round in a circle something like this: *Poor Chris. A widow. Got him in her clutches. And what a name. Cumfrit. Good God. Poor Chris. . . .*

From the next room there came sounds of walking up and down—careful walkings up and down, as of one desiring not to attract attention and yet impelled to walk—and Lewes's thoughts went round in their circle faster and more emphatically than ever: *Poor Chris. A widow. Cumfrit. Good God. . . .*

The worst of it was, he thought, shutting up Donne with a bang and throwing him on the table, that on these occasions friends could only look on. There was nothing to be done whatever, except to watch as helplessly as at a death-bed. And without even, he said to himself, the hope, which sometimes supports such watchers, of a sure and glorious resurrection. His friend had to go through with it, and disappear out of his, Lewes's, life; for never, he had observed, was any one the same friend exactly afterwards as before, whether the results of the adventure were happy or unhappy. *Poor Chris. A widow. Clutches. . . .*

The sounds of walking about presently left off. Lewes would have liked to have been able to look in and see for himself that his unfortunate and probably doomed friend was safely asleep, but he couldn't do that; so he lit his pipe again and reached over for Donne and had another go at him, able to concentrate better, now that the footsteps had left off, but still with a slightly cocked ear.

What was his surprise at breakfast next morning to see Christopher looking happy, and eating eggs and bacon with his usual simple relish. "Hullo," he couldn't help saying, "you seem rather pleased with life."

"I am. It's raining," said Christopher.

"So it is," said Lewes, glancing at the window; and he poured out his coffee in silence, because he was unable to see any connection.

"I can chuck that beastly golf," Christopher explained in a moment, his mouth full.

"So you can," said Lewes, well aware that up to now Christopher had looked forward with almost childish eagerness to his Saturdays.

"I've been out already and sent a telegram to my uncle," said Christopher.

"But I thought on occasions like this," said Lewes, "when

the weather prevented golf, you still went down and played chess with him."

"Damn chess," said Christopher.

And in Lewes's head once more began to revolve, *Poor Chris. Cumfrit. Clutches. . . .*

❧ III ❧

Christopher had had an inspiration—sudden, as are all inspirations—the night before, after walking up and down his room for the best part of an hour: he would throw over his uncle and golf the next day, and devote the afternoon to calling on Catherine, thus getting in ahead, anyhow, of Stephen. How simple. Let his uncle be offended and disappointed as much as he liked, let him leave his thousands to the boot-boy for all he cared. He would go and see Catherine; and keep on going and seeing her, the whole afternoon if needs be, if she were out at the first shot. Whereupon, having arrived at this decision, peace enfolded him, and he went to bed and slept like a contented baby.

He began calling in Hertford Street at three.

She was out. The porter told him she was out when he inquired which floor she was on.

"When will she be in?" he asked.

The porter said he couldn't say; and Christopher disliked the porter.

He went away and walked about in the park, on wet earth and with heavy drops falling on him in showers from the trees.

At half-past four he was back again. Tea time. She would be in to tea, unless she had it in some one else's house; in which case he would call again when she had had time to finish it.

She was still out.

"I'll go up and ask for myself," said Christopher, who disliked the porter more than ever; and at this the porter began to dislike Christopher.

"There's only this one way in," said the porter, his manner hardening. "I'd be bound to have seen her."

"Which floor?" said Christopher briefly.

"First," said the porter, still more briefly.

The first-floor flat of a building in Hertford Street seemed removed, thought Christopher as he walked up to it on a very thick carpet, and ignored the lift, which had anyhow not been suggested by the hardened porter, from the necessity for travelling by tube. Yet she had said she always went to *The Immortal Hour* by tube. Was it possible that there existed people who enjoyed tubes? He thought it was not possible. And to emerge from the quiet mahoganied dignity of the entrance hall of these flats and proceed on one's feet to the nearest tube instead of getting into at least a taxi, caused wonder to settle on his mind. A Rolls-Royce wouldn't have been out of the picture, but at least there ought to be a taxi.

Why did she do such things, and tire herself out, and get her lovely little feet wet? He longed to take care of her, to prevent her in all her doings, to put his great strong body between her and everything that could in any way hurt her. He hoped George had taken this line. He was sure he must have. Any man would. Any man—the words brought him back to Stephen, who was, he was convinced, a suitor, even if she did forget his name. Perhaps she forgot because he was one of many. What so likely? One of many. . . .

He felt suddenly uneasy again, and rang the bell of the flat in a great hurry, as if by getting in quickly he could somehow forestall and confound events.

The door was opened by Mrs. Mitcham, whom he was later so abundantly to know. All unconscious of the future they looked upon each other for the first time; and he saw a most respectable elderly person, not a parlourmaid, for she was without a cap, nor a lady's maid he judged for some reason, though he knew little of ladies' maids, but more like his idea—he had often secretly wished he had one—of a nanny; and she saw a fair, long-legged young man, with eyes like the eyes of children when they arrive at a birthday party.

"Will Mrs. Cumfrit be in soon?" he asked; and the way he asked matched the look in his eyes. "I know she is out—but how soon will she be in?"

"I couldn't say, sir," said Mrs. Mitcham, considering the eager-eyed young gentleman.

"Well, look here—could I come in and wait?"

Naturally Mrs. Mitcham hesitated.

"Well, I'll only have to wait downstairs, then, and I can't stand that porter."

Mrs. Mitcham happened not to be able to stand the porter either, and her face relaxed a little.

"Is Mrs. Cumfrit expecting you, sir?" she asked.

"Yes," said Christopher boldly; for so she was, the following Sunday week.

"She usually tells me—" began Mrs. Mitcham doubtfully; but she did draw a little aside, upon which he promptly went in. And as he gave her his hat and coat she hoped it was all right, for she thought she had her mistress's friends and acquaintances at her fingers' ends, and the young gentleman had certainly never been there before.

She took him towards the drawing-room.

"What name shall I say, sir, when Mrs. Cumfrit comes in?" she inquired, turning to him at the door.

"Mr. Christopher Monckton," he said—abstractedly, because he was going to see Catherine's room, the room she probably spent most of her time in, her shrine; and Mrs. Mitcham hesitating a little—for suppose she had done wrong, letting in a stranger, and the tea-table put ready with poor Mr. Cumfrit's silver spoons and sugar-basin on it? Ought she not rather to have asked the young gentleman to wait in the hall?—Mrs. Mitcham, with doubt in her heart, opened the door and allowed him to pass in, eyeing him as he passed.

No, he didn't look like that sort of person at all, she rebuked and encouraged herself. She knew a gentleman when she saw one. Still, she left the door a tiny crack open, so that she would be able to hear if— Also, she thought it as well to cross the hall with careful footsteps, and cast an appraising eye over his coat.

It was the coat of a gentleman; a rough coat, a worn coat, but unmistakable, and she went softly back into her kitchen, leaving its door wide open, and while she as noiselessly as possible cut bread and butter she listened for the sound of her mistress coming in, and, even more attentively, in order to be quite on the safe side, for the sound of any one going out.

The last thing, however, in the world that the young man who had just got into the drawing-room wanted to do was to go out of it again. He wanted to stay where he was for ever. Wonderful to have this little time alone with her things before she herself appeared. It was like reading the enchanting preface to a marvellous book. Next to being with her, this was the happiest of situations. For these things were as much expressions of herself as the clothes she wore. They would describe her to him, let him into at least a part, and a genuine part, of her personality.

And then, at his very first glance round, he felt it was not her room at all, but a man's room. George's room. George still going on. And going on flagrantly, shamelessly, in his great oak chairs and tables, and immense oil paintings, and busts, marble busts, corpsey white things on black pedestals in corners. Did nobody ever really die, then? he asked himself indignantly. Was there no end to people's insistence on somehow surviving? Hardened into oak, gathered up into busts and picture frames, the essence of George still solidly cohabited with his widow. How in such a mausoleum could she ever leave off remembering him? Clearly she didn't want to, or she would have chucked all this long ago, and had bright things, colour, flowers, silky soft things, things like herself, about her. She didn't want to. She had canonised George, in that strange way people did canonise quite troublesome and unpleasant persons once they were safely dead.

He stood staring round him, and telling himself that he knew how it had happened—oh yes, he could see it all—how at the moment of George's death Catherine, flooded with pity, with grief, perhaps with love now that she was no longer obliged to love, had clung on to his arrangements, not suffering a thing to be touched or moved or altered, pathetically anxious to keep it exactly as he used to, to keep him still alive at least in his furniture. Other widows he had heard of had done this; and widowers—but fewer of them—had done it too. He could imagine it easily, if one loved some one very much, or was desperately sorry because one hadn't. But to go on year after year? Yet, once one had begun, how stop? There was only one way to stop happily and naturally, and that was to marry again.

And then, as he was looking round, his nose lifted in impatient scorn of George's post-mortem persistence, and quite prepared to see whisky and cigars, grown dusty, on some table in a corner—why not? they would only be in keeping with all the rest—he caught sight of a little white object on the heavy sofa at right angles to a fireplace in which feebly flickered the minutest of newly lit fires. A bit of her. A trace, at last, of her.

He darted across and pounced on it. Soft, white, sweet with the sweetness he had noticed when he was near her, it was a small fox fur, a thing a woman puts round her neck.

He snatched it up, and held it to his face. How like her, how like her. He was absorbed in it, buried in it, breathing its delicate sweet smell; and Catherine, coming in quietly with her latchkey, saw him like this, over there by the sofa with his back to the door.

She stood quiet in the doorway, watching him with surprised amusement, because it seemed so funny. Really, to have this sort of thing happening to one's boa at one's age! Queer young man. Perhaps having all that flaming red hair made one. . . .

But, though he had heard no sound, he was aware of her, and turned round quickly, and caught her look of amusement, and flushed a deep red.

He put the fur carefully down on the sofa again and came over to her. "Well, why shouldn't I?" he said defiantly, throwing back his head.

She laughed and shook hands and said she was very glad he had come. She was so easy, so easy; taking things so much as a matter of course, things that were so little a matter of course that they made him tremble—things like drying her shoes the night before in the taxi, or feeling on his face the soft white fur. If she would be shy, be self-conscious for even an instant, he thought, he would be more master of himself as well as of her. But she wasn't. Not a trace of it. Just simple friendliness, as if everything he said and did was usual, was inevitable, was what she quite expected, or else didn't matter one way or the other. She wasn't even surprised to see him. Yet he had assured her he never could get away on Saturdays.

"I couldn't help coming," he said, the flush fixed on his face. "You didn't expect me to wait really till Sunday week, did you?"

"I'm very glad you didn't," she said, ringing the bell for tea and sitting down at the tea-table and beginning to pull off her gloves.

They stuck because they were wet with the rain she had been out in.

"Let me do that," he said, eagerly, watching her every movement.

She held out her hands at once.

"You've been walking in the rain," he said reproachfully,

21

pulling away at the soaked gloves. Then, looking down at her face, the grey hard daylight of the March afternoon full on it from the high windows, he saw that she was tired—fagged out, in fact—and he added, alarmed, "What have you been doing?"

"Doing?" she repeated, smiling up at the way he was staring at her. "Why, coming home as quickly as I could out of the rain."

"But why do you look so tired?"

She laughed. "Do I look tired?" she said. "Well, I'm not a bit."

"Then why do you look as if you had walked hundreds of miles and not slept for weeks?"

"I told you you ought to see me in daylight," she said, with amused eyes on his face of concern. "You've only seen me lit up at night, or in the dark. I looked just the same then, only you couldn't see me. Anybody can look not tired if it's dark enough."

"That's nonsense," he said. "You've been walking about, and going in tubes. Look here, I wish you'd tell me something—"

"I'll tell you anything," she said.

What sweet eyes she had, what incredibly sweet eyes, if only they weren't so tired. . . .

"But you must sit down," she went on. "You're so enormous that it hurts my neck to have to look up at you."

He threw himself into the chair next to her. "What I want to know is—" he began, leaning forward.

He broke off as the door opened, and Mrs. Mitcham came in with the tea.

"Go on," said Catherine encouragingly. "Unless it's something overwhelmingly indiscreet."

"Well, I was only going to ask you—do you *like* tubes?"

She laughed. She was always laughing. "No," she said, pouring out the tea.

The teapot was impressive; all the tea arrangements were impressive, except the part you ate. On that had descended a severely restraining hand, thinning the butter on the bread, withholding the currants from the cake. Not that Christopher saw anything of this, because he saw only Catherine; but afterwards, when he went over the visit in his head, he somehow was aware of a curious contrast between the tea and the picture frames.

"Then why do you go in them?" he asked, Mrs. Mitcham having gone again and shut the door.

"Because they're cheap."

His answer to that was to glance round the room—round, in his mind's eye, Hertford Street as well, and Park Lane so near by, and the reserved expensiveness of the entrance hall, and the well-got-up, even if personally objectionable, porter.

She followed his glance. "Tubes and this," she said. "Yes, I know. They don't match, do they. Perhaps," she went on, "I needn't be so frightfully careful. But I'm rather scared just to begin with. I shall know better after the first year—"

"What first year?" he asked, as she paused; but he wasn't really listening, because she had put up her hands and taken off her hat, and for the first time he saw her without her being half extinguished.

He gazed at her. She went on talking. He didn't hear. She had dark hair, brushed off her forehead. It had tiny silver threads in it. He saw them. She was, as he had felt, as he had somehow known she was, older than himself—but only a little; nothing to matter; just enough to make it proper that he should adore her, that his place should be at her feet. He gazed at her forehead—so candid, with something dove-like about it, with something extraordinarily good, and reassuring, and infinitely kind, but with faint lines on it as though she were worried. And then her grey eyes, beautifully spaced, very light grey with long dark eyelashes, had a pathetic look in them of having been crying. He hadn't noticed that before. At the theatre they had shone. He hoped she hadn't been crying, and wasn't worried, and that her laughing now wasn't only being put on for him, for the visitor.

She stopped short in what she had been saying, noticing that he wasn't listening and was looking at her with extreme earnestness. Her expression changed to amusement.

"Why do you look at me so solemnly?" she asked.

"Because I'm terribly afraid you've been crying."

"Crying?" she wondered. "What should I have been crying about?"

"I don't know. How should I know? I don't know anything."

He leaned over and timidly touched her sleeve. He had to. He couldn't help it. He hoped she hadn't noticed.

"Tell me some things," he said.

"I have been telling you, and you didn't listen," she said.

"Because I was looking at you. You know, I've never seen you once in my life before without your hat."

"Never once in your life before," she repeated smiling. "As if you had been seeing me since your cradle."

"I've always known you," he said solemnly; and at this she rather quickly offered him some cake, which he ignored.

"In my dreams," he went on, gazing at her with eyes which were, she was afraid, a little—well, not those of an ordinary caller.

"Oh—dreams. My *dear* Mr. Monckton. Do," she said, waving intangiblenesses aside, "have some more tea."

"You must call me Chris."

"But why?"

"Because we've known each other always. Because we're going to know each other always. Because I—because I—"

"Well but, you know, we haven't," she interrupted—for who could tell what her impetuous new friend might be going to say next? "Not really. Not outside make-believe. Not beyond *The Immortal Hour*. Can you see the cigarettes anywhere? Yes—there they are. Over there on that table. Will you get them?"

He got up and fetched them.

"You've no idea how lonely I am," he said, putting them down near her.

"Are you? I'm very sorry. But—are you really? I should imagine you with heaps and heaps of friends. You're so— so—" She hesitated. "So warm-hearted," she finished; and couldn't help smiling as she said it, for he was apparently very warm-hearted indeed. His heart, like his hair, seemed incandescent.

"Heaps and heaps of friends don't make one less lonely as long as one hasn't got—well, the one person. No, I won't smoke. Who is Stephen?"

How abrupt. She couldn't leap round with this quickness. "Stephen?" she repeated, a little bewildered. Then she remembered, and her face again brimmed with amusement.

"Oh yes—you thought I was going to take him to the Zoo to-morrow," she said. "The Zoo! Why, he's preaching to-morrow evening at St. Paul's. You'd better go and listen."

He caught hold of her hands. "You must tell me one thing," he said. "You *must.*"

"I told you I'll tell you anything," she said, pulling her hands away.

"Is Stephen—are you—you're not going to marry Stephen?"

For a moment she stared at him in profound astonishment. Then she burst into laughter, and laughed and laughed till her eyes really did cry.

"Oh, my dear boy—oh, my dear, dear boy!" she laughed, wiping her eyes while he sat and watched her.

And at that moment Mrs. Mitcham appeared at the door and announced two ladies—their miserable name sounded like Fanshawe—and two ladies, who might well be Fanshawes, immediately swam in and enveloped Catherine in arms of enormous length, it seemed to him, kissing her effusively— how deeply he hated them—and exclaiming in incoherent twitters that they had come to carry her off, that the car was there, that they wouldn't take no, that Ned was waiting—

Lord, what snakes.

He went away at once. No good staying just to see her being clawed away by Fanshawes to the waiting Ned. And who the devil was Ned? Yes, there he was—waiting right enough, sitting snugly in a Daimler that looked very new and expensive, while the porter, a changed man, hovered solicitously near. Ned needed every bit of the new Daimler and the fur rug and the hideously smart chauffeur to make up for the shape of his silly nose, thought Christopher, scornfully striding off down the street.

❧ IV ❧

Till the following Friday his week was harassed. It was wonderful to be in love, to have found her, but it would have been still more wonderful if he had known a little more about her. He wanted to be able to think of her and follow her through each minute of the day—picture her, see her in his mind's eye doing this and doing that, going here and going there; and there was nothing but a blank.

They were such strangers. Only, of course, strangers on the lower level of everyday circumstances. On the higher level, the starry level of splendid, unreasoning love, he had, as he told her, always known her. But to know her on that level and not on any other was awkward. It cut him off so completely. He couldn't think what to do next.

Once, before he met her, in those dark days when he was still a fool and reasoned, he had remarked to Lewes that he thought it a pity and liable to lead to disappointment that love should begin, as it apparently did begin, suddenly, at the top of emotion. There ought, he said, to be a gradual development in acquaintanceship, a steady unfolding of knowledge of each other, a preparatory and of course extremely agreeable crescendo, leading up to the august passion itself. As it was, ignorant of everything really about the woman except what she looked and sounded like, why—there you were. It was bad, finished Christopher, aloofly considering the faulty arrangements of nature, to start with infatuation, because you couldn't possibly do anything after that but cool off.

Now, remembering this when he couldn't sleep one night, he laughed himself to scorn for a prig and an idiot. That's all one knew about it when one wasn't in love oneself. Love gave one a sixth sense. It instantly apprehended. The symbol of the sweet outer aspect of the loved one was before one's eyes; from it one was aware of her inward and spiritual grace. The beloved looked so and so; therefore she was so and so. Love knew. But, on a lower level, on the level of mere convenience, it would be better, he admitted, to have had some preliminary acquaintance. He worshipped Catherine, and they were strangers. This was awkward. It cut him off. He didn't know what to do next.

"*I must see you,*" he wrote, after three evenings at *The Immortal Hour* by himself. "*When can I?*"

And he sent the note with some roses—those delicate pale roses in bud that come out so exquisitely in a warm atmosphere. They reminded him of her. They too were symbols, he said to himself, symbols of what would happen to her also if only she would let him be her atmosphere, her warmth; and though these roses were very expensive—ever so much for each bud—he sent three dozen, a real bunch of them, rejoicing in the extravagance, in doing something for her that he couldn't really afford.

She wrote back: "*But you are coming to tea on Sunday. Didn't we say you were? Your roses are quite beautiful. Thank you so very, very much.*"

And when he saw the letter, her first letter, the first bit of her handwriting, by his plate at breakfast, he seized it so quickly and turned so red that Lewes was painfully clear as to who had written it. *Poor Chris. Cumfrit. Clutches. . . .*

So he wasn't to see her till the next Sunday. Well, this state of things couldn't be allowed to go on. It was simply too starkly ridiculous. He must get on quicker next time; manage somehow to explain, to put things on their right footing. What the things were, and what the right footing was, he was far too much perturbed to consider.

Of course he had gone to St. Paul's on the Sunday after his visit, but he had not seen her. He might as easily have hoped to find the smallest of needles in the biggest of haystacks as Catherine at that evening service, with the lights glaring in one's eyes, and rows and rows of dark figures, all apparently exactly alike, stretching away into space.

Stephen he had seen, and also heard, and had dismissed him at once from his mind as one about whom he needn't worry. No wonder she had laughed when he asked if she were going to marry him. Marry Stephen? Good God. The same age as she was, indeed! Why, he was old enough to be her father. Standing up in the pulpit he looked like a hawk, a dry hawk. What he said, after the first sentence, Christopher didn't know, because of how earnestly he was still searching for Catherine; but his name, he saw on the service paper a sidesman thrust into his hand, was Colquhoun—the Rev. Stephen Colquhoun, Rector of Chickover with Barton St. Mary, wherever that might be, and he was preaching, so Christopher gathered from the text and the first sentence, in praise of Love.

What could he know about it, thought Christopher, himself quivering with the glorious thing—what could he know, that hawk up there, that middle-aged bone? As well might they put up some congealed spinster to explain to a congregation of mothers the emotions of parenthood. And he thought no more about Stephen. He no longer wanted him stoned. It would be waste of stones.

Of Ned that week he did sometimes think, because although Ned was manifestly a worm he was also equally manifestly a rich worm, and might as such dare to pester Catherine with his glistening attentions. But he felt too confident in Catherine's beautiful nature to be afraid of Ned. Catherine, who loved beauty, who was so much moved by it—witness her rapt face at *The Immortal Hour*—would never listen to blandishments from anyone with Ned's nose. Besides, Ned was elderly. In spite of the fur rug up to his chin, Christopher had seen that all right. He was an elderly, puffy man. Elderliness and love! He grinned to himself. If only the elderly could see themselves. . . .

Monday, Tuesday, and Wednesday he went to *The Immortal Hour,* and sat and wilted because she wasn't there. Thursday morning he sent her the roses. Friday morning he got her letter, and spent several hours when he ought to have been working in assuring himself that this couldn't go on, this being separated, this having to wait two more whole days and a half, and then perhaps call there only to find ossifications like the Fanshawes calling there too, and turgescences like Ned, and that callosity Stephen.

At lunch-time on Friday he telephoned to her, and held his breath while he waited, for fear she should be out.

No—there was her voice, her heavenly little coo. "Oh, my *darling!*" he was within an ace of crying down the thing in his relief. Only just did he manage not to, and as it took him a moment to gulp the word back again she repeated with gentle inquiry—what a perfect telephone voice—"Yes—who is it?"

"It's me. Chris. Look here—"

"Who?"

"Chris. Oh, you know. You said you'd call me Chris. Christopher, then. Monckton. Look here, I wish you'd come and dine, will you? To-night? There's an awfully jolly little restaurant—what? You can't? Oh, but you *must.* Why can't you? What? I can't hear if you laugh. You're not going to that thing *again?* Why, what nonsense. It's becoming an obsession. We'll go to it to-morrow night. Why didn't you go last night? And the night before? No—I want to talk. No—we can't talk there. No, we *must* talk. No it isn't—not at all the same thing. I'll come and fetch you at half-past seven. Yes but you *must.* I think I'd better be at your place at seven. You'll be ready, won't you? Yes I know—but that can wait till to-morrow night. All right then—seven. I say, it's simply frightfully ador—nice of you. Hullo—hullo—are you there? They tried to cut us off. Look here—I'd better fetch you a little before seven—say a quarter to—because the place might be crowded. And I say, look here—hullo, hullo—don't cut us off—oh, damn."

The last words were addressed to deafness. He hung up the

receiver, and snatching at his hat went off to the restaurant, an amusing one that specialised in Spanish dishes and might, he thought, interest her, to choose and secure his table. He then went out and bought some more of the roses she said were quite beautiful, and took them to the head waiter, who was all intelligence, and instructed him to keep them carefully apart in water till a quarter to seven, when they were to be put on his table. Then he went to Wyndham Place to see if Lewes, who was working at economics and sat indoors writing most of the day, would come out and play squash with him, for he couldn't go back to his office as if it were a day like any other day, and exercise he must have—violent exercise, or he felt he would burst.

Lewes went. He sighed to himself as he pushed his books aside, seeing in this break-up of his afternoon a further extension of the Cumfrit clutches. Poor Chris. He was in the bliss-stage now, the merest glance at his face showed it; but—Lewes, besides being a highly promising political economist, was also attached to the poets—

> Full soon his soul would have her earthly freight,
> And widows lie upon him with a weight
> Heavy as frost . . .

Alas, alas, how could he have committed such a profanity? Lewes loathed himself. The woman, of course, goading him— Mrs. Cumfrit. And his feeling towards a woman who could lower him to parody a beautiful poem became as icily hostile as Adam's ought to have been to Eve after she had lowered him to the eating of half the apple; instead of which the inexperienced man was weak, and let himself be inveigled into doing that which had ultimately produced himself, Chris, and Mrs. Cumfrit.

Adam and Chris, reflected Lewes, sadly going to the club where they played, and not speaking a word the whole way, were alike in this that they neither of them could do without a woman. And always, whenever there was a woman, trouble began; sooner or later trouble began. Or, if not actual trouble, what a deadly, what a disintegrating dulness.

Lewes knew from his friend's face, from the way he walked, from the sound of his voice, and presently also from the triumphant quickness and accuracy with which he beat him at squash, that something he considered marvellous had happened to him that day. What had the widow consented to? Neither of them now ever mentioned her; and if he, Lewes, said the least thing about either women or love—and being so deep in Donne and wanting to discuss him it was difficult not to mention these two disturbers of a man's peace—if ever he said the least thing about them, his poor friend at once began talking, very loud and most unnaturally, on subjects such as the condition of the pavement in Wyndham Place, or the increasing number of chocolate-coloured omnibuses in the streets. Things like that. Stupid things, about which he said more stupid things. And he used to be so intelligent, so vivid-minded. It was calamitous.

"Shall we go and dine somewhere together to-night, old man?" he couldn't resist suggesting, as Christopher walked back with him, more effulgent than ever after the satisfaction of his triumphant exercise, and chatting gaily on topics that neither of them cared twopence for. Just to see what he would say, Lewes asked him.

"I can't to-night," said Christopher, suddenly very short.

"The Immortal Hour again, I suppose," ventured Lewes after a pause, trying to sound airy.

"No," snapped Christopher. "I'm dining out."

And Lewes, silenced, resigned, and melancholy, gave up.

✂ V ✂

When Christopher got to Hertford Street Catherine wasn't ready because he was earlier than he had said he would be; but Mrs. Mitcham opened the door, wide and welcomingly this time, and looked pleased to see him and showed him at once into the drawing-room, saying her mistress would not be long.

The fire had been allowed to go out, and the room was so cold that his roses were still almost as much in bud as ever. People had been there that afternoon, he saw; the chairs were untidy, and there were cigarette ashes. Well, not one of them was taking her out to dinner. They might call, but he took her out to dinner.

Directly she came in he noticed she had a different hat on. It was a very pretty hat, much prettier than the other one. Was it possible she had put it on for him? Yet for whom else? Absorbed in the entrancingness of this thought he had the utmost difficulty in saying how do you do properly. He stared very hard, and gripped her hand very tight, and for a moment didn't say anything. And round her shoulders was the white fox thing he had held to his face the other day; and her little shoes—well, he had better not look at them.

"This is great fun," she said as he gripped her hand, and she successfully hid the agony caused by her fingers and her rings being crushed together.

"It's heaven," said Christopher.

"No, no, that's not nearly such fun as—just fun," she said, furtively rubbing her released hand and making a note in her mind not to wear rings next time her strong young friend was likely to say how do you do.

The pain had sent the blood flying up into her face. Christopher gazed at her. Surely she was blushing? Surely she was no longer so self-possessed and sure? Was it possible she was beginning to be shy? It gave him an extraordinary happiness to think so, and she, looking at him standing there with such a joyful face, couldn't but catch and reflect some at least of his light.

She laughed. It really was fun. It made her feel so young, frolicking off like this with a great delighted boy. He was such an interesting, unusual boy, full of such violent enthusiasms. She wished he need never grow older. How charming to be as young and absurd as that, she thought, laughing up at the creature. One never noticed how delightful youth was till one's own had finished. Well, she was going to be young for this one evening. He treated her as if she were; did he really think it? It was difficult to believe, yet still more difficult not to believe when one watched his face as he said all the things he did say. How amusing, how amusing. She had been solemn for so long, cloistered in duties for such years; and here all of a sudden was somebody behaving as if she were twenty. It made her *feel* twenty; feel, anyhow, of his own age. What fun. For one evening. . . .

She laughed gaily. (No, he thought, she wasn't shy. She was as secure as ever, and as sure of her little darling self. He must have dreamed that blush.) "Where are we going?" she asked.

31

"I haven't been to a restaurant for ages. Though I'm not sure we wouldn't have been happier at *The Immortal Hour.*"

"I am," said Christopher. "Quite sure. Don't you know we've got marvellous things to say to each other?"

"I didn't," she said, "but I daresay some may come into my head as we go along. Shall we start? Help me into my coat."

"What a jolly thing," he said, wrapping her in it with joyful care. He knew nothing about women's clothes, but he did feel that this was wonderful—so soft, so light, and yet altogether made of fur.

"It's a relic," she said, "of past splendour. I used to be well off. Up to quite a little while ago. And things like this have lapped over."

"I want to know all about everything," he said.

"I'll tell you anything you ask," she answered. "But you must promise to like it," she added, smiling.

"Why? Why shouldn't I like it?" he asked quickly, his face changing. "You're not—you're not going to be married?"

"Oh—don't be silly. There. I'm ready. Shall we go down?"

"I suppose you insist on walking down?"

"We can go in the lift if you like," she said, pausing surprised, "but it's only one floor."

"I want to carry you."

"Oh—don't be *silly,*" she said again, this time with a faint impatience. The evening wouldn't be at all amusing if he were going to be silly, seriously silly. And if he began already might he not grow worse? George, she remembered, used to be quite different after dinner from what he was before dinner. Always kind, after dinner he became more than kind. But he was her husband. One bore it. She had no wish for more than kindness from anybody else. Besides, whatever one might pretend for a moment, one *wasn't* twenty, and one naturally didn't want to be ridiculous.

She walked out of the flat thoughtfully. Perhaps she had better begin nipping his effusiveness in the bud a little harder, whenever it cropped up. She had nipped, but evidently not hard enough. Perhaps the simplest way—and indeed all his buds would be then nipped for ever at once—would be to tell him at dinner about Virginia. If seeing her as he had now done in full daylight hadn't removed his misconceptions, being told about Virginia certainly would. Only—she hadn't wanted to yet; she had wanted for this one evening to enjoy the queer, sweet, forgotten feeling of being young again, of being supposed to be young; which really, if one felt as young as she quite often very nearly did, amounted to the same thing.

"You're not angry with me?" he said, catching her up, having been delayed on the stairs by Mrs. Mitcham who had pursued him with his forgotten coat.

She smiled. "No, of course not," she said; and for a moment she forgot his misconceptions, and patted his arm reassuringly, because he looked so anxious. "You're giving me a lovely treat. We're going to enjoy our evening thoroughly," she said.

"And what are you giving *me?*" he said—how adorable of her to pat him; and yet, and yet—if she had been shy she wouldn't have. "Aren't you giving me the happiest evening of my whole life?"

"Oh," she said, shaking her head, "we mustn't talk on different levels. When I say something ordinary you mustn't answer"—she laughed—"with a shout. If you do, the conversation will be trying."

"But how can I help what you call shouting when I'm with you at last, after having starved, starved—"

"Oh," she interrupted quickly, putting her hands up to her ears, "you wouldn't like it, would you, if I went deaf?"

He must go slower. He knew he must. But how go slower? He must hold on to himself tightly. But how? How? And in another minute they would be shut up close and alone in one of those infernal taxis. . . . Perhaps they had better go by tube; yet that seemed a poor way of taking a woman out to dinner. No, he couldn't possibly do that. Better risk the taxi, and practise self-control.

"You know," she said when they were in it—fortunately it was a very fast one and would soon get there—"only a few days ago you used to sit at *The Immortal Hour* all quiet and good, and never say anything except intelligent things about Celts. Now you don't mention Celts, and don't seem a bit really intelligent. What has happened to you?"

"You have," he said.

"That can't be true," she reasoned, "for I haven't seen you for nearly a week."

"That's why," he said. "But look here, I don't want to say things that'll make you stop your ears up again, and I certainly shall if we don't talk about something quite—neutral."

"Well, let's. What is neutral enough?" she smiled.

"I don't believe there's anything," he said, thinking a moment. "There's nothing that wouldn't lead me back instantly to you. There's nothing in the whole world that doesn't make me think of you. Why, just the paving stones—you walked on them. Just the shop-windows—Catherine has looked into these. Just the streets—she has passed this way. Now don't, don't stop up your ears—please don't. Do listen. You see, you fill the world—oh *don't* put your fingers in your ears—"

"I wasn't going to," she said. "I was only just thinking that I believe I'm going to have a headache."

"A headache?"

"One of my headaches."

"Oh no—not really?"

He was aghast.

"You'll be all right when you've had some food," he said. "Are they bad? Do you get bad ones?"

"Perhaps if we don't talk for a little while—" she murmured, shutting her eyes.

He went as dumb as a fish. His evening . . . it would be too awful if it were spoiled, if she had to go home. . . .

She sat in her corner, her eyes tight shut.

He sat stiff in his, as if the least movement might shake the taxi and make her worse, stealing anxious looks at her from time to time.

She didn't speak again, nor did he.

In this way they reached the restaurant, and as he helped her out, his alarmed eyes on her face, she smiled faintly at him and said she thought it was going to be all right. And to herself she said, "At dinner I'll tell him about Virginia."

❦ VI ❧

But she was weak; it was such fun; she couldn't spoil it; not for this one evening.

There were the roses, sisters to the roses in her room, making the table a thing apart and cared for among the flock of tables decorated cynically with a sad daffodil or wrinkled tulip stuck in sprigs of box and fir; and there the welcoming head waiter, himself hovering over the proper serving of dishes which all seemed to be what she chanced to like best, and there sat Christopher opposite her, flushed with happiness and so obviously adoring that the other diners noticed it and sent frequent discreet glances of benevolent and sympathetic interest across to their corner, and nobody seemed to think his attitude was anything but natural, for she couldn't help seeing that the glances, after dwelling benevolently on him, dwelt with equal benevolence on her. It was too funny. It wouldn't have been human not to like it; and whatever misconception it was based on, and however certainly it was bound to end, while it lasted it was—well, amusing.

On the wall to her left was a long strip of looking-glass, and she caught sight of herself in it. No, she didn't seem old—not unsuitably old, even for Christopher; in fact not old at all. It was really rather surprising. When did one begin? True, the rose-coloured lights were very kindly in this restaurant, and besides, she was amused and enjoying herself, and amusement and enjoyment do for the time hide a lot of things in one's face, she reflected. What would Stephen say if he saw her at this moment?

She looked up quickly at Christopher, the thought laughing in her eyes; but meeting his, fixed on her face in adoration, the thought changed to: What would Stephen say if he saw Christopher?—and the laughter became a little uneasy. Well, she couldn't bother about that to-night; she would take the good the gods were providing. There was always to-morrow, and to-morrow and to-morrow to be dusty and dim in. For the next two hours she was Cinderella at the ball; and afterwards,

35

though there would be the rags, all the rags of all the years, still she would have been at the ball.

"What are you laughing at?" asked Christopher, himself one large laugh of joy.

"I was wondering what Stephen—your friend Stephen—would say if he saw us now."

"Poor old Jack-in-the-Box," said Christopher with easy irreverence. "I suppose he'd think us worldly."

She leaned forward. "What?" she asked, her face rippling with a mixture of laughter and dismay, "what was it you called him?"

"I said poor old Jack-in-the-Box. So he is. I saw him in his box on Sunday at St. Paul's. I went, of course. I'd go anywhere on the chance of seeing you. And there he was, poor old back number, gassing away about love. What on earth he thinks *he* knows about it—"

"Perhaps—" She hesitated. "Perhaps he knows a great deal. He has got"—she hesitated again—"he has got a quite young wife."

"Has he? Then he ought to be ashamed of himself. Old bone."

She stared at him. "Old what?" she asked.

"Bone," said Christopher. "You can't get love out of a bone."

"But—but he loves her very much," she said.

"Then he's a rocky old reprobate."

"Oh Christopher!" she said, helplessly.

It was the first time she had called him that, and it came out now as a cry, half of rebuke, half of horrified amusement; but in whatever form it came out the great thing to his enchanted ears was that it had got out, for from that to Chris would be an easy step.

"Well, so he is. He shouldn't at that age. He should pray."

"Oh Christopher!" cried Catherine again. "But she loves him too."

"Then she's a nasty girl," said Christopher stoutly; and after staring at him a moment she went off into a fit of laughter, and laughed in the heavenly way he had already seen her laugh once before—yes, that was over Stephen too—so it was; Stephen seemed a sure draw—with complete abandonment, till she had to pull out her handkerchief to wipe her eyes.

36

"I don't mind your crying that sort of tears," said Christopher benignly, "but I won't have any others."

"Oh," said Catherine, trying to recover, diligently wiping her eyes, "oh, you're so funny—you've no idea how funny—"

"I can be funnier than that," said Christopher proudly, delighted that he could make her laugh.

"Oh, don't be—don't be—I couldn't bear it. I haven't laughed like this since—I can't remember when. Not for years, anyhow."

"Was George at all like his furniture?"

"His furniture?"

"Well, you're not going to persuade me that that isn't George's, all that solemn stuff in your drawing-room. Was he like that? I mean, because if he was naturally you didn't laugh much."

"Oh—poor darling," said Catherine quickly, leaving off laughing.

He had been tactless. He had been brutal. He wanted to throw himself at her feet. It was the champagne, of course; for in reality he had the highest opinion of George, who not only was so admirably dead but also had evidently taken great care of Catherine while he wasn't.

"I say, I'm most awfully sorry," he murmured, deeply contrite—whatever had possessed him to drag George into their little feast? "And I like George most awfully. I'm sure he was a thoroughly decent chap. And he can't help it if he's got a bit crystallised—in his furniture, I mean, and still hangs round—"

His voice trailed out. He was making it worse. Catherine's face, bent over her plate, was solemn.

Christopher could have bitten out his tongue. He was amazed at his own folly. Had ever any man before, he asked himself distractedly, dragged in the deceased husband on such an occasion? No kind of husband, no kind at all, could be mentioned with profit at a little party of this nature, but a deceased one was completely fatal. At one stroke Christopher had wiped out her gaiety. Even if she hadn't been fond of George, she was bound in decency to go solemn directly he was brought in. But she was fond of him; he was sure she was; and his own folly in digging him up at such a moment was positively fantastic. He could only suppose it must be the champagne. Impatiently he waved the waiter away who tried to give him more, and gazed at Catherine, wondering what he could say to get her to smile again.

She was looking thoughtfully at her plate. Thinking of George, of course, which was absolute waste of the precious, precious time, but entirely his own idiotic fault.

"Don't," he murmured beseechingly.

She lifted her eyes, and when she saw his expression she couldn't help smiling a little, it was such intense, such concentrated entreaty. "Don't what?" she asked.

"Don't think," he begged. "Not now. Not here. Except about us."

"But," she said, "that's exactly what I was doing till—"

"I know. I'm a fool. I can't help somehow blurting things out to you. And yet if you only knew the things I've by a miracle managed *not* to blurt. Why, as if I didn't know this is no place for George—"

Again. He had done it again. He snapped his mouth to, pressing his lips tight together, and could only look at her.

"Perhaps," said Catherine smiling, for really he had the exact expression of an agonisedly apologetic dog, "we had better talk about George and get it over. I should hate to think he was something we didn't mention."

"Well, don't talk about him much then. For after all," pleaded Christopher, "I didn't ask *him* to dinner." And having said this he fell into confusion again, for he couldn't but recognise it as tactless.

Apparently—how grateful he was—she hadn't noticed, for her face became pensively reminiscent (imagine it, he said to himself, imagine having started her off on George when things had been going so happily!) and she said, breaking up her toast into small pieces and looking, he thought, like a cherub who should, in the autumn sunshine, contemplate a respectable and not unhappy past—how, he wondered, did a comparison with autumn sunshine get into his head?—she said, breaking up her toast, her eyes on her plate, "George was very good to me."

"I'm sure he was," said Christopher. *"Any* man—"

"He took immense care of me."

"I'm sure he did. *Any* man—"

"While he was alive."

"Yes—while he was alive, of course," agreed Christopher; and remarked that he couldn't very well do it while he wasn't.

"But that's just what he tried to do. That's just what he thinks—oh, poor darling, I don't know if he's able to think now, but it's what he *did* think he had done."

"What did he think he had done?"

"Arranged my future as carefully as he was accustomed to arrange my present. You see, he was very fond of me—"

"Any man—"

"And he was obsessed by a fear that somebody might want to"—her face, to his relief, broke into amusement again—"might want to marry me."

"Any man—" began Christopher again, with the utmost earnestness.

"Oh, but listen," she said, making a little gesture. "Listen. He never thought he'd die—not for ages, anyhow. One doesn't. So he naturally supposed that by the time he did I'd be too old for anybody to want to marry me for what"—her eyes were smiling—"is called myself. George was rich, you see."

"Yes, I've been imagining him rich."

"So he thought he'd keep me happy and safe from being a prey to wicked men only wanting money, by making me poor."

"I see. Sincerely anxious for your good."

"Oh, he was, he was. He loved me devotedly."

"And are you poor?"

"Very."

"Then why do you live in Hertford Street?"

"Because that was his flat when he had to come up on business, and was just big enough for me, he thought. Where we really lived was in the country. It was beautiful there—the house and everything. He left all that in his will to—to another relation, and nearly all his money of course, so as to keep it up properly, besides so as to protect me, and I got the flat, just as it is, for my life, with the rent paid out of the estate, and the use of the furniture and a little money—enough, he thought, for me by myself and one servant, but not enough to make me what he called a prey to some rascally fortune-hunter in my old age."

She smiled as she used George's phrase; how well she remembered his saying it, and things like it.

"What a cautious, far-seeing man," remarked Christopher, his opinion of George not quite what it was.

"He loved me very much," said Catherine simply.

"Yes—and whom the Lord loveth He chasteneth," said Christopher. "As no doubt Stephen has pointed out."

"Well, but when George made his will, five hundred a year and no rent to pay at all and all the furniture to use, wasn't in the least chastening for one woman by herself," she said.

"Five hundred? Why, I've got nearly double that, and I feel as poor as a rat!" exclaimed Christopher.

"Yes, but when George made his will it was worth much more."

"Was it? Why, when did he make his will?"

And Catherine, suddenly realising that in another moment at this rate she would inevitably tumble right into Virginia, paused an instant, and then said, "Before he died, of course—" and refused after that to say another word about him.

∾ VII ∾

Well, Christopher didn't want her to; he was only too glad that she wouldn't go on. He now thought of George as a narrow man, with a head shaped like a box and a long upper lip. But she had been right to bring him out and air him conversationally, once he had been thrust between them by his own incredible idiocy, and it did seem to have quieted poor old George down a bit, for he didn't again leap up unbidden to Christopher's tongue. His ghost was laid. The dinner proceeded without him; and they had begun it so early that, even drawn out to its utmost limit of innumerable cigarettes and the slowest of coffee-drinking and sipping of unwanted liqueurs, it couldn't be made to last beyond nine o'clock. What can you expect if you will begin before seven, thought the head waiter, watching the gentleman's desperate efforts to stay where he was. Impossible to take her home and be parted from her before ten. It would be dreadful enough to have to at eleven, but the sheer horribleness of ten flashed an inspiration into Christopher's mind: they would go to *The Immortal Hour* for whatever was left of it.

So they went, and were in time for the love scene, as well as for the whole of the last act.

Now, indeed, was Christopher perfectly happy, as he sat beside Catherine in the thrice-blessed theatre where they had first met and compared the past with the present. Only a week ago they were there—together indeed, but met as usual without his being sure they were going to meet, and he hadn't even known where she lived. They were strangers—discussing, as strangers would on such an occasion, the Celtic legends; and George, and Stephen, and the Hertford Street drawing-room, and even Ned in his car and the fluttering Fanshawes, now such vivid permanences in his mind, were still sleeping, as far as he was concerned, in the womb of time. Only a week ago and he had never touched her, never shaken hands, never said anything at all to her that could be considered—well, personal. Now he had said many such things; and although she had been restive over some of them, and although he knew he must proceed with such prudence as he could manage, yet please God, he told himself, he'd say many more of them before another week had passed.

There they sat together, after dining together, and there before her eyes on the stage was a lesson going on in how most beautifully to make love. He knew she always thrilled to that scene. Did she, he wondered, even vaguely take the lesson to heart? Did she at all, even dimly, think, "How marvellous to do that too"? Well, he would bring her steadily to this place, not leave it to chance any more, but go and fetch her and bring her to seats taken beforehand, bring her till it did get through to her consciousness that here was not only an exquisite thing to watch other people doing, but to go home and do oneself. How long would it take to get her to that stage? He felt so flaming with will, so irresistible in his determination, that he never doubted she would get there; but it might take rather a long time, he thought, glancing sideways at the little untouchable, ungetatable thing, sitting so close to him and yet so completely removed. If once she loved him, if once he could make her begin to love him, then he felt certain she would love him wonderfully, with a divine extravagance. . . . He would make her. He could make her. She wouldn't be able to resist such a great flame of love as his.

When it was over she said she wanted to walk home.

"You can't walk, it's too far," he said; and signalled to a taxi.

41

She took no notice of the taxi, and said they would walk part of the way, and then pick up an omnibus.

"But you're tired, you're tired—you can't," he implored; for what a finish to his evening, to trudge through slums and then be jolted in a public conveyance. If only it were raining, if only it weren't such an odiously dry fine night!

"I'm not tired," she said, while the merciless lights outside the theatre made her look tired to ghastliness, "and I want to walk through the old Bloomsbury squares. Then we can get an omnibus in Tottenham Court Road. See," she finished, smiling up at him, "how well I know the ropes of the poor."

"What I see is how badly you need some one to take care of you," he said, obliged to do what she wanted, and slouching off beside her, while she seemed to be walking very fast because she took two steps to his one.

"Mrs. Mitcham takes the most careful care of me."

"Oh—Mrs. Mitcham. I mean some one with authority. The authority of love."

There was a pause. Then Catherine said softly, "I've had such a pleasant evening, such a charming evening, and I should hate it to end up with one of my headaches."

"Why? Why?" he asked, at once anxious. "Do you feel like that again?"

"I do rather."

"Then you'll certainly go home in a taxi," he said, looking round for one.

"Oh, no—a taxi would be fatal," she said quickly, catching his arm as he raised it to wave to a distant rank. "They shake me so. I shall be all right if we walk along—quietly, not talking much."

"Poor little thing," he said looking down at her, flooded with tenderness and drawing her hand through his arm.

"Not at all a poor little thing," she smiled. "I've been very happy this evening, and don't want to end badly. So if you'll just not talk—just walk along quietly—"

"I insist on your taking my arm, then," he said.

"I will at the crossings," said Catherine, who had drawn her hand out as soon as he had drawn it in.

In this way, first on their feet, and then at last, for walking in the silent streets was anyhow better than being in an omnibus and he went on and on till she was really tired, in an omnibus, and then again walking, they reached Hertford Street, and good-night had to be said in the presence of the night porter.

What an anti-climax, thought Christopher, going home thwarted, and bitterly disappointed at having been done out of his taxi-drive at the end.

"Next time I see him," thought Catherine, rubbing the hand he had lately shaken, "I'll have to tell him about Virginia. It isn't fair. . . ."

Next time she saw him was the very next day—a fine Saturday, on which for the second time running he didn't go down to his expectant uncle in Surrey. Instead, having telegraphed to him, he arrived at Hertford Street in a carefully chosen open taxi directly after lunch, when she would be sure to be in if she were not lunching somewhere, and picked her up, carrying her off before she had time to think of objections, to Hampton Court to look at the crocuses and have tea at the Mitre.

It was fun. The sun shone, the air was soft, spring was at every street corner piled up gorgeously in baskets, everybody seemed young and gay, everybody seemed to be going off in twos, laughing, careless, just enjoying themselves. Why shouldn't she just enjoy herself too? For this once? The other women—she had almost said the other girls, but pulled herself up shocked—who passed on holiday bent, each with her man, lightly swept her face and Christopher's with a sort of gay recognition of their brotherhood and sisterhood, all off together for an afternoon's happiness, and when the taxi pulled up in a block of traffic in Kensington High Street, a flower-seller pushed some violets over the side and said, "Sweet violets, Miss?" Oh, it was fun. And Christopher had brought a rug, and tucked her up with immense care, and looked so happy, so absurdly happy, that she couldn't possibly spoil things for him.

She wouldn't spoil things. Next time she saw him would be heaps soon enough to tell him about Virginia; and on a wet day, not on a fine spring afternoon like this. A wet day and indoors: that was the time and place to tell him. Of course if he became very silly she would tell him instantly; but as long as he wasn't—and how could he be in an open taxi?—as long as he was just happy to be with her and take her out and walk her round among crocuses and give her tea and bring her home again tucked in as carefully as if she were some extraordinarily precious brittle treasure, why should she interfere? It was so amusing to be a treasure—yes, and so sweet. Let her be honest with herself—it was sweet. She hadn't been a treasure, not a real one, not the kind for whom things are done by enamoured men, for years—indeed, not ever; for George from the first, even before he was one, had behaved like a husband. He was so much older than she was; and though his devotion was steady and lasting he had at no time been infatuated. She had been a treasure, certainly, but of the other kind, the kind that does things for somebody else. Mrs. Mitcham, on a less glorified scale, was that type of treasure. She, Catherine, on a more glorified scale, had been very like Mrs. Mitcham all her life, she thought, making other people comfortable and happy, and being rewarded by their affection and dependence.

Also, she had been comfortable and happy herself, undisturbed by desires, unruffled by yearnings. It had been a sheltered, placid life; its ways were ways of pleasantness, and its paths were peace. The years had slipped serenely away in her beautiful country home, undistinguished years, with nothing in any of them to make them stand out afterwards in her memory. The pains in them were all little pains, the worries all little worries. Friendliness, affection, devotion—these things had accompanied her steps, for she herself was so friendly, so affectionate, so devoted. Love, except in these mild minor forms, had not so much as peeped over her rose-grown walls. As for passion, when it leaped out at her suddenly from a book, or she tumbled on it lurking in music, she thrilled a moment and quivered a moment, and then immediately subsided again. Somewhere in the world people felt these things, did these things, were ruined or exalted for ever by these things; but what discomfort, what confusion, what trouble! How much better to go quietly to bed every night with George, to whom she was so much used, and wake up next morning after placid slumbers, strengthened and refreshed for—

Sometimes, but very seldom, she paused here and asked, "For what?" Sometimes, but very seldom, it seemed to her as if she spent her whole life being strengthened and refreshed for an effort that never had to be made, an adventure that never happened. All those meals—to what end was she so carefully, four times a day, nourished? "The machine must be stoked," George would say, pressing her to eat, for he believed in abundant food, "or it won't work." More preparations for exertions that never were made. Nothing but preparations. . . .

Sometimes, but very seldom, she thought like this; then the

thought was lulled to sleep again, lapped quiet by the gentle waves of affection, devotion, dependence that encircled her. She made people happy; they made her happy in return. It was excessively simple, excessively easy. It really appeared that nothing more was needed than good nature. Not to be cross: was that the secret? As she didn't know what it was like to feel cross, to be impelled to behave disagreeably or to want to criticise anybody, it was all very easy. Wherever she was there seemed to gather round her a most comfortable atmosphere of sunny calm. So, she sometimes but very seldom thought, do vegetables flourish in well-manured kitchen gardens.

George called her throughout his life his little comfort. He had no trouble with her, ever. His gratitude for this increased as he grew busier and richer and had to be more and more away from home. To think of his Catherine, safe and contented, waiting affectionately down in the country for his return, looking forward, thinking of him, depending on him for all her comforts as he depended on her for all his joy, filled him with a satisfaction that never grew stale. His only fear was lest she should marry disastrously after he was dead. He was so much older. It was bad to be so much older, and in all likelihood have to die and leave her. He did what he could to save her by a most carefully-thought-out will; and when the horrid moment arrived and he was forced to go, at least he knew his wing would still, in a way, stretch protectingly over her little head, that he had made her safe from predatory fortune-hunters by making her poor. The last thing he did, the very last thing, was solemnly to bless and thank her; and then with extremest reluctance, for it was a miserable thing to have to do, George died.

But she didn't think much about him that afternoon at Hampton Court. He belonged to so long ago by now—ten years since his death; and Christopher was careful not to say anything this time that might set her off in widow-reveries. Nothing here reminded her of George. They had never been here together. He had never in his life taken her off like this, for an unpremeditated excursion, in a taxi, to tea at an inn. Of course he hadn't. He was her husband. Husbands didn't. Why should they? When she and George had wanted airing, they had gone out in their car; when they had wanted tea, they had had it in their drawing-room; when, and if, they had wanted crocuses, they had admired them either from the window or from the safe dryness of a gravel path.

How old she had been then compared to now! She laughed up at Christopher, who was leading her very fast by the elbow along wet paths shining in the sun, where the earth and grass smelt so good after London, out to lawns flung over with their little lovely coat of spring, their blue and gold and purple embroidered coat; and he laughed back at her, not asking why she laughed, nor knowing why he laughed, except that this was bliss.

The times that Christopher on this occasion managed not to seize her in his arms and tell her how frantically he loved her were not to be counted. He began counting them, but had to leave off, there were so many. His self-control amazed him. True he was terrified of offending her, but his terror was as nothing compared to his love. The wind on the drive down had whipped colour into her face, and though her eyes, her dear beautiful grey eyes, homes of kindness and reassurance, still had that pathetic tiredness, she looked gayer and fresher than he had yet seen her. She laughed, she talked, she was delighted with all she saw, she was evidently happy—happy with him, happy to spend an afternoon alone with him.

They had the cheerfullest tea in a window of the Mitre, and compared to them the other people at the other tables were solemn and bored. Not that they saw any other people; at least Christopher didn't, for he saw only Catherine, and he ate watercress and jam and radishes and rock-cakes quite unconsciously, drinking in every word she said, laughing, applauding, lost in wonder at what seemed to him evidences of a most unusual and distinguished intelligence. Once he thought of Lewes, no doubt at that moment with his long nose in his books, and how for hours he would prose on, insisting on the essential uninterestingness and unimportance of a woman's mind. Fool; ignorant fool. He should hear Catherine. And even when she said quite ordinary things, things which in other people would be completely ordinary, the way she said them, the soft turned-upness of her voice at the ends of her sentences, the sweet effect as of the cooing of doves he had noticed the first day, made them sound infinitely more important and arresting than anything that idiotic Lewes, churning out his brain stuff by the yard, could ever say. *Male and female created He them,* thought Christopher, gazing at her, entranced by the satisfaction, the comfort, the sense of being completed, her presence gave him. Admirable arrangement of an all-wise Providence, this making people in pairs. To have found one's other half, to be with her after the sterile loneliness with Lewes and the aridity of his own sketchy and wholly hateful previous adventures in so-called love, was like coming home.

"You're such a little *comfort,"* he said, suddenly leaning across the table and laying his hand on hers.

And she stared at him at this with such startled eyes and turned so very red that he not only took his hand away again instantly but begged her pardon.

"I'm sorry," he said, turning red in his turn. "I didn't mean to do that."

He mustn't even touch her hand. How was he going to manage? He wasn't going to. He couldn't. He loved her too much. He must get things on a satisfactory basis. He must propose to her.

He proposed that evening.

Not in the taxi, because it was open, it rattled, and there were tram-lines. Also she had gone pensive again, and it frightened him to see how easily she took fright. If her gaiety had been ruffled aside by that one brief touch of her hand at tea, what mightn't happen if he proposed? Suppose she sent him away and wouldn't ever see him again? Then he would die; he knew he would. He couldn't risk such a sentence. He would wait; he would manage; he would continue to exercise his wonderful self-control.

But he wasn't able to after all.

When they got to Hertford Street he reminded her that she had said she would go with him that evening to *The Immortal Hour,* and Catherine, sobered by having heard herself once more called by George's pet name, as if George from his grave were using this young man as a trumpet through which to blow her a warning of the perils of her behaviour, thanked him in a subdued and rather conscience-stricken voice, and said she was too tired to go out again.

Christopher's face fell to a length that was grotesque. "But I've been counting on it!" he cried. "And you said—"

"Well, but this afternoon was instead. And how lovely it was. I think for a change even more lovely than *The Immortal Hour.* Those crocuses with the sun slanting through them—"

"Never mind the crocuses," interrupted Christopher. "Do you mean to say I'm not going to see you again to-night?"

"Oh, aren't you a baby," she said, unable not to laugh at his face of despair.

He was walking up the stairs to her flat beside her, her wrap on his arm. He had refused to give it to her downstairs, because as long as he held on to that he couldn't, he judged, be sent away.

"Don't laugh at me," he said. "It isn't a bit funny to be separated from you."

Her face was instantly grave again. "I couldn't go anywhere to-night," she said, taking out her latchkey, "because I'm beginning to have one of my headaches."

"And I'm beginning to think," he said quickly, "that those headaches are things you get directly I say anything a little— anything the least approaching what I feel. Look here, I'll do that," he went on, taking the key from her and opening the door. "Isn't it true, now, about the headaches?"

He was becoming unmanageable. She must apply severity. So she held out her hand, the door being opened, and said good-bye. "Thank you so very much," she said with immense politeness. "It has been delicious. You were too kind to think of it. Thank you a thousand times."

"Oh, what an absurd way to talk!" exclaimed Christopher, brushing away such stuff with a gesture of scornful impatience. "As if we were strangers—as if we were mere smirking acquaintances!"

"I have a great opinion," said Catherine, becoming very dignified, "of politeness."

"And I haven't. It is a thing you put on as you're putting it on now to keep me off, to freeze me—as if you'd ever be able to freeze *me* when I'm anywhere near you!"

"Good-bye," said Catherine at this, very cool indeed.

"No," said Christopher. "Don't send me away. It's so early. It isn't seven yet. Think of all the hours till I see you again."

"What I do think," said Catherine icily, for it was grotesque, this refusal to go away, he was humiliating her with his absurdities, "is that you say more foolish things in less time than any person I have ever yet come across."

"That's because," said Christopher, "you've never yet come across any one who loves you as I love you. There. It's out. Now what are you going to do?"

And he folded his arms, and stood waiting with burning eyes for the door to be shut in his face.

She stood a moment looking at him, a quick flush coming and disappearing across her face.

"Oh," she then sighed faintly, "the *silliness. . . .*" For she was right up against it now. Her amusing little dream of resurrected youth was over. She was right up against Virginia.

"Well, what are you going to do?" asked Christopher, defiant on the threshold, waiting for his punishment. He knew it would be punishment; he saw by her face. But whatever it was, if it didn't kill him he would bear it, and then, when it was over, begin again.

She moved aside and pointed to the drawing-room door. "Ask you to come in," she said.

∽ VIII ∾

Christopher stared.

"I'm to—come in?" he stammered, bewildered.

"Please."

"Oh, my darling!" he burst out, throwing down her cloak and coming in with a rush.

But she held up her hand, exactly as if he were the traffic in Piccadilly, and remarked, so coldly that all that was left to him was once more bewilderment, "Not at all."

"Not at all?" he could only stupidly repeat.

"Please come into the drawing-room," said Catherine, walking into it herself. "I want to tell you something."

"Nothing you can tell me can ever—"

"Yes it can," said Catherine.

Mrs. Mitcham appeared, following them into the room. "Shall I light the fire, m'm?" she inquired. "It seemed warm, and Mr. Colquhoun thought—"

"Was Mr. Colquhoun here?"

"Yes, m'm. He's only been gone a few minutes."

"What a pity," said Catherine.

"What a mercy," said Christopher.

"I would have liked you to meet him," she said. "No, thank you—I won't have a fire," she added, turning to Mrs. Mitcham, who went away and shut the door.

"Why? Why on earth should you want me to meet Stephen?"

"He would so very nicely have pointed the moral of what

49

I'm going to tell you," she said smiling, for she felt safe again, knowing that Virginia would bring him to his senses once and for ever.

"Catherine, if you smile at me like that—" he began, taking a step forward.

"Christopher, it's my conviction that you're mad," she said, taking a step backward. "I never heard of a young man behaving as you do in my life before."

"I'd kill any other young man who did. And look here—whatever it is you want to say, let me tell you you may say what you like, and tell me what you like, and send me away as much as you like, and it'll have no effect whatever. I love you too much. I'll always come back, and back, however often you send me away, till at last you'll be so tired of it that you'll marry me."

"Marry you!"

"Yes, Catherine. It's what one does. When people love frantically—"

She looked at him aghast at his expressions.

"But who loves frantically?" she inquired.

"I do. All by myself at present. But you will too, soon. You won't be able to help it. It's the most absolutely catching thing—"

"Oh, my dear boy," she interrupted, shocked at such a picture of herself, "don't talk like that. It's really dreadful. I've never done anything frantically in my life."

"I'm going to make you."

"Oh—oh. . . ."

She was scandalised. She said quickly, "I ought to have told you ages ago about Virginia—when first you began saying foolish things."

"I don't care a hang about Virginia, whoever she may be."

"She's my daughter."

"What do I care?"

"She's grown up."

"She must have grown very fast, then."

"Please don't be silly. She's not only grown up, she's married. So now, perhaps, you'll understand—"

"George was married before, then?" he said.

"No. She's my daughter. My very own. So now you'll understand—"

"That you're older than I am. I knew that. I could see that."

How unaccountable one is, thought Catherine; for when he said this she was conscious of a small stab of chagrin.

"But you see now how *much* older," she said.

"Much! Little! What words. I don't know what they mean. You're you. And you're me as well. As though I cared for any Virginia, fifty times married. My business is only with you, and yours only with me——"

"I haven't got any business with you."

"Shut her out. Forget her——"

"Shut out Virginia?"

"Be just you. Be just me."

"Oh, you're absolutely mad."

"Catherine, you're not going to let the fact that you were born before me separate us?"

She stared at him in astonishment and dismay. Virginia as a cure had failed. It was at once excessively warming to her vanity and curiously humiliating to her sense of decency. The last twelve years of her life, since George's death, as the widowed mother of a daughter who during them grew up, was taken out, became engaged and married, had so much accustomed her to her position as a background—necessary, even important, but only a background for the young creature who was to have all the money directly she married with her mother's consent or came of age—that to be dragged out of this useful obscurity, so proper, as she had long considered, to her age, and her friends and relations had considered it so also, to be dragged out with real violence into the very front of the stage, forced to be the prima donna of the piece of whom it was suddenly passionately demanded that she should sing, shocked and humiliated her. Yet, over and through this feeling of wounded decency washed a queer warm feeling of gratified vanity. She was still, then, if taken by herself, away from Virginia, who up to three months before had always been at her side, attractive; she was still so apparently young, so outwardly young, that Christopher evidently altogether failed to visualise Virginia. It really was a feather in a woman's cap. But then the recollection that this young man was just the right age for Virginia overwhelmed her, and she turned away with a quick flush of shame.

"I have my pride," she remarked.

"Pride! What has pride to do with love?"

"Everything with the only sort of love I shall ever know——

family love, and the affection of my child, and later on I hope
of her children."

"Oh Catherine, don't talk such stuff to me—such copy-
book, renunciated stuff!" he exclaimed, coming nearer.

"You see," she said, "how much older I am than you,
whatever you may choose to pretend. Why, we don't even talk
the same language. When I talk what I'm sure is sense you call
it copy-book stuff. And when you talk what I know is
nonsense, you're positive it is most right and proper."

"So it is, because it's natural. Yours is all convention and
other people's ideas, and what you've been told and not what
you've thought for yourself, and nothing to do with a simple
following of your natural instincts."

"My natural instincts!"

She was horrified at his supposing she had such things. At
her age. The mother of Virginia.

"Well, are you going to dare tell me you haven't been happy
with me, you haven't liked going out with me?"

"Yes. I did. It was queer—I oughtn't to have."

"It was natural, that's why. You were being natural then,
and not thinking. It's natural you should be loved—"

"But not by you," she said quickly. "That's most unnatural.
The generations have to keep together. You would have to be
twenty years older before it could even begin to be decent."

"Love isn't decent. Love is glorious and shameless."

She put up her hand again, warding off his words. "Christopher, good-bye," she said very firmly. "I can't listen to any
more foolish things. As long as you didn't know about
Virginia I could forgive them, but now that you know I simply
can't bear them. You make me ridiculous. I'm sorry. I ought to
have told you at the beginning, but I couldn't believe you
wouldn't see for yourself—"

"What is there to see except that you are what I have always
dreamed of?"

"Oh—*please*. Good-bye. I'm really very sorry. But you'll
laugh over this in a year's time—perhaps we'll laugh over it
together."

"Yes—when you're my wife, and I remind you of how you
tormented me."

Her answer to that was to go towards the fireplace to ring the
bell for Mrs. Mitcham to show him out. There was nothing to
be done with Christopher. He was mad.

But he got to the fireplace first. "No," he said, standing in front of the bell. "Please. Listen to me. One moment more. I can't go away like this. Please, Catherine—my darling, my darling—don't send *love* away—"

"Mr. Colquhoun, m'm," said Mrs. Mitcham opening the door; and in walked Stephen.

"Why, Stephen," cried Catherine, almost running to him, so very glad was she to see him, so much gladder than she had yet been in her life, "I *am* pleased!"

"I was here earlier in the evening," began Stephen—and paused on catching sight of the flaming young man in the corner by the fireplace.

"Oh, yes—this is Mr. Monckton," said Catherine hastily. And to Christopher she said, "This is Mr. Colquhoun—" Adding, with extreme clearness, "My son-in-law."

❧ IX ❧

The manner of Christopher's departure was not creditable. He shouldn't behave like that, thought Catherine, whatever his feelings might be. He pretended not to be aware of Stephen's outstretched hand, scowled at him in silence, and then immediately said good-bye to her; and as he crushed her fingers— she hadn't time to pull off her rings—he said out loud, "The generations don't do what they should, you see, after all."

"I have no idea what you mean," she said coldly.

"Just now you laid down as a principle that they should keep together." And he glanced at Stephen.

Stephen and Virginia. Yes; but how absurd of him to compare—

"That's different," she said quickly and defiantly.

"Is it?" he said; and he was gone, and twilight seemed suddenly to come into the room.

"What a very odd young man," remarked her son-in-law, after a pause during which they both stood staring at the shut door as if it might burst open again, and again let in a flood of something molten. "What did he mean about the generations?"

"I don't think he knows himself," she said.

"Perhaps not. Perhaps not," said Stephen with that thoughtfulness which never forsook him. "At his age they frequently do not."

She shivered a little, and rang the bell for Mrs. Mitcham to light the fire. Stephen looked so old and dry, as if he needed warming, and she too felt as though the evening had grown cold.

But how nice it was to sit quietly with Stephen, the virtuous and the calm. So nice. So what one was used to. She hadn't half appreciated him. He was like some quiet pond, with heaven reflected on his excellent bosom. She liked to sit by him after the raging billows of Christopher; it was peaceful, secure. What a great thing peace was, and the company of a person of one's own age. But he did look very old, she thought. He was tiring himself out with all the improvements on the estate he and Virginia were at work on, besides preaching a series of Lenten sermons in different London churches, which obliged him to come up for the week-ends, leaving Virginia, who was not travelling just now, down at Chickover Manor with the curate to officiate on the Sundays.

"You are tired, Stephen," said Catherine gently.

"No," he said thoughtfully. "No."

How peaceful were these monosyllables; how soothing, after the turbulent speech of that demented young man.

"Virginia is well?"

"Quite well. That is, as well as one can expect."

"She must take care of herself."

"She does. I was to give you her love."

"Darling Virginia. I hope you are dining with me to-night?"

"Thank you—I should like to, if I may. Did you say that young fellow's name was Monckton?"

"Yes."

"Do I know him? Or, I should perhaps say, do I know anything about him?"

"I don't think so."

Stephen sat thoughtful, looking at the fire.

"A little overwhelming, is he not?" he said presently.

"He is young."

"Ah."

He paused again; reflecting, his thin cheek leaning on his hand, that to be young was not necessarily to be overwhelming. Virginia, the youngest of the young—what inexhaustible, proud delight her youth gave him!—was not at all overwhelming.

But Christopher did not really interest him. The world was full of young men—all, to Stephen, very much alike, all with spirits that had to be blown off. The Chickover ones, his own parishioners, blew theirs off on Saturday afternoons at football or cricket according to the time of year, and the rest of the week it was to be presumed that work quieted them. Of whatever class, they seemed to Stephen noisy and restless, and the one he had just seen reminded him of a lighted torch, flaring away unpleasantly among the sober blacks and greys of the late Mr. Cumfrit's furniture.

But he was not really interested. "I preach to-morrow at St. Clement's," he remarked after a silence.

"On the same subject?"

"There is only one. It embraces every other."

"Yes—Love," she said; and her voice at the word went very soft.

"Yes—Love," he repeated, still thoughtfully gazing at the fire, his cheek on his hand.

His subject on these Lenten Sundays was Love. After having preached not particularly well all his life on other subjects, since his marriage he had begun to preach remarkably well on this one. He knew what he was talking about. He loved Virginia, and had only been married to her three months, and his warm knowledge of love in particular burned in a real eloquence on Love in general. He loved and was loved. The marriage about which Catherine had had misgivings, because she thought him a little too wooden—what mistakes one makes—for a girl so young, had been completely successful. They adored each other in the quiet, becoming way a clergyman and his wife, when they adore, do adore; that is, not wantonly at all, in public, but nicely, in the fear of God. And both were determined to use Virginia's money only for ends that were noble and good.

Virginia was like her father—made for quiet domestic bliss. Also she had never been very pretty, and that too was suitable. The Church has no use, Stephen knew, for beauty. A beautiful woman married to a clergyman easily produces complications; for we are but weak creatures, and our footsteps, even if we are a bishop, sometimes go astray. But she was quite pretty enough, with lovely eyes, and was so entrancingly young, besides being such a good little girl, and rich.

Stephen, who was first the curate and then the rector of Chickover, having been presented to the living by George Cumfrit its patron, who liked him, had had his thoughtful eye on Virginia from the beginning. When he went there she was five and he was thirty-four. Dear little child; he played with her. Presently she was fifteen, and he was forty-four. Sweet little maid; he prepared her for confirmation. Again presently she was eighteen, and he was forty-seven. Touching young bud of womanhood; he proposed to her. Catherine hesitated, for Virginia was so very young, while Stephen compared to her was so very old; and Stephen explained that age, difference in age, had nothing to do with love. Love loved, Stephen pointed out, and there was an end of it. No objections in face of that great fact could be valid, he said. Seeing that Virginia returned his love, whatever were their respective ages it surely had nothing to do with anybody except themselves. Should Mrs. Cumfrit think fit to refuse her consent she would merely be depriving her daughter of three years' happiness, for they would certainly marry directly Virginia was of age.

Thus, before young men had had time to become aware of Virginia, Stephen had carried her off. She wasn't nineteen when he married her. He loved her with the excessive love of a middle-aged man for a very young girl, though of course decorously in public. She, having been trained to it from childhood by him, thought there was no one in the world like him. He was to her most great, most brilliant, most good. She worshipped him. Never was a girl so proud and happy as she was when Stephen married her. Their loves, however, were private. No one was offended by demonstrations. His mother-in-law, who was of his own age, or even slightly younger—one year younger, to be exact—wasn't made to feel uncomfortable. Indeed, he had too high an opinion of his mother-in-law not to wish in every way to please her. She had behaved admirably. With the whole of the income of George Cumfrit's fortune at her disposal till Virginia was either twenty-one or married with her consent under that age, and able, merely by refusing her consent, to continue in its enjoyment for another three years, she had relinquished everything with perfect grace the moment he had convinced her that it was for her daughter's happiness. Stephen could not but consider himself the most fortunate of men. Here, by simply resisting the desire to marry—and he was a man naturally disposed to marriage— until Virginia had grown up, he had secured a delightful young wife with money enough to carry out all his most ardent dreams of benevolence, and a really remarkable mother-in-law. Indeed, his mother-in-law was exactly what the mother-in-law of a clergyman should be: a modest, unassuming, non-interfering, kind, contented Christian gentlewoman. Great had been his satisfaction when he discovered she was contented. The drop from the Cumfrit thousands and Chickover to £500 a year and a small London flat was big enough to unsettle most women. His mother-in-law dropped without a murmur. She was not in the least unsettled. She remained as kind as ever. She made no demands at all, either on Virginia or himself. When they invited her, she went, but not otherwise. When he came to see her, she welcomed him with the same pleasant friendliness. A kind, quiet woman, who didn't mind being poor. St. Paul would have liked her.

He and she presently had the mild meal she spoke of as dinner in George Cumfrit's little *pied-à-terre* dining-room— the most excellent of men, poor George Cumfrit, ripe in foresight and wisdom—and Stephen invoked God's blessing on two cups not quite full of broth, and some scrambled eggs.

Catherine walked delicately among words with Stephen, and in his presence called that dinner which to Mrs. Mitcham she called supper, or, even more simply, something to eat, in order that Stephen, now so splendidly established in what used to be her shoes, should not be made in any way to feel the difference his marriage had made in her circumstances; while Stephen for his part always went out of his way to praise the quality and abundance of whatever food she gave him, lest she should perhaps notice that she did not now have particularly much to eat. Enough, of course; enough, and most wholesome —heavy meals at night were a mistake. And once, when he had happened to come in when there was only a milk pudding, he had behaved to it as ceremoniously and as reverently as he would have behaved to ducks and green peas, of which he was particularly fond, and said grace over it, and, as it were, carved it—she liked him to preside—with all the air of pleased anticipation of a man rubbing his hands before a banquet. Catherine had been much concerned at his chancing to come in on a milk-pudding night, and had explained, what was true, that she had not been well, and the pudding was in the nature of a sanitary precaution; and Stephen had assured her that a good rice pudding, properly made, was one of the very best of God's gifts.

There they sat, then, on this evening of her excursion to Hampton Court, quietly eating their scrambled eggs and talking of calm things. It was strange to her to remember that such a few hours earlier she had been an ostensibly young woman out for the afternoon with her adorer, moving swiftly, laughing gaily, petted, cherished, of infinite importance. How unsuitable, how unsuitable, thought Catherine, flushing hotly —"Yes, Stephen? Old Mrs. Dymock—?"

"She is dead at last."

"Poor old thing."

"A blessed release."

It had been all wrong, of course. It was merest make-believe. These were the sober facts of life; this was really where she belonged—"Did you say young Andrews? His leg?"

"Broken playing football."

"Poor boy. I am very sorry."

"It is his own fault. A rough customer, a very rough customer."

Now she had entered again into her dim kingdom, in which she negatively reigned as Stephen's mother-in-law. He was well disposed towards her she knew, and so was she towards him; but she also knew they were not interesting to each other except in their quality of satisfactory son-in-law, satisfactory mother-in-law. She wasn't to Stephen a woman; Stephen was not to her a man—"But do I remember Daisy? I don't seem—"

"She is my mother's housemaid at the Rectory. She is marrying the cowman up at Tovey's farm."

"Your mother will miss her."

"That is what I fear."

Virginia had assured her, on becoming engaged, that he was of a distinguished mind; she knew for herself, since he had begun so unexpectedly to preach eloquently on love, that he had a tender and understanding heart; but neither of these things came to the surface and lit up his conversation when he was with her. Strange dehumanisation of a human being produced by their relationship. . . .

"Bathrooms did you say?"

"In every cottage. And the new cottages are going to have lavatory basins in each bedroom."

"But that is really splendid."

"It is my idea, and also Virginia's, of true religion: Love and Cleanliness. They go hand in hand. Give the poor the opportunity of washing—*easy* washing—there must be no difficulty about it of any sort, or they won't—and they will begin to respect themselves. And from a decent self-respect to a decent courting of a decent girl is but one step."

She did feel, however, that George's will was calculated to make any son-in-law a little awkward and uncomfortable when with her, and was very sorry for Stephen. He would of course get used to it soon, but he had only had three months as yet of Chickover Manor, so tremendously associated in his eyes, who had lived next door for fourteen years, with her as its mistress, and she did her best to make him understand by every sort of friendliness that she was perfectly content. Why, she was content already; and as soon as she had had time to turn round, and was really settled in her new life, and knew exactly what she could do with her income and what she couldn't, she suspected she was going to be happier than she had ever been. Because, for the first time, she was free; and just to be able to do things such as go to *The Immortal Hour* as often as she wanted to—George hadn't cared for music—and see what friends she liked—George had been happiest when he had her to himself—and read as much as she felt inclined —George loved her to listen to him, and nobody can both listen and read—was already most agreeable, and would go on, as her life developed, becoming more and more so. Only she mustn't, of course, behave like a fool. She had behaved very like a fool, she was afraid, in letting Christopher become so intimate, and it was her fault that he had dared be so familiar. Yet who could have dreamed, who could possibly have imagined. . . . Still, there it was.

Again she flushed hotly, wondering what Stephen, tranquilly eating eggs, would say if he knew.

But even if he had been looking at her, his mother-in-law might have flushed the vividest red and he wouldn't have seen it, because it is not what one expects of mothers-in-law. They are not women, of like emotions to oneself, they are institutions. And if she to him seemed like an institution, he to her seemed oddly like a public building. A museum; a temple; a great, cool place through whose echoing emptiness one wandered. On a hot day, what a relief. These last days for Catherine had been hot—hot, and disturbing; and she did find it refreshing to sit like this among Stephen's shadows. Presently her thoughts faded dim and quiet. Christopher's image faded dim and quiet. Presently in the accustomed atmosphere—George's atmosphere too had been a quiet one—she paled down till she matched it. By the end of the meal she was like a mouse, a grey mouse the colour of her surroundings, sitting unassumingly nibbling its food.

"For these and all Thy blessings—" said Stephen, towering tall and lean over the empty egg-dish, his eyes closed, his hands folded, his voice sounding as if it came out of somewhere hollow.

"Amen," murmured Catherine with propriety.

Yes—it was soothing; it was what one knew.

And the evening in the drawing-room continued to soothe. He sat in what had been George's chair on one side of the small fire, and she sat on the big sofa facing him. So had she and George sat when she had come up from Chickover to go out with him to some unavoidable festivity. If George could, he avoided festivities; and she, born with that spirit of adaptability which made her so pleasant to live with, born with that fortunate and convenient disposition which squeezed its happiness out of acquiescences, out of what she had, rather than waiting to be happy when she should have got something else, had gladly shared in his desire to avoid them. But if they were not avoidable, then she cheerfully came up to London and supported him; and afterwards, when whatever it was they had been to was over, with what a sigh of satisfaction did George sink into his chair before going to bed and rest his eyes on his Catherine sitting opposite him. He didn't even like her to take up the evening paper and glance at the headlines, so much did he love to have her whole attention. Never did any one listen as sweetly as his Catherine. It was the best conversation he ever had, George considered, this talk to Catherine who so sweetly listened. Now she sat opposite Stephen, and Stephen gazed at the fire and hardly spoke, so that even her talent for listening was able to rest. Peace, perfect peace, she thought, her head in the cushions and her eyes inclined to shut.

At nine o'clock Stephen looked at his watch. He had been

prepared to take it out, look at it, exclaim that time had flown, get up, and go.

But time had not flown. Both of them had been supposing it must be ten o'clock—at least ten, probably much later; so that when he saw it was only nine he was disconcerted as well as astonished.

He didn't quite know what to do. To leave so early would not be respectful, he felt, to his excellent mother-in-law; to hold his watch up to his ear in order to make sure it hadn't stopped—it *must* have stopped—was an impulse he resisted as discourteous. Yet he wanted to go away. Whatever his watch declared, he felt it was long past bedtime.

"Would you like me," he suggested, fidgeting in his chair a little, "to say prayers for you and your household before I go?"

"Very much," said Catherine politely, waking up; she was the last person to baulk any clergyman who should want to pray. "Only there isn't—"

She hesitated, anxious not to seem to complain. She had been going to say there wasn't any household; instead, she inquired whether she should call Mrs. Mitcham.

"Pray do," said Stephen.

Mrs. Mitcham came.

Then it appeared there wasn't a prayer-book. The prayer-books, both hers and Mrs. Mitcham's—it was most unfortunate—had been left behind at Chickover.

Stephen stood thoughtfully on the hearth-rug. Mrs. Mitcham, with the expression of one already in church, waited with decent folded hands for whatever of unction should descend on her. Catherine reflected that she hadn't left her furs behind at Chickover, nor her trinkets, and wondered whether perhaps Stephen might be reflecting this too and drawing his conclusions.

But Stephen was not. He was merely turning over in his mind what, cut off from the assistance of the prayer-book, he should say to these two women as a good-night benediction, and so with grace be able to go back to his lodging to bed.

The thought of that bed, all solitary and cold, recalled Virginia, and with her his great discovery of Love. He suddenly raised his hands over his mother-in-law and her servant—instinctively they bowed their heads—and with complete simplicity and earnestness bade them love one another.

"Little children, love one another," Stephen said simply.

It was the best he could do for them, he felt; it was the best that could be done for any one in the world. Then, abruptly, he wished Catherine good-night.

"Do you come to St. Clement's to-morrow evening?" he inquired of her.

"I will certainly come," she said.

Mrs. Mitcham helped him into his coat with reverence. She liked having texts said over her; it gave her a peculiar, pleasant feeling in her chest. She couldn't imagine how she had come to forget her prayer-book and not even notice she hadn't got it. It must have been the confusion of Miss Virginia's wedding, and moving up to London and settling in. She wrote that very evening to the housekeeper at Chickover, and begged her to send it to her, and also her mistress's, at once.

X

By this time it was a quarter past nine; quite early, and yet how late it seemed. Catherine went back to the sofa, and turning out the light on the table by her side, for she was being very cautious this first year of her limited income and not wasting anything, put her feet up and lay in the firelight, feeling a little tired.

Stephen, as a cool refuge from the warmths of Christopher, had been restful, but only up to a certain point. He had provided the sort of relief the cool air of a cellar gives those coming rather blinded out of the heat of the sun, and, like a cellar, he had presently palled. She had long ago found, and it had been greatly to her regret, that it was difficult to keep her eyes open after a short time alone with Stephen. She thought this must be due to his conversation. There was nothing to lay hold of in it. It was bony. One slipped off. Besides, he didn't talk to her as if she were anything but another bone. Bones to bones; how dreary; how little one likes being behaved to as if one were a bone. Yet he knew now about love, and nobody could hear him preach without being thrilled by his appreciation of it. He appreciated it in his sermons in all its branches. At present in his life there was only one branch really living, and that was married love. All those other loves he praised— brotherly love, which he entreated might continue; the love of friends, surpassing, he declared, in beauty and dignity the love of the sexes; that large love of humanity, which needs must well from every thinking heart—were theories to him. Well, perhaps by sheer talking about them from pulpits to impressed congregations they would gradually become real. One did, in a very remarkable way, talk oneself into attitudes of mind that altered one's entire behaviour; or was talked into them by somebody else, which was less excellent—in fact, should be guarded against.

She shut her eyes. She was tired.

Little children, love one another. . . . He could say that beautifully—and how beautiful it was—but he didn't *do* it himself. Except Virginia, the rest of the world was at present left out from Stephen's loving. The exhortation had been for her and Mrs. Mitcham, who had long loved one another in the form of affection and daily mutual courtesies.

Little children, love . . .

She was tired. She hadn't walked so fast or so much for ages as she had that afternoon at Hampton Court. And the spring air was relaxing. And Christopher had such long legs, and strode easily over ground that took her innumerable small steps to cover. And, being clearly mad as well, it wasn't only her feet he had fatigued, but her spirit. Stephen, so passive and indifferent; Christopher, so active and not indifferent enough; and she between them being agreeable, and agreeable, and for ever agreeable. Why did a woman always try, however fruitlessly, as with Stephen, or dangerously, as with Christopher, to be agreeable? She feared it was, at bottom, vanity. Anyhow it was very stupid, when it was so tiring, so tiring. . . .

Little children, love . . .

She dozed; she more than dozed; she went to sleep. And she hadn't been asleep five minutes before Christopher came back.

There was her wrap—he hadn't given her her wrap yet, and found it when he went out where he had dropped it on the carpet outside her door. In any case he had meant to wait in the street till that incredible old son-in-law—that *she* should dare to try to put him off with stuff about the generations!—

had gone, and then see her again unless it was very late. But the wrap made it his duty to see her again; and when he beheld, from the opposite pavement, Stephen emerge and go away at a quarter past nine, he walked up and down for another ten minutes in case the old raven should have forgotten something and come back, and then, the wrap on his arm, went in and up the stairs with all the dignity and composure that legitimate business bestows.

But he was not really composed; not inside. When Mrs. Mitcham opened the door at his ring and, still under the influence of Stephen's exhortation to love one another, smiled brightly at him, he could hardly stammer out that he had something of Mrs. Cumfrit's—her wrap—

"Oh, thank you, sir. I'll take it," said Mrs. Mitcham.

"Well, but I want to see Mrs. Cumfrit a minute—it isn't late—it's quite early—I'll go in for just a minute—"

And thrusting the wrap into her hand he made for the drawing-room.

She watched him shut the door behind him, and hoped it didn't matter, her not announcing him. After all, he had but lately left; it wasn't as if he were calling that day for the first time. On the contrary, this was the third time since lunch that he had come in.

She stood uncertain a moment in the hall, ready to let him out again if he did only stay a minute; then, when he did not reappear, she went back to the kitchen.

Now Christopher might have behaved quite differently if he had found Catherine wide awake in her chair, properly lit up, and reading or sewing. He had meant, in coming back, only to reason with her. He couldn't be sent away, cut short in the middle of a sentence and cast out as he had been by Stephen's entrance, and not see her again at least to finish what he had to say. If she wouldn't listen now, at least they might arrange an hour the next day when she would. He couldn't go home to just black misery. He couldn't. He was a human being. There were things a human being simply couldn't do. He would see her again that evening, if only to find out when she would let him call and talk quietly. Surely she owed him this. He hadn't done anything to offend her really, except tell her that he loved her. And was that an offence? No; it was most natural, inevitable and right, he assured his shrinking heart. For his heart did shrink; it was very fearful, because he knew she would be angry when she saw him. He could barely get the words out to Mrs. Mitcham at the door, so short was he of breath because of his heart. It was behaving as if he had been tearing up six flights of stairs, instead of walking slowly up one.

Then, inside the room, instead of light, and Catherine looking up from whatever she was doing at him with surprise and reproach, he found first darkness, and presently, as he stood uncertain and his eyes grew more accustomed to it, the outline of Catherine in the dull glow of the fire, motionless on the sofa. He couldn't see if she was asleep. She said nothing and didn't move. She must be asleep. And just at that moment a flame leapt out of the coals, and he saw that she was asleep.

The most extraordinary feeling flooded his heart. All the mothers in his ancestry crowded back to life in him. She looked so little, and helpless and vulnerable. She looked so tired, with no colour at all in her face. Not for anything in the world would Christopher have disturbed that sleep. He would creep away softly, and simply bear the incertitude as to when he was to see her again. Such an immense tenderness he had never in his life felt. He knew now that he loved her beyond all things, and far beyond himself.

He turned to go away, holding his breath, feeling for the door handle, when his foot knocked against the leg of George's big chair.

Catherine woke up. "Mrs. Mitcham—" she began, drowsily. And then as no one answered, for though he tried to he couldn't, she put out her hand and turned on the light.

They blinked at each other.

Astonishment, succeeded by indignation, spread over Catherine's face. She could hardly believe her eyes. Christopher. Back again. Got into her flat like a thief. Stealing in in the dark. . . .

She sat up, leaning on her hands. "You!" was all she could find to say.

"Yes, I had to. I had to bring you back your—"

He was going to shelter behind her cloak, and then was ashamed of such trifling.

She made a movement to get up, but the sofa was a very low one, and she rather ridiculously bumped down on it again; and before she could make another attempt he had flown across to help her.

"No, no," said Catherine, whose indignation was greater than any she had felt in her life, pushing aside his outstretched hands.

So then he lifted her up bodily, indifferent to everything else in the world; and having set her on her feet he held her like that, tightly in his arms, and didn't care if he had to die for it.

There was a moment's complete silence. Catherine was so much amazed that for a moment she was quite still.

Then she gave a gasp—muffled, because of his coat, against which her face was pressed. *"Oh—"* she gasped, faint and muffled, trying to push him away.

She might as well have tried to push a rock away.

"Oh—" she gasped again, as Christopher, still not caring if he had to die for it, began kissing her. He kissed what he could—her hair, the tip of one ear, and she, aghast, horrified, buried her face deeper and deeper into his coat in her efforts to protect it.

Oh, the outrage—never in her life—how dared he, how dared he—just because she was alone, and had no one to defend her—

Not a word of this came out; it was entirely muffled in his coat. Aghast and horrified, Catherine continued to have the top of her head kissed, and her aghastness and horror became overwhelming when she realised that she—no, it wasn't possible, it *couldn't* be that she—that this—that she was somehow, besides being horrified, strangely shot through by a feeling that was not unpleasant? Impossible, impossible. . . .

"Let me go," she gasped into his coat. "Let me *go*—"

For answer he took her head in his hands and held it back and kissed her really, right on her mouth, as no one in her life before had ever kissed her.

Impossible, impossible. . . .

She stood, her arms hanging by her side, her body quivering. She didn't seem able to move. She seemed as if she were becoming every instant more drawn into this, more absorbed in what was happening—as profoundly absorbed as he was, as remote from realities. The room disappeared, the relics of George disappeared, the world disappeared, and all the reminders of the facts of her life. Youth had swept down out of the skies and caught her up in its arms into a strange, warm oblivion. He and she were not any longer Christopher and Catherine—Catherine tied up in a tangle of relationships, of obligations, of increasing memories, Christopher an impetuous young man who needed tremendously to be kept in his proper place: she was simply the Beloved, and he was Love.

"I worship you," murmured Christopher.

Through her dream she heard him murmuring, and it woke her up to consciousness.

She opened her eyes and looked up at him.

He was gazing down at her—beautiful, all light. She stared at him an instant, still held in his arms, collecting her thoughts.

What had she done? What was she doing? What was this? Oh, but it was shameful, shameful. . . .

She made one immense effort, and with both her hands pushed him away; and before he could stop her, for he too was in a dream, she had run to the door and flown along the passage to her bedroom and locked herself in.

Then she rang violently for Mrs. Mitcham, and told her through the shut door to let Mr. Monckton out—she was going to bed at once—she had a terrible headache. . . . And she sat down on her bed and cried bitterly.

∾ XI ∾

Virginia, coming back to the house on Sunday from a short after-luncheon stroll in the garden, where the daffodils were making a great show and the blackbirds a great noise, with the intention of putting her feet up till tea and lying quietly in her boudoir, was surprised to see her mother standing on the terrace.

Her first thought was of Stephen. Her mother had never yet come uninvited and unexpected. Was anything wrong with him?

She hastened her steps. "Anything wrong?" she called out anxiously.

Her mother shook her head reassuringly, and came down to meet her.

They kissed.

"I had such a longing to see you," said Catherine, in answer to Virginia's face of wonder; and, clinging to her a little, she added, "I felt I wanted to be close to you—quite close."

She took Virginia's arm, and they walked back slowly towards the house.

"Sweet of you, mother," said Virginia, who was taller than her mother, having taken after George in height as well as features; but still she wondered.

She wondered even more when later on she saw her mother's luggage. It suggested a longer stay than any she had yet made. But even as they strolled towards the house she felt a little uneasy. Her mother had been so satisfactory till now, so careful not to intrude, not to mar the felicities of the early married months. Stephen had warmly praised her admirable tendency to absence rather than presence, and Virginia had been very proud of having provided him with a mother-in-law he admitted could not be bettered. She loved to lay every good gift in her possession at Stephen's feet, and had rejoiced that her mother should be another of them. Was there going now to be a difference?

She said nothing, however, except that it was a pity she hadn't known her mother was coming, so that her room might have been ready for her.

"And how did you manage at the station, mother, with nothing to meet you?" she asked.

"I got the fly from the Dragon. I had to wait, of course, but not long. Old Mr. Pearce was so kind, and drove me himself. I would have let you know, but I hadn't time. I—I suddenly felt I *must* be with you. I had a longing to be just here, peacefully. It doesn't put you out, dearest?"

"But of course not, mother. Only you have missed hearing Stephen preach to-night."

"Yes. I'm sorry. I saw him yesterday, though. He dined with me."

"Oh, did he?" said Virginia, suddenly eager. "How was he? How did he seem? Had he had a good journey up? Did he say anything about the sandwiches? I've got a new cook, and I don't know if her sand—"

"Has Mrs. Benson gone?"

"Yes. We decided she was too expensive. You see, our idea is to cut down unnecessary expenses in the house so as to have more to carry out our schemes with, and this is the first time the new one has had to cut sandwiches. Did Stephen say anything about them?"

"No; so I expect they were all right."

"I do hope they were. He hates restaurant cars, you know, and won't go and have a proper lunch in them. And it's important—"

"Of course. How are you, darling?"

"*Quite* well. It's wonderful how well I feel. How did you think Stephen was looking?"

"Quite well."

"Not tired? That journey every week is so tiring. I must say I shall be glad when Lent is over. Isn't it wonderful, mother, how he works, how he gives up his life—"

"And how very well he is preaching. *You* have made him preach like that."

"I?"

"Yes. By just loving him."

Virginia blushed. "But who could help it?" she asked.

"And by believing in him."

"I think everybody must believe in Stephen," she said.

Her mother pressed her arm. "Darling," she said softly; and thought how strange a thing love was, how strange that Virginia, by taking this spinster-man, this middle-aged dry man, and just loving him with all her simple young heart and entirely believing in him, had made him, so completely commonplace before in all his utterances, suddenly—at least in the pulpit—sing. Was it acute, personal experience that one needed? Did one only cry out the truth really movingly when under some sort of lash, either of grief or ecstasy?

They went up the broad steps on to the familiar terrace. George's peacocks—George had been of opinion that manors should have peacocks—were behaving as peacocks ought. In the great tubs on each side of the row of long windows— George had seen pictures of terraces, and they all had tubs— the first tulips were showing buds. The bells had begun to ring for afternoon service, and the sound floated across the quiet tree-tops as it had floated on all the Sundays of all the years Catherine had spent in that place. Such blameless, such dignified years. Every corner of them open to the light. Years of clear duties, clear affections—family years. And here was her serious young daughter carrying on the tradition. And here was she too come back to it, but come back to it disgracefully, to hide. She hiding! She winced, and held on tighter to Virginia's arm. What would Virginia say if she knew? It seemed to Catherine that even her soul turned red at the bare thought.

They went into the boudoir, so recently her own—"I was just going to rest a little," said Virginia. "Yes, you must take great care not to stand about too much," said her mother—and Catherine tucked her up on the sofa, as she had so often tucked her up in her cot, and there they stayed talking, while the sweet damp smells a garden is so full of in early spring came in through the open window, and filled the room with delicate promises.

Throughout the afternoon Virginia talked, and Catherine listened. So it had always been in that family: Catherine listened. How thankful she was to listen now, not to be asked questions, not to have it noticed that she looked pale and heavy-eyed, leaning back in her own old chair, her head, which ached, on a cushion she remembered covering herself. Her humiliated head; the head Christopher only a few hours before had held in both his hands and—no, she wouldn't, she couldn't think of it.

Virginia had much to tell of all that she and Stephen were doing and planning and hoping and intending. Drastic changes were being made; the easy-going old days at the Manor were over for ever. She did not say this in so many words, because it might, perhaps, have been tactless, for were not the old easy-going ways her mother's ways? But it was evident that a pure flame of reform, of determination to abolish the old arrangements and substitute arrangements that improved, helped, and ultimately sanctified, was sweeping over Chickover. Her father's money, so long used merely on the unimaginative material well-being of a small domestic circle—she didn't quite put it this way, but so it drifted into Catherine's consciousness—was to be spread out like some rich top-dressing—nor did she say just this, yet Catherine had a vision of a kind of holy manure, and Stephen, girt with righteousness, digging it diligently in—across the wide field of the whole parish, and the crop that would spring up would be a crop of entirely sanitary dwellings. No one, said Virginia—it seemed to Catherine that it was the voice of Stephen—could live in an entirely sanitary dwelling without gradually acquiring an entirely sanitary body, and from a sanitary body to a sanitary soul was only a step.

"Stephen said something about that yesterday," said Catherine, her eyelids drooping as she lay back in her chair.

"He puts it so wonderfully. I can't explain things as he does, but I'd like just to give you an idea, mother—"

"I'd love to hear," said Catherine, her voice sounding very small and tired.

On the table beside Virginia's sofa were estimates and plans in a pile. She explained them to her mother one after the other, and the most convoluted plumbing, set forth in diagrams that looked exactly like diagrams Catherine had seen of people's insides, were as nothing to Virginia. She knew them by heart; she understood them clearly; she could and did tell her mother things about drains that Catherine would never have dreamed of left to herself. Lucidly she described the different drainage systems available, and their various advantages and drawbacks. No detail of plumbing was too small to be explored. For half an hour she talked of taps; for another she expounded geysers; and as for plugs, Catherine had no idea of all the things a plug could do to you and your health and happiness if you didn't in the first instance approach it with care and caution.

She lay back in her chair and listened. It was like listening to water running from one of Virginia's newest type of tap. It went on and on, and only an occasional word, or even a mere sound of agreement was required of her. Outside, the afternoon sun lit up the beautiful leafless beeches, and when the bells left off ringing she could hear the blackbirds again. Blessed, blessed tranquillity. She felt as people do after an illness—just wanting to rest, to be quiet.

And here she knew she was entirely safe from questions. Virginia never asked her questions about herself or what she was doing. George had been like that, too, pouring out everything to her, but not demanding that she should pour back. What a precious quality this was really, though she remembered it had sometimes made her feel lonely. How valuable, though, now. No solicitous questionings embarrassed her. She was aware she was pale and puff-eyed, but Virginia wouldn't notice. She couldn't have stood her daughter's young gaze of inquiry. Oh, she would have been ashamed, ashamed. . . .

Her head ached badly. She hadn't had any breakfast, in her wild desire to get away, to escape from Hertford Street before anything more could happen to her, and the slow Sunday train had offered no occasion for lunch. But she wasn't in the least hungry; she only wanted to sit there quiet and feel safe. Virginia, absorbed in all she had to talk about, hadn't thought of the possibility of her mother's not having had lunch. The arrival at such an unusual time had surprised her out of her customary hospitable solicitudes, for she took her duties as hostess of the Manor with much seriousness, and wouldn't for worlds have failed in any of them. Catherine, too, had forgotten lunch. She wanted nothing in the world but to get here, to sit quiet, to be safe.

While they were having tea, Mrs. Colquhoun the elder, Stephen's mother, called in to see her daughter-in-law.

She now lived alone in her son's abandoned rectory, and daily walked across the park to inquire how Virginia did. She was immensely surprised to see Catherine, who had not before arrived uninvited and unprepared for, but welcomed her nevertheless, for she too had a high opinion of her.

Nobody could have given less trouble than Mrs. Cumfrit, or been more sensible in the matter of the marriage. Also, not a breath of gossip or criticism had blown upon her during the whole long time between her husband's death and her daughter's marriage, when it well might have if she had been of a less complete propriety and quietness of behaviour. For, after all, she had only been in the early thirties when poor Mr. Cumfrit—a heart of gold, that man, but self-made, and not educated at either Oxford or Cambridge, nor even at a public school, which had been such a pity for Stephen, who otherwise might have found him more interesting to talk to—died, and being quite a pretty little thing, with something really very taking in the way she spoke and looked up at one, it wouldn't have been surprising if her name had been coupled from time to time with that of some man. It never had been. If there were suitors, the Rectory never heard of them. People came and stayed at the Manor, but they were all relations—either rather odd ones of poor Mr. Cumfrit's, or much more desirable ones of Mrs. Cumfrit's, whose mother had been a daughter of the first Lord Bognor. A quiet, decent, well-bred woman was Mrs. Cumfrit, content to devote herself to her home, her child, and the doing of kind acts in the parish; an excellent mother-in-law, tactful and unobtrusive; a good neighbour, a firm friend. The only thing about her which Mrs. Colquhoun could have wished, perhaps, different, was her personal appearance: she still looked younger than the mother of a married daughter should—though to do her justice it was in no way, apparently, because she tried to. Well, no doubt later on, when all the expensive clothes surviving from her extravagant days had had time to wear out, and she dressed more ordinarily, in sensible things like plain serges and tweeds, this would be remedied, and of course each year now would make a great difference. For Stephen's sake she ought to look older. People had smiled, Mrs. Colquhoun knew, at her being his mother-in-law. This seemed to his mother a pity. She was a little sensitive about it; the more so that there had been a time when she had secretly hoped Stephen would marry Mrs. Cumfrit—before, of course, his own splendid plan had dawned on her, and Virginia was still in socks. But Stephen, wise boy, knew what he was about, and waited patiently for little Virginia, of whom he had always been so fond.

The two mothers-in-law met with propriety. They kissed, and expressed pleasure.

"This is surely a surprise," said Mrs. Colquhoun, looking at Virginia but with a smile of welcome for Catherine on her face. She was very like her son—tall and thin, and of an avian profile. She towered above the small, round Catherine.

"Yes," said Virginia, putting her papers neatly together; Stephen did so much dislike disorder, and two mothers at once might presently create it.

"What brought you down on a Sunday, dear Mrs. Cumfrit?" asked Mrs. Colquhoun, sitting on the end of the sofa, and patting Virginia's feet, reassuringly to show they were not in her way, and approvingly because they were, as she daily told her daughter-in-law they should be, up.

Catherine wanted to say "A train," but discarded this as childish. In her conversations with Mrs. Colquhoun she was constantly being impelled towards the simple truth, and constantly discarding it as unsuitable.

She really didn't know what to give as a reason. She looked at her fellow-mother-in-law helplessly.

Mrs. Colquhoun was struck by an air of dilapidation about her. "Ageing," she commented to herself.

"I had a longing to see Virginia," said Catherine at last; and it seemed a lame sort of reason, in spite of its being true.

Mrs. Colquhoun privately hoped this mightn't be the first of a series of such longings, for it was in her opinion essential that a young couple should be left undisturbed by relations, and especially should they not be allowed to get a feeling that at any moment they might unexpectedly be descended upon. It made them jumpy; and what could be worse for a young married woman than to be made jumpy? For three months Virginia's mother had left her most properly alone, only coming down occasionally for a night, and never without being asked. Was she now going to inaugurate an era of surprise visits? Stephen wouldn't like it at all, and Mrs. Colquhoun couldn't help feeling, even as Virginia had felt, a little uneasy. If she had seen the luggage she would have felt still more so, for it was not, as Virginia had already noticed, the luggage of a mere week-end.

"How natural," said Mrs. Colquhoun. "And dear Virginia will, I am sure, have been delighted."

"Yes," said Virginia, removing her pile of papers out of reach of the jam to which her mother seemed to be helping herself a little carelessly; Stephen did so much dislike stickiness.

"But I hope you weren't worried about her," Mrs. Colquhoun continued. "She is in very good hands here, you know, and you may be sure that when her husband is away I look after her—don't I, Virginia."

"Yes," said Virginia, anxiously watching her mother, who seemed about to put her cup down on the top of the pile of papers. She got up, and quietly drew the table away into safety; Stephen did so much dislike smudges.

"Indeed I know that," said Catherine politely.

She and Mrs. Colquhoun had always been politeness itself to each other. She tried to smile as she spoke. She ought to smile. She always did smile when addressing Mrs. Colquhoun. And she couldn't. An awful vision of what Mrs. Colquhoun's face would change into if she could have seen her the night before froze her mouth stiff.

"She looks ill," thought Mrs. Colquhoun; and fervently hoped she wasn't going to be ill there.

Virginia offered them bread and butter. Mrs. Colquhoun would not eat; she would just have a cup of tea, and be off again. Virginia mustn't think she came there only for what she could get.

Virginia smiled, for this was one of her mother-in-law's little jokes; but she was of so grave a type of countenance that even when she smiled she somehow managed still to look serious. She had strongly marked dark eyebrows, and her hair was drawn off her forehead and neatly brushed back from her ears. She looked very young—rather like a schoolgirl in her last term, dressed with the plainness Stephen and her own taste preferred. She was not pretty, she was merely young; but what grace, what charm there was in that!

Her mother-in-law watched her presiding over the massive silver tea service—George had wished Catherine's tea service to be handsome—with proud and affectionate possessiveness. Virginia called both the mothers-in-law mother—what else was she to call them? Impossible to address Mrs. Colquhoun by a hybrid like mamma or, even more impossible and grotesque, mummy—and it led to confusion. For, unless their eyes were fixed on her face, they couldn't know which of them she was talking to. Conversation was constantly being tripped up and delayed by this when the three were together, and Virginia, who was anxious to be a good hostess, besides dutifully loving them both, sometimes found this a strain, and wished she could deal with them separately. Not that, owing to the rareness and shortness of her mother's visits, it had often happened that she had had them at the same time, for on those occasions her mother-in-law, apprised of the arrival, refrained, as she put it, from intruding. This had been easy when a visit only lasted from Saturday to Monday; but if the present one were going to last longer—and what about all that luggage?—it was not to be expected nor wished that Stephen's mother shouldn't come round as usual.

What she and Stephen's mother wanted most to know at that moment was how long Virginia's mother meant to stay. But no one can ever ask what most they want to know. What one most wants to know does invariably seem outside the proprieties, thought Virginia, slightly frowning at life's social complications as she ate her bread and butter, thankful that she and Stephen lived in the country where there were fewer of them.

And Catherine, lying back in her chair—Mrs. Colquhoun never lay back in her chair unless she was definitely unwell and in a dressing-gown—didn't in any way help. She said nothing whatever about her intentions, and hardly anything about anything else; she merely sat there and looked dilapidated. Evidently, thought Mrs. Colquhoun, observing her, she was worn out. But why? One journey by train from London to Chickover, even by a slow Sunday train, oughtn't to make a normal woman look yellow. Mrs. Cumfrit looked excessively yellow. Why?

"Do have some of this cake, mother," said Virginia; and as Catherine's gaze was fixed on the open window and Mrs. Colquhoun's was fixed on Catherine, they both together said they wouldn't, thank you; and then, as usual when this happened, there was a brief upheaval of explanations.

"And how is the excellent Mrs. Mitcham?" inquired Mrs. Colquhoun, pleasantly. "How does she like her transplantation from a quiet country parish to London? Does she take root in Mayfair?"

Catherine said she was as kind as ever, and made her most comfortable.

"We were sure she would, weren't we, Virginia. Dear Mrs. Cumfrit, I do so like to know that you are in clover with that devoted creature to look after you. And so does Virginia—don't you, Virginia."

Virginia said she did, and Catherine said she was.

"But how does the good soul like it when you leave her alone and come away?" inquired Mrs. Colquhoun. "Oh well, of course you never do leave her for long, do you. A day or two—at the outside a day or two, or really one can imagine her beginning to fret, she is so devoted to you."

"Stephen might have stayed in the flat," said Virginia, "as you're not in it this week-end, mother. Poor Stephen—he does get so very tired of hotels. I wish we had known."

"Oh—" exclaimed Catherine, startled at the picture her imagination instantly presented of Stephen loose in her bedroom—there were only two bedrooms in the flat, hers and Mrs. Mitcham's—sleeping in her bed, ranging at will among her excessively pretty odds and ends, among all those little charming things that collect on the dressing-table of a wealthy man's adored wife, and naturally don't wear out as fast as he does. But she pulled herself up, and after a tiny pause deftly ended what had so unpropitiously begun with, "What a pity."

"Perhaps it might be arranged another time," suggested Mrs. Colquhoun, hoping that Catherine would on this let them know whether the next Sunday was to find her still at poor little Virginia's. Surely not; surely, surely she couldn't suddenly have become, after so much tactfulness, entirely without any?

But Catherine only said in her small voice, as politely as ever, "Indeed it might"—and wondered to herself how many more Sundays there were in Lent. Not many, she thought;

Easter must be quite close now; Stephen had been in London for what seemed to her innumerable week-ends, and Lent, she knew, only contained six of them. Yet even if there were only one more, the picture of Stephen in her bed. . . .

Mrs. Colquhoun now saw that only a direct question would extract from Catherine what she wanted to know, and getting up with her customary briskness—she was well on the way to seventy, but yet was brisk—remarked that she really must be going; and having bent over Virginia and kissed her—"No, no, don't dream of moving, my dear child," she said—she approached Catherine, who had got out of her chair, and held out her hand.

"Shall I see you again, dear Mrs. Cumfrit?" she asked.

And Catherine, instead of, as Mrs. Colquhoun had trusted she would, saying, "I'm afraid not—I go home to-morrow early," only said warmly, "Indeed I hope so."

Which left Mrs. Colquhoun where it found her.

‹ö XII ‹ö

Mr. Lambton came to supper. He was the curate; and, during these Lenten Sundays of Stephen's absence, after evening service supped at the Manor.

Mrs. Colquhoun, it transpired, supped on these occasions too, otherwise, Virginia pointed out, Mr. Lambton couldn't have supped, it needing two women to make one man proper. She didn't put it quite like this, but that is how it arrived in Catherine's mind. On this evening Mrs. Colquhoun didn't sup because Catherine's presence made hers unnecessary; and by absenting herself when she needn't have, and thus leaving Catherine to enjoy her daughter's society untrammelled, gave her colleague in the office of mother-in-law a lesson in tact which she hoped, as she ate her solitary meal at home and didn't like it, for she hadn't been expected back to supper and there was nothing really worth eating, would not be lost.

Mr. Lambton was young, and kind, and full of reverences. He reverenced his Rector and his Rector's wife and his

Rector's mother and his Rector's mother-in-law; he was ready to reverence their man-servants and their maid-servants and anything that was theirs as well. He was not long from Cambridge, and this was his first curacy.

On the quiet surface of the evening he hardly caused an extra ripple. He was attentive to both ladies, offering them beet-root salad and bringing them footstools, and afterwards in the drawing-room he brought them more footstools. Catherine kept on forgetting he was there; and Mr. Lambton, having established his Rector's wife's mother in an easy-chair out of a draught, and inquired if she didn't wish for a shawl—having discharged, in fact, his duty to the waning generation, forgot in his turn that she was there, and with Virginia discussed the proposed improvements, going with a quiet relish through all the papers Catherine had been taken through that afternoon.

Catherine sat in her chair and dozed. She felt just as old as they made her. With drowsy wonder she remembered this time yesterday, and the afternoon at Hampton Court, when she had raced—yes, actually raced—about the gardens, propelled by Christopher's firm hand on her elbow and keeping up with his great strides, laughing, talking, the blood quick in her veins, the scent of spring in her nostrils, the gay adoring words of that strange young man in her ears. Mr. Lambton must be about Christopher's age, she thought. Yet to Mr. Lambton she was merely some one, perhaps more accurately something, to be placed carefully in a chair out of a draught and then left. Which of them was right? It was most unsettling. Was she the same person to-night as last night? Was she two persons? If she was only one, which one? Or was she a mere vessel of receptiveness, a transparent vessel into which other people poured their view of her, and she instantly reflected the exact colour of their opinion?

Catherine didn't like this idea of herself—it seemed to make her somehow get lost, and she shifted uneasily in her chair. But she didn't like anything about herself these days; she was horribly surprised, and shocked, and confused. After all, one couldn't get away from the fact that one was well on in the forties, and supposing that there were people in the world who did seem able to fall in love with one even then—silly people, of course; silly, violent people—surely one felt nothing oneself but a bland and creditable indifference? On the other hand she didn't believe she was nearly old enough to be planted among cushions out of a draught and left. It was very puzzling, and tiresome too. Here she felt almost rheumatic with age. Last night—

The mere thought of last night woke her up so completely and made her so angry that she gave the footstool an impatient push with her foot, and it skidded away along the polished oak floor.

Mr. Lambton looked up from the papers he and Virginia were poring over, and mildly contemplated the figure by the fire a moment, collecting his thoughts. Something rather vigorous seemed just to have been done. There had been a noise, and the footstool was certainly a good way off.

He got up, and went across and replaced it under Catherine's feet. "You're sure you're quite comfortable, Mrs. Cumfrit?" he asked, in much the same voice with which, when district visiting, he addressed the aged poor—a hearty, an encouraging, a rather loud voice. "You wouldn't like another cushion, would you?"

Catherine thanked him, and just to please him and make him feel he was pleasing her, said she thought another cushion would be very nice indeed, and let him adjust it with care in what he described, evidently from his knowledge of where his older parishioners chiefly ached, the small of her back.

The small of her back. She wanted to laugh. All these elderly places she seemed to have about her—feet needing supporting on footstools, shoulders needing sheltering in shawls, backs needing propping with cushions. . . . But she didn't laugh; she sat quiet, having nicely thanked Mr. Lambton, and on the whole did feel very comfortable like that, cushioned and footstooled, and no demands of any sort being made on her. It anyhow was peace.

Down here she was still simply somebody's mother, and it was a restful state. Except for the last three months she had continually in her life only been somebody's something. She had begun by being somebody's daughter—such a good little girl; she clearly remembered being a good little girl who gave no trouble, and played happily for hours together by herself. Then she passed straight from that to being somebody's wife; again a great success, again doing everything that was expected of her and nothing that wasn't. Then, when this phase was over, for twelve years she became exclusively somebody's mother; but how had she not, when that too ended, stretched out her arms to the sun and cried out all to herself, "Now I'm going to be me!"

Three months she had had of it, three months of freedom in London; and friends had seemed to spring up like daisies under her feet, and Mrs. Mitcham was always making tea, and cigarette ends were always being emptied out of ash-trays, and some cousins she had in London, who had cropped up the minute she had got there, brought friends, and these friends instantly became her friends, and it was a holiday, the three months, a very happy little holiday as different as possible from anything she had ever known, in which every one she met was kind and gay, and nobody in any way restricted her movements, and when she wanted to be alone and go for her solitary enjoyments, such as music, which she best loved alone, or visits to Kew to see whether spring wasn't anywhere about yet, she could be alone and go, and when she wanted to see people and talk, she could see them and talk, and there was no clash anywhere of some one else's opposing tastes and wishes.

A pleasant life. An amusing, independent, dignified small life; opening out before her with that other life of faithfully fulfilled duties and expectations at the back of her like a pillow to rest her conscience on. She hadn't had time to arrange anything yet, but she certainly meant to do good as well as be happy, to find some form of charitable activity and throw herself into it. She wasn't going to be idle, to drift into being one of those numerous ex-wives and mothers, unhappy specialists out of a job, who roam through their remaining years unprofitably conversing.

All this had seemed to open out before her like a bland afternoon landscape, and what had she done? Behaved so idiotically that she had been forced to run away; and not only run, but not know in the least when she would be able to go back again.

It was most unfortunate that she should have chanced to meet and make friends with the one young man in, she supposed, ten millions, who could be mad enough to fall in love with her and was of an undisciplined disposition into the bargain. Why, he might have been a quite meek young man—one of those who worship in secret, reverence from afar, one controlled by a lifted finger or a flickered eyelash. But nothing controlled Christopher. He was an elemental force, and he swept her with him—she had certainly been swept somewhere unusual that brief moment she became so strangely quiescent in his arms. In his arms! Disgraceful. It rankled. It gnawed. The only thing to do, with such a memory scorching one, was to take to one's heels. But imagine at her age having to take to any such things. The *indignity*. . . .

Once more the footstool skidded across the shiny floor.

The heads bent over the table turned towards her inquiringly.

"Have you the fidgets, mother?" asked Virginia gravely.

"I think I'll go to bed," said Catherine, getting up from her cushions.

Mr. Lambton hastened across to help. An odd desire to slap Mr. Lambton seized her. She blushed that she should wish to.

"But not before prayers?" said Virginia, surprised.

"Oh yes—I forgot prayers," said Catherine, slightly ashamed.

Virginia, though, was more ashamed. It did seem to her unfortunate that her mother should have said that before Mr. Lambton. Bad to forget them, but worse to say so.

She got up and rang the bell.

"We'll have them now, as you're tired," she said.

There usedn't to be prayers in Catherine's day, because George in his day hadn't liked them, and she had kept things up exactly as he had, so that it was natural she should forget the new habits, besides finding it difficult to remember that the Manor was really a rectory now, a place in which family prayers the last thing at night and the first thing in the morning were inevitable.

In came the servants, headed by the parlourmaid bearing a tray of lemonade and soda water, and it seemed to Catherine, watching for the faces of old friends, that they had been much thinned out. They trickled in where, in old days, if there had been prayers, they would have poured. Manifestly they were being rapidly exchanged for cottages. There was hardly one left to smile furtively at her before settling down with folded hands and composed vacant face to listen to Mr. Lambton.

He officiated in Stephen's absence. He did it in a clear tenor. The room growled with muffled responses. Virginia's voice firmly led the growls. They all knelt with their faces to the walls and the soles of their shoes towards Mr. Lambton. Catherine became very conscious of her shoes, aware that their high heels were not the heels of the absolutely pure in heart. Before her mind floated a picture she had once seen of a pair of German boots that had belonged to a German woman who had been wicked, but, by the time she wore the boots, was good. They were the very opposite of the shoes she herself had on at the moment, and below the picture of them was written:

> O wie lieblich sind die Schuhe
> Demuthsvolle Seelensruhe. . . .

She wondered what Mr. Lambton would think of them as outward signs of inward grace, and, if he thought highly, what would he think of hers? Ashamed, she collected her wandering thoughts; for the words Mr. Lambton was repeating were so beautiful that they sanctified everything—himself, herself, the assembled upturned shoe-soles. She suddenly felt very small and silly, as though she were one of the commoner insects, hopping irreverently at the feet of some great calm angel. She laid her cheek on her folded arms and listened attentively to the lovely words Mr. Lambton was praying—*Lighten our darkness, we beseech Thee* . . . How often she had heard them; how seldom she had noticed them. They were more beautiful than music; they were nobler. . . .

Virginia saw—it was her business to see how the servants behaved, and her glance naturally took in Catherine too—her mother's attitude, and hoped that Mr. Lambton didn't. The only decent way of praying in a drawing-room was to kneel up straight, hands folded and eyes either shut or looking at the seat of one's chair. Her mother was crouching, almost sitting, on the floor, her arms resting on her chair, her head laid sideways on her arms. Mothers oughtn't to do that. A child who was very tired might, but it would certainly be reproved afterwards. Fortunately the servants couldn't see because of their backs, but Mr. Lambton, if he raised his eyes, wouldn't be able not to. She hoped he wouldn't raise his eyes. How very keenly one felt everything one's mother did or didn't do. Strange how sensitive one became about her when one was grown up, and how, in some uncomfortable way, responsible.

Prayers were over in ten minutes, the servants filed out, Mr. Lambton, having drunk some soda water and said what was proper about his evening, went away, and Virginia, reluctant to go upstairs to her frigid solitude, came and stood by the fire warming her hands so as to put off the melancholy moment a little longer, and talked of Stephen.

"I do so miss him these week-ends," she said, strangling a sigh.

Catherine sympathetically stroked her arm.

"I can so well understand how much one would miss some one one loved as you love Stephen," she said.

("Mother," thought Virginia, "is really very nice, in spite of her queer ways.")

"You've no idea," she said aloud, her eyes bright with pride, "how wonderful he is."

("Who," thought Catherine, "could have imagined it. That solemn old Stephen.")

"I'm so glad," she said aloud, putting her arm round Virginia. "You know I used to be afraid—I wasn't quite sure—whether perhaps the difference in age—"

"Age!"

Virginia looked down at her mother pityingly. "I wish you understood, mother," she said gravely, "how little age has to do with it so long as people love each other. Why, what can it matter? We never think of it. It simply doesn't come in. Stephen is Stephen, whatever his age may be. He never, never could be anything else."

"No," agreed Catherine rather wistfully, for if Stephen could only be something else she might find him easier to talk to.

However, that was neither here nor there. He wasn't Virginia's husband in order to talk agreeably to her mother. The great thing was that he succeeded in bringing complete bliss to his wife. How right the child had been to insist on marrying him; how unerring was her instinct. What had she cared for the reasoning of relations, the advice so copiously given not only by Catherine herself, but by various uncles and cousins, both on her father's and mother's side? And as for the suggestion that she would look ridiculous going about with a husband old enough to be her father, she had merely smiled gravely at that and not even condescended to answer.

"I wonder," said Catherine, pensively gazing into the fire, her cheek against Virginia's sleeve, "how much happiness has been prevented by fear."

"What fear?"

"Of people—and especially relations. Their opinion."

"I am sure," said Virginia, blushing a little, for she wasn't used to talking about these things to anybody but Stephen, "that one should give up everything to follow love."

"But what love?"

Virginia blushed again. "Oh, mother—of course only the right love."

"You mean husbands?"

"Well, of course, mother."

Virginia blushed a third time. What could her mother imagine she was thinking of?

She went on with grave shyness: "Love—the right love—shouldn't mind anything any one in the world says."

"I suppose it shouldn't," said Catherine. "And yet—"

"There isn't any 'and yet' in love, mother. Not in real love."

"You mean husbands," said Catherine again.

"Well, of course, mother," said Virginia, impatiently this time.

"I suppose there isn't," said Catherine pensively. "But still—"

"There isn't any 'but still' either."

Before this splendid inexperience, this magnificent unawareness, Catherine could only be mute; and presently she held up her face to be kissed, and murmured that she thought she would now go to bed.

Virginia fidgeted. She didn't seem to want to leave the fire. She raked out the ashes for quite a long time, and then pushed the chairs back into their proper places and shook up the cushions.

"I hate going to bed," she said suddenly.

Catherine, who had been watching her sleepily, was surprised awake again—Virginia had sounded so natural.

"Do you, darling?" she asked. "Why?"

Virginia looked at her mother a moment, and then fetched the bedroom candles from the table they had been put ready on, the electric light being now cut off by Stephen's wish at half-past ten each night.

She gave Catherine her candle. "Didn't you—" she began.

"Didn't I what?"

"Hate going to bed when my father was away?"

"Oh. I see. No, I didn't. I—I liked being alone."

They stood looking at each other, their candles lighting up their faces. Catherine's face was surprised; Virginia's immensely earnest.

"I think that's very strange, mother," she said; and added after a silence, "You do understand, don't you, that in all I've been saying about—about love, I only"—she blushed for the fourth time—"mean *proper* love."

"Oh, quite, darling," Catherine hastened to assure her. "Husbands."

And Catherine, not used to bedroom candles, held hers crooked and dropped some grease on the carpet, and Virginia had the utmost difficulty in strangling an exclamation. Stephen did so much dislike grease on the carpets.

⋐ XIII ⋑

Stephen came back by the first train next morning, suppressing his excitement as he got out of the car and on the doorstep saw Virginia, standing there as usual, in her simple morning frock and fresh neatness, waiting to welcome him home. Outwardly he looked just a sober, middle-aged cleric, giving his wife a perfunctory kiss while the servants brought in his things; inwardly he was thirty at the sight of her, and twenty at the touch of her. She, suppressing in her turn all signs of joy, received his greeting with a grave smile, and they both at once went into his study, and shutting the door fell into each other's arms.

"My wife," whispered Stephen.

"My husband," whispered Virginia.

It was their invariable greeting at this blissful Monday morning moment of reunion. No one would have recognised Stephen who saw him alone with Virginia; no one would have recognised Virginia who saw her alone with Stephen. Such are the transformations of love. Catherine kept out of the way; she went tactfully for a walk. They were to themselves till lunch-time, and could pour out everything each had been thinking and feeling and saying and doing since they parted such ages ago, on Saturday.

Unfortunately this time Virginia had something to pour out which wasn't going to give Stephen pleasure. She put it off as long as she could, but he, made quick by love, soon felt there was something in the background of her talk, and drawing his finger gently over her forehead, which usually was serene with purest joy, said, "A little pucker. I see the tiniest pucker. What is it, Virginia love?"

"Mother," said Virginia.

"Mother? My mother?"

Stephen couldn't believe it. His mother causing puckers?

"No. Mine. She's come."

"Come here?"

Stephen was much surprised. And on Saturday night not a word, not an indication of this intention.

"Had you asked her?" he inquired.

"Oh, Stephen—as though I would without your consent!"

"No. Of course not, darling. But when—?"

"Yesterday."

"On a Sunday?"

"Yes. And I'm afraid—oh, Stephen, I do think she doesn't mean to go away very soon, because she has brought two trunks."

Stephen was much moved by this news. He looked at his wife in real dismay. He considered he was still in his honeymoon. What were three months? Nothing. To people who loved as he and Virginia loved they were absolutely nothing, and to have a parent come and interrupt, and especially a parent to whom the whole place had so recently belonged. . . . Unfortunate; unfortunate; unfortunate to the last degree.

"How very odd," said Stephen, who till now had regarded his mother-in-law as a monument of tact; adding, after a pause, "Two trunks, did you say? You counted them, I suppose. Two trunks. That is certainly a large number. And your mother said nothing at all of this when I dined with her on Saturday—"

"I do hope, darling," interrupted Virginia anxiously, "that you had enough to eat?"

"Plenty, plenty," said Stephen, waving the recollection of the scrambled eggs aside. "She said no word at all, Virginia. On the contrary, she assured me she was coming to St. Clement's to hear me preach last night."

"Oh, Stephen—I simply can't understand how she could bear to miss that!"

"Have you any idea, my love, what made her come down unannounced?" asked Stephen, the joy of his homecoming completely clouded over.

"No, darling. I can't make it out. It really puzzles me."

"You have no theory at all?"

"None."

"Nor any idea as to the length of her proposed stay?"

"Only the idea of the two trunks. Mother hasn't said a word, and I can't very well ask."

"No," said Stephen thoughtfully. "No." And added, "It is very disquieting."

It was; for he saw clearly what an awkward situation must arise with the abdicated monarch alongside of the reigning one for any time longer than a day or two, and also, since nothing particular appeared to have brought her down, she must have come idly, on an impulse, because she had nothing else to do—and to be idle, to drift round, seemed to him really a great pity for any human being. It led inevitably to mischief. Fruitful activity was of the first importance for every one, he couldn't but think, especially for one's wife's mother. But it must take place somewhere else. That was essential: it must take place somewhere else.

"Well, perhaps," he said, stroking Virginia's hair, endeavouring to give and get comfort, "in spite of the trunks it will only be for a day or two. Ladies do take large amounts of luggage about with them."

Virginia shook her head. "Mother doesn't," she said. "Each time before she only brought a bag."

They were silent. He left off stroking her hair.

Then Stephen pulled himself together. "Well, well," he said. "Come, come. Whatever it is that happens to us, Virginia love, we must do our best to bear it, mustn't we."

"Oh, of *course,* Stephen darling," said Virginia. "You know I'll do whatever you do."

She laid her head on his breast, and they gave themselves up to those happy lawful caresses that are at once the joy and the duty of the married. Exquisite arrangement, Stephen considered, who had been starved of caresses till middle age, and now, let lawfully loose among them, found them more delightful than in his most repented-of dreams he had dared imagine —exquisite arrangement, by which the more you love the greater is your virtue.

"After all, my darling," he whispered, "we have got each other."

"Indeed and indeed we have," whispered Virginia, clinging to him.

"My own dear wife," murmured Stephen, holding her close.

"My own darling husband," murmured Virginia, blissfully nestling.

Catherine, meanwhile, was hurrying back across muddy fields and many stiles so as not to be late for lunch. Anxious to leave her children—was not Stephen by law now also her child? fantastic thought—to themselves as long as possible, she had rather overdone it, and walked farther than there was time for, so that at the end her walk had almost to become a run. Stephen, she felt sure, was a punctual man. Besides, nobody likes being kept waiting for meals. She hoped they wouldn't wait. She hurried and got hot. Her shoes were caked in mud, and her hair, for the March wind was blowing, wasn't neat. She hoped to slip in unseen and arrange herself decently before facing Stephen, but when she arrived within sight of the house they both, having been standing at the window ever since the gong went, came out to meet her.

"Oh, you shouldn't have!" she cried, as soon as they were near enough to hear. "You shouldn't have waited. I'm dreadfully sorry. Am I very late?"

"Only a quarter of an hour," said Stephen courteously—how wonderful he was, thought Virginia. "Nothing at all to worry about. How do you do. This is an unexpected pleasure."

"I hope you don't mind?" said Catherine, smiling up at him as they shook hands. "I've been impulsive. I came down on a sudden wave of longing to be with Virginia. You'll have to teach me self-control, Stephen."

"We all need that," said Stephen.

He hid his feelings; he contrived to smile; he was wonderful, thought Virginia.

"And on my very first day I'm late for lunch," said Catherine. "I wish you hadn't waited."

The expression "my very first day" seemed to Stephen and Virginia ominous; nobody spoke of a first day unless there was to be a second, a third, a fourth, a whole row of days. There was, therefore, a small pause. Then Stephen said, as politely as if he were a man who wasn't hungry and had not had breakfast ever so much earlier than usual, "Not at all"—and Catherine felt, as she had so often felt before, that he was a little difficult to talk to, and Virginia, who knew how particularly he disliked being kept waiting for meals, even when he wasn't hungry, loved him more than ever.

Indeed, his manner to her mother was perfect, she thought

—so patient, so—the absurd word did describe it—
gentlemanly. And he remained patient and gentlemanly even
when Catherine, in her desire to be quick, only gave her
muddy shoes the briefest rubbing on the mat, so that she made
footmarks on the hall carpet, and Stephen, who was a clean
man and didn't like footmarks on his carpets, merely said,
"Kate will bring a brush."

Lunch went off very well considering, Virginia thought. It
was thanks to Stephen, of course. He was adorable. He told
her mother the news of the parish, not forgetting anything he
thought might interest her about the people she had known,
such as young Andrews breaking his leg at football, and
foolish Daisy Logan leaving her good situation to marry a
cowman and begin her troubles before she need; and afterwards in the drawing-room, where they had coffee—when she
and Stephen were alone they had it cosily in the study, the
darling study, scene of so many happy private hours—he sent
Kate to fetch the plans and estimates, and went through them
with her mother so patiently and carefully, explaining them
infinitely better and more clearly than she had been able to do
the day before, and always in such admirable brief sentences,
using five words where she, with her untrained mind, had used
fifty, and making her mother feel that they liked her to know
what they were doing, and wanted her to share their interests.
Her mother was not to feel out in the cold. Dear Stephen.
Virginia glowed with love of him. Who but Stephen could, in
the moment of his own disappointment, think and act with
such absolute sweetness?

Time flew. It was her hour for putting up her feet, but she
couldn't tear herself away from Stephen and the plans. She sat
watching his fine face—how she loved his thinness, his
clean-cut, definite features—bent over the table, while with
his finger he traced the lines her mother was having explained
to her. Her mother looked sleepy. Virginia thought this queer
so early in the day. She had been sleepy the evening before, but
that was natural after the journey and getting up so early.
Perhaps she had walked too far, and tired herself. After all, she
wasn't any longer young.

"You see how simply it can be worked," said Stephen. "You
merely turn this tap—a—and the water flows through b and c,
along d, and round the curve to f, washing out, on its way, the
whole of e."

Her mother murmured something—Virginia thought she

said, "I'd like to be *e"*—and if this was really what she did say, it was evident that she not only looked sleepy, but was very nearly actually asleep. In which case Stephen's pains were all being wasted, and he might just as well leave off.

"Not only," said Stephen, "is this the simplest device of any that have been submitted, and as far as one can humanly tell absolutely foolproof, but, as is so often the case with the best, it is also the cheapest."

There was a long pause. Her mother said nothing. Virginia looked at her, and it did seem as if she really had gone to sleep.

"Mother," said Virginia gently. She couldn't bear that Stephen should be taking all this trouble to interest and inform somebody who wasn't awake.

Her mother started and gave herself a little shake and said rather hastily, "I see." And then, to save what she felt was a delicate situation and divert Stephen's attention from herself —he was looking at her thoughtfully over the top of his glasses—she pointed to a specially involuted part of the plan, where pipes seemed twisted in a frenzy, and asked what happened there, at that knot, at—she bent closer—yes, at *k.*

Stephen, simple-minded man, at once with the utmost courtesy and clearness told her, and before he was half-way through his explanation Virginia noticed—it was really very queer—her mother's eyelids shutting again.

This time she got up a little brusquely; she couldn't let Stephen's kindness and time be wasted in such a manner. "It's my hour for resting," she said, standing gravely at the table, one hand, a red young hand with a slender wedding ring, resting on her husband's shoulder. "I suppose I ought to go and lie down."

Her mother at that moment came to life again. "Shall I come and tuck you up?" she asked, making a movement as if she were going to accompany her.

"Sweet of you, mother—but if Stephen doesn't mind, I thought I'd rest on the couch in his study to-day. It's so comfortable."

"Certainly," said Stephen.

He refrained from calling her his love; he and she both refrained from any endearments in public—on principle, as unseemly in a clergyman's family, and also because they feared that if once they began they mightn't be able to stop, so excessive was their mutual delight, at this early stage, in lovemaking, and so new were they both at the delicious game. And, besides this, they were shy, and unable either of them in their hearts to get away from a queer feeling of guilt, in spite of the Law and the Church both having shed their awful smiles and blessings on whatever they might choose to do.

"Oh, I won't profane Stephen's study," said her mother, smiling at him. "I'll only just come and tuck you up and then leave you to sleep. Thank you so much, Stephen," she added, turning to him; "it has been so good of you. I think your ideas are marvellous."

But how many of them had her mother heard, Virginia wondered as, after a pressure of her husband's shoulder which meant, "Be quick and come to the study and we can be by ourselves till tea," and a brief answering touch of her hand by his which meant that he'd follow her in five minutes, she and Catherine walked together down the long, beautiful old room, while Stephen laid his papers carefully in the wicker tray kept for the purpose. Very few, surely. Yet her mother spoke enthusiastically. It did slightly shake one's belief in a mother who obviously slept most of the time ideas were being expounded to her, that she should, with that easy worldly over-emphasis Virginia hadn't heard now for three months, that pleasant simulation of an enthusiasm which Virginia had always, ever since she began really to think, suspected couldn't be quite real, declare them marvellous, on waking up.

"I mustn't be unfair, though," thought Virginia as they went into the study arm in arm—it was Catherine who had put her arm through Virginia's. "After all, I explained things yesterday, so mother did know something of our ideas, even if she didn't listen to-day. But *why* should she be so tired?"

"Didn't you sleep well last night, mother?" she asked, as Catherine arranged the cushions comfortably for her.

"Not very well," said Catherine, turning a little red and looking oddly like a child caught out in ill behaviour, thought Virginia.

How strange the way the tables of life turned, and how imperceptibly yet quickly one changed places. Here was her mother looking just as she was sure she herself used to look when she was caught out doing wrong things with the fruit or the jam. But why? Virginia couldn't think why she should look so.

"I shall sleep better when I've got more used to the bed,"

said Catherine, who was unnerved by the knowledge that Stephen's conversation did inevitably dispose her to drowsiness, and that Virginia was on the verge of finding it out.

Used to the bed. Virginia turned this expression over in her mind with grave eyes fixed on her mother, who was smoothing her skirt over her ankles.

Used to the bed. It suggested infinity to Virginia. You couldn't get used to a bed without practice in spending nights in it; you couldn't get used to anything without many repetitions. How she wished she could be frank with her mother and ask her straight out how long she meant to stay. But could one ever be frank with either one's mother or with one's guest? And when both were combined! As a daughter she wasn't able to say anything, as a hostess she wasn't able to say anything, and as a daughter and a hostess rolled into one her muzzling was complete.

Virginia watched her mother gravely as she busied herself making her comfortable. It was for her mother to give some idea of her intentions, and she hadn't said a word.

"Are you quite comfortable, dearest?" Catherine asked, kissing the solemn young face before going away.

"Quite, thank you. Sweet of you, mother," said Virginia, closing her eyes.

For some reason she suddenly wanted to cry. Things were so contrary; it was so hard that she and Stephen couldn't be left alone; yet her mother was so kind, and one would hate to hurt her. But one's husband and his happiness—did not they come first?

Her mother went away, shutting the door softly. Virginia lay listening for Stephen's footsteps.

Her forehead had a pucker in it again.

Used to the bed. . . .

✍ XIV ✍

Catherine was safe at Chickover; for that much she was thankful. But, apart from safety, what a strange, different place it now seemed to her.

Each night throughout that week as she undressed, she had a fresh set of reflections to occupy her mind. It was a queer week. It had an atmosphere of its own. In this developing dampness—for so at last it presented itself to her imagination —she felt as if her wings, supposing she had any, hung more and more stiffly at her side. As the solemn days trudged one by one heavily past she had a curious sensation of ebbing vitality. Life was going out of her. Mists were closing in on her. The house was so quiet that it made her feel deaf. After dark there were so few lights that it made her feel blind. Oh yes, she was safe—safe from that mad young man; but there were other things here—strange, uncomfortable things. There was this depressing feeling of a slow, creeping, choking, wet fog gradually enveloping her.

On Monday night as she undressed she didn't think like this, she hadn't got as far. All she did on Monday night was to go over the events of the day with mild wonder. She had said a great many prayers that day; for not only had there been family prayers before breakfast and the last thing at night, but Stephen had asked her after tea whether she wouldn't like to go with him to evening service.

A host's suggestions are commands. When he invites, one must needs accept. Indeed, she had accepted with the propitiatory alacrity common in guests when their hosts invite, aware that he was doing his best, with the means at his disposal, to entertain her, and anxious to show herself grateful. Where other hosts take their guests to look at ruins, or similar unusual sights, Stephen took his to church.

"Oh—delightful," she had exclaimed on his proposing it; and only afterwards reflected that this was perhaps not quite the right word.

Virginia didn't go with them, because so much kneeling and

standing mightn't be good for her, and she and Stephen set out
after tea in the windy dusk by themselves, Stephen carrying
the lantern that would be lit for their walk home in the dark.
Catherine, accordingly, had had two *tête-à-tête* talks with
Stephen that day, but as she was walking rather fast during
them, and there was a high wind into the bargain, flicking her
blood, she had had no trouble in keeping awake. Also there
was the hope of the quiet relaxing in church at the end, with no
need to make any effort for a while, to support her.

But there in the pew that used to be hers, sitting in it
established and spread out, was Stephen's mother; and Stephen's mother was of those who are articulate in church, who
like to set an example of distinctness in prayer and praise, and
look round at people who merely mumble. Catherine, who
was a mumbler, had had to speak up and sing up. There was
no help for it. One of Mrs. Colquhoun's looks was enough, and
she found herself docilely doing, as she so often in life had
found herself docilely doing, what was expected of her.

Afterwards she and Mrs. Colquhoun had waited together in
the porch for Stephen to come out of his vestry, the while
exchanging pleasant speech, and then they had all three gone
on together to a meeting in the schoolroom—Catherine
hadn't known there was to be a meeting as well as the
service—at which Stephen was giving an address.

"Would you care to come round to the schoolroom?" he had
asked her on joining his two mothers in the porch, buttoning
his coat as he spoke, for it was flapping wildly in the wind. "I
am giving an address."

At this point Catherine had felt a little overwhelmed by his
hospitality; but, unable to refuse, had continued to accept.

He gave an informing address. She hadn't known till she
heard it that they were at the beginning of the week before the
week that ends in Easter, the busiest fortnight of the clerical
year, and she now discovered that there were to be daily
morning and evening services, several sermons, and many
meetings, between that day and the following Sunday.

Would she have to come to them all? she asked herself, as
she sat with Mrs. Colquhoun, after having been stopped
several times on her way to her seat by old friends in the
parish, people she had known for years; and always *tête-à-tête*
with Stephen during the walk there and back, and always
under Mrs. Colquhoun's supervision in the pew?

Up on the platform, in front of an enormous blackboard,

stood Stephen, giving his address. He told his parishioners they were entering the very most solemn time of the whole year, and exceptional opportunities were being offered of observing it. He read out a list of the opportunities, and ended by exhorting those present to love one another and, during this holy season, to watch without ceasing and pray. Yes, she would have to come to them all. A guest is a helpless creature; a mother-in-law guest is a very helpless creature; an uninvited mother-in-law guest is a thing bound hand and foot.

Soberly, when the meeting was over, she walked out of the stuffy schoolroom with its smell of slates, into the great wind-swept cleanness of the night. It was nearly half-past seven, and she and Stephen were unable therefore to accept Mrs. Colquhoun's invitation to go into the Rectory and rest. She had had, however, to promise to look in the next day but one—"That is, dear Mrs. Cumfrit," Mrs. Colquhoun had said, suggesting the next day but one as a test of the length of her visit, "if you will still be here. You will? Delightful."

As she undressed on Monday night and thought of her day, her feeling, though she regarded its contents since Stephen's arrival with surprise, was still that she was thankful to be there. It was sweet to be with Virginia, sweet and natural to be able, in moments of stress, to take refuge in her old home, in her Virginia's home. And Stephen, though he took his duties as host too seriously, was such a good man; and Virginia was evidently supremely happy in her undemonstrative little way. If only she could manage, when Stephen talked, to keep awake better. . . . What was it about him, whom she so much respected, that sent her to sleep? But really, after the silliness of her recent experiences in London, it was like getting into a bath to come into this pure place—a big, cool, clean, peaceful bath.

Thus did Catherine think on Monday night in her bedroom; and, while she was doing so, Stephen was saying to Virginia: "What, my love, makes your mother so drowsy? This afternoon—and again this evening—"

"Don't people always get drowsy when they get old?" Virginia asked in reply.

"Ah," said Stephen thoughtfully. "Yes. I suppose they do." Then, remembering that Catherine was a year younger than himself, he added, "Women, of course, age more rapidly than men. A man your mother's age would still be—"

"A boy," interrupted Virginia, laying her face against his.

"Well, not quite," said Stephen smiling, "but certainly in the prime of life."

"Of course," said Virginia, rubbing her cheek softly up and down. "A boy in the prime of life."

"Yes—had he had the happiness of marrying you."

"Darling."

"My blessed child."

On Tuesday evening, once more in her room preparing for bed, with another day past and over to reflect upon, her thoughts were different, or, rather, they were maturing. She continued to feel that Virginia's home was her natural refuge, and she still told herself she was glad she was in it, but she had begun to be aware of awkwardnesses. Little ones. Perhaps inseparable from the situation.

If Christopher had forced her down to Chickover in a year's time instead of now, these awkwardnesses would probably not have occurred. But the servants, indoors and out, hadn't had time to forget her, and they showed a flattering but embarrassing pleasure at her reappearance. She had had no idea that they had liked her as much as all that. She couldn't imagine why they should. It was awkward, because they conveyed, most unfortunately, by their manner that they still looked upon her as their real mistress. This was very silly and tiresome of them. She must draw into her shell. But naturally on coming across a familiar face she had been pleased, and had greeted it amiably, for of those who were still there she knew all the history, and for years they had looked after her, and she them. Naturally on meeting them she had inquired after their family affairs. Their response, however, had been too warm. It amounted to a criticism of the new *régime*.

Out in the garden, for instance, the gardeners that day had seemed to come and garden wherever she happened to be walking, and then of course—how natural it all was—she had talked to them of the last autumn bulbs which had been planted under her directions, and had gone round with them looking at the results, at the crocuses in full glory, the daffodils beginning their beauty, and the tulips still stuck neatly in their buds; and she had become absorbed, as people who are interested in such things do become absorbed, in the conversation.

Stephen, passing through on his way to some work in the parish, had found her like this, poring over a border, deep in talk with the head gardener, and hadn't liked it. She saw by his face he hadn't liked it. He had merely raised his hat and gone by without a word. She must be cooler to the gardeners. But as though it mattered—as though it mattered. *Little children, love one another.* . . . She sighed as she thought what a very happy world it would be if they really did.

Then there was Ellen, the under-housemaid, now promoted to be head, and one of the few indoor servants left. In the old days a model of reserve, Ellen now positively burst with talk. She was always hovering round her, always bringing her hot water, and clean towels, and more flowers—watching for her to come upstairs, wanting to know what she could do next. That morning, when she came back from church, Ellen was there in her room poking the fire into a blaze, and had insisted that her stockings must be damp after the muddy walk, and had knelt down and taken them off.

Catherine, amused at her care for her, had said, "Ellen, I believe you quite like me."

And Ellen, turning red, had exclaimed, "Oh, ma'am!"

The excessive devotion in her voice was another criticism of the existing *régime.* It was a warning to Catherine that she must not encourage this. Servants were like children—the past was always rosy to them, what they had had was always so much better than what they were having. She must furbish up her tact, and steer a little more carefully among these unexpected shallows. She sighed faintly. Tact was so tiring. Still, she was thankful, she told herself, to be there.

And while she was thinking this, Stephen was saying to Virginia: "We must make allowances."

He had just been describing what he had seen in the garden. "No one," he had finished thoughtfully—"no one would have supposed, from their general appearance and expression, that your mother was not the mistress and Burroughs her servant. Burroughs, indeed, might easily have been mistaken for a particularly devoted servant. I was sorry, my darling, because of you. I was, I confess, jealous on my Virginia's behalf."

"And there's Ellen, too," said Virginia, her brow puckered. "She's always in mother's room."

At this fresh example of injudiciousness Stephen was silent. He couldn't help thinking that perfect tact would have avoided, especially under the peculiar and delicate circumstances, long and frequent conversations with some one else's servants. He didn't say so to Virginia, for had he not often, and with sincerity, praised precisely this in his mother-in-law, her perfect tact? She appeared after all not to possess it in quite the quantity he had believed, but that was no reason for hurting his Virginia's feelings by pointing it out. Virginia loved her mother; and perhaps the lapse was temporary.

"We must make allowances," he repeated presently.

"Yes," said Virginia, who would have given much not to have been put by her mother in a position in which allowances had to be made. After having been so proud and happy in the knowledge that Stephen considered her mother flawless as a mother-in-law, was it not hard?

On Wednesday night, when Catherine went to bed, her reflections were definitely darker. This was the day she had, at Mrs. Colquhoun's invitation, looked in at the Rectory after lunch, bearing with her a message from Virginia to the effect that she hoped her mother-in-law would come back with her mother to tea.

Mrs. Colquhoun had refused.

"No, no, dear Mrs. Cumfrit," she had said. "We must take care of our little girl. She mustn't be overtired. Too many people to pour out for aren't at all good for her just now."

"But there wouldn't be anybody but us," Catherine had said. "And Virginia says she hasn't seen you for ages."

"Yes. Not since the day you arrived. It does seem a long while to me too, but believe me it wouldn't be fair to the child to have all of us there at once."

She had then busily talked of other matters, entertaining her visitor with tales of her simple but full life, explaining how she didn't know, owing to never being idle a moment, what loneliness meant, and couldn't understand why women should ever want to be anywhere but in their own homes.

"At our age one wants just one's own home, doesn't one, dear Mrs. Cumfrit. However small it is, however modest, it is *home*. Don't you too feel how, as one gets older, one's own little daily round, one's own little common task, gone cheerfully, done thoroughly, become more and more satisfying and beautiful?"

Catherine said she did.

Mrs. Colquhoun begged her to take some refreshment after her walk, declaring that after a certain age it was one's duty not to overtax the body.

"We grandmothers—" she said, smiling.

Catherine endeavoured to respond to Mrs. Colquhoun's playfulness, by more on the same lines of her own.

"Oh, but we mustn't count our grandchildren before they're hatched," she had said with answering smiles.

And Mrs. Colquhoun had seemed a little shocked at that. The word hatched, perhaps . . . in connection with Stephen's child.

"Dear Mrs. Cumfrit—" she had murmured, in the tone of one overlooking a lapse.

But it wasn't her visit to Mrs. Colquhoun that was making her undress so thoughtfully on Wednesday night, but the fact, most disagreeable to have to admit, that she was tired of Stephen. From the beginning of the *tête-à-tête* walks she had been afraid that presently she might get a little tired of him, and now, after the tenth of them, the thing she feared had happened.

This dejected her, for it was her earnest wish not to get tired of Stephen. He was her Virginia's loved husband, he was her host; and she wished to feel nothing towards him but the warmest affectionate interest. If she saw less of him, she reflected as she slowly, and with the movements of fatigue, got ready for bed, it would be easier. Wisdom dictated that Stephen should be eked out; but how could one eke out a host so persistent in doing his duty? It was difficult. It was very, very difficult.

She sat a long time pensive by the fire, wondering how she was going to bear any more of these walks to and from church. Good to have a refuge, but sometimes its price. . . .

And while she was sitting thus, Stephen in their bedroom was saying to Virginia: "I miss our mother."

"Which one?" asked Virginia, not at first quite following.

"Ours," said Stephen. "She hasn't been here since yours arrived. Have you noticed that, darling?"

"Indeed I have. And I miss her very much, too. I asked her to come to tea this afternoon, but she didn't. The message mother brought back wasn't very clear, I thought."

There was a pause. Then Stephen said: "She is full of tact."

"Which one?" asked Virginia again, who felt—and how mournfully—that he could no longer mean her mother, but tried to hope he did.

"Ours," said Stephen, stroking Virginia's hair; and presently added, "We must make allowances."

Virginia sighed.

On Thursday night, when Catherine was once more going to bed, she sat for a long while without undressing, staring into the fire. She was too tired to undress. Her mind was as tired as her body. Her spirits were low. For, while the night before she had been facing the fact that she was tired of Stephen, to-night she was facing the much worse fact that he was tired of her. She hadn't been able to help noticing it. It had become obvious on their twelfth walk; and it had added immensely to her struggles.

For what can one say to somebody who, one feels in one's bones, is tired of one? How difficult, in such a case, is conversation. It had been difficult enough before, but that day, on making her discovery, it had become as good as impossible. Yet there were the conventions; and for two grown-up people to walk together and not speak was absurd. They simply had to. And as Catherine was more practised than Stephen in easy talk, it was she who, struggling, had had to do more and more of it until, as he grew ever dumber, she had to do it all.

In the house, too, the same thing had happened. The meals had been almost monologues—Catherine's—for the honest Virginia was incapable of talking if she had nothing she wished to say, or, rather, nothing she considered desirable should be said. They would have sat at the table in dead silence but for Catherine's efforts. As it was, she only succeeded in extracting occasional words, mostly single, from the other two.

Well, it was evident that in ordinary cases, having tired one's host, one would go away. But was this quite an ordinary case? She couldn't think so. She couldn't help remembering, though it was a thing she never thought of, that she had made way without difficulty for Stephen to come and live in this very house, giving him everything—why, with both hands giving him everything—and she couldn't help feeling that to be allowed to stay in it for a few days, or even weeks, wasn't so very much to want of him. Not that he didn't allow her to stay in it; he was still assiduous in all politenesses, opening doors, and lighting candles, and so on. It was only that she knew he was tired of her; tired to the point of no longer being able to speak when she was there.

Catherine wasn't very vain, but what vanity she had was ruffled. She tried, however, to be fair. She had been tired of Stephen first, and had thought it natural. Now that he, in his turn, was tired of her, why should she mind? She did, however, mind. She had taken such pains to be agreeable. She had walked backwards and forwards to church so assiduously—walked miles and miles, if one counted all the times up. And she had really tried very hard to talk on subjects that interested him—the parish, the plans, the services, even adventuring into the region of religion. Why should he be tired of her? Why had this blight descended on him? Why had he become speechless? Why?

As she sat by her fire on Thursday night she felt curiously down and lonely. Stephen and Virginia, she had become conscious during the week, were very much one, and a fear stole into her heart, a small flicker of fear, gone as soon as come, that perhaps they were one too in this, and that Virginia too might be . . .

No, she turned her head away and wouldn't even look in the direction of such a fear. But, sitting there in the night, with the big house with all its passages and empty rooms on the other side of her door dark and silent, the feeling came upon her that she was a ghost injudiciously wandered back to its old haunts, to find, what it might have known, that it no longer had part nor lot in them.

From this feeling too she turned away, and impatiently, for it was a shame to feel like that when there was Virginia.

And while she sat looking at the fire, her hands hanging over the sides of the chair, too weary to go to bed, Stephen in their room said to Virginia: "What a very blessed thing it is, my darling, that each day has to end, and that then there is night."

And Virginia said, "Oh, Stephen—isn't it!"

∽ XV ∾

On Saturday Stephen would have to go up to London for his two last Lenten sermons in the City, and Catherine made up her mind that she would stay over the week-end, because he wouldn't then be there to be oppressed by her, and she would go away on Monday before he came back.

Gradually, in bed on Friday morning during the interval between drinking her tea and getting up, she came to this decision. In the morning light—the sun was shining that day—it seemed rather amusing than otherwise that her son-in-law should so quickly have come to the end of his powers of enduring her. Hers, after all, was to be the conventional fate of mothers-in-law. And she had supposed herself so much nicer than most! She thought, "How funny," and tried to see it as altogether amusing; but it was not altogether amusing. "You're vain," she then rebuked herself.

Yes; she would follow Mrs. Colquhoun's example, and stay in her own home. Perhaps that was the secret of Mrs. Colquhoun's success as a mother-in-law, and she, very obviously, was a success. She would emulate her; and from her own home defy Christopher.

It was all owing to him that she had ever left her home. How unfortunate that she should have come across somebody so mad. Oughtn't Stephen and his mother, if they knew the real reason for her appearance in their midst, applaud her as discreet? What could a woman do more proper than, in such circumstances, run away? But they would be too profoundly shocked by the real reason to be able to do anything but regard her, she was sure, with horror. Her, not Christopher. And she was afraid their attitude would be natural. "We grandmothers . . ."

Catherine turned red. Mercifully, no one would ever know. Down here, in this atmosphere where she was regarded as coeval with Mrs. Colquhoun, those encounters with Christopher seemed infinitely worse than in London—so bad, indeed, that they hardly seemed real. She would go back on Monday, declining to be kept out of her own home longer, and take firm steps. Christopher should never see her again. If he tried to, she would write a letter that would clear his mind for ever, and she would, for what was left to her of life, proceed with undeviating dignity along her allotted path to old age. And after all, what could he really do? Between her and him there was, first, the hall porter, and then Mrs. Mitcham. To both of these she would give precise instructions.

In this state of mind, a state more definite than any she had been in that week, as if a ray of light, pale and wintry, but yet light, had straggled for a moment through the mists, did Catherine get up that morning; but not in this state of mind did she that evening go to bed, for by the evening she had made a further discovery, and one that took away what still was left of her vitality: Virginia was tired of her too.

Virginia. It seemed impossible. She couldn't believe it. But, believe it or not, she knew it; and she knew it because that afternoon at tea, before Virginia had had time to take care, her face had flashed into immense, unmistakable relief when her mother said, in answer to some inquiry of Mrs. Colquhoun's, who had at last consented to come round, that she would have to go back to London on Monday. Instantly the child's face had flashed into light; and though she had, as it were, at once banged the shutters to again, the flash had escaped, and Catherine had seen it.

After this her spirits were at zero. She allowed herself to be taken away to church—though why any longer bother to try to please Stephen?—because she was too spiritless to say she preferred to stay at home. She went there one of four this time, Mr. Lambton having come in too to tea, and walked silent among them. The others were very nearly gay. The effect of her announcement had been to restore speech to Stephen, to make Mrs. Colquhoun more cordial than ever, and even to produce in Mr. Lambton, who without understanding the cause yet felt the sudden rise of temperature, almost a friskiness. It was nice, thought Catherine drearily, trying to be sardonic so as not to be too deeply hurt, to have the power of making four people happy by just saying one was going away.

She walked among them in silence, unable to feel sardonic long, and telling herself that it wasn't *really* true that Virginia was tired of her, for it wasn't Virginia at all—it was Stephen. Virginia, being so completely one with him, had caught it from him as one catches a disease. The disease wasn't part of Virginia; it would go, and she would be as she was before. Catherine, however, would not stay a minute longer than Monday morning. She would have liked to go away the very next day, but to alter her announced intention now might make Virginia afraid her mother had noticed something, and then she would be so unhappy, poor little thing, thinking she had hurt her. For, after that one look of relief, she had blushed painfully, and what she was feeling had opened out before Catherine like a book: she was glad her mother was going, and was unhappy that she should be glad.

No; Catherine would stay till Monday, so that Virginia shouldn't be hurt by the knowledge that she had hurt her mother. Oh, these family tangles and tendernesses, these unexpected inflamed places that mustn't be touched, these complicated emotions, and hurtings, and avoidances and concealments, these loving intentions and these wretched results! It wasn't easy to be a mother successfully, and she began to perceive it was difficult successfully to be a daughter. The position of mother-in-law, which she had taken on so lightly as a natural one, not giving it a thought, wasn't at all easy to fill either, being evidently a highly complicated and artificial affair. She thought she saw, too, that sons-in-law might have their difficulties; and she ended, as the party approached the churchyard, by thinking it extraordinarily difficult successfully to be a human being at all. She felt very old. She missed George.

Mr. Lambton opened the gate for the ladies, and, with his Rector, stood aside. Mrs. Colquhoun was prepared to persuade Catherine to pass through first, but Catherine, in deep abstraction, and seeing an open gate in her path, passed through it without persuasion.

"Absent-minded," thought Mrs. Colquhoun, explaining this otherwise ruffling lapse from manners. "Ageing," she added, explaining the absent-mindedness; and there was something dragging about Catherine's walk which really did look rather old.

The others caught her up. "A penny, dear Mrs. Cumfrit," said Mrs. Colquhoun, rallying her, "for your thoughts."

They happened to be passing George's tomb—George, the unfailingly good, the unvaryingly kind, the steadfastly loving, George who had been so devoted to her, and never, never got tired of her—and Catherine, roused thus suddenly, said absently, "I miss George."

It spread a chill, this answer of hers. It was so unexpected. Mr. Lambton, though unaware of the cause, for he didn't know, being new in the parish, what George was being missed, felt the drop in the temperature and immediately dropped with it into silence. Neither Mrs. Colquhoun nor Stephen could think for a moment of anything to say. Poor Mr. Cumfrit had been dead twelve years, and to be missed out loud after twelve solid years of death seemed to them uncalled for. It put them in an awkward position. It was almost an expression of dissatisfaction with the present situation. And, in any case, after twelve years it was difficult to condole with reasonable freshness.

Something had to be done, however, if only because of Mr. Lambton; and Stephen spoke first.

"Ah," he said; and then, because he couldn't think of

anything else, said it again more thoughtfully. "Ah," said Stephen a second time.

And Mrs. Colquhoun, taking Catherine's arm, and walking thus with her the rest of the way to the porch, said, "Dear Mrs. Cumfrit, I do so understand. Haven't I been through it all too?"

"I can't think why I said that," said Catherine, looking first at her and then at Stephen, lost in surprise at herself, her cheeks flushed.

"So natural, *so* natural," Mrs. Colquhoun assured her; to which Stephen, desirous of doing his best, added, "Very proper."

That night in their bedroom Stephen said to Virginia: "Your mother misses your father."

Virginia looked at him with startled eyes. "Oh? Do you think so, Stephen? Why?" she asked, turning red; for how dreadful if her mother had felt, had noticed, that she and Stephen . . . Yet why else should she suddenly begin to miss . . .

"Because she said so."

Virginia stood looking at Stephen, the comb with which she was combing out her long dark hair suspended. It wasn't natural to begin all over again missing her father. Her mother wouldn't have if she hadn't noticed . . . How dreadful. She would so much hate her to be hurt. Poor mother. Yet what could she do? Stephen, and his peace and happiness, did come first. Except that she couldn't imagine such expressions applied to either of them, she did feel as if she were between the devil and the deep sea.

"Do you think—do you suppose—" she faltered.

"It is not, is it my darling, altogether flattering to us," said Stephen.

"Oh, Stephen—yes—I know you've done all you could. You've been wonderful—"

She put down the comb and went across to him, and he enfolded her in his arms.

"I wish—" she began.

"What do you wish, my beloved wife?" he asked, laying one hand, as if in blessing, on her head. "I hope it is something nice, for, you know, whatever it is you wish I shall be unable not to wish it too."

She smiled, and sighed, and nestled close.

"Darling Stephen," she murmured; and after a moment said, with another sigh, "I wish mother didn't miss father."

"Yes," said Stephen. "Indeed I wish it too. But," he went on, stroking the long lovely strands of her thick hair, "we must make allowances."

✿ XVI ✿

The next morning Catherine went to church for the last time—for when Stephen was in London, and not there to invite her to accompany him, which he solemnly before each separate service did, there would be no more need to go—and for the last time mingled her psalms with Mrs. Colquhoun's.

The psalms at Morning Prayer were said, not sung, and she was in the middle of joining with Mrs. Colquhoun in asserting that it was better to trust in the Lord than to put any confidence in man, which at that moment she was very willing to believe, when she felt she was being stared at.

She looked up from her prayer-book, but could see only a few backs, and, one on each side of the chancel, Stephen and Mr. Lambton tossing the verses backwards and forwards across to each other, as if they were a kind of holy ball. She went on with her psalm, but the feeling grew stronger, and at last, contrary to all decent practice, she turned round.

There was Christopher.

She stood gazing at him, her open prayer-book in her hand, for such an appreciable moment that Mrs. Colquhoun had to say the next verse without her.

The same stone, said Mrs. Colquhoun very loud and distinctly, and in a voice of remonstrance—for really, what had come over Virginia's mother, turning her back on the altar in this manner?—*which the builders refused is become the head-stone of the corner.*

She had to say all the other verses without her as well, and all subsequent responses, because Virginia's mother, though she presently resumed her proper eastward position, was thenceforth—such odd behaviour—dumb.

Perhaps she was not feeling well. She certainly looked pale,

or, rather, yellow, thought Mrs. Colquhoun, observing her
during the reading of the first lesson, through which she sat
with downcast eyes and grew, so it seemed to Mrs. Colquhoun,
steadily yellower.

"Dear Mrs. Cumfrit," whispered Mrs. Colquhoun at last,
bending towards her, for she really did look sick, and it would
be terrible if she—"would you like to go out?"

"Oh *no*," was the quick, emphatic answer.

The service came to an end, it seemed to Catherine, in a
flash. She hadn't had time to settle anything at all in her mind.
She didn't in the least know what she was going to do. How
had he found her? Had Mrs. Mitcham betrayed her? After her
orders, her strict, exact orders? Was everybody failing her,
even Mrs. Mitcham? How dared he follow her. It was persecu-
tion. And what was she to do, what *was* she to do, if he
behaved badly, if he showed any of his idiotic, his mad
feelings?

She knelt so long after the benediction that Mrs. Colquhoun
began to fidget. Mrs. Colquhoun couldn't get out. She was
hemmed into the pew by the kneeling figure. The few worship-
pers went away, and still Virginia's mother—really most
odd—knelt. The outer door of the vestry was banged to,
which meant Stephen and Mr. Lambton had gone, and still
she knelt. The verger came down the aisle with his keys
jingling to lock up, and still she knelt. "This," thought Mrs.
Colquhoun, vexed by such a prolonged and ill-timed devout-
ness, "is ostentation." And she touched Catherine's elbow.
"Dear Mrs. Cumfrit—" she reminded her.

Catherine got up, very pale. The moment had come when
she must turn and face Christopher.

But the church was empty. No one was in it except the
verger, waiting down by the door with his keys and looking
patient. If only Christopher had gone right away—if only
something in the service had touched him, and made him see
he was behaving outrageously, and he had gone right
away. . . .

The porch, too, was empty. Perhaps he had really gone.
Perhaps—she almost began to hope he had never been there,
that she had imagined him. She walked slowly beside Mrs.
Colquhoun along the path to the churchyard gate. Stephen had
hurried off to a sick-bed, Mr. Lambton had withdrawn to his
lodgings to prepare his Sunday sermons.

"I'm afraid you felt unwell in church," said Mrs.

Colquhoun, suiting her steps to Catherine's, which were small and slow, which, in fact, dragged.

"I have rather a headache to-day," said Catherine, in a voice that trailed away into indistinctness, for, on turning a bend in the path, there once more was Christopher.

He was examining George's tomb.

Mrs. Colquhoun saw him at the same moment, and her attention was at once diverted from Catherine. Strangers were rare in that quiet corner of the world, and she scrutinised this one with keen, interested eyes. The young man in his leather motoring-clothes pleased her, for not only was he a well-set-up young man, but he was reading poor Mr. Cumfrit's inscription bareheaded. So, in her opinion, should all *hic jacet* inscriptions be read. It showed, thought Mrs. Colquhoun, a rather delicate reverence, not usually found in these wild scorchers of the road. If Mr. Cumfrit had been the Unknown Warrior himself his inscription couldn't have been read more respectfully.

She was pleased, and wondered complacently who the stranger could be; and almost before she had had time to wonder, he turned from the tomb and came towards them.

"Why, he seems——" she began; for the young man was showing signs of recognition, his face was widening in greeting, and the next moment he was holding out his hand to her companion.

"How do you do," he said, with such warmth that she concluded he must be Mrs. Cumfrit's favourite nephew. She had never heard of any nephews, but most families have got some.

"How do you do," replied her companion, with no warmth at all—with, indeed, hardly any voice at all.

The newcomer, standing bareheaded in the sun, seemed red all over. His face was very red, and his hair glowed. She liked the look of him. Vigour. Life. A relief after her bloodless companion.

"Introduce us," she said briskly, with the frankness she felt her age entitled her to when dealing with young folk of the other sex. "I am sure," she said heartily, holding out her hand in its sensible, loose-fitting wash-leather glove, "you are one of Mrs. Cumfrit's nephews, and our dear Virginia's cousin."

"No, I'm dashed if I am," exclaimed the stranger. "I mean"—he turned an even more fiery red—"I'm not."

"Mr. Monckton," said Catherine, in a far-away voice.

"She doesn't tell you who *I* am," smiled Mrs. Colquhoun, gripping his hand, still pleased with him in spite of his exclamation, for she liked young men, and there existed, besides, a tradition that she got on well with them, and knew how to manage them. "Have you noticed that people who introduce hardly ever do so completely? I'm the other mother-in-law."

A faint hope began to flutter in Catherine's heart. Christopher had the appearance of one who doesn't know what to say next. She had never known him not know that before. If Mrs. Colquhoun could reduce him to silence, she might yet get through the next few minutes not too discreditably. "Mrs. Cumfrit and I," explained Mrs. Colquhoun, putting her arm through Catherine's, as though elucidating her, "are both the mothers-in-law of the same delightful couple—I of her daughter, she of my son. We are linked together, she and I, in indissoluble bonds."

Christopher wished to slay her as she stood. The liberal days were past, however, when one could behave simply, and as he couldn't behave simply and slay her, he didn't know how to behave to her at all.

"The woman has a beak," he thought, standing red and tongue-tied before her. "She's a bird of prey. She has got her talons into my Catherine. Linked together! Good God."

Convention preventing his saying this out loud, or any of the other things he was feeling, he turned in silence and walked with them, on the other side of Catherine, towards the gate.

A faint desire to laugh stole like a small trickle of reviving courage through Catherine's cowed spirit. It was the first desire of the kind she had had since she got to Chickover, and it arrived, she couldn't help noticing, at the same time as Christopher.

Mrs. Colquhoun was a little surprised at the silence of her two companions. Mr. Monckton, whoever he might be, didn't respond to her friendliness as instantly as other young men she had dealt with, and Mrs. Cumfrit said nothing either. Then she remembered her friend's attack in church, and made allowances; while as for Mr. Monckton, whoever he might be, he probably was shy. Well, she knew how to manage shy young folk; they never stayed shy long with her.

"Mrs. Cumfrit," she explained over the top of Catherine's head to Christopher, "isn't feeling very well to-day."

"Oh?" said Christopher quickly, with a swift, anxious look at Catherine.

"No. So we mustn't make her talk, Mr. Monckton. She turned a little faint just now in church"—again the desire to laugh crept through Catherine. "She'll be all right presently, and meanwhile you and I will entertain each other. You shall tell me all about yourself, and how it is you've dropped out of the clouds into our quiet little midst."

Christopher's earnest wish at that moment was to uproot one of the tombstones and with it fell Mrs. Colquhoun to the ground. That old jackdaw Stephen's mother . . . birds of a feather . . . making him look and be a fool. . . .

"Do tell us," urged Mrs. Colquhoun pleasantly, across the top of Catherine's head, as he said nothing.

Catherine, walking in silence between them, began to feel she was in competent hands.

"There isn't much to tell," said Christopher, thus inexorably urged, and flaming red to the roots of his flaming hair.

"Everything," Mrs. Colquhoun assured him encouragingly, "interests us here. All is grist to our quiet little mills—isn't it, dear Mrs. Cumfrit. Ah, no—I forgot. You are not to be made to talk. We will do it all for you, won't we, Mr. Monckton."

They had got to the gate. Christopher lunged at it to open it for them.

As Catherine went through it he said to her quickly, in a low voice, "You look years older."

She raised her eyes a moment. "I always was," she murmured, with, she hoped, blood-curdling significance.

"Older?" repeated Mrs. Colquhoun, whose hearing, as she often told her friends, was still, she was thankful to say, unimpaired. "That, my young friend, is what may be said daily of us all. No doubt Mrs. Cumfrit notices a change even in you. Have you not met for a long while?"

"Not for an eternity," said Christopher, in the sort of voice a man swears with.

A motor-cycle with a side-car was in the road outside the gate, and Mrs. Colquhoun paused on seeing it.

"Yours, of course, Mr. Monckton," she said. "This is the machine in which you have dropped out of the skies on us. And with a side-car, too. An empty one, though. I don't like to think of a young man with an empty side-car. But perhaps the young lady has merely gone for a little stroll?"

"I have brought it to take Mrs. Cumfrit back to London in,"

said Christopher stiffly; but of what use stiffness, of what use dignity, when one was being made to look and be such a hopeless fool?

"Really?" said Mrs. Colquhoun, excessively surprised. "Only, she doesn't go back till Monday—do you, dear Mrs. Cumfrit. Ah, no—don't talk. I forgot."

"Neither do I," said Christopher.

"Really?" said Mrs. Colquhoun again; and was for a moment, in her turn, silent.

A side-car seemed to her a highly unsuitable vehicle for a person of Mrs. Cumfrit's age. Nor could she recollect, during all the time she had, off and on, known her, ever having seen her in such a thing. Instinct here began to warn her, as she afterwards was fond of telling her friends, that the situation was not quite normal. How far it was from normal, however, instinct in her case, being that of a decent elderly woman presently to become a grandmother, was naturally incapable of guessing.

"You didn't tell us, dear Mrs. Cumfrit," she said, turning to her pale and obviously not very well companion, "that this was to be your mode of progress. Delightful, of course, in a way. But personally I should be afraid of the shaking. Young people don't feel these things as we do. Are you, then," she continued, turning to Christopher, "staying in the neighbourhood over Sunday?"

"Yes," said Christopher, taking a rug out of the side-car and unfolding it.

"I wonder where. You'll think me an inquisitive old woman, but really I wonder where. You see, I know this district so well, and there isn't—oh, I expect you're with the Parkers. They usually have a houseful of young people for the week-end. You'll enjoy it. The country round is—What, are you going on, dear Mrs. Cumfrit? Then good-bye for the present. I shall see you at lunch. Virginia always likes me to come in on these Lenten Saturdays while Stephen is away. It has become a ritual. Now take my advice, and lie down for half an hour. I'm a very sensible person, Mr. Monckton, and know that one can't go on for ever as if one were still twenty-five."

Christopher stepped forward, intercepting Catherine. "I'll drive you back," he said.

"I'd rather walk," she said.

"Then I'll walk with you." And he threw the rug into the side-car again.

"What? And leave your motor-cycle and rug and everything unprotected?" exclaimed Mrs. Colquhoun, who had listened to this brief dialogue with surprise. Mr. Monckton, whoever he might be, was neither Mrs. Cumfrit's son, for she hadn't got one, nor her nephew, for he had himself said, with the emphasis of the male young, that he wasn't, and his masterfulness seemed accordingly a little unaccountable.

"You'd better let me drive you," he persisted to her pale companion, taking no notice of this exclamation. "You oughtn't to walk."

Was he, perhaps, thought Mrs. Colquhoun, a doctor? A young doctor? Mrs. Cumfrit's London medical adviser? If so, of course. . . . Yet even then, her not having mentioned his expected arrival, and her plan for motoring up with him on Monday, was odd. Besides, nobody except the very rich had doctors dangling after them.

"Let me drive you," said the young man again.

And Mrs. Cumfrit said—rather helplessly, Mrs. Colquhoun thought, as if she were seriously lacking in backbone, "Very well."

It was all extremely odd.

"Virginia will wonder," remarked Mrs. Colquhoun, looking on with a distinctly pursed expression while her colleague was being rolled into the rug as carefully as if she were china—rolled right up to her chin in it, as if she were going thousands of miles, and at least to Lapland. "But no doubt you have told her Mr. Monckton was coming down."

"I shall only drive part of the way," answered Mrs. Cumfrit—there was a tinge of colour in her face now, Mrs. Colquhoun noticed; perhaps the tight rug was choking her—"but I shall get back quicker like this."

"I wonder," said Mrs. Colquhoun grimly.

She watched them disappear in a cloud of dust, and then turned to go home, where she had several things to see to before lunching at the Manor; but, pausing, she decided that she would walk round into the village instead, and see if she could meet Stephen. Perhaps he would be able to explain Mr. Monckton.

And Catherine did not, after all, get back quicker. No sooner was she off, at what seemed to her a great pace, than she began to have misgivings about it, for it occurred to her that on her feet she could go where she liked, but in Christopher's side-car she would have to go where he did.

"That's the turning," she called out—she found she had to speak very loud to get heard above the din the thing made—pointing to a road to the right a short distance ahead.

"Is it?" Christopher shouted back; and rushed past it.

∽ XVII ∾

The noise, the shaking, the wind, made it impossible to say much. Perhaps up there above her on his perch he really didn't hear; he anyhow behaved as if he didn't. Getting no answer to any of the things she said, she looked up at him. He was intent, bent forward, his mouth tight shut, and his hair—he had nothing on his head—blown backwards, shining in the sun.

The anger died from her face. It was so absurd, what was happening to her, that she couldn't be angry. All the trouble she had taken to get away from him, all she had endured and made Stephen and Virginia endure that week as a result of it, ending like this, in being caught and carried off in a side-car! Besides, there was something about him sitting up there in the sun, something in his expression, at once triumphant and troubled, determined and anxious, happy and scared, that brought a smile flickering round the corners of her mouth, which, however, she carefully buried in her scarf.

And as she settled down into the rug, for she couldn't do anything at that moment except go, except rush, except be hurtled, as she gave herself up to this extraordinary temporary abduction, a queer feeling stole over her as if she had come in out of the cold into a room with a bright fire in it. Yes, she had been cold; and with Christopher it was warm. Absurd as it was, she felt she was with somebody of her own age again.

They were through the village in a flash. Stephen, still on his way to the sick-bed he was to console, was caught up and passed without his knowing who was passing. He jumped aside when he heard the noise of their approach behind him—quickly, because he was cautious and they were close, and without looking at them, because motor-cycles and the ways of young men who used them were repugnant to him.

Christopher rushed past him with a loud hoot. It sounded

defiant. Catherine gathered, from its special violence, that her son-in-law had been recognised.

The road beyond Chickover winds sweetly among hills. If one continues on it long enough, that is for twenty miles or so, one comes to the sea. This was where Christopher took Catherine that morning, not stopping a moment, nor slowing down except when prudence demanded, nor speaking a word till he got there. At the bottom of the steep bit at the end, down which he went carefully, acutely aware of the preciousness of his passenger, where between grassy banks the road abruptly finishes in shingle and the sea, he stopped, got off, and came round to unwind her.

This was the moment he was most afraid of.

She looked so very small, rolled round in the rug like a little bolster, propped up in the side-car, that his heart misgave him worse than ever. It had been misgiving him without interruption the whole way, but it misgave him worse than ever now. He felt she was too small to hurt, to anger, even to ruffle; that it wasn't fair; that he ought, if he must attack, attack a woman more his own size.

And she didn't say anything. She had, he knew, said a good many things when they passed that turning, none of which he could hear, but since then she had been silent. She was silent now; only, over the top of her scarf, which had got pushed up rather funnily round her ears, her eyes were fixed on him.

"There. Here we are," he said. "We can talk here. If you'll stand up I'll get this thing unwound."

For a moment he thought she was going to refuse to move, but she said nothing, and let him help her up. She was so tightly rolled round that it would have been difficult to move by herself.

He took the rug off, and folded it up busily so as not to have to meet her eyes, for he was afraid.

"Help me out," she said.

He looked her suddenly in the face. "I'm glad I did it, anyhow," he said, flinging back his head.

"Are you?" she said.

She held out her hand to be helped. She looked rumpled.

"Your little coat—" he murmured, pulling it tidy; and he couldn't keep his hand from shaking, because he loved her so—"your little coat—" Then he straightened himself, and looked her in the eyes. "Catherine, we've got to talk," he said.

"Is that why you've brought me here?"

"Yes," said Christopher.

"Do you imagine I'm going to listen?"

"Yes," said Christopher.

"You don't feel at all ashamed?"

"No," said Christopher.

She got out, and walked on to the shingle, and stood with her back to him, apparently considering the view. It was low tide, and the sea lay a good way off across wet sands. The sheltered bay was very quiet, and she could hear larks singing above the grassy banks behind her. Dreadful how little angry she was. She turned her back so as to hide how little angry she was. She wasn't really angry at all, and she knew she ought to be. Christopher ought to be sent away at once and for ever, but there were two reasons against that—one that he wouldn't go, and the other that she didn't want him to. Contrary to all right feeling, to all sense of what was decent, she was amazingly glad to be with him again. She didn't do any of the things she ought to do—flame with anger, wither him with rebukes. It was shameful, but there it was: she was amazingly glad to be with him again.

Christopher, watching her, tried to keep up a stout heart. He had had such a horrible week that whatever happened now couldn't anyhow be worse. And she—well, she didn't look any the happier for it, for running away from him, either.

He tried to make his voice sound fearless. "Catherine, we must talk," he said. "It's no use turning your back on me and staring at the silly view. You don't see it, so why pretend?"

She didn't move. She was wondering at the way her attitude towards him had developed in this week. All the while she was so indignant with him she was really getting used to him, getting used to the idea of him. Helped, of course, by Stephen. Immensely helped by Stephen, and even by Virginia.

"I told you you'd never get away from me," he said to the back of her head, putting all he had of defiance into his voice. But he had so little; it was bluff, sheer bluff, while his heart was ignominiously in his boots.

"Your methods amaze me," said Catherine to the view.

"Why did you run away?"

"Why did you force me to?"

"Well, it hasn't been much good, has it, seeing that here we are again."

"It hasn't been the least good."

"It never is, unless it's done in twos. Then I'm all for it.

Don't forget that next time, will you. And you might also give the poor devil who is run from a thought. He has the thinnest time. I suppose if I were to try and tell you the sort of hell he has to endure you wouldn't even understand, you untouched little thing—you self-sufficing little thing."

Silence.

Catherine, gazing at the view, was no doubt taking his remarks in. At least, he hoped so.

"Won't you turn round, Catherine?" he inquired.

"Yes, when you're ready to take me back to Chickover."

"I'll be ready to do that when we've arrived at some conclusion. Is it any use my coming round to your other side? We could talk better if we could see each other's faces."

"No use at all," said Catherine.

"Because you'd only turn your back on me again?"

"Yes."

Silence.

"Aren't we silly," said Christopher.

"Idiots," said Catherine.

Silence.

"Of course I know you're very angry with me," said Christopher.

"I've been extraordinarily angry with you the whole week," said Catherine.

"That's only because you will persist in being unnatural. You're the absurdest little bundle of prejudices, and musty old fears. Why on earth you can't simply let yourself go—"

Silence.

She, and letting herself go! She struggled to keep her laughter safe muffled inside her scarf. She hadn't laughed since last she was with Christopher. At Chickover nobody laughed. A serious smile from Virginia, a bright conventional smile from Mrs. Colquhoun, no smile at all from Stephen; that was the nearest they got to it. Laughter—one of the most precious of God's gifts; the very salt, the very light, the very fresh air of life; the divine disinfectant, the heavenly purge. Could one ever be real friends with somebody one didn't laugh with? Of course one couldn't. She and Christopher, they laughed. Oh, she had missed him. . . . But he was so headlong, he was so dangerous, he must be kept so sternly within what bounds she could get him to stay in.

She therefore continued to turn her back on him, for her face, she knew, would betray her.

"You haven't been happy down here, that I'll swear," said Christopher. "I saw it at once in your little face."

"You needn't swear, because I'm not going to pretend anything. I haven't been at all happy. I was very angry with you, and I was—lonely."

"Lonely?"

"Yes. One misses—one's friends."

"But you were up to your eyes in relations."

Silence.

Then Catherine said, "I'm beginning to think relations can't be friends—neither blood relations, nor relations by marriage."

"Would you," asked Christopher after a pause, during which he considered this remark, "call a husband a relation by marriage?"

"It depends," said Catherine, "whose."

"Yours, of course. You know I mean yours."

She was quiet a moment, then she said cautiously, "I'd call him George."

He took a quick step forward, before she had time to turn away, and looked at her.

"You're laughing," he said, his face lighting up. "I felt you were. Why, I don't believe you're angry at all—I believe you're glad I've come. Catherine, you *are* glad I've come. You're fed up with Stephen and Virginia, and the old lady with the profile, and I've come as a sort of relief. Isn't it true? You *are* glad?"

"I think they're rather fed up, as you put it, with me," said Catherine soberly.

"Fed up with you? They? That ancient, moulting, feathered tribe?"

He stared at her. "Then why do you stay till Monday?" he asked.

"Because of Virginia."

"You mean she, of course, isn't fed up."

"Yes, she is."

"She too?"

He tried to take this in. "Then why on earth stay?" he asked again.

"Because I don't want her to know I know she *is* fed up. Christopher, how catching your language is—"

His face broadened into a grin. "Lord," he said, "these twists-up one gets into with relations."

"Yes," agreed Catherine.

"Thank heaven I haven't got any."

"Yes," agreed Catherine; and added with a faint sigh, her eyes on the distant sea, "I oughtn't to have come at all."

"Well, as though that wasn't abundantly clear from the first."

"I mean, because young people should be left undisturbed."

"Young people! Stephen?"

"Well, young couples."

"He isn't a young couple."

"Virginia has made him young. They ought to be left to themselves. It isn't that Virginia doesn't love me—it's that she loves Stephen more, and wants to be alone with him."

"She's a horrid girl," said Christopher with conviction.

"She's mine," said Catherine, "and I love her. Don't forget that, please. It's very important in my life."

He took her hands and kissed them. "I adore you," he said simply.

"Well, it's not much good doing that," she said.

"Doing what?"

"Adoring somebody old enough to be your mother."

"Mothers be damned," said Christopher.

"Oh, that's what I've been thinking all the week!" cried Catherine—and then looked so much shocked at herself that Christopher burst out laughing, and so, after a minute, did she, and they stood there laughing, he holding both her hands, and happiness coming back to them in waves.

"Aren't we friends," she said, looking at him in a kind of glad surprise.

"Aren't we," said Christopher, kissing her hands again.

They wandered along the sands for a little after that, after their simultaneous laughter had loosened them from their reserves and fears, both feeling that an immense stride had been made in intimacy. Catherine, as they wandered, expounded her view of the nature and manifestations of true friendship, as other women have done on similar occasions, and Christopher, even as other men on such occasions, pretended that he thought just like that too.

He wasn't going to frighten her away again. She had been flung back to him in this unexpected frame of mind, this state of relief and gladness, because it happened that Stephen was Stephen and Virginia was Virginia—but suppose she had chanced to run to appreciative friends, friends delighted to

have her, who petted her and made her happy, to the enthusiastic Fanshawes, for instance, he would have had a poor hope
of anything but being avoided for the rest of his life. And he
had suffered, suffered. It had been the blackest week of misery.
He wasn't going to risk any more of it. He would walk along
the sands with her and talk carefully with her of friendship.

And Catherine, used only to George, and without experience of the endless variety of the approaches and disguises of
love, was delighted with Christopher, and felt every minute
more reassured and safe. He agreed, it appeared, completely
with her that in a world where nobody can get everything it is
better to take something rather than have nothing, and that
friendship between a man and a woman, even a warm one, is
perfectly possible—only reverting to his more violent way of
speech when she added, "Especially at our unequal ages,"
upon which he said, in his earlier manner, "Oh, damn unequal
ages."

For a moment he had difficulty in not holding forth on this
subject, and her ridiculous obsession by it, but stopped
himself. He wasn't going to spoil this. It was too happy, this
wandering alone together on those blessed solitary sands—
too, too happy, after the dark torments of the week, to risk
spoiling it. Let her say what she liked. Let her coo away about
being friends; in another moment she would probably assure
him that she would like to be his sister, his own dear sister, or
his mother to whom he could always turn in trouble, or some
absurd female relation of that sort. He wouldn't stop her. He
would only listen and laugh inside himself. His Catherine. His
love. As sure as she walked there, as sure as there behind her,
reaching farther and farther back, was a double ribbon of her
little wobbly footprints in the sand, she was his love. And
presently she too would know it, and all the sister and mother
and friend talk go the way such talk always went, and be
remembered some day only with wonder and smiles.

"Catherine," he said, "just to walk with you makes me so
happy that it's as clear as God's daylight we're the wonder-
fullest, most harmonious of friends."

The *relief* of being with Christopher! To be wanted again, to
have some one pleased to be with her, preferring to be with her
than anywhere else in the world—what a contrast to her
recent experiences at Chickover. She no longer had the
amused feeling of gratified vanity that had warmed her in
London before he began to behave badly; what she felt now

was much simpler and more sincere—not trivial like that. They had both been through their rages, and had come out into this fresh air, these sunlit waters. They were friends.

"I'm so glad I came away," she said, smiling up at him; and she very nearly added, as she looked at him and saw him such a part of the morning, and of the fresh sea and the clear light, so bright-haired and young-limbed, "I do *love* you, Christopher—" but was afraid he would misunderstand. Which he certainly would have.

They arranged, before they turned back, that he should drive her up to London that afternoon. Her luggage could be sent by train. It seemed silly, he said, to stay till Monday when she didn't want to, and Virginia didn't want her to, and nobody wanted her to, while in London there were her friends, all wanting her—

"One friend," she smiled.

"Well, one friend is enough to change the world."

"Oh *yes,*" she agreed, her eyes shining.

Still, it would be difficult, she said. Virginia would be astonished at the motor-cycle—

"She knows all about that by now," said Christopher. "You bet the old lady has told her about it long ago. Rushed straight round on purpose."

Well then, in that case, on the principle of being hung for a whole sheep while one was about it, Catherine thought she might as well drive up with him that day. Especially—

"Now don't say especially at our ages."

"I wasn't going to. I was going to say, especially as it will make everybody happy all round."

"Yes, my love—I mean, my friend. Even though they won't admit it," said Christopher.

He was to leave her, they decided, at the Chickover gates, and at lunch she would explain him to Virginia, and then he would call for her at two o'clock and take her away. Introduced, however, to Virginia first.

"Must I be?" he asked.

"Of course," said Catherine.

With what different feelings did Christopher pack her up in the rug this time. There was no fear now, no anxiety. She laughed, and was the Catherine of the afternoon at Hampton Court—only come so much nearer, come so close up to him, come indeed, and of her own accord, almost right into his heart.

"My blessed little angel," he thought, propping her up in the seat when she was wound round and couldn't move her arms; and her eyes were so bright, and her face so different from the face that he had seen in church two hours before, that he said, "You looked ten years older this morning than you did in London, and now you look twenty years younger than you did then."

"What age does that make me?" she asked, laughing up at him.

"So you see," he said, ignoring this, "how wholesome, how necessary it is to be with one's friend."

ເ໑ XVIII ໑ວ

Meanwhile the morning at the Manor was passing in its usual quiet yet busy dignity. Virginia attended to her household duties, while her mother and Stephen were at church, and herself cut the sandwiches that Stephen was to take up with him to London, because the ones the week before had been, he told her, highly unsatisfactory.

The cook looked on with the expression natural to cooks in such circumstances, and Virginia, who had never made sandwiches, but knew what they ought to taste like, was disconcerted by their appearance when she had done.

"It's how the master likes them," she said rather uncertainly, as she herself arranged the strange-shaped things in the aluminium box they were to travel in.

"Yes, m'm," said the cook.

She came out of the kitchen and into her own part of the house with a sigh of relief. It was always a relief to get through those baize doors. The servants made her shy. She wasn't able, somehow, to get into touch with them. What she aimed at in her relations with them was perfect justice and kindness, combined with dignity. She most earnestly wished to do her duty by them, and in return it seemed merely fair to demand that they should do their duty by her. Her mother's reign had been lax. She had found, on looking into things on her marriage, many abuses. These she had removed one by one, and after much trouble had put the whole household on a decent economic footing.

Up to now the servants hadn't quite settled down to it, but her mother-in-law, who was experienced in frugalities, assured her they would in time, and be all the happier and the better for it. She had gone so far as to explain to them, her serious young face firm in the belief that once they were told they would understand and even co-operate, that the more carefully the house was run the more would the poor, the sick, and the aged of the parish benefit. "No one," she said, earnestly striving to make herself clear, "has more than a certain amount of money to spend, and if it is spent in one way it can't possibly be spent in another."

The servants were silent.

She even tried, overcoming her shyness, to talk to them of noble aims, and love for one's fellow-creatures.

The servants continued silent.

She went further, and in a voice that faltered because of her extreme desire to run away and hide, talked to them of God.

The servants became really terribly silent.

Carrying her aluminium box, she passed on this Saturday morning, with her customary sigh of relief, through the baize doors that separated the domestic part of the house from the part where one was happy, and went into the study to put the sandwiches in Stephen's suit-case, along with his sermons and pyjamas. He, she knew, would only be back a short time before starting for the station, because of the sick-bed he had to visit, poor Stephen, but her mother would be back.

Virginia had made up her mind to devote herself entirely this week-end to her mother, and do her best to remove any suspicion she might have that she had not been, perhaps, quite wanted; and having shut the sandwiches in the suit-case she went in search of her.

Poor mother. Virginia wished, with a sigh, that she need never be hurt. She was so kind, and so often so sweet. But what problems mothers were after a certain age! Unless they were as perfectly sensible as Stephen's, or else were truly religious. Religion, of course, was what was most needed, especially when one was old. Virginia had, however, long felt that her mother was not truly religious—not truly and seriously, as she and Stephen were. No doubt she thought she was, and perhaps she was, in some queer way; but were queer ways of being religious permissible? Weren't they as bad, really, as no ways at all?

Virginia sighed again. One did so long to be able to look up to one's mother, to revere. . . .

The house seemed empty. All the big rooms, glanced into one after the other, were empty. Nothing in them but the mild spring sunshine, and furniture, and silence.

She went upstairs, but in her mother's bedroom was only Ellen, arranging another bunch of flowers—another, when yesterday's were still perfectly good—on the writing-table. Stephen disliked flowers in bedrooms, but suppose he hadn't, would Ellen so assiduously see that they were always fresh? Virginia thought she wouldn't, and very much wished at that moment to point out the extravagance of picking flowers unnecessarily at a time of year when they were scarce; but she was handicapped by their being for her mother.

She said nothing, therefore, and went away, and Ellen was relieved when she went. Just as Virginia was relieved when she got away from the servants, so were the servants relieved when they saw her go.

She fetched a wrap from her bedroom—the room already looked forlorn, as if it knew it was to be empty of Stephen for two whole nights—and went downstairs and out on to the terrace. Probably her mother was lingering in the garden this mild morning, and Virginia took two or three turns up and down, expecting every moment to see her approaching along some path.

Nobody approached, however: the garden remained as empty as the house. And time was passing; Stephen would be due soon to come back; her mother would want to say good-bye to him, and couldn't have gone for a walk on this morning of departure. She would particularly want to say good-bye, quite apart from the fact that she would be gone before his return on Monday, because she wasn't letting him stay in Hertford Street over the week-end. Stephen did so hate hotels. It seemed hard when no one was in the flat that he couldn't use it. Her mother had made excuses—said something or other about Mrs. Mitcham having a holiday, but Virginia didn't think she had felt quite comfortable about it. She would therefore certainly wish to make him some parting little speech of more than ordinary gratitude for his hospitality, seeing how from him she was withholding hers. And here was Stephen, coming across the grass, and in a few minutes he would have started, and her mother still nowhere to be seen.

"What has become of mother?" she called, when he was within earshot.

He didn't answer till he was close to her. Then he said, looking worried, "Isn't she back yet?"

"No. Where is she?"

He stared at Virginia a moment, then made a gesture of extreme impatience. "I can't imagine," he said, pulling out his watch and beginning to walk quickly across the terrace to the open windows of the drawing-room, for he hadn't much time, he saw, before his train left, "what possessed your mother."

"Possessed her?" echoed Virginia, her eyes and mouth all astonishment.

"Anything more unsuitable—" said Stephen, quickly going through the drawing-room, followed by Virginia. "Tut, tut," he finished, in a most strange way.

Virginia's heart gave a queer kind of drop. "Unsuitable?" she repeated faintly.

It was the word of all others she dreaded hearing applied to her mother, and applied by Stephen. She herself had felt many little things unsuitable in her mother during this visit, the first real visit since her marriage, but she had so much hoped Stephen hadn't noticed, and she did so much want him to continue in the warm respect and admiration for her mother he had felt before. What had she done now? What could she have done to produce this fluster of annoyance in the quiet, controlled Stephen?

"She all but ran over me in my own village street," he said, going into the study and hastily collecting his things.

Virginia could only again echo. "All but ran over you?" she repeated blankly.

"Yes. You know how strongly I feel about motor-cycles, and the type of scallywag youth who uses them. Where is my muffler?"

"Motor-cycles?" said Virginia, her mouth open.

"I naturally hadn't the remotest idea it could be your mother, but mother—our mother—met me and told me—yes, yes, Kate, I know—I'm coming immediately. Good-bye, my love—I shall miss my train—"

"But Stephen—"

"Mother will tell you. Really I find the utmost difficulty in believing it. And not back yet. Still scorching—"

He was out in the hall; he was in the car; he was gone.

Virginia stood staring after him. Stephen gone, and in such a way. No good-bye hardly, no lingering, sweet farewell, nothing but hurry and upset. What had happened? What had her mother done?

His incredible last word beat on her ears—scorching. She wished she had flung herself into the car and gone with him to the station, and so at least had a little more time to be told things. But Stephen disliked impetuosity, and, for that matter, so did she. There were, however, moments in life when indulgence in it was positively right.

Virginia stood there feeling perhaps more unhappy than she had ever yet felt. One couldn't have a mother all one's life and not be attached to her; at least, she couldn't. She was made up of loyalties. They differed in intensity, but each in its degree was complete. Passionately she wanted the objects of her loyalties to have the invulnerableness of perfection. Stephen had it. She had supposed, till this last visit, that her mother had it—in an entirely different line, of course, with all sorts of little things about her Virginia didn't understand but was willing to accept as also, in their way, in their different way, good. *There is one glory of the sun, and another glory of the moon,* Virginia, observing her mother, had sometimes quoted to herself. Both of them glories, but different—greater and lesser. Stephen had the glory of the sun; her mother had the moon one. During this unlucky visit, though, how had it not, thought Virginia standing on the steps, looking down the empty avenue, been obscured. And now, just at the end, just as she was going to make such an effort to set everything right again, her mother had evidently done something definitely dreadful, with a motor-cycle. Her mother, her mouse-like mother. What could she *possibly*. . . .

She turned away and went indoors, her eyes fixed on the carpet, her brows knitted in painfullest perplexity.

Should she go and meet Stephen's mother, who was coming to lunch and evidently knew what had happened? There was still half an hour before lunch, and before Stephen's mother, who never came a minute sooner or a minute later than the exact appointed time, would arrive. But her own mother might come back at any moment, and it would be better to hear things from her, wouldn't it, than from Stephen's mother. She was very fond of Stephen's mother—indeed, how should she not be, when he was?—and admired her many qualities

excessively, but she didn't love her as she did her own mother.
One began so young with one's own mother, of course one felt
differently about her from what one did about any one else's.
She shrank from hearing, from Stephen's mother, whatever it
was her own mother had done.

Family pride, loyalty, and the queer little ache of love,
sometimes disapproving, sometimes wistful, sometimes disappointed, sometimes pitiful, but always love, that she felt for
her mother, made her not want to hear Stephen's mother tell
her what had happened. Stephen was different. If he told and
blamed he had a right to, he belonged. It would be painful to
her to the point of agony, seeing how much she loved them
both, but he had the right. His mother, though, hadn't. She felt
she couldn't bear to listen to even the most tactful disapproval
from his mother. No, she wouldn't go to meet her. Her mother
would certainly be in time for lunch, and get there before
Stephen's mother. Oh, all these mothers! There were too many
of them, Virginia thought with sudden impatience, and then
was ashamed—she, the wife of one of God's priests.

The drawing-room door was open, and opposite it was the
widely-flung-up William and Mary window, and through the
window she saw, coming across the terrace and walking with
even more than her usual briskness, Stephen's mother.

Such a thing had never happened before, that she should
arrive before her time. *What* had her mother done?

Virginia stood in the hall, rooted, wanting to run up to her
bedroom and hide, but unable to make up her mind quickly
enough, and Mrs. Colquhoun saw her the minute she was
through the window, and it was too late.

"Oh, my dear Virginia," she cried out, "I am concerned for
your mother. I hope she got home safely? I couldn't rest. I had
to come and hear that she wasn't too much shaken. The young
man went off at such a pace. And Stephen told me they nearly
ran over him in the village. I thought it so courageous of Mrs.
Cumfrit. I do hope she is none the worse?"

"I haven't seen mother yet," said Virginia, getting nearer
prevarication than in her transparent life she had yet been.

But Mrs. Colquhoun was not to be put off by prevarication.
"What? Isn't she back?" she exclaimed.

"I haven't seen her," said Virginia obstinately.

Mrs. Colquhoun stared at her. "But then, where—?" she
began.

"I don't see," said Virginia, very red, and straight of eyebrow, "why mother shouldn't motor-cycle if she wants to."

"But of *course* not. *Certainly* not. And Mr. Monckton is an old friend, isn't he—that's to say, as old a friend as one can be at such a very young age. I expect he's your friend really, isn't he? Though I don't remember seeing him at Chickover before."

"Tell me what happened, mother," said Virginia, leading the way to her boudoir.

"But is Mrs. Cumfrit safely back yet? That's what I'm really anxious to hear," said Mrs. Colquhoun, taking off her gloves and woollen scarf, and sitting as far from the fire as she could, so as to convey, with the delicacy of action rather than the clumsiness of words, that a fire on such a sunny morning was unnecessary.

"No," said Virginia.

"Well, you mustn't be agitated, dearest child. Mr. Monckton is a safe rider, I'm sure. And careful. Young, of course, and in so far headstrong, but I'm sure careful. Especially when taking some one of your mother's age with him. How long have you known him?"

"I haven't known him," said Virginia stiffly.

She wouldn't admit to herself that all this amazed and shook her. She would let no thought get through into her mind except that it was natural and perfectly ordinary, if one wanted to, to go off motor-cycling, natural and perfectly ordinary for anybody, her mother included.

"Not known him?" exclaimed Mrs. Colquhoun.

"Mother has many friends I haven't met," said Virginia, sitting very straight.

"Quite. Of course. In London."

"Yes. You haven't told me what happened, mother."

"Well, this *very* tall and *quite* good-looking Mr. Monckton was waiting in the churchyard at your poor father's tomb, when we came out after the service—"

"Waiting for mother?"

"Yes. He said he had come down on purpose to drive her up to London in his side-car—"

"But mother isn't going till Monday."

"Exactly. Nor, he said, was he. His motor-cycle was outside the gate, and he persuaded your mother to get in and let him drive her back here, and she did, and off they went. Off, really, like a flash. Such courage in your dear mother. I did so admire it at her age. Perfectly splendid, I thought. It means, you know, Virginia, vitality—the most important of all possessions. Without it one can do nothing. With it one can do everything. However—to go on. I watched them, and saw they didn't take the first turning home, and then I met Stephen in the village, and they had been through it and just missed running over him by inches. Now, now, Virginia, don't turn pale, dear child. They didn't run over him, or of course I wouldn't have told you. Now, my dearest child, there's nothing at all exciting and upsetting in this, so don't allow yourself to be upset. It's very bad for you, you know—"

"I'm not upset, mother. Why should I be?" said Virginia, holding herself up. She hadn't been able to help turning pale at the terrible idea of Stephen so narrowly missing being run over by her mother—oh, what a horrible combination of circumstances!—but what else, she asked herself, was there to mind in this? Why shouldn't her mother, meeting a friend, go for a little turn in his side-car on such a fine morning?

"I never knew your mother do anything in the least like this before," said Mrs. Colquhoun.

"No," said Virginia. "But don't you think there always has to be a beginning?"

"A beginning?"

Mrs. Colquhoun was surprised. Virginia was almost arguing with her. Besides, it was an unexpected view to take. Beginnings were not suitable, she felt, after a certain age, especially not for women. Mothers of the married, such as herself and Mrs. Cumfrit, should be concerned rather with endings than beginnings.

But she would not be anything but broad-minded; she was determined to remain, however much surprised, broad-minded. So she said, "Certainly," with hearty agreement. And repeated, "Certainly. Certainly there must be a beginning. Always. To everything. Only—I was wondering whether perhaps—well, anyhow it shows a wonderful vitality, and as no one recognised your mother in the village—"

"Is it wrong to go in a side-car?" asked Virginia, again surprisingly.

"My dearest child, of course not. It's only that—well, it's a little unusual for your mother. It's not quite what people here are used to in her, is it. It's a—a young thing to do. Girls go in side-cars, and other wild young persons, but not—well, as I say, one can but admire such vitality and courage. I confess I wouldn't have dared. I do believe there isn't the young man living who could have induced me to."

Virginia felt very unhappy. Fancy having to sit there defending her mother—her *mother,* who had always been on such a pinnacle. It was like a bad dream. And where was she? Why didn't she come back? Suppose something had happened to her? Something must have happened to her, or surely she wouldn't have missed saying good-bye to Stephen?

A sick little fear began to creep round Virginia's heart. She hadn't much imagination; she didn't dramatically visualise an accident, her mother lying crumpled up and lifeless in some lonely lane, but she did think it possible something unpleasant might have happened, and it made her look with very wide, anxious eyes at Mrs. Colquhoun, and wonder what in the world it could matter really whether her mother got into fifty side-cars and rushed through fifty villages as long as she safely got out of them again.

The gong sounded.

"Lunch," said Mrs. Colquhoun brightly, for Virginia's expression rather startled her, and it was above all things necessary that the child should, in her present condition, be kept calm. "Shall you wait?"

"Listen," said Virginia, holding up her hand.

In another moment Mrs. Colquhoun heard it too—the noise of a motor-cycle, far away but coming nearer.

"What quick ears," she smilingly congratulated her daughter-in-law; but Virginia was on her feet, and running out to meet her mother.

She ran through the hall and on to the steps, expecting to see the motor-cycle careering along the avenue; and there was nothing to be seen, and the noise had left off too. It must have been some one else's. The avenue was empty.

She stood staring down it, thrown back on her fears. Then in the distance, round the bend, she saw a small figure walking quickly towards the house. It was her mother, safe and sound.

Virginia's immediate impulse in her glad relief was to run down the steps to meet her and hug her, but instantly the reaction set in. Nothing had happened, her mother was unharmed, and it was really too bad that she should have gone in the foolish side-car. One surely had a right to expect at least dignity in one's mother, a sense of the suitable; especially when she belonged, too, to Stephen, a man in a public position, with a sacred calling.

Sore and puzzled, Virginia stood stiffly on the steps. Her mother came along very quickly and lightly, like a little leaf being blown up the avenue; and when she got nearer, and began to wave her hand with what appeared to be, and no doubt was, forced gaiety, Virginia noticed her face had the look on it she had seen once before during this unfortunate visit, the look of a child caught by its elders stealing the jam.

&ᴏ XIX ᴏ&

Catherine had walked very fast up the avenue, afraid she was late. Her face was hot with exercise, and her eyes bright with Christopher. She didn't look like the same person who had set out that morning, listless and pale, with Stephen for church. She had somehow entirely wiped out Christopher's behaviour in London, and felt she had started again with him on a new footing. She was happy, and wanted to tell Virginia of her new arrangements quickly, before their naturalness and desirability, so evident and clear while she was with Christopher, had faded and become obscure. She felt they might do that rather easily without him, especially as Mrs. Colquhoun was going to be at lunch.

She must be quick, while she still saw plain. Everybody wanted her to go, and she wanted to go; then why not go? Yes, but they wouldn't be able to let her go without criticism, without disapproval. Dear me, she thought, how pleasant to be quite simple and straight. How pleasant to be free from sentimentalism, and all its grievances and tender places. How very pleasant not to mind if one's children did sometimes get bored with one, and for them not to mind if you sometimes got bored with them.

She laughed a little at these aspirations, as she hurried towards her tall, unmoving daughter and waved her hand in greeting, because they sounded so very like a desire to be free of family life altogether. And she didn't desire to be free of it, she clung to what remained of it for her, she clung to Virginia, her last shred of it, however different they were, however deeply they didn't understand each other. Blood; strange, compelling, unbreakable link. Could one forget that that tall creature there, so aloof, so critical, had once been tiny and helpless, depending on her for her very life?

A fresh wave of love for her daughter washed over her. She felt so able to love and be happy at that moment. "I'm late—I know I'm late," she said breathlessly, running up the steps and kissing her. "Did you think I was lost, darling?"

"I was afraid something might have happened, mother," said Virginia, very stiff and grave.

"Darling—I'm so sorry. It didn't upset you?"

"I was a little afraid. But it's all right now that you've come back. Lunch is ready, and mother is waiting. Shall we go in?"

"She will have told you, hasn't she, of my escapade," said Catherine a little nervously as they went indoors, for Virginia was so very grave.

"I hope you had a pleasant drive," said Virginia, wincing at the word escapade. Mothers didn't have escapades. Such things were for them, and indeed for most people who wished to live the lives of plain Christians, unsuitable.

She ached with different emotions. The only way to keep her feelings out of sight, safely hidden, was to encase herself in ice.

She sat at the head of the table, a mother on either hand, and helped them in turn icily to mince. On the Saturdays of Stephen's absences both parlourmaids, once he had been seen off, were given a holiday, and the dishes were placed on the table by Ellen. There was always mince for lunch on these Saturdays, because mince rested the cook. Also, it didn't have to be carved. But it is not a food to promote good-fellowship; impossible to be really convivial on mince. The three, however, wouldn't have been convivial that day even if the table had been covered with, say, quails; for in the consciousness of each was, enormous and vivid, that side-car and the young man who belonged to it.

Both Virginia and Mrs. Colquhoun earnestly desired that neither it nor he should be mentioned during lunch, because of Ellen, and Mrs. Colquhoun did her best to talk well and brightly about everything except just that. But Catherine was anxious to tell them quickly, before she became any more congealed, what was going to happen next. She knew it was past one already, and that at two Christopher and the motor-cycle would appear to fetch her, and that the entire household would be aware of her departure in the side-car. She was obliged to talk of it, and at the very first pause in Mrs. Colquhoun's conversation began to do so.

How difficult it was. Worse than she had feared. Her cheeks got hotter. Virginia's face, and her grieved, astonished eyes, made her stammer. And Mrs. Colquhoun, when she heard of the drive planned for that afternoon to London, on top of the drive that morning to goodness knew where, merely raised her hands and ejaculated "Insatiable!"

For some reason Catherine found this brief ejaculation curiously disconcerting.

"If you must go to-day, mother," said Virginia, stung and perplexed, "you might have gone with Stephen."

"Ah, but the fresh air, dear child—the fresh air," cried Mrs. Colquhoun, desiring to do what she could for her colleague in the eyes of Ellen. "Your mother looks a different creature already, after just her outing this morning. There's nothing like fresh air. Air, air—it's what we all need. And our windows—" she glanced severely at Ellen, "opened *wide* at night."

"Besides," went on the wounded Virginia, "I thought you said Mrs. Mitcham was having a holiday."

"Darling, I *must* go up," murmured Catherine, mechanically eating mince. She couldn't now go into what she had said about Mrs. Mitcham; she didn't remember what she had said, and she couldn't get involved in explanations, for if once she began there would be no end to them. "I—well, I must. I've been away from home so long this time."

No, she didn't know what to say. She had nothing to say. There was no reason nor explanation in the least suited to either Virginia's or Mrs. Colquhoun's ears. It was strange how people, when they were getting what they really wanted, yet disapproved, yet didn't like it, she thought.

"Of course, of course," said Mrs. Colquhoun heartily, desirous of dropping the subject as soon as possible because of Ellen. "Homes can't be left. Homes are there so as *not* to be left. Or why have them? I do so approve, dear Mrs. Cumfrit. We shall miss you, of course, but I do so approve."

She leant across the table and smiled. She had put the seal on her colleague; she had wrapped her in her own cloak. The servants, in the face of such protection, would be able to notice and wonder nothing.

They had prunes to finish up with. Nobody is long over prunes, and the three were out of the dining-room twenty minutes after they had gone into it.

Catherine went upstairs to see, she said, to her things. Virginia followed her. Mrs. Colquhoun assured them she didn't mind being left, that she was never dull alone, would wait quite happily in the drawing-room, and they were not to give her a thought.

"Mother—" began Virginia, when they had got into the bedroom, her eyes dark with perplexity.

"You don't mind, darling?" said Catherine, putting her arm round her. "I mean, my going all of a sudden like this?"

Then she laughed a little. "I came all of a sudden, and I'm going all of a sudden," she said. "Am I a very uncomfortable sort of mother to have?"

Virginia flushed a deep red. How could she say Yes, which was the truth? How could she say No, which was a lie?

"Mother," she said painfully, for the question insisted on forcing its way through her protective coating of ice, "you're not going away to-day because you think—because you think—"

She stopped, and looked at her mother.

And Catherine, as unable not to lie when it came to either lying or hurting, as Virginia was unable, faced by such an alternative, to be anything but stonily silent, kissed her softly on each cheek and said, "No, darling, I'm not. And I don't think anything."

It wasn't quite a lie. She wasn't going away that day because of Virginia; she was going away now because of Christopher. Life was intricate. Lies were so much mixed up with truth. And as for love, it got into everything, and wherever it was one seemed to have to lie. Ah, to be able to be simple and straight. The one thing that appeared to be really simple and straight and easy was ordinary, affectionate friendship. Not too affectionate; not, either, too ordinary; but warm, and steady, and understanding. In fact, what hers and Christopher's was going to be.

Ellen came in and asked if she should pack. Nothing had been said to Ellen, Virginia knew, yet here she was, full of a devotion she never showed in her ordinary work.

Catherine explained that she couldn't take her luggage with her, and Ellen said, just as if Catherine were still her mistress and Virginia still a little girl, that she would see that it went up by the next train. She then got out Catherine's fur coat, and gave her her gloves and a thick veil, and insisted that she should wear gaiters, kneeling down and buttoning them for her.

Virginia might have been a stranger standing looking on. And her mother was laughing and talking to Ellen, rather after the fashion of a child going off for a holiday. In a way it was a relief, because it did seem as if she hadn't noticed anything, but it was an odd mood in her mother; Virginia couldn't remember any mood quite like it.

"I'll go down to mother," she said, taking refuge in the other one.

"Do, darling," said Catherine, busy being buttoned up.

And Virginia, going down into the drawing-room, found a young man in brown leather there, being talked to by Mrs. Colquhoun, who turned round quickly when she came in, and whose face changed from eager to rather disagreeable, she thought, when he saw her.

"This, Virginia, my child," said Mrs. Colquhoun with even more than her usual briskness, "is your mother's old friend Mr. Monckton. Mr. Monckton, this is my daughter-in-law, Mrs. Stephen Colquhoun. Conceive its falling to my lot to make you two acquainted! I should have thought you would have lisped together in infant numbers, tumbled about like puppies together on lawns, been nursed upon the self-same hill. I hope, Mr. Monckton, you admire with me the poet I am quoting from?"

No; young people could never remain shy long when she was there. Yet presently she had to admit that with these two, anyhow, it was heavy going. They couldn't be got to talk to each other. Dear little Virginia, of course, never did go in much for small chat, and Mr. Monckton's disposition appeared after all not to correspond with his glowing exterior. He was as silent as if he had been puny and sallow. A picture of splendid youth, standing there on the hearth-rug—he wouldn't sit down, he wouldn't have coffee, he wouldn't smoke, he wouldn't talk, he wouldn't do anything—he seemed to have really nothing in him. Except perhaps obstinacy; and possibly a hasty temper. Who and what he was, and why Mrs. Cumfrit should be friends with him, she couldn't imagine. To all her questions—of course, tactfully put—he only made evasive answers, chiefly in monosyllables. Little Virginia was as silent as he was. Indeed, she seemed to take a dislike to him from the first. Later on, describing the meeting to her friends, Mrs. Colquhoun was fond of dwelling on the unerring instinct of that dear child.

"We ought to be starting," said Christopher, looking at his wrist-watch.

It was intolerable to him being there alone with these two women, in the house that used to be Catherine's, faced by the girl who was, he was certain, the living image of George, and who stood watching him with great critical eyes while the old lady enfiladed him with a non-stopping fire of God knew what.

"I wish you'd tell your mother," he said, turning with a quick movement of impatience to Virginia.

She stared at him a moment without answering. Then she said slowly, "My mother will come when she is ready."

"Hoity toity," Christopher all but said aloud; and added under his breath, "young Miss."

Then he remembered that she wasn't a Miss at all, but the wife of that ancient bustard Stephen. Horrible as it was of her to go and marry anybody so moth-eaten with age, it yet gave him an argument, and a very mighty one, to use against Catherine when occasion should—and would—arise. In as far as this went, he was much obliged to Virginia; but except for this he didn't mind admitting that he regarded her with aversion. She oughtn't to be there at all. Unborn, she would have been perfectly all right and comfortable, and Catherine wouldn't have had any of her ideas about being the mother of a married daughter, and what would Virginia say, and all such stuff. Directly he saw the girl, and her cold eyes and her determined mouth, he knew he was going to have trouble with Catherine when things had reached their crisis—as they were bound to do—about what Virginia would say, and think, and feel. He knew it, he knew it.

"Oh, damn—" he muttered; and jerked up his elbow to look at his wrist-watch again.

"If your mother doesn't come soon," he said, "I see no prospect of our reaching London to-night." And to himself, his spirit grinning, he added, "That'll fetch them."

It did.

"Really, Virginia," Mrs. Colquhoun instantly said, turning to her with a kind of shocked bristling, "do go up and tell your mother she must hurry. Or shall I? The stairs—"

But there was Catherine, coming in like light and warmth, he thought, into a dark and frost-bound place.

"Oh, Christopher!" she exclaimed in her surprise at seeing him there—("Christopher," noted Mrs. Colquhoun)—"You here already? I didn't hear you arrive. Aren't you very early?"

"Far from being very early," said Mrs. Colquhoun, rising from her chair preparatory to going into the hall to witness this unique departure, "Mr. Monckton says it is very late. Hardly time, indeed, to get to London."

"Oh, but let us go at once, then. Have you been introduced to Virginia? Oh, yes, I've got a fur coat—it's in the hall. Virginia darling, take care of yourself, won't you. Good-bye, Mrs. Colquhoun—oh yes, I know you will—I do know she is perfectly safe in your hands. And whenever you want me, dearest—when*ever* you want me, you've only got to send me one little word, and I'll come."

"Sweet of you, mother."

Even with her mother the girl was like a poker—a cold poker, thought Christopher, who felt he might have forgiven her being a poker if only she had been a red hot one. But how excessively he hated all this, how excessively he hated seeing Catherine in these relationships. Why had she made him come in? Why need he ever have seen Virginia, and been introduced, and have to make the fool grimaces of convention? Well, he would soon have put miles between themselves and Chickover, and he fervently hoped he might never see the beastly place again.

Once more he tucked Catherine in the rug up to her chin. This time she was laughing. The two women on the steps, watching the departure, weren't laughing. Virginia's face was expressionless; Mrs. Colquhoun's had the smile on it of hospitality got down to its dregs—the fixed smile of determination not to relax one hairs-breadth of proper geniality till the door was shut and the guest round the corner. On her son's behalf, she told herself, she saw his late guest off. Virginia, of course, was doing it on her own behalf, but Mrs. Colquhoun was even more important, for she represented the master of the house. How thankful she was that he wasn't there to do it himself. What would he have thought of it all?

She put on her eyeglasses in order to see better what was going on down there. The young man, busy with the rug, no longer looked as he had looked in the drawing-room; his face now shone with smiles. So did Mrs. Cumfrit's. Mrs. Colquhoun could not help being struck by this air of gaiety. And she remembered Mrs. Cumfrit's yellowness and fatigue on her arrival the previous Sunday, and the way she had remained yellow and had got visibly older all the week, ending up in church that morning by being on the verge either of being sick or fainting—perhaps both. There was no sign of this now. On the contrary, she looked remarkably healthy. Odd; very odd.

"Oh—*good*-bye. *Good*-bye. Now, Mr. Monckton, be very careful, won't you—"

They were gone. In an instant, it seemed, they were a speck down the avenue, and then the bend hid them, the sound of them died away, and she and Virginia had Chickover to themselves again.

The word harum-scarum entered Mrs. Colquhoun's mind. She dismissed it. She couldn't admit a word like that in connection with her Stephen's mother-in-law.

She looked at Virginia. Virginia was staring straight in front of her at the avenue, at the afternoon sun lying along its emptiness.

"I do think it good of your dear mother to bother about that young man," said Mrs. Colquhoun. "Let us hope she will teach him better manners. And now," she added briskly, laying an affectionate arm round her daughter-in-law's shoulder, "isn't it time our little Virginia put her feet up?"

❧ XX ❧

Christopher's was the slowest motor-cycle on the road that day. At times it proceeded with the leisureliness of a station fly. They loitered along in the sunshine, stopping at the least excuse—a view, an old house, a flock of primroses. They had tea at Salisbury, and examined the Cathedral, and talked gaily of *Jude the Obscure,* surely the most unfortunate of men, and from him they naturally proceeded to discuss death and disaster, and all very happily, for they were in the precisely opposite mood of the one praised by the poet as sweet, and the sad thoughts evoked by Sarum Close brought pleasant thoughts to their mind.

How much they had to say to each other. There was no end

to their talk, their eager exchange of opinions. Chickover was
dim as a dream now in Catherine's mind; and the Catherine
who had gone to bed there every evening in a growing
wretchedness was a dream within a dream. With Christopher
she was alive. He himself was so tremendously alive that one
would indeed have to be a hopeless mummy not to catch life
from him and wake up. Besides, it was impossible to be—
anyhow for a short time—with some one who adored one,
unless he was physically repulsive, and not be happy. That
Christopher adored her was plain to the very passers-by. The
men who passed grinned to themselves in sympathy; the
women sighed; and old ladies, long done with envy, smiled
with open benevolence between their bonnet-strings.

Unconscious of everybody except each other, they walked
about Salisbury looking at the sights and not seeing them, so
deeply were they engaged in talk. What could be more
innocent than to walk, talking, about Salisbury? Yet if Stephen, Virginia, or Mrs. Colquhoun had met them they would
have been moved by unpleasant emotions. Once during the
afternoon this thought crossed Catherine's mind. It was when,
at tea in a confectioner's, Christopher was holding out a plate
of muffins to her, his face the face of a seraph floating in glory;
and she took a muffin, and held it suspended while she looked
at him, arrested by the thought, and said, "Why mayn't one be
happy?"

"But one may, and one is," said Christopher.

"One is," she smiled, "but one mayn't. At least, one mayn't
go on being happy. Not over again. Not in this way. Not—"
she tried to find the words to express it—"out of one's turn."

"What one's relations think, or wish, or approve, or de-
plore," said Christopher, who scented Stephen somewhere at
the back of her remarks, "should never be taken the least
notice of if one wishes to go on developing."

"Well, I seem to be going on developing at a breakneck
rate."

"Besides, it's jealousy. Nearly always. Deep down. The
grudge of the half dead against the wholly alive, of the not
wanted against the wanted. They can't manage to be alive
themselves, so they declare the only respectable thing is to be
dead. The only pure thing. The only holy thing. And they
pretend every sort of pious horror if one won't be dead too.
Relations," he finished, lighting a cigarette and speaking from
the depths of an experience that consisted of one uncle, and he

the most amiable and unexacting of men, who never gave advice and never criticised, and only wanted sometimes to be played golf with, "are like that. They have to be defied. Or they'll strangle one."

"It seems dangerous," said Catherine, pursuing her first thought, "to show that one likes anything or anybody very much."

"Isn't it the rankest hypocrisy," said Christopher with a face of disgust.

"If you were bald, and had a long white beard—" she began. "But even then," she went on after a pause, "if we looked pleased while we talked and seemed very much interested, we'd be done for."

She smiled. "They wouldn't mind at all," she said, "if you were eating muffins happily with a girl of your own age. It's when somebody like me comes along, who has had her turn, who is out of her turn."

"They would have people love by rule," said Christopher.

"I don't know about love, but they would have them be happy by rule," said Catherine.

"They must be defied," said Christopher.

She laughed. "We *are* defying them," she said.

Proceeding from Salisbury with the setting sun behind them, they continued with the same leisureliness in the direction of Andover and London.

"Oughtn't we to go a little faster?" Catherine asked, noticing the lowness of the sun.

"If you're home by nine o'clock, won't that be soon enough?" he asked.

"Oh, quite. I love this."

"I'd like to go on for ever," said Christopher.

"Aren't we friends," said Catherine, looking up at him with a smile.

"*Aren't* we," said Christopher, in deep contentment.

The chimney stacks of an old house on their right among trees attracted her, and they turned off the main road to go and look at it. The house was nothing specially beautiful, but the road that led to it was, and it went winding on past the house through woods even more beautiful.

They followed it, for the main road was uninteresting, and this one, though making a detour, would no doubt ultimately arrive at Andover.

Charming, this slow going along in the soft, purple evening.

The smell of the damp earth and grass in the woods they passed through was delicious. It was dead quiet, and sometimes they stopped just to listen to the silence.

Companionship: what a perfect thing it was, thought Catherine. To be two instead of one, to be happily two, with no strain, no concealing or pretending, quite natural, quite simple, quite relaxed—so natural and simple and relaxed that it was really like being oneself doubled, but oneself at one's best, at one's serenest and most amusing. Could any condition be more absolutely delightful? And, thought Catherine, to be two with some one of the opposite sex, some one strong who could take care of one, with whom one felt safe and cosy, some one young, who liked doing all the things the eternal child in oneself liked doing so much, but never dared to for want of backing up, for fear of being laughed at—how completely delightful.

They came, on the outer edge of the woods, to a group of cottages; a little hamlet, solitary, tucked away from noise, the smoke of its chimneys going straight up into the still air, so small that it hadn't even got a church—happy, happy hamlet, thought Catherine, remembering her past week of church—and in one of the cottage gardens, sheltered and warm, was the first flowering currant bush she had seen that year.

It stood splendid against the grey background of the shadowy garden, brilliant pink and crimson in the dusk, and Christopher stopped at her exclamation, and got off and went into the cottage and asked the old woman who lived there to sell him a bunch of the flowers; and the old woman, looking at him and Catherine, was sure from their faces of peace that they were on their honeymoon, and picked a bunch and went to the gate and gave it to Catherine, and wouldn't take any money for it, and said it was for luck.

It seemed quite natural, and in keeping with everything else that afternoon, to find a nice old woman who gave them flowers and wished them luck. In Salisbury people had all seemed extraordinarily amiable. This old woman was extraordinarily amiable. She even called them pretty dears, which filled their cup of enjoyment to the brim.

After this the country was very open, and solitary, and still. No signs of any town were to be seen; only rolling hills, and here and there a little group of trees. Also a few faint stars began to appear in the pale sky.

"Oughtn't we to go faster?" asked Catherine again, her lap full of the crimson flowers.

"We'll make up between Andover and London," said Christopher. "If it's half-past nine instead of nine before we get to Hertford Street, will it be early enough?"

"Oh, quite," said Catherine placidly.

They jogged along, up and down the windings of the lane, which presently grew grassier and narrower, into hollows and out of them again. Not a house was to be seen, not a human being. Stillness, evening, stars. It seemed to Catherine presently, in that wide place of rolling country and great sky, that in the whole world there was nothing except herself, Christopher, and the stars.

About seven miles beyond the hamlet of the flowering currant bush, just at the top of an incline, the motor-cycle stopped.

She thought, waking from the dream she had fallen into, that he was stopping it, as so often before that afternoon, to listen to the silence; but he hadn't stopped it, it had stopped itself.

"Damn," said Christopher, pulling and pushing and kicking certain parts of the thing.

"Why?" asked Catherine comfortably.

"The engine's stopped."

"Perhaps it wants winding up."

He got off, and began to stoop and peer. She sat quiet, her head back, her face upturned, gazing at the stars. It was most beautiful there in the great quiet of the falling night. There was still a dull red line in the sky where the sun had gone down, but from the east a dim curtain was drawing slowly towards them. The road, just at the place they were, curved southwards, and she had the red streak of the sunset on her right and the advancing darkness on her left. They were on the top of a rising in the vast flatness, and it was as if she could see to the ends of the world. The quiet, now that the motor had stopped, was profound.

Christopher came and looked at her. She smiled at him. She was perfectly content and happy.

He didn't smile back. "The petrol's run out," he said.

"Has it?" said Catherine placidly. In cars, when petrol ran out, one opened another can of it and ran it in again.

"There isn't any more," said Christopher. "And from the

look of this place I should say we were ten miles from anywhere."

He was overwhelmed. He had meant to have his tank filled up at Salisbury, and in his enchanted condition of happiness had forgotten. Of all the infernal, hopeless fools . . .

He could only stare at her.

"Well, what are we going to do?" she asked, waking up a little to the seriousness of his face.

"If we were near anywhere—" he said, looking round.

"Can't we go back to those cottages?"

"The thing won't budge."

"Walk?"

"At least seven miles."

They stared at each other in the deepening dusk.

"Well, but, Christopher—"

"I know," he said. "We're in a hell of a fix, and it's entirely my fault. I simply forgot to have her filled up at Salisbury."

"Well, but there must be some way out."

"Not unless some one happens to come along, and I could persuade him to go to the nearest petrol place and fetch us some."

"Can't you go?"

"And leave you here?"

"Can't I go?"

"As though you could!"

In silence they gazed at each other. The stars were growing brighter. Their faces stood out now as something white in the darkening landscape.

"Well, but, Christopher—" began Catherine incredulously.

"If I thought we could by walking get anywhere within reasonable time, I'd leave the blighted machine here to its fate. But we might get lost, and wander round for hours. And besides, where would we find a railway station? Miles and miles we might have to go."

"That wouldn't matter. I mean, however late we got to London wouldn't matter as long as we did get there."

"I quite see we've jolly well got to get there. What beats me is how."

Catherine was silent. They were indeed, as Christopher said, in a fix. She would even, mentally, agree with him that it was a hell of a one.

"Catherine, I'm sorry," he said, laying his hand on hers.

The words but feebly represented his feelings. He was

crushed by his folly, by his idiotic forgetfulness in Salisbury. Would she ever trust herself with him again? If she didn't, he deserved all he got.

"I was so happy in Salisbury," he said, "that I never thought about the petrol. I'm the most hopeless blighter."

"But what are we to *do?*" asked Catherine earnestly.

"I'm hanged if I know," he said.

Again they stared at each other in silence. The night seemed to have descended on them now with the suddenness of a huge swooping bird.

"I suppose we had better leave it here and walk on," she said. "It seems a dreadful thing to do, but there's a chance perhaps of our meeting some one or getting somewhere. Or couldn't we push it? Is it very heavy?"

"I could push it for two miles, perhaps, but that would be about the limit."

"But I'd help."

"You!"

He smiled at her, miserable as he was.

"We might strike the main road," he said, gazing across the dim space to where—how many miles away?—it probably lay.

"It can't be very far, can it?" she said. "And then perhaps a car passing might help us."

He struck a match and lit the lamps—their light comforted them a little—and took out his map and studied it.

As he feared, this obscure and attractive cart-track was not to be found on it, nor was the group of solitary cottages.

Far away to the north, in some distant trees, an owl hooted. It had the effect of making them feel more lost than ever.

"I think we'd better stay where we are," he said.

"And hope some one may come along?"

"Yes. We'll have the lights on. They ought to be seen for miles round. Somebody may wonder what they're doing up here, not moving. There's just a chance. People are so damned incurious, though," he added.

"Especially if being curious would mean walking up here in the dark."

She tried to talk in her usual voice, but it was difficult, for she was aghast at the misfortune that had overtaken them.

"Perhaps if you shouted—?" she suggested.

He shouted. It sounded awful. It emphasised the loneliness. It made her shiver. And after each shout, out of the silence that succeeded it, the owl away in the distant trees hooted. It was the only answer.

"Let us wait quietly," she said, laying her hand on his arm. "Some one is sure to see the lights, sooner or later."

A little wind began to creep round them, a mere stirring, to begin with, of the air, but it was a very cool little wind, not to say cold, and any more of it would be decidedly unpleasant.

He looked round him again. The ground dropped on the left of the track into one of the many hollows they had been down into and up out of since leaving the cottages.

"We'll go and sit down there," he said. "It'll be more sheltered, and we shall hear all right if anybody comes along the road."

She got on to her feet, and he helped her out, unwinding the rug as he had done that morning—was it really only that morning?—in the sunny cove by the sea.

"What a day we're having!" said Catherine, trying to be gay; but never did anybody feel less so.

He carried the rug and cushions across the grass and down the slope. He had nothing he could say. He was overwhelmed by his folly. Of what use throwing himself at her feet and begging her to forgive him? That wouldn't help them. Besides, she wasn't angry with him, she couldn't forgive an offence she didn't recognise. She was an angel. She was made up of patience and sweet temper. And he had got her into this incredible mess.

Silently Christopher chose, by one of the lamps he took off his machine, a little hollow within the hollow, and spread the rug in it and arranged the cushions. "It's not much past eight," he said, looking at his wrist-watch. "Quite early. With any luck—"

He broke off, and covered her up, as she sat on it, with the ends and sides of the rug, for what did he mean by luck? If anybody were to come across that plain and consent to go and fetch petrol, what hours before it could be found and brought! Still, to get her back to Hertford Street in the small hours of the night, even in the very smallest, would be better than not getting her back till next day.

"You stay here," he said, "and I'll go up to that confounded machine again, and do a bit more shouting."

"It sounds so gruesome," she said, with a shiver. "As if we were being murdered."

"You won't hear it so much down here."

He went up the slope, and presently the forlorn sound echoed round again. The night rang with it. It seemed impossible that the whole world should not be startled into activity by such a noice.

When he was hoarse he came back to her, and sat listening with a cocked ear for any sounds of approaching footsteps.

"You're not cold?" he asked. "Oh, Catherine—forgive me."

"Quite warm," she answered smiling. "And I don't mind this a bit, you know. It really is—fun."

He said no more. He who was so ready of tongue had nothing to say now. In silence he sat beside her, listening.

"I'm glad we ate all those muffins for tea," she said presently.

"Are you hungry?"

"Not yet. But I think I shall be soon, and so will you."

"And soon you'll be cold, I'm afraid. Oh, Catherine—"

"Well, I'm not cold yet," she interrupted him, smiling again, for what was the good of poor Christopher reproaching himself?

Peering into her face, white in the darkness, he could see she was smiling. He tucked the rug closer round her. He wanted to kiss her feet, to adore her for being so cheerful and patient, but what was the good of that? Nothing he did could convey what he thought of himself. There they were; and it was getting cold.

He fancied he heard a sound on the track above, and leapt up the bank.

Silence up there. Silence, and the stars, and the lonely lights of his deserted machine, and black down below, and all round emptiness.

He shouted again. His shout seemed to come back to him mournfully, from great distances.

By this time it was half-past nine.

He stayed up there, shouting at intervals, for half an hour, till his voice gave out. When he scrambled down again into the hollow, Catherine was asleep.

He sat down carefully beside her. He didn't dare light a cigarette for fear the smell would wake her. It was better that she should sleep.

He sat cursing himself. Suppose she caught cold, suppose she was ill from fatigue and exposure? Beyond this, and her natural, and he was afraid inevitable, loss of trust in him, he saw no other danger for her. These were bad enough, but he saw no others. Nobody would know about this. None of her detestable relations would ever hear that she did not after all get home till—when? How should they? It wouldn't enter Mrs. Mitcham's head, or the porter's, to mention it. Why on earth should they? His mind was quiet as to that. But Catherine out there, in a damp field, at night, perhaps for hours—Catherine who was so precious a jewel in his eyes that he felt she ought never to be let out of the softest, safest nest—Catherine brought there by him, marooned there by his fault—these were the things that made him swear under his breath, sitting beside her while she slept.

It got colder, much colder. A mist gathered below them, and crawled about among the hillocks. No wind could reach them in their hollow, but a mist, he knew, is a nasty clammy thing to have edging up over one's boots.

Perhaps it wouldn't come so high. He watched it anxiously. He was in despair. They could get warm, he knew, by walking, and he himself would get more than warm pushing his machine, but he couldn't push it for anything like two miles, as he had told her, on that rough track, and when he was obliged to stop from exhaustion they would both very soon be colder than ever. Besides, imagine Catherine, with her little feet, slithering and stumbling about in the mud and the dark! And anyhow they'd get nowhere now there was that mist. Better stick where they were. At least they were sheltered from wind. But it was fantastic to think, as he was beginning to be forced to think, that they might have to stay there till daylight.

He sat with his hands gripped round his knees, and stared at the stars. How hard and cold they looked. What did they care? Cruel brutes. He wondered why he had ever admired them.

Catherine moved, and he turned to her quickly, and gently tucked the loosened rug round her again.

This woke her, and she opened her eyes and looked for a moment in silent astonishment at his head, dark and shadowy, with stars behind it in a black sky, bending over her.

It seemed to be Christopher's, but why?

Then she remembered. "Oh," she said faintly, "we're still here. . . ."

She tried not to shiver, but she was very cold, and what is one rug and damp grass to lie on to a person used at that time of night to a bed and blankets? Also, her surface was small, and she got cold more quickly than bigger people.

He saw her shiver, and without asking leave, or wasting time in phrases, moved close up to her and took her in his arms.

"This is nothing to do with anything, Catherine," he explained, as she made a movement of resistance, "except a determination not to let you die of cold. Besides, it will keep me warm too—which I daresay I wouldn't be, towards the small hours of the morning, if I kept myself to myself."

"The morning?" she echoed in a very small voice. "Are we—do you think we shall be here all night?"

"It looks like it," he said.

"Oh, Christopher—"

"I know."

She said no more, and he held her and her coat and the rug tightly in his arms. As a mother holds her babe, so did Christopher hold Catherine, and with much the same sort of passionate protective tenderness. One arm was beneath her shoulders, so that her head rested on his breast, the other was round her body, keeping her coverings close round her. His own head was on the cushion from the side-car, and his cheek leaned against her soft motoring cap.

Like this they lay in silence, and what Catherine felt was, first, amazement that she should be there, on an unknown hillside in a lonely country at night with Christopher, forced by circumstances to get as close to him as possible; and secondly, as she became warmer and drowsier, and nature accordingly prevailed over convention, a queer satisfaction and peace. And what Christopher felt, as he lay leaning his cheek against her head and gazing up at the stars, was that he had never seen anything more beautiful than the way those blessed stars seemed to understand—twinkling and flashing down at them as if they were laughing for joy at the amount of happiness that was flung about the world. His precious little love—his precious, precious little love. . . .

"Of course—you know—" murmured Catherine, on the verge of sleep, "this is only—a kind of—precautionary measure—"

"Quite," whispered Christopher, holding the rug closer round her.

But sleep is a great loosener of the moral sense. How is one to know right from wrong if one is asleep? How can one, in that state, be expected to be responsible? Catherine slept, and Christopher kissed her. Dimly through her dreams she knew she was being kissed, but it was so gentle a kissing, so tender, it made her feel so safe . . . and up there there was no one to mind, no one to criticise . . . and yesterday was infinitely far away . . . and to-morrow might never come. . . .

She was not so much asleep that she did not know she was happy; she was too much asleep to feel she ought to stop him.

✎ XXI ✎

Mrs. Mitcham, not expecting her mistress back till Monday, went on that Saturday to visit a friend in Camden Town, and when she came back soon after nine was surprised to find Miss Virginia's husband on the mat outside the door of the flat ringing the bell. He, of all people, should know her mistress wasn't there, thought Mrs. Mitcham, seeing that it was in Miss Virginia's house she was staying.

The carpet on the stairs was thick, and Mrs. Mitcham arrived at Stephen's side unnoticed. He was absorbed in ringing. He rang and rang.

"I beg your pardon, sir," said Mrs. Mitcham respectfully.

He turned quickly. "Where is your mistress?" he inquired.

"My mistress, sir?" said Mrs. Mitcham, much surprised. "I understood she was coming back on Monday, sir."

"She left the Manor this afternoon on her way home. She ought to have been here long ago. Have you had no telegram announcing her arrival?"

"No, sir."

"Well, I have," he said, looking quite upset, Mrs. Mitcham noticed, and pulling a telegram out of his overcoat pocket. "My wife telegraphed her mother had started, and asked me to see if she got here safely."

"Safely, sir?" echoed Mrs. Mitcham, surprised at the word.

"Mrs. Cumfrit was—motoring up. As you know, my wife should not be worried and made anxious just now," said Stephen frowning. "It is most undesirable—most undesirable."

"Yes, sir," said Mrs. Mitcham. "But I'm sure there is no cause. Mrs. Cumfrit will be here presently. It's not more than nine o'clock, sir."

"She left at half-past two."

"Allowing for punctures, sir—" suggested Mrs. Mitcham respectfully. "Will you come in, sir?" she added, unlocking the door and holding it open for him.

"Yes—and wait," said Stephen in a determined voice.

He went straight into the drawing-room without taking off his overcoat. That Miss Virginia's husband was upset was plain to Mrs. Mitcham. He hardly seemed like the same gentleman who had on his last visit so nicely called her and her mistress little children and told them to love one another. She was quite glad to get away from him into her calm kitchen.

Stephen was very much upset. He had received Virginia's telegram at six o'clock, just as he was quietly sitting in his hotel bedroom going over his sermons and giving them the last important touches. These were valuable hours, these afternoon and evening hours of the Saturdays before he preached, and to be taken away from them for any reason was most annoying. To be taken away from them for this one was more than annoying, it was gravely disturbing. Again that side-car; again that young man; as if a whole morning in it and with him were not sufficiently deplorable. No wonder his poor little darling at home was anxious. She said so in the telegram. It ran: *Mother left for Hertford Street in Mr. Monckton's side-car 2:30. Do see if arrived safely. Anxious.*

Two-thirty; and it was then six. He went round at once. He didn't know much about motor-cycles, but at the pace he had seen them going he judged that Monckton, not less swift than his confrères in upsetting the peace of God's countryside, would have had time to get to London.

No one, however, was in the flat, not even Mrs. Mitcham, who was bound to it by duty. He rang in vain. As he went away he inquired of the hall porter why no one was there, and learned that Mrs. Mitcham had gone out at three o'clock and had not yet returned, and that Mrs. Cumfrit had been away for the last week in the country—which he already only too well knew.

At half-past seven he called again—his sermons would suffer, he was painfully aware—but with the same result. It was dark then, and he too began to feel anxious; not on his mother-in-law's account, for whatever happened to her would be entirely her own fault, but on Virginia's. She would be in a terrible state if she knew her mother had not reached home yet. That Mrs. Mitcham should still be absent from her duties he regarded as not only reprehensible and another proof of Mrs. Cumfrit's laxness, but as a sign that she was unaware of her mistress's impending return, which was strange.

Immediately after dinner—a bad one, but if it had been good he could not have appreciated it in his then condition of mind—he went back to Hertford Street, and unable to believe, in spite of the hall porter's assurances, that the flat was still empty, rang and rang, and was found by Mrs. Mitcham ringing. His mother-in-law must be there by now. She was inside. He felt she was inside, and had gone to bed tired.

But directly he got in he knew she was not. There was a chill, a silence about the flat, such as only places abandoned by their inhabitants have. The drawing-room was as cold and tidy as a corpse. He kept his coat on. The idea of taking it off in such bleakness would not have occurred to him. He would have liked to keep his hat on too, for he had gone bald early, but the teaching of his youth on the subject of ladies' drawing-rooms and what to do in them prevented him.

Mrs. Mitcham, coming in to light the fire, found him staring out of the window in the dark. The room was only lit by the shining in of the street lamps. She was quite sorry for him. She had not supposed him so much attached to Mrs. Cumfrit. Mrs. Mitcham was herself feeling rather worried by now, and as she made Catherine's bed and got her room ready she had only kept cheerful by recollecting that a car had four tyres, all of which might puncture, besides innumerable other parts, no doubt equally able to have things the matter with them.

"I'll light the fire, if you please, sir," she said.

"Not for me," said Stephen, without moving.

She lit it nevertheless, and also turned on the light by the sofa. She didn't like to draw the curtains, because he continued to stand at the window staring into the street. Watching, thought Mrs. Mitcham; watching anxiously. She was quite touched.

"Is there anything you would like, sir?" she inquired.

"Nothing," said Stephen, his gaze riveted on the street.

Throughout that dreadful night Stephen watched at the window, and Mrs. Mitcham came in at intervals to see what she could do for him. She made coffee at eleven o'clock, and brought it to him, and fetched it away again at midnight cold and untouched. She carried in an armful of blankets at one o'clock, and arranged a bed for him on the sofa, into which he did not go. At five she brought him tea, which he did not drink. At eight she began to get breakfast ready. Throughout the night he stood at the window, or walked up and down the room, and each time she saw him he seemed to have grown thinner. Certainly his face looked sharper than it had the night before. Mrs. Mitcham could not but be infected by such agitation, though being naturally optimistic she felt somehow that her mistress was delayed rather than hurt. Still, it was impossible to see a gentleman like Mr. Colquhoun, a gentleman of great learning, she had heard, who must know everything about everything and had preached in St. Paul's Cathedral—it was impossible to see such a gentleman grow thinner with anxiety before one's eyes without becoming, in spite of one's secret faith, anxious too. And the hard fact that her mistress's bed had not been slept in stared her in the face.

"I must wash," said Stephen hoarsely, when she told him breakfast was ready and would do him good.

She conducted him to the bathroom.

"I must shave," he said, looking at her with hollow eyes. "I have to preach this morning. I must go back to my hotel and shave."

"Oh no, sir," said Mrs. Mitcham; and brought him George's razors—a little blunt, but yet razors.

He stared at them. His eyes seemed to become more hollow. "Razors?" he said. "Here?"

That there should be razors in the apartment of a widow—

"The late Mr. Cumfrit's, sir," said Mrs. Mitcham.

Of course. Really his control was gone; he was no longer apparently able to keep his thoughts from plunging into the most incredible places.

He stropped the razors, thinking of the probable last time they had been stropped by his father-in-law before being folded away by him who would never strop again, and shaved in front of the glass in the bathroom before which the excellent man must so often have stood. *Pulvis et umbra sumum,* said Stephen to himself in his profound dejection, forgetting for a moment the glorious resurrection he so carefully believed in. At what point did one, he wondered, his mind returning to his troubles—at what point did one, in the circumstances in which he found himself, inform the police?

He forced himself to eat some breakfast for fear he might otherwise collapse in the pulpit, and he drank a cup of strong coffee with the same idea of being kept up. The thought that it was his own mother-in-law who had brought all this trouble on him had a peculiar sting. Quite evidently there had been an accident, and God knew how he would get through his sermon, with the fear crushing him of the effect such terrible news would have on the beloved mother of his child to be. There was no blessing, he told himself, outside the single straight path of one's duty. If his mother-in-law had continued in that path as she used to continue in it, instead of suddenly taking to giving way to every impulse—that she should still have impulses was in itself indecent—this misery for Virginia, and accordingly for himself, would have been avoided. To go rushing about the country with a young man—why, how scandalous at her age. And the punishment for this, the accident that had so evidently happened, fell most heavily, as punishments so mysteriously often did—only one must not question God's wisdom—on the innocent. What living thing in the whole world could be more innocent than his wife? Except the child; except the little soul of love she bore about with her beneath her heart; and that too would suffer through her suffering.

Stephen prayed. He couldn't bear the thought of what Virginia was going to suffer. He bowed his head on his arms and prayed. Mrs. Mitcham found him like this when she came to clear away the breakfast. She was deeply sorry for him; he seemed to have been so much more attached to her mistress than one would have ever guessed.

"You'll feel better, sir," she consoled him, "when your breakfast has had more time." And she ventured to ask, "Was it Miss Virginia's car bringing Mrs. Cumfrit up? I beg pardon, sir—I mean, your car? Because if so, I'll be bound she'll be safe with Smithers."

Stephen shook his head. He could bear no questions. He could not go into the story of the motor-cycle with Mrs. Mitcham. He felt ill after his night walking about the drawing-room; his head seemed to be bursting. He got up and left the room.

He had to go to the hotel on his way to St. Jude's to fetch his sermon. He waited till the last possible minute, still hoping that some news might come; and then, when he dared wait no longer, and Mrs. Mitcham was helping him into his coat, he told her he would come back immediately after morning service and consider what steps should be taken as to informing the police.

"The police?" repeated Mrs. Mitcham, much shocked. The police and her mistress. Out of her heart disappeared the last ray of optimism.

"We must somehow find out what has happened," said Stephen sharply.

"Yes, sir," said Mrs. Mitcham, opening the door for him.

The police and her mistress. She had a feeling that the mere putting the police on to search would make them find something dreadful—that if nothing had happened, the moment they began to look something would have happened.

Feeling profoundly conscious of being only a weak woman in a world full of headstrong men, she opened the door for Stephen, and he, going through it without further speech, met Catherine coming out of the lift—Catherine perfectly sound and unharmed—and with her was Christopher.

They all three stopped dead.

"You, Stephen?" said Catherine after a moment, very faintly. "Why, how—?"

"I have," said Stephen, "been waiting all night. Waiting and watching for you."

"I—we—broke down."

He made a sign to the lift boy that he was coming down with him.

"Enough—enough," he said, with a queer gesture of pushing her and everything connected with her out of his sight; and hurried into the lift and disappeared.

Catherine and Christopher looked at each other.

∾ XXII ∾

That was an awful day for Stephen.

Men have found out, with terrible pangs, that their wives, whom they regarded as models of blamelessness, were secretly betraying their homes and families, but Stephen could not recall any instance of a man's finding this out about his wife's mother. It was not, he supposed, quite so personally awful as if it were one's wife, but on the other hand it had a peculiar awfulness of its own. A young woman might descend declivities, impelled by the sheer momentum of youth; but for women of riper years, for the matrons, for the dowagers, for those whose calm remaining business in life is to hold aloft the lantern of example, whose pride it should be to be quiet, to be immobile, to be looked-up to and venerated—for these to indulge in conduct that disgraced their families and ruined themselves was, in a way, even more horrible. In any woman of riper years it was horrible and terrible. In this one—what it was in this one was hardly to be uttered, for she—ah, ten times horrible and terrible—was his own mother-in-law.

He preached his sermon mechanically, with no sense of what he was reading, never lifting his eyes from his manuscript. The dilapidated pair—they had looked extraordinarily dilapidated as they stood there, guilty and caught, in the unsparing light of Sunday morning—floated constantly before him, and made it impossible for him to attend to a word he was saying.

What was he to do next? How could he ever face Virginia, and answer her anxious, loving questions about her mother's safety? It must be kept from her, the appalling, the simply unutterable truth; at all costs it must be kept from her in her present condition, or it well might kill her. He felt he must tell his mother, for he could not bear this burden alone, but no one else must ever know what he knew. It would be the first secret between him and Virginia, and what a secret!

His thoughts whirled this way and that, anywhere but where he was, while his lips read out what he had written in those days last week of innocent peace, that now seemed so far away, about Love. Love! What sins, thought Stephen, were committed in its name. Incredible as it was, almost impossible to imagine at their different ages, and shocking to every feeling of decency and propriety, the word had probably frequented the conversations of those two.

He shuddered away. There were some things one simply could not think of. And yet he did think of them; they haunted him. "We broke down," she had said. Persons in her position always said that. He was man of the world enough to know what that meant. And then their faces—their startled, guilty faces, when they found him so unexpectedly confronting them.

"*Love,*" read out Stephen from his manuscript, quoting part of his text and with mechanically uplifted hand and emphasis impressing it on his congregation, "*thinketh no evil. . . .*"

After the service he went straight back to Hertford Street. Useless to flinch from his duty. His first impulse that morning, and he had followed it, was to remove himself at once from contact with his mother-in-law. But he was a priest; he was her nearest living male relative; he was bound to do something.

He went straight back to Hertford Street, and found her sitting in the dining-room quietly eating mutton.

It had always seemed grievous to Stephen, and deeply to be regretted, that no traces of sin should be physically visible on the persons of the sinners, that a little washing and tidying should be enough to make them indistinguishable from those who had not sinned. Here was this one, looking much the same as usual, very like any other respectable quiet lady at her Sunday luncheon, eating mutton as though nothing had happened. At such a crisis, he felt, at such an overwhelming moment of all their lives, of his, of hers, of his dear love's, whitely unconscious at home, whatever his mother-in-law did it ought anyhow not to have been that.

She looked up when he came in, walking in unannounced, putting Mrs. Mitcham aside when she tried to open the door for him.

"I'm glad you've come back, Stephen," she said, leaning forward and pushing out the chair on her right hand for him to sit on—as though he would dream of sitting!—"I want to tell you what happened."

He took no notice of the chair, and stood facing her at the end of the table, leaning on it with both hands, their thin knuckles white with his heavy pressure.

"Won't you sit down?" she said.

"No."

"Have you had lunch?"

"No."

"Will you have some?"

"No."

There was nothing for it, Catherine knew, but to face whatever music Stephen should make, but she did think he might have said "No, thank you." Still, her position was very weak, so she accepted his monosyllables without comment. Besides—poor Stephen—he did look wretchedly upset; he must have had a dreadful night.

She was very sorry for him, and began to tell him what had happened, how the petrol had run out just when they were in that bare stretch of country between Salisbury and Andover—

Stephen raised his hand. "Spare me all this," he said. "Spare me and yourself."

"There's nothing to spare," said Catherine. "I assure you I don't mind telling you what happened."

"You should *blush,"* said Stephen, leaning forward on his knuckles. "You should *blush."*

"Blush?" she repeated.

"Do you not know that you are fatally compromised?"

"My dear Stephen—"

He longed to forbid her to call him by that name.

"Fatally," he said.

"My dear Stephen, don't be ridiculous. I know it was most unfortunate that I shouldn't get back till this morning—"

"Unfortunate!"

"But who will ever hear about it? And I couldn't help it. You don't suppose I *liked* it?"

Then, as she said the words, the remembrance of herself being kept warm in Christopher's arms, and of him softly kissing her eyes, came back to her. Yes; she had liked that. Yes; she knew she had liked that, and been happy.

A deep red flooded her face even as she said the words, and she lowered her eyes.

Stephen saw; and any faint hope he had had that her story might be true went out. His soul seemed to drop into a pit of blackness. She was guilty. She had done something unthinkable. Virginia's mother. It was horror to be in the same room with her.

"This thing," he said in a low voice, his eyes wide open and blazing, as though he indeed beheld horror, "must be made good somehow. There is only one way. It is a shame, a shame to have to utter it in connection with a boy of his age and a woman of yours, but the only thing left for you to do is to marry him."

"Marry him?"

She stared at him, her mouth open in her amazement.

"Nothing else will save you, either from man's condemnation or God's punishment."

"Stephen," she said, "are you mad?"—that *he* should be urging her to marry Christopher!—"Why should I do anything of the sort?"

"Why? You ask me why? Am I to suffer the uttermost shame, and be forced to put into words what you have done?"

"You are certainly mad, Stephen," said Catherine, trying to keep her head up, but terribly handicapped, she being of so blameless a life that the least speck on it was conspicuous and looked to her enormous, by the memory of those dimly felt kisses.

If only she had trudged all night in the mud, trudged on, however much exhausted she had been, she could have faced Stephen with the proper indignation of virtue unjustly suspected; but there were those hours asleep, folded warm in Christopher's arms, and through her sleep the consciousness of his kisses. She would probably have been very ill if she had trudged all night, but she could have held up her head and ordered Stephen out of her presence. As it was, her head wouldn't hold up, and Stephen was as certain as if he had seen the pair in some hotel that there had been no breakdown, and his mother-in-law was lying.

Hideous, he thought; too hideous. So hideous that one couldn't even pray about it, for to speak about such matters to God . . .

"I have nothing more to say," he said slowly, his face as cold and hard as frozen rock, "except that unless you marry him you will never be allowed to see my wife again. But the *disgrace* of such a marriage—the *disgrace*—"

She stared at him, pale now.

"But Stephen—" she began.

She stared at him, across the absurd mutton, the mutton he had felt was so incongruous, gone cold and congealed on its dish. This silliness, this madness, this determination to insist on sin! She might have laughed if she had not been so angry; she might have laughed, too, if it had not been for the awkward, the mortifying memory of those kisses; she might, even so, have laughed, if he had not had the power to cut her off from Virginia. But he had the power—he, the stranger she had let in to her gates when she could so easily have been ungenerous and shut him out. Why, it wouldn't even have been ungenerous, but merely prudent. Three years more of freedom she would have gained, of freedom from him and possession of her child, by just saying one word. And she hadn't said it. She had let him in. And here he was with power to destroy her.

She looked at him, very pale. "It's at least a mercy, then," she said, her eyes full of bright tears of indignation at the injustice, the cruelty of the man she had made so happy, "that I love Christopher."

"You love him!" repeated Stephen, appalled by the shamelessness of such a confession.

"Yes," said Catherine. "I love him very much. He loves me so much, and I find it impossible—I find it impossible—"

Her voice faltered, but with a great effort she got it steady again, and went on, "I find it impossible not to love people who are good, if they love me."

"You dare," said Stephen, "to mention love? You dare to use that word in connection with this boy and yourself?"

"But would you have me marry him and not love him?"

"It is shameful," said Stephen, beside himself at what seemed to him her ghastly effrontery, "that some one so much older should even think of love in connection with some one so much younger."

"But what, then," said Catherine, "about you and Virginia?"

It was the first time she had ever alluded to it. The instant she had said it she was sorry. Always she had rather be hurt than hurt, rather be insulted than insult.

He looked at her a moment, his thin face white with this last outrage. Then he turned, and went away without a word.

✎ XXIII ✎

She spent the afternoon walking up and down the drawing-room, even as Stephen had spent the night walking up and down it.

She was trying to arrange her thoughts, so that she could see a little more clearly through the tangle they were in, but as they were not so much thoughts as feelings, and all of them agitated and all of them contradictory, it was difficult.

What had happened to her was from every point of view most unpleasant. Sometimes she cried, and sometimes she stopped dead in the middle of the room, smitten by a horrid sensation of sickness when she thought of Virginia. Stephen would be as good as his word, she knew, and cut her off from Virginia, and how could he cut her off from Virginia without explaining the reason for it, his reason for it? The alternative was to marry Christopher. But what would Virginia think of *that?* And if she did marry him—how incredible that she should find herself being forced by Stephen, of all people, even to consider it—it would prove to Stephen that he had been right, and that she had been guilty.

Guilty! She went scarlet with anger and humiliation at the word. She, at her age; she, with her record of unvaryingly correct wifehood and motherhood and widowhood, her single-minded concentration of devotion, first on George and then on Virginia. Years and years of it there had been, years and years of complete blamelessness. One would have supposed, she said to herself, clenching her hands, that it ought to be possible, after a lifetime of crystal-clear propriety, for a woman to be in a motor break-down at night without instantly being suspected of wickedness. Only clergymen, only thoroughly good clergymen, could have such thoughts. . . .

Oh, she would write at once to Virginia. She would tell her what had happened. But how shameful to have to defend herself to her daughter against such an accusation. And never again, of course, never, never again could things be the same between them, because how could they be, after all that Stephen had said?

Up and down the room walked Catherine. It was intolerable she told herself; the whole situation was intolerable. She wouldn't endure it. She would go away to the ends of the earth—away, away, and never come back to a country inhabited by Stephen. She would turn her back on everybody, shake their horrid dust from her feet, settle somewhere in Africa or Australia, give herself up to forgetting. . . .

And hardly had she declared this than she was declaring that she wouldn't. No, she wouldn't be driven out of her own country by Stephen and his base mind. She would stay and brave him out. She would tell everybody what had happened —not only Virginia, but Mrs. Colquhoun, and all her friends both in London and at Chickover, and she would tell them the sequel too, and what her clergyman son-in-law demanded of her as the price she was to pay for being readmitted into the ranks of honest women—she would make him ridiculous, turn the laugh against him. . . .

And hardly had she declared this than she was declaring that she wouldn't. No, she wouldn't be bitter, she wouldn't make Stephen ridiculous, of course she would do nothing of the kind. How could she so desperately hurt Virginia? But she would write to Virginia, and describe the night's misfortunes, and as tactfully as possible explain how Stephen, in his anxiety, took an extreme view of what people might say of her adventure, but that she was sure when he had had time to think it over he would see that he was unnecessarily alarmed, and that nobody would say anything.

She would restrict herself to this. She couldn't, to Virginia, bring herself to mention Stephen's command that she should marry Christopher. Marry Christopher! She threw back her head and laughed out loud, standing alone among George's frowning furniture, and went on laughing till she found she wasn't laughing at all, but crying; for there were certainly tears rolling down her cheeks, and they were certainly not tears of amusement. So then she wiped her face and began to walk up and down again.

But struggle through the tangle of her mind as she might, Catherine could see no real daylight. Always beneath her anger, her indignation at Stephen's odious instant jumping to the worst conclusions—"And he a priest of God," she said to herself, rolling her damp handkerchief into a ball—was that memory of kisses on her closed eyelids. What things one did in the dark! How differently one behaved. The memory of these kisses pulverised her morale, made the bones of her pride go to water within her. If only, only she had insisted on walking on. But it had seemed so natural to sit down, especially when there was nowhere to walk to. And once she had sat down, the rest had followed in the simplest sequence.

At intervals of half an hour the telephone bell rang, and Mrs. Mitcham came in and said Mr. Monckton was at the telephone.

"Tell him I'm asleep," said Catherine each time, turning her face away so that Mrs. Mitcham should not see she had been crying.

At five o'clock Mrs. Mitcham came to say that Mr. Monckton was asking when he might come round.

"Tell him I'm still asleep," said Catherine, looking out of the window.

Christopher. What was she going to do about him? She

could say she was asleep that afternoon, but she couldn't be asleep for ever; sooner or later she would have to see him. That morning, after the dreadful encounter with Stephen on the door-mat, she had sent Christopher away at once. Overwhelmed by the shocking bad fortune of running straight into Stephen, by the shocking bad fortune of having Christopher with her, who had carried up her things for her when it wasn't in the least necessary, only one doesn't think, one says yes without thinking—naturally one does, for one can't suspect life of going to hit one at every twist and turn—she had told him to go away, had almost pushed him away, as if, now that the mischief was done, his going or staying mattered any more.

But what was she going to do about him? Was she strong enough to defy Stephen and go on seeing Christopher just as before, without marrying him? And Virginia? Whatever she did in regard to Stephen included Virginia; if she defied one she defied and cut herself off from the other. How could she let go of Virginia, her only flesh and blood, her one baby, so tenderly loved and cared for? How could she bear to know that Virginia would believe she had done something abominable? It was a nightmare . . . she didn't know how to shake herself free . . . all because of Stephen. . . .

Seeing nothing, because she was blind with tears, she stood at the window that looked out into the grey and gloomy street. To think that this had happened just as she had got her relationship with Christopher on to a clear and comfortable footing, freed him from all the nonsense in his mind! Oh, well—last night—it was true there was last night—but that didn't count, that was an accident, that was because it was so cold and dark, and anyhow she wasn't awake—no, that didn't count. She *had* freed his mind, she *had* cleared him up, and here comes Stephen, and with his awful points of view, his terrible saintly suspiciousness, smashes the whole of her friendship to bits. And however much she might have wished to marry Christopher—she never, never would have wished to, but *supposing* she had—she couldn't do it now, because it would be an admission that she must.

She leant her forehead against the cold window-pane. The houses opposite stared across from out of their blank, curtained faces. It was raining, and the street looked a grimy, sooty place, chill and lonely on that wet Sunday afternoon, indifferent and hard. What did one do when one was in trouble and had no one to go to? What did one *do?*

"Mr. Monckton, m'm," said Mrs. Mitcham, opening the door.

"However often he telephones," said Catherine in a smothered voice, her face carefully turned to the street, "tell him I'm still a—asleep."

The door shut, and there was silence in the room behind her.

Then some one came across it—she supposed Mrs. Mitcham, going to make up the fire, and she resented the impossibility, when one was unhappy, of getting away from the perpetual interruptions of routine. Fires to be made up, meals to sit down to and pretend to eat, clothes to be put on and taken off—how could one be thoroughly unhappy, get to grips with one's wretchedness, have it out, if one were always being interrupted?

Then she suddenly knew it wasn't Mrs. Mitcham, it was Christopher.

She turned round quickly to send him away, but found him so close behind her that by merely turning she tumbled up against him.

Instantly his arms were round her, and instantly she had the feeling she had had the night before, when going to sleep, of comfort, and warmth and safety.

"You mustn't—" she tried to protest; but he held her tight, and even while she said he mustn't she knew he must, and she must.

"Oh, Chris," she whispered, her cheek pressed against his coat, "I'm so *ashamed*—so *ashamed*—"

"What of?" asked Christopher, holding her so tight that even if she had wanted to she couldn't have got away. But she didn't want to.

"Stephen has been here, saying the most awful things—"

"Has he, by Jove," said Christopher, his head on hers, one hand softly stroking her face. "He's a very good chap, though," he added.

"What? Stephen? Why, you know he isn't."

"But he is. He came to see me too, this afternoon."

"Oh."

"And I think he's a thorough sensible chap."

"Why, what did he—what did he—?"

"Narrow, of course, and an infernal ass in places, as I told him several times in the clearest language, besides being a disgusting swine with a regrettably foul mind—"

"Oh, then did he—did he—?"

"But as good and sensible really, within his limits, as any one I'd wish to speak to."

"Oh, Chris—then he—?"

"Yes. And we're going to."

❧ PART II ❧

❧ I ❧

Between the end of March, when these things happened, and the end of April, when Catherine married Christopher, all taxi-drivers, bus-conductors and railway-porters called her Miss.

Such was the effect Christopher had on her. Except for him, she reflected, they probably would have addressed her as Mother, for except for him she would have been profoundly miserable at this time, in the deep disgrace and pain of being cut off from Virginia, from whom her letters came back unopened, re-addressed by Stephen; and there was nothing like inward misery, she knew, for turning women into apparent mothers, old mothers, just as there was nothing like inward happiness for turning them into apparent misses, young misses. She had this inward happiness, for she had Christopher to love her, to comfort her, to feed her with sweet names; and she flowered in his warmth into a beauty she had never possessed in the tepid days of George. Obviously what the world needed was love. She couldn't help thinking this when she caught sight of her own changed face in the glass.

Her friends, seeing her, marvelled at the wonderful effect the visit to Chickover had had. They had feared this visit for her, feared its inevitable painful awkwardness; and here she was back again, looking so much younger and happier that they could scarcely believe their eyes.

Headed by the Fanshawes, they decided that so attractive a little thing, whose only child was now married and out of the way, should no longer be allowed to waste in widowhood, and that a suitable husband with plenty of money must be found for her as quickly as possible. A series of dinners, beginning at the Fanshawes, was arranged, at each of which Catherine was to meet, one after the other, some good fellow with plenty of money. But these plans were all frustrated; first by the fact that most good fellows with plenty of money had wives already, and if they hadn't they had something just as bad, such as extreme old age, broken-down health, or confirmed ferocious bachelorhood; and secondly, by the fact that Catherine wouldn't come.

She wouldn't come. She wouldn't at last come to anything, not even to the telephone, and was never to be found at home. In those days, in the middle of April, her friends sought her in vain, for she was absorbed altogether in Christopher and the arrangements for their marrying. The arrangements were simple enough, seeing that Christopher would merely leave his rooms and come and live in her flat. Mrs. Mitcham would sleep out, and her room be his dressing-room. Between them, Catherine and Christopher would have fourteen hundred a year and no rent to pay. It was enough. He would, of course, earn more later on, and end, he assured her, by making her quite rich; at which she smiled, for she cared nothing for that. The arrangements were in themselves quite simple, but she had to hide them from her friends. She was terribly afraid they might find out, and add their surprise to her own surprise at what fate seemed to be hurling her into.

For no one could be more surprised than Catherine. She had tried, she had kept on trying, to keep only to an affectionate friendship with Christopher, but wasn't able at last to stand up against him. He was so young and strong and determined. He never got tired. Her arguments were as nothing compared to his. He brushed her counsels of prudence, of wisdom aside. He merely was very angry when she gave their ages as a reason, the reason, why they shouldn't marry; and when she gave Stephen's command that they should as a reason why they simply couldn't, not for very pride they couldn't, he looked at her with the calm pity of one who watches a child hurting itself to spite its elders.

At night she lay awake and told herself she couldn't possibly do this thing, harm him so profoundly, handicap his whole future. Seeing that he was so reckless, it behoved her to be wise and sane for them both. What would she look like in ten years, and what would he look like coming into a room with her? How plainly she saw at night that whatever she did she ought not to marry Christopher, and how what she saw vanished like shadows fleeing before the morning light when he came back to her next day. He had all the fearless hopefulness, the fresh resolves of morning. He swept her away with him into a region where nobody cared for prudence, and wisdom was thrown to the winds. Not so had George loved her; not so had any one, she began to believe, ever been loved before. Christopher loved her with the passion of youth, of imagination, of poetry, of all the fresh beginnings of wonder and worship that have been since Love first lit his torch and made in the darkness a great light.

What was age if one didn't feel it? Why should she mind it if he didn't? No stranger seeing them would suppose there was a difference that mattered. He made her young; and she would stay young for ever in his love. *La chair de femme se nourrit de caresses* . . . she had read that somewhere, in the old days of George, and thought what stuff. Now she began to believe it. Look at her in the glass—quite young, really quite young. Love. Miraculous love, that could do all things. And suppose after a while she did begin to grow old, he would have got used to her by then, and perhaps not notice it.

So one day, tired of fighting, and in a sudden reckless mood, she said she would marry him; and as soon as possible after that they were married at the registrar's in Princes Row, the witnesses being Mrs. Mitcham, as usual hoping for the best and in new bonnet-strings, and Lewes, who was so much upset that he could hardly sign the certificate, from which stared out at him in plain words the disastrous facts—widow, forty-seven, bachelor, twenty-five—and together went straight into what Christopher knew was heaven but Catherine spoke of placidly as the Isle of Wight.

Up to this point Catherine had loved Christopher, but not been in love with him. It was a happy state. It had a kind of agreeable, warm security. He was in love, and she only loved. He poured out his heart, and she took it and was comforted. He made her forget Chickover, and Stephen and Virginia, and he woo'd and woo'd till her face was all lit up with the reassurance of his sweet flatteries. Her vanity was fed to the point of beatitude. She smiled even in her sleep. But she remained fundamentally untouched, and would have said, if obliged to think it out, that her love for him didn't differ much in degree from the love she had had for Virginia. That was a great love, this was a great love. They were different in kind, of course, but not in degree. One couldn't do more, she thought, than just love.

After she was married, however, she found that one could: one could not only love but fall in love—two entirely distinct things, as she at once and rather uneasily became aware. He had said, in the early days when she used to be angry with him, that being in love was catching. She hadn't caught it from him during the whole of his wooing, but she did on their honey-moon, and fell in love with a helpless completeness that amazed and frightened her. So this was what it was like. This was that thing they called passion, that had lurked in music and made her cry, and had flashed out of poetry and made her quiver—at long intervals, at long, long intervals in the sunny, empty years that had been her life. Now it had got her; and was it pain or joy? Why, it was joy. But joy so acute, so excessive, that the least touch would turn it into agony, a heaven so perfect that the least flaw, the least shadow, would ruin it into hell. How would she bear it, she thought, staring aghast at these violent new emotions, if he were ever to love her less? There were no half measures left now, she felt, no half tones, no neutral zones. It was either all light, or would be, and how terrifyingly, all black.

They had taken a furnished cottage on the pleasant road that runs along near the sea between St. Lawrence and Blackgang. The little house faced the sea, which lay at the end of a meadow full of buttercups, for it was the time of buttercups, on the other side of the road. A woman from St. Lawrence came and looked after them by day, and at night they had the house and the tiny garden and the quiet road and the whispering pine trees and the murmuring sea to them-selves. These were the days of her poetry, and she said to herself—and she said it too to him, her lips against his ear—that he had made the difference in her life between an unlit room and the same room when the lamp is brought in; a beautiful lamp, she whispered, with a silver stem, and its flame the colour of the heart of a rose.

And Christopher's answer was the answer of all young lovers not two days married, and it did seem to them both that they were actually in heaven.

Such happiness had not appeared to either of them possible, such a sudden revelation of what life could be, what life really was, when filled to the brim with only love. She loved him passionately, she no longer thought of anything or any one in the world but him. Now that it had come upon her at last, late in her life, it seemed to catch her up into an agonising bliss. Who was she, what had she done, to have this extraordinary young love flung at her feet? And Christopher told himself that he had always known it, he had always known that if he could only wake her up, rouse her out of her sleep, she would be the most wonderful of lovers.

They never laughed. They were dead serious. They talked mostly in whispers, because passion always whispers; and for three days in that happy, empty island, from whence the Easter tourists had departed and to which the summer tourists had not yet come, down by the sea, up in the woods, along through the buttercups, the sun shone on them by day and the stars by night, and there was no smallest falling off in ecstasy.

Three days. The third day is usually the crucial one of a honeymoon, but never having been on honeymoons before—the sweet word could not, she felt, be applied to George's wedding tour, and anyhow she had forgotten that—they neither of them knew it, and Christopher was so young that they passed through this day too at the highest pitch of happiness.

Then, on the fourth morning, Christopher breakfasted alone, for Catherine was asleep when the bell rang and he had told the woman not to disturb her, and after breakfast, going into the little garden with his pipe and leaning on the gate staring across the bright and glorious carpet of brisk buttercups at the sea, he suddenly felt overwhelmingly disposed to meditation. Private meditation. By himself for a couple of hours. Or, failing that, he felt he would like a game of golf. Exercise. Out of doors. With a man.

He wondered where the golf links were; he wondered whether, if he went to them, he might by some lucky chance find a man he knew. Catherine didn't play golf, and he didn't want her to. He wanted for a bit to be with a man, to stalk about with a man, and not say anything, except, if it were necessary, swear, and know all the while that he was going back to her, going back, amazingly, to his own wife. Or he would like to run down to the sea and swim a long way, and then dry himself in the sun, and then go off for a quick, striding walk up the cliffs behind the house, out into the open where the wind blew fresh, and jolly little larks sang. Catherine didn't swim, and couldn't walk like that, and he didn't want her to; he wanted to go off alone, so as to have the joy of coming back, amazingly, to his own wife.

He went indoors and upstairs to look in at her and see if she were awake, so that he might tell her he thought of going for a quick run somewhere. But when he softly opened the door and crept into the room and found her still asleep, he couldn't resist kneeling down by the bed and kissing her; whereupon she opened her eyes, and smiled so incredibly sweetly at him that he slid his arm round her, and they began, his face on the pillow beside hers, whispering again.

He went nowhere that day. In the afternoon they lay about together in the field and read poetry. She asked him to. The desire for silent meditation was stronger upon him by this time than ever, and he didn't want just then to read poetry.

She instantly noticed that he was reading it differently from the way he had read it on the other days, reading it—but how could this be when he was so fond of it?—almost reluctantly.

"Is anything the matter, Chris?" she asked, bending her face anxiously over him.

He took it in his two hands. "I love you," he said.

How tired she looked. He was struck by it, out there in the afternoon light, as he held her face in his hands.

He became attentive and anxious. "Aren't you well, my darling?" he asked, still holding her face.

"Yes. Quite. Why?" she answered, wondering. Then added rather quickly, drawing back, "Do I look tired?"

"You're so pale."

"I don't *feel* pale," she said, turning her head away so that he could only see her profile.

She tried to laugh, but she discovered she found it unpleasant to be asked by Christopher if she didn't feel well. It meant she must be looking worn; and passionately she didn't want to look worn—not now, not on her honeymoon, not married to Christopher, not ever. A most undesirable thing to look, and to be avoided by every means in her power.

"I don't feel pale at all," she said again, trying to laugh and keeping her face turned away from him and the bright sunlight. "Inside, anyhow, I feel all rosy."

She jumped up. "Let's go for a walk, Chris darling," she said, shaking the buttercups he had stuck about her out of her dress. "We haven't been for a real good long walk since we got here."

"Are you sure you're not too tired?" he asked, getting up too.

"Tired!"

And to show him what she could do, she started off at a great pace and climbed over the five-barred gate into the road before he could reach her to help.

But she was tired; and though the quick walk and climb made her hot and hid her paleness, when she was in her room getting ready for the evening meal and the heat had faded out of her cheeks, she was startled by her face. Why, she looked ghastly. Her face seemed to be drooping with fatigue. The corners of her mouth were pitiful with it, her eyes appeared sunk in black shadows. And how white she was. She stared at herself aghast; and a recollection of those pleasant bus-conductors and taxi-men came into her mind, all smiling at her and calling her Miss as lately as a week ago, and of her own image in the glass at that time when, radiant with the cool happiness of not being in love, with the peace of gratified vanity at having somebody extraordinarily in love with her, while she herself loved him quite enough but not too much, she might have been and was so easily taken for really young.

Really young . . . ah, what a lovely thing to be . . . married to Christopher and really young. . . .

The lamp in the cottage was like all lamps in cottages, and unpleasantly glared. There was only one, and that one was now in the living-room, and at meals stood on the table; and it had a white glass shade, and who older than twenty-five could expect to stand light from a lamp with a white glass shade after a long, hot, hilly walk? Even in her bedroom, lit up only by two hesitating candle-flames, she looked worn out, so what would she look like down there, faced by Christopher's searching eyes and that intolerable lamp?

It was as she had feared, and he did stare at her—at first with open concern and questioning, and afterwards furtively, for she couldn't help showing she shrank from having her fatigue noticed. At the beginning of their acquaintance she used to laugh when he told her she looked tired, and say she wasn't tired a bit, and it was merely age made her seem so; she was perfectly frank and natural about it; she didn't in the least care. Now she couldn't laugh, she found—she couldn't bring herself to say, with the gay indifference, the take-me-as-I-am-or-leave-me attitude that was hers at the beginning, a word about age.

She hurried through the meal, and got up before he had finished, and went and stood at the open window, looking at the stars.

"What is it, my darling?" asked Christopher anxiously, pushing away his plate and coming after her.

"It's such a lovely night. Let's put out that stupid lamp, and then we can see the stars."

"But then we shan't see each other."

"Do we want to?"

That was true; why see, when you can feel?

They put out the lamp, and sat at the open window smelling the sweet night air, full of scents of damp grass and the sea, and he forgot his fears, for in the dark she seemed quite well again, and he talked sweetly to her, his arms round her, her head upon his breast, of their happiness, and their love, and the perfect life they were going to have together for the rest of their days; and she listened, pressing close to him, painfully adoring him, shutting her mind against the remembrance of that face in the glass, of that frightening face, of that face as it would be every day soon when she was a little older, as it would be now already each time she was overtired, or nervy, or the least thing happened to worry her. Only she wouldn't be overtired or nervy; and as for things happening to worry her, what could do that in this haven of safety she had got into with Christopher? And she would take the utmost care of herself, now that she was so precious to somebody so dear, and see to it that she kept well and strong; and nerves after all had never in her life yet afflicted her—the utmost sunny tranquillity of mind and body had been hers always; why should she even think of such things? The idea must have got into her head because of the funny feeling she had had that day, the fourth of her happiness, of being on wires. She had been jumpy. The smallest noise or sudden movement made her start. And her body had a queer kind of tingling sensation in it, an uncomfortable sensation of being exposed, raw at the surface; and her skin felt sensitive, as though it were all rubbed the wrong way; and besides, quite without any reason that she could discover, she had wanted several times that afternoon to cry.

She shook herself. Silly thoughts. All imagination. Here was Christopher, so real, dear, and close. . . .

She put her arm round his neck and pulled herself up a little higher, and laid her cheek against his. "I didn't know one could be so happy," she said, clinging to him.

"My darling love," he said, holding her tight.

They began to whisper.

⊷ II ⊷

But though night is good, and stars are good, and sweet communion is very good, with one's beloved lying soft and warm in one's arms, day also is good, and the stir and zest of it, and men's voices, and the wind along the heath.

Such were Christopher's conclusions when he had been married a week. He leant on the gate after breakfast on the first weekly anniversary of his wedding day, smoking and gazing at the field of buttercups that so gorgeously embroidered the edges of the sea, and reflected that you have to have both—the blissful night, the active day, so as completely to appreciate either. That is, if your life is to be as near perfect as possible. And why shouldn't his life be as near perfect as possible? It had all the necessary ingredients—youth, health, and Catherine. Only, for a day to be happy it must not be too much like the night; there must be a contrast, and there must be a complete contrast. In the days and nights of the last week there had been hardly any contrast, and wasn't contrast in life as indispensable as salt in cooking? Bliss there had been, bliss in quantities, wonderful quantities; wild bliss, then quiet bliss, then wild bliss again, then quiet bliss, but always bliss. He adored Catherine. Life was marvellous. On that fine May morning he was certain he was the happiest human being in the island, for nobody could possibly be happier, nor could anybody be as happy, for nobody else had Catherine; but he wished that that day—

Well, what did he wish that day? It wasn't possible that he wanted to be away from Catherine, yet he did want to—for a few hours, for a little while; why, if only to have the joy of coming back to her. He was conscious, and the consciousness surprised him, that he didn't want to kiss her for a bit. No, he didn't. And fancy not wanting to, when a month ago he would have sold everything he had, including his soul, to be allowed to! That came, thought Christopher, narrowing his eyes to watch a white sail out at sea bending in the wind—Jove, how jolly it looked, scudding along like that—of not having contrast. There had to be interruption, pause, the mind switched off on to something else. How could one ever know the joy of coming back if one didn't first go?

He wanted to go that day, to go by himself, to do things she couldn't do, and then come back all new to her again. He wanted to tramp miles in the wind he knew was blowing gloriously beyond their sheltering cliff—look how that yacht cut through the sea—up out into the open country where the larks were singing; miles and miles he wanted to tramp in the sun, and stretch all his slack muscles, and get into an almighty sweat, and drink great draughts of beer, and rid himself of the sort of sticky languor that was laying hold of him. He couldn't spend another day just sitting about or strolling gently round; he must be up and doing.

Catherine wasn't able to come with him, and he didn't want her to. She said the spring always made her lazy at first, till she got used to it. She certainly wasn't able to walk as she had walked with him before her marriage, and was very evidently soon tired, and sometimes looked so extraordinarily tired that it frightened him. She ought to rest, these first spring days, then, just as he ought to take violent exercise. She slept now very late into the morning, and he was glad she did, his tired little love; but even that didn't seem to make her be able to be active for the rest of the day. He was glad she did sleep late, only it did break up the day a bit, not knowing when she was coming down. It kept one hanging about, unable to plan anything. If he could be certain she wouldn't wake up, say, till lunch time, he could do a lot in the morning, but as it was he couldn't do anything but just wait. And he always forgot at night to tell her that if she found he wasn't there next day when she came down it would be because he had gone for a tramp, but he would be back to lunch. He always forgot at night, because at night the thing called next morning seemed so completely unimportant and uninteresting. He forgot everything at night, except Catherine and love. And then, in its turn, came morning; and it was important, and it was interesting.

He opened the gate and went out into the road. The baker's cart from Ventnor was swinging round the corner on its two high wheels, the boy cracking his whip and whistling. Enough to make any one whistle, a day like that. The boy grinned at him as he passed, and he grinned back. He would have liked to be driving that fast little mare himself, and shouting out triumphant epithalamiums as he drove. What was the plural of epithalamium? He must ask Lewes. Dash it all, why couldn't one have one's friends about one more? They were always somewhere else. If Lewes were there now they could join the golf club and have a gorgeous time. Lewes was very good at golf. Lewes was good at everything, really; and it wasn't his fault if he was so damned clever into the bargain and nosed away most of his life in books. Besides, one could swear at Lewes, be absolutely natural, say any old thing that came into one's head. With a woman, with the dearest of women, with her whom one worshipped body, soul and mind, there was a being-in-the-drawing-room flavour about things; and after a bout of drawing-room one wanted a bout of public-house—putting it roughly, that is, putting it very roughly. Catherine, his beloved, to whom he whispered things he could never tell another human being, to whom he told every thought he had of beauty and romance, was more or less the drawing-room, and Lewes, who drank only water, and who, though he listened unmoved to any oath on any subject, was himself in his language most choice, was more or less the public-house.

He strolled aimlessly about the road, kicking stones out of his path. He wished old Lewes would appear round the bend from St. Lawrence, and see for himself what happiness was like. He had been a fool from the start about Catherine, Lewes had. All wrong. The poor chap hadn't a notion what love was. But if he didn't know about love he knew about most other things, and it would be jolly to have a yarn with him, and listen to him being clever.

Christopher looked up the road, and down the road, almost as if, in answer to his wish, Lewes must appear. The young leaves were bursting out in the woods on either side, making delicate shadows on the dust. The sky was intensely blue, and a warm wind full of the scent of hawthorns tossed the small fat white clouds across it. God, what a day, what a day to do something tremendous in!

He turned quickly, and went back to the cottage, and looking up at Catherine's window whistled softly. If she were awake she would come to the window, and he would tell her he was going for a quick walk; if she wasn't awake he would leave a note for her and be off.

The bedroom window was open, but the curtains were drawn.

He whistled again, and watched for a movement behind them.

Nothing stirred.

He went indoors, scribbled a note saying he would be back to lunch, left it on the table of the sitting-room, seized a stick, and started down the path and up the road with great energetic strides in the direction of Blackgang. It was eleven o'clock, and he would walk as hard as he knew how for two hours. That ought to do him good; that ought to take the slackness out of him. Oh, jolly, jolly to be walking again, really walking. . . .

But hardly had he got a few yards from the cottage when he heard Catherine calling. He heard her little voice through all the scrunchings of his footsteps on the road and the rustlings of spring in the trees, as he would hear it, he was sure, if she should call him from the sleep of death.

He stopped, and went back slowly.

She was at the bedroom window, holding the curtains a tiny strip apart, for she shrank from showing herself to him at the window in the morning light before she had had time to do what she could for her silly face, which was being so tiresome these days and looking so persistently haggard.

"Chris—Chris—where are you going?" she called.

"I left you a note, darling."

"A note? Why?"

"I didn't want to wake you. I'm going for a walk."

"Oh I'd love to come too—wait five minutes—"

"But I want to go very quick, and as far as I can before lunch."

"Don't let's come back to lunch, then we needn't hurry. I'll be down in five seconds."

And he heard sounds of hasty moving about the room.

He sat down on the verandah-step and lit his pipe. Well, it couldn't be helped; he must wait till to-morrow for his exercise.

She wasn't five seconds but twenty-five minutes, but when she did come down in a broad-brimmed hat that shaded her face, and smiled her sweet smile at him and slipped her hand through his arm, he cheerfully gave up the idea of fierce solitary exercise and was glad she was there. His darling. His Catherine. His dream of happiness come true. His astonishing angel-wife.

"Let's stay out all day," she said, as they walked up the road, again in the direction of Blackgang but at a moderate pace that would never, he knew, however long it went on, get a drop of the sweat he craved for out of him.

"But we haven't brought food."

"We'll get the hotel at Blackgang to cut us some sandwiches and take them with us. Oh Chris, isn't it a gorgeous day! Did you ever know anything like it? Oh, I'm so happy. By the way—good morning."

She stopped and held up her face. He laughed and kissed it.

"Darling," he said, kissing her again. Yes; it would have been beastly of him to go off and leave her, to go off and let her wake up and find herself alone.

At the hotel they asked, as Catherine had suggested, for lunch to take with them, and while it was being got ready went out through the heat and hot-house flowers of the glass verandah to the fresh garden glowing and blowing with the blossoms of May. It was a sight, that garden on the cliffs above the sea, jewelled with tulips, frothed with fruit-blossom, and just beyond it, splendidly holding it in with a golden circlet, gorse.

"It's much more beautiful here than at our cottage," said Catherine, looking about her.

"How could anything ever be more beautiful than our cottage?" he answered; and she smiled at him, love in her eyes, and softly slid her hand along his sleeve.

In the garden, reading *The Times,* was Mr. Jerrold, the eminent editor of the *Saturday Judge,* who with his daughter Sybil to keep him company had come down from London for a fortnight's rest and quiet. He had rested now for a whole week, and was beginning to feel that quiet can be overdone. His daughter Sybil had long been aware of it. The hotel was empty—he had hoped it would be when he engaged his rooms, but now thought that perhaps some one else in it might not be wholly disagreeable—and when, on raising his eyes from *The Times* he saw two visitors emerging from the glass verandah in which he spent his solitary evenings reading among pots of cinerarias, he was glad.

So was his daughter Sybil, who had been down the cliff and up again three times already since breakfast, and was wondering what she could do with the rest of the morning till lunch-time.

Mr. Jerrold watched the new arrivals with deep interest. They would be a great addition to the party, if he and his daughter could properly be described as a party. The young man was a good type of clean, nice-looking young English-man, public school and university, and would do admirably to play about with poor Billy, thwarted in her desire for pro-longed and violent exercise by his inability to take it with her, while he would find the lady, who seemed just about that agreeable age when conversation is preferred to activity, a pleasant companion meanwhile.

He awaited their passing where he and Billy were sitting in basket-chairs under some hawthorns; when they did, he would ask them if they had seen that morning's *Times,* and thus open up channels of friendship.

But the new arrivals edged away across the grass, not yet realising, no doubt, how rare was intercourse in that lonely spot and accordingly how precious. So he got up and strolled after them—("Poor father," thought his daughter, who only knew him as reserved, "I had no idea he has been as bored as all that")—and overtook them at the edge of the garden, where they were gazing at the sea, brilliant blue between the great orange-coloured branches of the gorse.

"Wonderful colour, isn't it," said Mr. Jerrold pleasantly, waving his *Times* at the gorse and the sea.

"Marvellous," said the young man heartily.

"Too wonderful," cooed the lady.

In a few minutes they were talking as friends, the young man in particular, who on closer view was even more what Mr. Jerrold felt sure would amuse poor Billy, being very friendly.

Mr. Jerrold called to his daughter, who had stayed in her basket-chair.

"Come and be introduced, Billy," he called; and when she had come he presented her to the lady.

"My daughter Sybil," said Mr. Jerrold, expecting in return to be told the names of the attractive new arrivals.

He was told. "Our name is Monckton," said the young man, laughing and turning redder than ever—why should he laugh and turn red? wondered Mr. Jerrold, unaware that this was the very first time Christopher had spoken of himself and Cather-ine collectively as Monckton.

"Ours is Jerrold," said Mr. Jerrold; and proceeded pleasant-ly to assure the lady that she would find the hotel comfortable.

It was a real disappointment, so much did he like the look of both of them, so admirably did their ages fit in with his and

Billy's, to be told they were not going to stay there but had only come over from St. Lawrence, where they had a cottage, to get some food to take with them on a walk.

Both the Jerrolds' faces fell at this. Billy's broad smile seemed to contract by about half a yard. She had two long rows of very white teeth, endless rows they seemed, so wide was her smile, and they looked even whiter than they were because the sea wind had tanned her face. Her eyes, too, looked bluer than they were for the same reason, and the sunshine of a week spent hatless had bleached her hair the colour of flax. She was a sturdy creature, firm on solid ankles, and not particularly pretty, but as she stood there bareheaded, and the wind blew her fair hair across her forehead, and she smiled immensely at everybody, she fitted in with complete harmony to the young jollity of the morning and the month.

Christopher thought she looked like a good-natured young shark.

"What an awful pity," she said. "We might have gone for excursions together."

And she said it with such a heartiness of chagrin that they all laughed.

The end of it was that when the sandwiches came and the Moncktons went, the Jerrolds, still talking, went with them, first to the entrance of the hotel garden, then into the road, then, still talking, along the road.

The Jerrolds not having talked for a week were unable now to leave off. Mr. Jerrold found himself wishing to tell the small agreeable lady who he was, and why, and how, and did so with a completeness that surprised himself. His daughter, striding on ahead with the young man—they seemed naturally to shoot ahead together, the two young ones, the minute they got on to the road—explained just as completely to her companion, who appeared at once to tumble to it, the dreadful feeling of being about to burst after a week's flopping round with somebody who couldn't be left while one rushed all over the island, and couldn't, owing to age and infirmity and being a father and all that, rush too.

"Just look at those youngsters forging along," said Mr. Jerrold, smiling complacently at the two figures in front, at their four worsted-stockinged legs moving so quickly in step, at their swinging arms, and their bare heads turned to each other while they talked and laughed.

His companion looked, but said nothing. He wondered

what relation she was to the young man that she too should be a Monckton, and decided that she must be either his father's second wife or his aunt by marriage. Not a blood relation, clearly; they were too much unlike.

"Is there anything more delightful in the world," said Mr. Jerrold, gazing benevolently at the pair ahead, "than a wholesome English boy and girl?"

At this his companion murmured something that he understood meant that the two would soon be out of sight, which they certainly would be if they went on at that pace, and he said, "Yes—quite. Hi, there," he called, "you youngsters! Steady—we can't keep up!"

But the wind was against him, and they strode on unheeding.

"Not that," said Mr. Jerrold, turning gallantly to the lady, "it would be anything but my gain if they did go on. Why not let them? And you and I sit down somewhere and talk."

"But Christopher has got the sandwiches," said his new friend.

"So he has. Christopher. Delightful name. Attractive youth. Well, let Christopher eat them, sharing them with Billy somewhere at the end of their first twenty miles or so, and allow me the pleasure of offering you lunch in the hotel."

"How very kind of you. But Christopher—"

"Well, you see he doesn't hear," said Mr. Jerrold. "I don't suppose he'll even notice that we're not following. When young people get together . . . I assure you it would give me the greatest pleasure to entertain you, and we can sit afterwards in that nice garden in comfortable chairs till they come back."

Mr. Jerrold paused persuasively in the road. After a week of not speaking to a soul but his daughter he ached to entertain. The two on in front turned a corner and disappeared. Mr. Jerrold, whose wife had been dead some years, felt the situation unfolding romantically. This was a dear little lady, and she looked as though she needed taking care of. He had a strong wish to give her lunch.

"But—" she began.

"We will consider no buts," said Mr. Jerrold, even more gallantly. "Your nephew—is he your nephew?—won't notice—"

"He's my husband," said the little lady, flushing a very bright scarlet.

Well; what a surprise. Mr. Jerrold was really most surprised. Not that the lady wasn't, he was sure, a most agreeable wife for any man to have, but that the young man seemed so very young to have one at all; and if at all she ought, to match him, be a mere slip of a girl—somebody about Billy's age.

Yes; it was a surprise. Mr. Jerrold didn't quite know what to say.

"In that case—" he began.

But really he hadn't an idea what to say, and stood in the middle of the road staring down at the little lady through his monocle—he wore a monocle—and she stared back at him, while the flush slowly ebbed away out of her face.

ꞏ꧁ III ꧂ꞏ

Her nephew. So that was what Christopher seemed to be to this impartial stranger. It gave Catherine more than a shock, it made her heart feel as if it stood still. And his surprise, his humiliating surprise, when she said Christopher was her husband, and her own discomfort when she told him. . . .

Was it so much marked, then, the difference between them? It hadn't been in London. Why, in London before they married they had often stood arm in arm in front of a glass and laughed to see how no one would guess, really no one could possibly guess, that they were not very nearly of an age. Besides what about all those bus-conductors and people calling her Miss? One of them had even called her Missie— "Take care, now, Missie," he had said, catching her by the arm, "don't you go jumping off before we're stopped and breaking your neck and getting us into trouble with your young man"—but he, she was afraid, had been drinking. It must be because she was so tired now always that she looked older. To-day she was tired, yesterday she had been tired—oh, but so tired, so *tired*.

She stared up at Mr. Jerrold, while the flush faded out of her face, and thought how dreadful it was going to be if every time she was tired people took her for Christopher's aunt. What a humiliation. And inevitably sooner or later he would notice it himself, and hear it too from strangers, just as she was hearing it from this stranger.

"Let us sit down," said Mr. Jerrold sensibly, "and wait for them to come back."

And a day or two afterwards, when Christopher, impelled by his desire for movement, by a terrific longing to do something, anything, that wasn't lying in grass reading poetry to Catherine—if he didn't read poetry to her she was surprised and asked him why, because at the beginning he had wanted to do nothing else—hired a two-seater and drove her round the island, stopping for the night at a little place on the west side where there was a small hotel they liked the look of, on their going in and asking if they could be put up for the night the young lady in the office, glancing at them, said she was very sorry but she had only one room vacant.

"But we only want one," said Christopher, surprised at this answer. "We want a double room, that's all."

"Oh, I'm sorry—" said the young lady, turning red and bending over her ledger to hide her confusion. "Yes—" she said, running her finger down the page, "I can give you No. 7."

"Do you think she thought we weren't married?" said Christopher, amused, when they were in No. 7 undoing their suit-cases. "Or do you think she thought we were so grand that we couldn't do without a sitting-room?"

Catherine, very busy it seemed with her suit-case, said nothing. She couldn't have. She felt sick, as if some one had hit her head. Again she had been taken for Christopher's aunt. Or even for his—no, her mind swerved aside from that word; it simply refused to look at it.

They saw no more of the Jerrolds, though Christopher had talked of long and violent scrambles with the eagerly acquiescent Billy while they sprinted on ahead that morning before he realised that Catherine had been left behind out of sight. When he did discover this he had turned back at once. "Come on," he had said to the surprised Billy, seizing her wrist, "we must run."

And he had run; and she had run, thinking it great fun but wondering why they should be running; and after that, when they all joined up again, her father had taken her back to the hotel and the Moncktons had gone for their picnic by themselves, and she had never set eyes on them again nor heard anything more of the promised scrambles.

But one thing she had heard, and with astonishment, from

her father, and that was that Mr. Monckton was Mrs. Monckton's husband.

"No!" cried Billy, her eyes very round; adding, after a silence, "Good Lord."

"Quite," said her father.

A few days more and the honeymoon was at an end. Christopher had not attempted again to leave Catherine, for she didn't seem well, though she assured him she was— assured him eagerly, almost painfully eagerly, and that it was only the spring. He wasn't quite able to believe this, and stayed with her and petted her. She loved to lie quite quiet in his arms, out of doors or anywhere, while he read to her or they both snoozed. He suppressed his fidgetings, because he knew if he said he wanted to walk she would want to walk with him, and then she would be tired out and he after all not exercised. It struck him once as odd how little they talked. They used to talk and talk before they were married. Now they hardly said anything, except when they began to whisper, and then it wasn't talk, but emotion clothing itself scantily in words. Still, it had been a heavenly, heavenly time; something to remember joyfully all one's days.

"When we're old," he said, the last evening, "how we shall think of this."

Just as if, she thought, pressing close to him so as to hide from the thought, when he had got to the stage of being old she wouldn't, far ahead of him, be long past thinking at all.

He had to be back at his office the end of the second week, and the last night in their abode of bliss they hardly slept at all, so loth were they to lose any minutes of what was left of their honeymoon in unconsciousness; and the effect of this was that in the morning, while Christopher was as blithe as a lark and breakfasted cheerfully and packed up with zeal, Catherine could hardly move for fatigue, and was really shocked by her leaden face when she saw it in the glass.

Luckily he noticed nothing that time; he was too busy packing up, too much pleased in the fresh morning to be doing something different, to be starting on a journey. Besides, wasn't he going to work like a navvy now? Hadn't he got something to work for—responsibilities, the sweetest, most wonderful in the world? He itched to be at it, to do well, make her proud of him, earn money for her as that old George had earned money for her.

With gusto he swept his scattered things into his suit-case, whistling the love music out of *The Immortal Hour* as he packed, with gusto he settled the bills and tipped the woman, with gusto he walked, his arm through Catherine's, down the path to the gate for the last time, and waved to the buttercup-field in which he would not again have to lie. He was in high spirits. It was jolly getting back to work, beginning it again in these new delicious conditions, with Catherine to speed him in the morning and welcome him back at night. Now he would have variety; now he would have work and love, absence and presence, in their right proportion.

He was very happy. It seemed incredible to him, as he fondly looked down at her when they were in the bright warm sunshine on the ferry, that he had actually attained his heart's desire and got Catherine. Life was splendid—packed with possibilities, a thing of the utmost magnificence. The waters of the Solent danced and sparkled; white wings flashed out of the deep blue of the sky; the sun lay hot across the back of his neck; the wind was fresh and salt in his face; the world looked as it must have looked on the morning of its first day. Old Lewes—he would go and dig out old Lewes to-morrow, and make him come and lunch in one of those jolly little restaurants where the food was good and ladies didn't go, and yarn his head off. And on Saturday he would take Catherine down and introduce her to his uncle, who would certainly adore her, and she would wander about the garden and enjoy her darling little self while he gave the old boy the round of golf he knew he was thirsting for. So was he thirsting for it. His honeymoon had been wonderful, but a fortnight is enough. It wouldn't of course be enough, and one would never then want it to end, if one were going to be torn from one's beloved when it was over. But here they were, he and she, entering into the joys, the varied joys of married life, with him, the male, girding up his loins in the morning and going forth to labour until the evening, as men from time immemorial had girded themselves and gone forth, and coming back at night to his nest and his mate. And this after all was better in the long run than a honeymoon, just as real good bread and butter was better than everlasting cake.

"I'm so happy," he said, slipping his arm round her and giving her a quick hug when no one was looking. He couldn't see her face; she was sitting too close to him, besides having put on a gauze motor-veil.

"Darling Chris," she murmured, smiling through her veil.

But she would have liked it better if he hadn't been quite so exuberantly happy on that particular morning. After all, it was the finish of their honeymoon, and they would never have one again. Yet perhaps it was as well it was finished. Once at home and he at work, she would be able to sleep at least all day. . . .

In London Mrs. Mitcham, anxious to do the right thing, had filled George's different bits of china with white flowers, and the drawing-room with its heavy black furniture looked more like a carefully kept-up memorial than ever. She herself was very clean and spruce in her best apron, and her face was wreathed in the proper welcoming smiles, though she was in fact excessively nervous and embarrassed. She had always liked Christopher, with the indulgent liking of the elderly female servant for the irrepressible young gentleman, and she was thoroughly aware that marriage was marriage, yet she couldn't help turning a little red when he marched into her mistress's bedroom as if it were his. So it was his; but for years and years it hadn't been his, and for years and years before that it not only hadn't been his but had been poor Mr. Cumfrit's. It was her vivid recollection of poor Mr. Cumfrit— the times she had taken him and Mrs. Cumfrit their morning tea into that very room, and they always so pleasant and content together in their double bed—that gave her this feeling of shock when she saw Christopher walking in.

Mrs. Mitcham, who was so well trained that her very thoughts were respectful, wouldn't have dreamed of comparing Christopher to a cuckoo, but she had heard of the bird's habits in regard to nests not originally its own, and deep down in the vast dark regions of her subconsciousness, where no training had ever set its foot and simple candour prevailed, was the recognition of the fact that her mistress was the natural prey of cuckoos—first Stephen, turning her out of her original nest, now Christopher, taking possession of this one.

She could only hope that all would be well. What wasn't well, plain enough for any one to see, was her mistress. Mrs. Mitcham couldn't have believed such a change possible in that short time. "It's them honeymoons," she said to herself, shaking her head over her saucepans. They did no good to a woman, she thought, not after a certain age. You had to be very strong to put up with them at any time. No rest. No regular hours. Never knew where you were. *He* looked all right, the young gentleman did, and it wasn't for not being happy that her mistress didn't, for already, in the quarter of an hour since they had arrived, Mrs. Mitcham had seen more love about in the flat than she could remember during the whole of poor Mr. Cumfrit's time in it. She couldn't help wondering what that poor gentleman would say if he could see what was happening in his flat. He wouldn't much like it, she was afraid; but perhaps hardly anybody who was dead would much like what they would see, supposing they were able to come back and look. Even Mitcham wouldn't. What Mitcham wouldn't like seeing, if there was nothing else for him to grumble about, would be how well she had got on without him.

She carried the asparagus into the dining-room. Once again, as she opened the door, she felt uncomfortable. How should she have thought of knocking first? She had never had to knock at any except bedroom doors since she had been in service. Whenever she happened to go into a room everything would be just as nice and what you'd expect as possible: Mr. Cumfrit at the head of the table, taking a sip of claret, Mrs. Cumfrit on his right hand, quietly eating her toast. "I've done a good stroke of business to-day," Mr. Cumfrit would be saying. "I'm so glad, George dear," Mrs. Cumfrit would be answering. Things like that would be going on in the room, things you'd expect. Or, in the drawing-room, Mr. Cumfrit would be one side of the fire, Mrs. Cumfrit the other, reading out bits of the evening paper to each other. "Seems to me this wretched Government doesn't know what it wants," Mr. Cumfrit would be saying. "It does seem so, doesn't it, George dear," Mrs. Cumfrit would be answering, quiet and ladylike.

But this . . .

Impossible for Mrs. Mitcham not to start and draw back when she opened the door. She all but scattered the lovely asparagus over the carpet. She wasn't used—and her mistress, too—she couldn't have believed—

"Come in, come in, Mrs. Mitcham," the young gentleman called out gaily, picking up his napkin which had fallen on to the floor. "We're married, you know. It's all right. You signed the certificate yourself."

Mrs. Mitcham smiled nervously. The sauce-boat rattled in its dish as she handed it to her mistress. She wasn't used to this sort of thing.

⤳ IV ⤵

That evening, sentimentally, they went to *The Immortal Hour*. In this very place, only two months back, they had been sitting apart hardly aware of each other, hardly more than looking at each other out of the corners of their eyes.

"Do you remember the night I first moved up next to you?" Christopher whispered.

"Don't I," she murmured.

"Oh, Catherine—isn't it wonderful to think we're married!" he whispered.

"Sh-sh," hissed the audience, still sparse and still ferocious.

She was in bliss again. He loved her so. He had been so utterly charming in Hertford Street, boyishly delighted with everything, filling the dull little flat with youth, and all that youth trails with it of clouds of glory—laughter, happiness, radiant confidence. Amazing to have this there after George, after the quiet years since George.

By the evening she was tired, horribly tired, and knew she looked like a ghost; but she didn't mind as long as it was dark and he couldn't see her silly white face and smudged, haggard eyes. There was only one interval, and her hat would hide her then. *The Immortal Hour* was such a nice dark opera: pitch dark for ages in the first act—so restful, so soothing.

She went sound asleep, her head against his arm. He didn't know she was asleep, and was thinking all the time of how they were both thinking and feeling the same things exactly, he and she who owed each other to the for-ever-to-be-adored *Immortal Hour*.

"Darling, darling," he murmured, stooping and trying to kiss her at the darkest moment. This bliss of unity with the perfect love, this end of loneliness, this enveloping joy. . . .

She slept profoundly.

However, she woke when the curtain went down before the second part of the act, and those of the audience who were new to it clapped in spite of the music going on, and those who weren't new indignantly hissed at them, and sat up and pulled her hat straight. It was the same funny little extinguishing hat she used to wear at the beginning; he had specially asked her to put it on.

"Yes, we must be proper now," said Christopher, smiling at her.

"Sh-sh," hissed the outraged audience.

How familiar it all was; how happy they were. She was glad he didn't know she had been asleep. It was awful to have gone to sleep on such an occasion, but then she was so appallingly tired. Never in her life had she been tired like this. Ah, here was the love scene beginning . . . she wouldn't go to sleep now. . . .

Her hand slid into his; his shut tight over it; they sat close, close, thrilled by memories, by all that the music meant to them; and in the most beautiful part Catherine felt her thrills grow fainter and fade away and go out, and again her head drooped against his shoulder and again she went sound asleep.

"Oh, I love you, love you," whispered Christopher, putting his arm round her, sure her drooping head was the gesture of abandonment to irresistible emotion.

"Sh-sh," hissed the audience.

Afterwards he wanted to take her somewhere to supper.

"Supper?" echoed Catherine faintly, who was dying with fatigue.

"Yes. We must celebrate—drink the health of our home-coming," said Christopher, drawing her hand through his arm and proudly walking her off to a taxi. His wife. Marvellous. No more slipping away in the crowd and escaping him now, thank you. "Let's go somewhere where we can dance. I shall blow up if I don't let off steam somehow."

"Dance?" echoed Catherine again, still more faintly, as she was swept up into the taxi.

"Do you realise we've never danced together once yet?"

"But we can't go anywhere like that in these clothes."

That was true. He hadn't thought of that. Well then, they would dress properly the next night and go and dance and dance.

Catherine sat back in the seat. Dance? She hadn't danced for years, not since before her marriage with George—never since.

She told Christopher this, and he only laughed and said it was high time she did dance; he adored dancing; he longed to dance with her; they would often go.

"Oh, Christopher," said Catherine, sliding close up to him, "the best thing of all will be being alone together at home, you and I, in your precious evenings. Won't we go there now? Do we really want supper?"

"Tired, darling?" he asked, instantly anxious, stooping to look under her hat.

"Oh no—not a bit. Not in the least. Really not," said Catherine quickly. "But—our first evening—it's so lovely at home—"

He hung out of the window and redirected the driver. "Yes. Of course," he said, taking her in his arms. "That's far and away the best of all—"

And they began to whisper.

Next day he went back to work. When he left at ten o'clock Catherine was still in bed.

"Do you mind my not being at breakfast?" she had asked him when Mrs. Mitcham very gingerly beat, or, more accurately, delicately patted the gong.

Mrs. Mitcham had had some moments of painful indecision before doing anything with the gong. It was altogether a most awkward morning for her. She had never yet been placed in such a position. Husband and wife, of course, and all that— she knew all that; but still it did feel awkward, and she had a queer reluctance to rousing them—almost as if they were dangerous, as well as embarrassing, to have loose about the flat. Yet it was breakfast time. Orders were for nine sharp. She did finally get herself to the gong and timidly tapped it, divided between duty and her odd reluctance to see her mistress and the young gentleman come out of that room, to have to face them. . . .

"Stay there, my darling love," said Christopher, smoothing the pillows and tucking Catherine up as tenderly as if she were a baby. "I'll bring you your breakfast."

"I—never do get up to breakfast," she said, after a moment's hesitation, smiling at him as he bent over her—she, who had not once during the whole of George's time missed being down on the stroke of half-past eight to pour out his coffee for him and kiss him good-bye on the door-mat. "Good-bye, little woman," George used to say, waving to her before the lift engulfed him. In those days good husbands of good wives frequently called them little women.

Here now was her chance. She would establish a custom that might save her. And if she never had got up to breakfast it wouldn't worry Christopher that she never did, and he wouldn't, frowning with concerned perplexity, ask her searching questions as to being not well. So, by sleeping on into the mornings after he had gone to work, she might catch up with rest and dodge those horrid furrows exhaustion was dragging down her face.

So the habit was started, and Mrs. Mitcham learnt not to expect to see her till lunch-time. Sometimes she even slept later, and once or twice stayed in bed all day, not getting up till just in time to dress for dinner. This, however, only happened during the first two or three weeks. As time went on Mrs. Mitcham began to be able to count on her mistress's having her bath at twelve o'clock and being ready by one.

Mrs. Mitcham was all for her resting and taking care of herself, for she was much attached to Catherine, but she couldn't help feeling—she didn't permit herself to think it, but she couldn't help feeling—that there was something unbecoming in this turning of day into night. There was plenty of night, Mrs. Mitcham thought, for those who chose to take it, but of course if—

Mrs. Mitcham, folding up her mistress's garments, shook her head. And the garments too—she shook her head at them. Such things had not hitherto been part of Mrs. Cumfrit's outfit. Good things she had had, as good of their kind as one would wish to see—lawn, silk, fine embroideries—but never what Mrs. Mitcham called flimsies. These were flimsy, and not only flimsy but transparent. Every time Mrs. Mitcham saw them she was shocked afresh. She couldn't get used to them. Mrs. Cumfrit—she corrected herself, and said Mrs. Monckton—had gone out and bought them the first afternoon of her return from the Isle of Wight; and she so careful about coals, and turning the electric light out. There were six nightgowns that you could pull through a wedding-ring, they went so into nothing. Chiffon nightgowns. Different colours. Pink, lemon-colour, and so on; and all of them you could see through as plain as daylight. It was a mercy, thought Mrs. Mitcham, that it was dark at night. She, who prided herself on Catherine and had always thought her the ideal of what a lady should be, was much perturbed by these nightgowns. And the bathroom too—such a litter there now of scented dusting powder, and scented crystals, and flagons of coloured liquid that smelt good but improper, thought Mrs. Mitcham, furtively sniffing; what would poor Mr. Cumfrit say to his bathroom now, he who had never had a thing in it but a big sponge and a piece of Pears' soap?

It was after the visit of the Fanshawes that Mrs. Mitcham first found a lip-stick on Catherine's dressing-table. She was immensely upset. No lady she had had to do with had ever had such a thing on her dressing-table. Powder was different, because one needed powder sometimes for other things besides one's face, and also one powdered babies, and they, poor lambs, couldn't be suspected of wanting to appear different from what God had made them. But a lip-stick! Red stuff. What actresses put on, and those who were no better than they should be. Her mistress and a lip-stick—what would Miss Virginia say?

The Fanshawes, who were the immediate cause of the buying of the lip-stick, came to tea the second Sunday after the end of the honeymoon—Ned, his mother and sister. They had been extraordinarily taken aback by Catherine's appearance. The flat rang with their exclamations and laments. Catherine, who had been looking sixteen when they last saw her, Catherine the bright-eyed, the quick of movement, Catherine with her lovely skin and unruffled brow—they couldn't get over it.

Christopher had gone for a walk in the Park after lunch, straining at his leash, angry at being kept in London this beautiful afternoon because the Fanshawes insisted on coming and thrusting their inquisitive noses where they weren't wanted, and he hadn't got back when they arrived, so that Catherine had them to herself at first.

"Damn those women," he had remarked when, after persistent telephoning and letters and impassioned inquiries as to what had happened to her and when they might come and see her, Catherine had felt she had better face it and wrote and told them she was married and asked them to tea that Sunday to meet her husband. And when he heard that it wasn't only women but Ned too, he damned him particularly, on the ground that he had a silly nose and wore a fur rug up to his chin; and, expressing extreme disgust at being kept in on his and Catherine's only real afternoon by a blighter like that, he went off for a quick turn in the Park, promising faithfully to be back in time.

He wasn't; and the Fanshawes got there first, and the flat was echoing with exclamations when he opened the door.

Catherine was sitting on the sofa, wedged between the two female Fanshawes, whose arms encircled her and whose free hands stroked her, and that worm Ned was looking on from his, Christopher's, special chair.

"I've had influenza—that's why," Catherine was lying as he came in.

"But fancy not telling us you were married! Fancy not telling us a word!"

"Of course it's what we've been dying to have happen for ages—isn't it, Ned?"

"You sweet little thing, we're so delighted—aren't we, Ned?"

"Do tell us all about it. Isn't he off his head with happiness? How pleased Virginia must be—"

"So nice for her to have a father again—"

"Are they devoted to each other?"

"Have you been down to Chickover with him yet?"

"We're simply aching to see him—"

And there in the doorway he stood.

"Here *is* Christopher," said Catherine, flushing and half getting up.

They all turned their heads. For a moment nobody spoke. He advanced on them with outstretched hand, doing his best to smile broadly, to be the welcoming host.

That young man. That *boy.* The boy they had found with Catherine one day, who had rushed out the minute they came in, and Catherine had laughed when they asked who on earth he was, and said all she knew about him was that he was certainly mad. *That* fellow. The youth who had glared through the window of the car and almost shook his fist. . . .

The Fanshawes couldn't speak. They couldn't move either. They were stunned.

☙ V ☙

At Chickover there had been the most painful consultations between Stephen and Mrs. Colquhoun as to the best thing to do under the deplorable circumstances. Should they or should they not tell Virginia? Could they, indeed, help telling her? Not all, of course; she must never be told all. The night spent somewhere between Chickover and London—they both felt that the entire stretch of country between those two points was from henceforth polluted—the night that made the scandalous marriage a necessity, must be kept from Virginia for ever. But it became clear after a week that she must be told something, if only to account for her not hearing from her mother.

Stephen couldn't bring himself to let her have the letters. They came at first, as he had expected, one after the other and all very thick. He wondered, turning them over in his hand, whether it wasn't his duty to open them, but he resisted the strong leaning towards his duty that lifelong practice in doing it had induced in him, and took the more dignified course of sending them back unopened. Much more punitive too, he felt—leaving the wretched woman completely in the dark as to what was happening at Chickover and what Virginia was feeling.

Then, when the letters at last left off coming, he watched for telegrams; he rather expected telegrams.

None came.

Then he was on the look-out for an unannounced arrival; he quite thought there would be one.

Nothing happened. Just silence.

At the end of the week Virginia said, "I can't think why mother doesn't write"—and began to look worried, and write letters herself.

Stephen took them out of the box in the hall and burnt them. "Painful, painful necessities," he said to Mrs. Colquhoun; for this letter business went against the grain—the gentleman grain, he told his mother, who hardly left him, comforting and advising him as best she could.

At the end of another week Virginia sent a telegram, or rather was going to send it but was stopped by Stephen. Clearly she must be told something. She had said, while writing it: "If I don't get an answer to this I shall go up to London myself and see if anything is wrong."

"Poor child, poor child," murmured Mrs. Colquhoun, the moment for enlightenment having manifestly come. "Would you like me to be with you?" she whispered in Stephen's ear.

"Better not, I think," he whispered back.

Alone with Virginia he took her on his knee. She was holding the telegram she had just written, and was in a hurry to go and send it off.

"Yes, Stephen—what is it?" she asked, fretted at being held back, and worried by this strange silence of her mother's to the point of being unlike herself.

"I am but a clumsy creature," he began, overwhelmed by the thought of the blow about to be delivered—and delivered by his hand, too, his own loving hand.

He laid his head on her breast, his arms round her, as she sat on his knee.

This beginning made Virginia still more uneasy; Stephen had never called himself a clumsy creature before. "What is it, darling?" she asked, very anxious.

"What is it not," groaned Stephen, holding her tight. To think it was he, he who so deeply loved her. . . .

"Oh, Stephen"—Virginia was thoroughly frightened—"mother?"

"Yes. Yes. Yours. And Virginia, my loved wife," he said, raising his head and looking at her, "believe me I had rather, to spare you, it were mine."

Virginia sat like a stone. Her face was stiff and set. The worst had happened, then. Her little mother, her own sweet little mother, to whom she had been unkind, unloving, and who had never once failed in kindness and love to her, was dead.

"She is dead," said Virginia, in a voice so toneless that it sounded indifferent.

"How much better," thought Stephen, "for everybody as well as herself if she were."

Aloud he said, his face buried in Virginia's bosom, "No. She is not dead. Quite the contrary. She is remarrying."

And as Virginia said nothing, for her breath was taken away by these blows and counter-blows, he went on: "Darling, I would have spared you if I could. I have tried to spare you. I have tried all these days to find some way of keeping it from you. Indeed, indeed I have tried—"

"But, Stephen—why? Why shouldn't mother marry again?" asked Virginia, with the irritability natural to people who have been frightened without cause, but so unusual in her that Stephen could only account for it by her physical condition. "I think it very strange of her not to tell me, but why shouldn't she remarry? Now there'll be somebody to take care of her. I'm glad."

"Darling—"

He pressed his face still closer to her bosom. He wished he could hide it there for ever.

"But I do think," said Virginia, reaction against her mother setting in now she knew she wasn't dead, as it had set in the day she saw her trotting safe and sound up the avenue when she had been torn by fears of an accident, "I do think she might have told me. I do think that."

Her voice had tears in it. She strangled them, and held herself up very straight, offering no real hospitality to Stephen's head. She was deeply wounded.

"Ah, but there are some things one doesn't tell," said Stephen.

He was miserable. He would have given at least half Chickover to be able to spare her.

"Remarrying isn't one of them," she said; and for the first time he caught a glimpse of another Virginia, a Virginia who perhaps, ten years ahead, might argue.

He raised his head from her bosom and looked at her again.

"I know what I am talking about, my child," he said. "This remarrying is. She is marrying the young man with whom she motored up to London. You saw him yourself. Perhaps you will now agree that there are some things one does not willingly tell one's daughter."

Virginia stared at him a moment, her eyes very wide open. Then, without speaking a word, she got up off his knee and walked over to a window and stood at it with her back to him.

How strange of her, he thought. What a strange way of meeting trouble—to go away from him like that, to turn from the love that longed to help her.

He didn't know what to do or say next. He sat watching her in the utmost perplexity. His Virginia, getting up off his knee, withdrawing herself from his loving arms—

"Yes," she said after a long silence. "I can imagine there may be such things. But I don't think"—she turned and faced him—"this is one of them."

He got on to his feet and went towards her, his arms outstretched.

"My darling, my wounded darling," he cried, all understanding and pitifulness, "you are generous and young—"

"So is Mr. Monckton," was her unexpected answer.

Really it was like a blow in the face. It stopped him short. It *must* be her condition. But all that day the attitude continued, the strange, almost defiant attitude, and Stephen could only go into his study and pray that her heart might be softened, and her eyes opened to see things as they truly were.

Such a grave misfortune—she did not of course know how grave, how terrible it was—the first in their married life, and to take it this way, hardening her heart against the sympathy and understanding he and his mother offered her in such boundless measure, and persisting, with an obstinacy he wouldn't have dreamed her capable of, in upholding what her mother had done! True she said very little, but that little was all obstinate. She was quite unlike her usual self to his mother, too, whose one thought was to comfort, and would not admit that there was anything to be comforted about. And when that night he got into bed, and drew her to his heart in the exquisite contact of the body that had always till then soothed every trouble of the spirit, and she came apparently willingly, and clung to him, and was his own dear wife as he thought, and, happily sure of this, he whispered that he hoped she had remembered to pray for her poor mother, it was a grievous shock to feel her shrink away from him and hear her say she hadn't—not more than usual, not more than her childhood's "God bless my mummy," and most grievous to have her ask him, just as if they weren't in bed but downstairs conversing in their clothes, just as if they weren't in the sacred place and at the sacred moment never yet profaned by talk of anything but love, why he really thought it so dreadful for her mother to marry again.

"Do you not see it is terrible to marry some one young enough to be your son?" he had asked sternly—he couldn't have believed he would ever have to be stern with his own love in such a place, at such an hour.

And she had answered: "But is it any more terrible than marrying some one young enough to be your daughter?"

Virginia had answered that. His Virginia. In bed. In his very arms.

✺ VI ✺

Stephen was completely crushed by this. It was like the things children say, unanswerable in its simple rightness, and yet, the grown-up world being what it is, all wrong.

Virginia was nearer the fount of truth than he was. Where he stood, thirty years further from it, its waters naturally were muddier; but there they were, and had to be dealt with including their mud, and not as if they remained for ever, as she so near the source supposed, crystal clear.

On the other hand he couldn't do without his wife. He owed her everything, and above all he owed her his return to youth. She had come and released him from the darkening prison of deepening middle age. He worshipped her more than he knew. For instance, up to this he hadn't known he was wax in her hands, he had imagined he led, guided, was in absolute authority; now suddenly he knew he was wax. When his mother-in-law had dared compare his marriage with hers, the thing had been the deadliest outrage. Virginia pointed her finger at it, and instead of being outraged he was crushed— crushed by the truth as she saw it, crushed by the knowledge that in her clear young eyes he hadn't, in his condemnation of her mother's action, a leg to stand on.

Yet how many legs did Stephen not know he really had to stand on. Everybody, except children like Virginia, inexperienced and new, would agree that the difference between the two cases was such that one was accepted as natural and the other with derision. But Virginia said there was no difference —he had an uneasy feeling that Christ might have said so too—and declared that if her mother's marrying some one so much younger was terrible, then her marrying Stephen was terrible; more terrible, because there were actually eight years greater difference in their case.

All this she said that first tragic night in bed, and inquired, when she had finished, what was to be done about it.

He was wax. Not immediately; not for some black weeks of agonising separation, of days spent avoiding each other, of

199

nights spent with their backs turned; but inevitably, before her stubbornness, he melted. She had too many of the necessities of his life in her hands. To be out of harmony with Virginia was worse, far worse—he shuddered as he admitted it, but there it was—than being out of harmony with God.

And Virginia, though she kept up her stout exterior and went doggedly through these painful days of April and May— the estrangement lasted all that time—was most wretchedly unhappy. What was she to make of all this? In her heart she was as much shocked as Stephen. But how could she not stand up for and defend her mother? How could she deny her own blood? Deeply she resented having to defend her mother; it shattered the foundations of the whole of her childhood's faith. Was there ever anything more miserable, she thought, than to love some one and be horrified at them at the same time? She who ought to have been putting up her feet and resting more diligently than ever—"The fifth month, dear child," Mrs. Colquhoun anxiously reminded her, "we are in the fifth month now, you know, and have to be most careful" —walked ceaselessly instead in the garden, up and down, up and down, in all those paths where she was least likely to be found by her mother-in-law, trying her hardest to see clear, to think right, groping round for some way to get back to Stephen while at the same time not deserting her mother, to get back to his arms, to his heart, to the unclouded love without which she felt she couldn't live.

"You know, Virginia dearest," said Mrs. Colquhoun at last, whose only wish was to console and be confided in, and who was much upset by this marked and morbid avoidance, *"you* have nothing to be ashamed of."

"Has anybody?" Virginia asked, stopping short in the middle of the path she had been waylaid in, and looking her mother-in-law squarely in the eyes.

"That wretched, wretched mother of hers," groaned Mrs. Colquhoun to Stephen, describing this little scene to him and how uncomfortable and hurt she had been by the poor child's want of frankness. "What misery she has brought on us all."

"Nevertheless," said Stephen, looking up wearily from the sermon he was trying to write—his head, his heart, every part of him seemed to ache—"we must countenance her."

"Countenance? Countenance her? Do you mean behave as if we approved of her?"

"I do, mother. I have been thinking it over very seriously. Virginia's health, and with her health her child's health, is at stake. She—" his voice faltered, for he was most miserable— "she weeps at night. She—she weeps when she thinks I am asleep. If I try to console her it—it becomes heartbreaking."

He turned his face away and bent over the manuscript. Tears had come out of his own eyes, and were wetting his face. Impossible for any one to conceive the torments of his nights in bed with his beloved one and estranged from her. That turning of backs, that cold space between their two unhappy bodies. . . .

"Wretched, wretched woman," said Mrs. Colquhoun again, more bitterly than ever, for she saw her son's tears.

"Yes. But we must think of Virginia."

"Has she been writing to her mother?"

"I am sure she has not. She would do nothing without my knowledge."

He dug the nib of his pen into the blotting-paper.

"My wife is the soul of loyalty and straightness—" he began, but his voice quivering uncontrollably at the mention of her dear qualities, he broke off.

"Yes indeed, Stephen. Indeed I know it. She is the dearest child. Only at these times a woman isn't quite herself, and Virginia, I can see, has got into a curious morbid state—"

"I should leave her alone, mother," interrupted Stephen, his head bent so that she couldn't see his face.

Mrs. Colquhoun was hurt. All her affection and sympathy being thrown back, as it were, at her—told straight by her son, to whose welfare she had devoted the whole of her life, that she was taking the wrong line with Virginia. As though she didn't know better than he could what was the right line to take with some one in Virginia's condition!

"I think I was wrong about those letters," he said, continuing to jab his pen into the blotting-paper. "I ought to have let her have them."

"I don't at all agree with you. We did what we thought right, and more than that no mortal can be expected to do."

"No doubt. But we were mistaken, perhaps, as to what was right."

"Nonsense, Stephen. The child is only nineteen. She has to be protected from the influence of that woman. You caught the woman out yourself in the most scandalous, the most disgraceful immorality, and now you propose to countenance her

LOVE

and her—well, really there is only one word for him—her paramour."

"They are married. They have expiated their sin."

"Her late paramour, then."

"For Virginia's sake they must be countenanced."

"How?" asked Mrs. Colquhoun, greatly exasperated. Here was her son every bit as morbid as her daughter-in-law, and with no excuse of being in any particular month.

"I am going to ask Virginia to write and invite them to pay us a visit."

"Here?"

"Where else?"

"I shall go away."

"As you please."

"Stephen—"

"Yes, mother?"

But without waiting to hear what she was going to say he went on: "I have mismanaged this whole business. I have adopted a line with Virginia which cannot be continued, for it makes her unhappy and ill. Except for that night they spent together, which has now been expiated, what is there after all in their marriage different from Virginia's and mine?"

"Stephen!"

"The sexes are reversed; the ages are the same—or rather the balance is on her side. She is eight years nearer his age than I am to Virginia's."

"Stephen!"

"It's a mere prejudice, in any case."

"Stephen!"

"My darling Virginia, so much closer to simple truth than I am—so much closer, indeed, to God—sees no difference."

"She says so to you, does she? I wager she does see a difference in her heart, then. She is only standing up for that woman from some warped idea of duty—standing up for her against her own husband, against the father of her child."

He made a gesture of weariness. He had suffered much. None but himself knew what his nights had been.

"I love Virginia," he said, as if to himself.

Mrs. Colquhoun stood staring at him. He did not look at her, but sat at his table with bowed head. She had never before seen him like this, broken down, his standards gone, giving in, winking at sin, prepared, as he himself put it, to countenance it.

"Stephen—" she began.

He got up. "I think," he said, "I'll go to Virginia now and put things straight."

"You really intend to have those shocking people here and whitewash them?"

He looked at her a moment in silence, bringing his attention back to what she was saying.

"You talk as if they were outbuildings, mother," he said, with a faint, wretched smile.

"Outbuildings! Sepulchres," said Mrs. Colquhoun. "Abodes of corruption. And nothing you can do in the way of whitening them will hide—will hide—"

She was becoming hysterical; in her life she had never been that. Words were failing her; in her life they had never done that. She must grip on to herself, she must shut her mouth tight. It frightened her, the behaviour of her hitherto absolutely reliable body.

Her son went out of the room and left her standing there.

∽ VII ∾

It was the very morning after this that Stephen was late for breakfast for the first time for years, and Virginia got down before him and found a postcard in her mother's handwriting among the letters, with a picture on it of some place in the Isle of Wight and these words: *You have helped me to happiness. Catherine Monckton.*

She stared at it puzzled. She was still more puzzled when, turning it over again and looking at the address, she saw it was for Stephen, not for her.

Stephen had helped her mother to happiness? It would be just like him, of course—their reconciliation the night before had been utter and wonderful—but how? What had he had to do with it? He who only now, only yesterday, had come round to not disapproving any longer of the marriage?

She was still holding the postcard in her hand, vainly trying to make head or tail of it, when he came in.

"It seems," she said, going to meet him with the quick steps and the radiant smile of love that is very proud, "that I still don't know all your goodness, dear husband."

"What is it, my own wife?" he asked, gazing at her upturned face with the glad content of the readmitted into paradise.

"Why, look—" And she gave him the postcard.

He turned a deep red. She took that for modesty, and laughed with pride in him. What he could have done and why he had done it she didn't know, but she loved him with a positively burning faith.

Stephen, reading the words on the postcard, deduced that the marriage, which he had supposed had taken place a month or six weeks before, had in fact only just done so, for he believed no lasting happiness could be the lot of the ex–Mrs. Cumfrit, and gave her and her unfortunate victim two or three days of it at most before remorse and disillusionment set in. They were evidently at the very beginning of their two or three days when the card was written. He had had no wish at all, he knew, to help his mother-in-law to happiness. Expiation only was what he had had in mind. That expiation should be a happiness-giving process had not occurred to him as possible. And here was Virginia, praising and blessing him; here was this young unsullied spirit once more making him, by her belief and pride in his goodness, feel ashamed of himself. Also, how awkward it was. Why could not Mrs. Cumfrit have announced she was now Monckton in an ordinary manner, without dragging him into it?

"Let us, my darling," he said, not knowing what to say and fervently wishing he really had done something to deserve the look of proud adoration on Virginia's face, "have breakfast. Otherwise it will be cold. And I am as hungry as a—" he was going to say hunter, but it sounded too unclerical, so he said rector instead; and they both laughed, being in the mood, that happy morning, when one laughs at anything.

She brought his coffee round to him, and stood behind his chair laying her cheek on his head. "You've got to confess, you know," she said, "however much you want to hide your light under a bushel. What did you do, Stephen darling, and why have we been so miserable all this time about mother's marrying, when it was really you who—?"

"I'll confess to you, my love, that I did enjoin marriage."

"You did? Then why—?"

"Virginia, love, you trust your husband?"

"Oh, Stephen—so *absolutely!"* she cried, putting her arms round his neck.

"Then if I ask you not to question me further on this matter?" he said, stroking the hand round his neck and looking up at the face so near his own.

"Oh Stephen—ask me something harder than that. I do so long to show what I would do for you. I do so long to be more like you—"

"My darling, God forbid," said Stephen very earnestly.

"Oh Stephen—" was all Virginia could say to a modesty, a humility so profound. She had married not only a lover but a saint.

Her cup was full. To be asked by Stephen not to question him . . . she went about as dumb as a mouse. To be asked by Stephen to believe in him . . . she went about bursting with belief. And she was so happy, restored to her husband after the black separation, that she didn't even any longer mind the idea of Christopher as a stepfather; and her happiness spilt over into the letter she wrote her mother asking them both to Chickover; and it was such a warm letter that Catherine, accustomed in her relations with Virginia to provide all the warmth, was as much puzzled as Virginia had been on reading the postcard to Stephen.

That Virginia, who rarely showed warmth, should show it now was really very puzzling. But, being at the moment in the first astonishment at the joy of falling in love, Catherine had no time for anything or any one but Christopher, and didn't think about Virginia's letter for long. She scribbled a little note—*"Thank you, darling, for your letter. We shall love to come some day"*—and forgot her. Nor did she remember her again, or think of Chickover and Stephen and all that strange dim life, till the Fanshawes' visit.

On that visit almost everything the Fanshawes said seemed to produce a climax. Their innocent questions were all, except one, very difficult to answer, and their comments could mostly only be met by silence. The one question that wasn't difficult was, "Have you been to Chickover with him yet?"—for the warm, forgotten invitation came back to Catherine's mind at these words; and though at the moment the Fanshawes hadn't given her time to answer, afterwards, before they left, when all the naturalness and glow had gone out of their visit and everybody was elaborately making conversation, she announced that Virginia had written urging them to go down as soon as possible and stay a long while, and that they thought of soon going.

At this Christopher had made a face at her, indicative of his amazement, for it was the first he had heard of any such invitation or visit; and Mrs. Fanshawe asked, "Have Virginia and Mr. Monckton already met?"—a little timidly, for by this time she too felt that any question was likely to turn out to be a bombshell.

"Oh yes," said Catherine, reddening again, a vision of that meeting flashing before her eyes—the Chickover drawing-room, herself coming in ready to start for London and finding three figures in it, figures stiff and silent as three hostile pokers.

Upon which the Fanshawes decided that there were things and people in life they couldn't understand, and gave up trying to. But their bosoms were benevolent, and the only criticism they permitted themselves was that Virginia, whom they didn't know, must be a little unusual.

✑ VIII ✑

But what was to be done about Chickover?

When she saw herself in the glass in the mornings before dressing, Catherine felt she had better not go. The exclamations of the Fanshawes had confirmed her worst fears, and she knew for certain she was looking worn out. How could she go down there with Christopher, looking worn out? Virginia would notice it at once, and think she wasn't happy and blame Christopher. Stephen would notice it too, and be sure she wasn't happy, and triumph. While as for Mrs. Colquhoun—

She put Chickover out of her thoughts, and went and bought a lip-stick. The Fanshawes were giving a dance that night, and had invited them, and Christopher insisted on going. Useless for her to say she couldn't dance; he said she wouldn't be able to help herself with him. It appeared that he loved dancing, and only hadn't danced much before his marriage because, as he explained, he couldn't stick the fool-girls one met at dances. After all, it wasn't possible to dance in absolutely stony silence, and what to say to these girls positively beat him. If one could have made love to them, now—Catherine winced—but one couldn't even do that, because then one would have got tangled up and have to marry them. Marry them! Good God.

Now came this invitation, and he jumped at it, and all she could do was to make the best of herself. So, as a first step, she went out and bought a lip-stick; and such had been the innocence of her life in these matters that she blushed when she asked for one. But she wasn't pleased with the effect, and, anxiously examining herself before Christopher came in to dinner, was inclined to think it only made her look older and certainly made her look less good.

He, however, noticed nothing, for by this time George's electric lights had been heavily shaded, and he kissed her with his usual delight at getting back to her, and the stuff all came off, and she wondered what other women did to keep it on, or whether one either had a lip-stick or a lover, but never both.

She didn't enjoy the dance. He couldn't make her dance, however much he tried and she tried; and after struggling round the room with her and treading lamentably on each other's toes, he gave up and let her sit down. But it wasn't possible for him, hearing that throbbing music, not to dance, and Catherine, looking on at him going round with one girl after the other, all of whom seemed miracles of youth and prettiness, didn't enjoy herself.

The girls appeared to languish at him. No wonder. He was far the most attractive young man there, she thought with an ache both of pride and pain. She didn't enjoy herself at all.

The Fanshawes were very kind—almost too kind, as though they were eager to hide the facts of her own situation from her—and kept on bringing up elderly men who weren't dancing and introducing them. But the elderly men thought the small lady with the wandering eyes and inattentive ears and reddened mouth rather tiresome, and soon melted away; besides, they preferred girls. So that whenever the Fanshawes looked her way they saw her, in spite of their efforts, sitting alone.

At last, after Ned Fanshawe had sat with her a long time, his mother came up with an elderly woman instead of an elderly man, and introduced her, and she did stick. Like Catherine, she appeared to know nobody there. They sat together the rest of the evening.

"That's my daughter," said the elderly woman, pointing out a very pretty girl dancing at that moment with Christopher. "Which is yours?"

No, Catherine didn't enjoy herself.

For the life of her she couldn't help being rather quiet in the taxi going home. Christopher had seemed to enjoy himself so much. All those girls . . .

"I loved that," he said, lighting a cigarette, and then drawing her to him.

"I thought you said you were bored by girls."

"Not if you're there too. It makes all the difference."

"But I wasn't much good to you."

"Why, just to know you were there, with me, in the room, made me happy."

"Do I make a good background?" she asked, trying to sound amused.

He threw away his cigarette and took her in his arms. "Darling, were you horribly fed up, sitting there? I tell you what—we'll get a gramophone, and I'll teach you to dance. You'll learn in no time, and then we'll dance together at these shows every night."

"Wouldn't I be *tired*," said Catherine, making an effort to laugh; and, instead of laughing, crying.

Crying. The worst thing possible for her eyes. She would be a real, unmistakable hag in the morning.

"Why, what is it, my precious little thing?" exclaimed Christopher, feeling her face suddenly wet, and greatly surprised and distressed.

"It's nothing—I'm just tired," she said, hurriedly wiping her eyes and determined no more tears should screw themselves out.

"I was a selfish idiot not to think how bored you must be," he said, anxiously kissing and loving her. "I saw you talking to Fanshawe, and thought you looked quite happy—"

"Oh yes—so I was."

"Catherine—little thing—"

He kissed her again and again, and she kissed him back, and managed to laugh.

"Darling Chris," she said, nestling close, "I don't believe I'm any good at dances."

"You will be when I've taught you. You'll dance like a little angel. We'll get a gramophone to-morrow."

"Oh no—don't get a gramophone. Please, Chris darling. I

can't learn to dance. I don't want to. I'm sure I never could. You must go to dances without me."

"Without you! I like that. As though I'd ever go to anything, or budge an inch, without you."

At this time they had been married five weeks.

There came another letter from Virginia; not quite so warm, because nobody can keep at the same temperature uninterruptedly for weeks, but still continuing to invite.

"We hope you and Mr. Monckton are soon coming here, dearest mother," she wrote in her round, childish handwriting. *"I have to lie up most of the time now, because I've begun the seventh month, and mother says that that is the one to be most careful in, so that if you were to come now we could have some nice quiet talks. Stephen is visiting in the parish, but I think if he were here he would ask me to give you his love."*

How far away it sounded. Another life, dim and misty. Stephen had evidently told her nothing of his monstrous suspicions. Virginia was prepared, dutifully as always, to accept her mother's new husband. She had disliked him very obviously that day at Chickover, but now she was going to do her duty by him, just as she did her duty by everybody who had a claim on it.

Catherine sighed, holding the letter in her hand. It seemed like the splashing of cool water, a distant, quiet freshness, compared to her fevered, strange, rapturous—but was it really rapturous?—life now.

An ache of longing to see Virginia stole into her heart. One's children and new husbands—how difficult they were to mix comfortably. Mothers, to be completely satisfactory, must be ready for sacrifice, and more sacrifice, and nothing but sacrifice. They mustn't want any happiness but happiness through, by, and with their children. They must make no attempt to be individuals, to be separate human beings, but only mothers.

She sat staring at herself in the glass, thinking. When the letter arrived she was at her dressing-table, going through the now long and difficult process of doing her face. Mrs. Mitcham had brought the post in on tiptoe—she always now approached Catherine on tiptoe—laid it on the table, and stolen out again quickly, neither looking to the right hand nor the left, for by this time experience had taught her that if she did look what she saw was likely to be upsetting.

Catherine paused in what she was doing to open the letter,

and then sat idly twisting it round her finger. She had been told of a woman in Sackville Street by Kitty Fanshawe who "did" faces, and had gone at once and had hers done, and had been enchanted by the result. No more elementary lip-sticks and powder for her. In this elegant retreat, at the back of the building away from all noise, soothing to the nerves merely to go into, she had lain back in a deep delicious chair, and an exquisite young woman, whose own face was a convincing proof of the excellence of the treatment, did things with creams and oils and soft finger-tips; and when at the end—it was so soothing that Catherine went to sleep—a hand-glass was given her and she was told to look, she couldn't help an exclamation of pleasure.

Well; this was a miracle. She not only looked ten, fifteen years younger and really, really pretty, but she looked so very fashionable. A little adventurous, perhaps, the last vestiges of the quiet country lady that still had survived the rubbings-off of Christopher all gone, but how—well, how *pretty*.

The only thing left to do was to go at once and buy a hat worthy of so distinguished a complexion. She went straight to Bond Street, and on the short walk discovered that people looked at her, saw her, instead of her being, as she had lately been, so completely uninteresting that it made her practically invisible.

Both the hat and the treatment were expensive—the treatment more so, because it didn't last, and the hat at least for a little while did. Impossible to have the treatment more often than very occasionally, as it cost so much, and she accordingly bought a box containing everything belonging to it except the young woman's finger-tips, and tried to give it to herself at home.

The results were rather unfortunate. She didn't look like anybody in the very least good. Mrs. Mitcham was secretly much worried. But she persisted, hoping by practice to become clever at it; and it was while she was in the middle of her daily struggles one morning, that Virginia's second letter arrived.

What was to be done about Chickover? How could she go there with Christopher? Though he swore he would never go near the accursèd spot again, she knew he would if she asked him to. But how painful, how impossible it would be. Stephen was holding out olive-branches, for of course Virginia would never have invited them without his approval; but Stephen's olive-branches were unpleasant things, she thought, remembering him as she had seen him last, on the day of his horrible accusations. To have met him last like that, and then find him on the doorstep being the pleasant host to Christopher! And Virginia, kept ignorant of everything except the fact of the marriage, bravely trying to do her duty all round, and Mrs. Colquhoun profoundly hostile and disapproving—why should her beloved Chris be exposed to such ordeals?

No, he shouldn't be. But how could she go without him? Such were her feelings for Christopher that the thought of being separated from him even for the shortest possible visit was unbearable to her. Yet how not go? Enmeshed though she was in her obsession, the natural longing of her blood to see Virginia again yet tugged at her heart. If she could see Virginia without the others! But that, she knew, was impossible.

Presently, when she had finished dressing, she went into the drawing-room and looked up trains. Suppose she went on a Monday, and came back on the Wednesday in time for dinner? No; she couldn't endure being away so long from Christopher. One night would be quite enough for Chickover; there would be the whole afternoon and evening to talk in. No; she couldn't endure that either. What mightn't happen to him while she was away? The whole time her heart would be in her mouth. Why not do it in a day? Go the first thing, and come back the last thing?

She looked up trains again. Chickover was so very far away; it took hours to get there. But by leaving Waterloo soon after eight in the morning she could be there by twelve, and the last train from there at seven-twenty would get her back by midnight.

Yes; she would do that. No, she wouldn't. There was another train at eleven something, getting down at three. It was most important she should look well and happy, and show those doubters and disapprovers what a success her marriage was. She who was so well and happy—surely there couldn't be anybody in the world *more* well and happy, except for sometimes being rather tired, which was nothing at all—must look it; and if she had lines and hollows in her face the three would at once jump to every sort of conclusion. The eleven o'clock train would give her time to go to Maria Rome, the Sackville Street lady, for face treatment first. There would still be four solid hours at Chickover. It made the whole thing very expensive, of course, but it was well worth it; for when they saw her so fresh and smooth they couldn't but feel that it was merely silly to think her marriage had been a mistake, or to insist on measuring age and behaviour by years instead of by appearance. How intensely she wanted to prove her happiness, to triumph in Christopher!

She wrote to Virginia and told her she was coming down alone for the afternoon the following Monday, just to be with her a little by herself; Virginia wouldn't want to see anybody she didn't yet know very well in her present state, and she and Christopher—she wrote of him as Christopher, for all other ways of describing him were, she felt, absurd—would come down together later on, after the baby was born and Virginia was up and about again.

Then, at dinner, she told Christopher what she was going to do.

He didn't like it. He hated the idea of her not being back till so late. She was far too precious and tiny to go racketing off alone. What mightn't happen to her? He wouldn't be able to do a stroke of work all Monday for thinking of her. In fact, he took the news exactly in the way Catherine would have wished him to, and she loved him, if possible, more than ever. Naturally at the same time he made some extremely disrespectful comments on Stephen's personal appearance and general character, though, as the old boy had been the means of making Catherine marry him, he couldn't help, he pointed out, liking him in spite of his various and glaring defects; and as for Virginia, his opinion of that girl was what it had always been, but he admitted that a mother might probably see something in her, and that if Catherine felt herself irresistibly impelled to go down and visit her, he supposed she had better go and get it over.

"She's going to have a—" began Catherine, but stopped. Really, she couldn't bring herself to tell him. She would have to sometime, but why before it was absolutely necessary? Virginia's baby would make her a grandmother. Christopher would be married to a grandmother. If he hadn't up to now felt the difference in their ages this must inevitably wake him up to it. To think of it made her feel raw, as if her skin had been pulled off, and she left exposed, shrinking in an agonised apprehension and sensitiveness. . . . Love, love—if only she didn't love him so much. . . .

"What is she going to have?" he asked, as she stopped short, looking up from the strawberries he was eating.

"A happy afternoon, I hope," said Catherine quickly, turning red and smiling nervously.

"I should think so indeed—with you there," said Christopher. And added under his breath, so that Catherine couldn't hear and have her darling little maternal affections hurt, "Young blighter."

∽ IX ∾

On the Monday, then, a pretty little lady of about thirty to thirty-five, whose prettiness was of the kind that is mostly disapproved of in country places, got out of the train at Chickover, and was met by an embarrassed clergyman.

The corners of her mouth were turned up in pleased smiles—it was so exciting and delightful to know one was looking really nice again—as she trotted along the platform to where he stood hesitating. She was, besides being very glad she looked nice, very glad to be going to see Virginia and very glad to be going back to Christopher that evening. Also, upheld by the knowledge of her attractiveness, the journey hadn't tired her; on the contrary, it had been amusing, with an eagerly friendly strange man in the carriage, concerned in every way for her comfort. Added to which, the day being hot, she was flushed through the fainter flush bestowed on her by Sackville Street, and this was always becoming to her. And, finally, her eyes were bright with the gaiety that takes hold of a woman after even a small success. So that, altogether, it was natural she should smile.

Stephen had been prepared for anything rather than this. He had nerved himself to a quite different encounter—certainly not to smiles. Bygones were to be bygones; his recent sacred experiences with Virginia had made him ardently determined to strive after the goodness she believed was his already, and his mother-in-law was to be received back with as much of the old respect for her as could possibly be scraped together. He would keep her before his mind as she used to be, and not dwell on that which she had since become. Besides, though she might have been happy when she wrote the postcard that had so unexpectedly intensified his own happiness, she couldn't, he opined, be happy now. It was eight weeks ago that she wrote the card. Much, in marriage, may happen in eight weeks. Eight days was sometimes enough, so he understood, to open the eyes of the married. And here she was smiling.

"How do you do," he said, grabbing at his soft hat with one hand and nervelessly shaking her hand with the other.

"How very nice of you to come and meet me," she said gaily. Funny old Stephen. One couldn't really be angry with him. And he was really very good. He looked extremely old, though, after having had Christopher before one's eyes.

"Not at all," said Stephen.

"How is Virginia?"

"Well."

"I'm so glad. I'm longing to see her. Oh, how do you do, Smithers. How are the children? I'm so glad——"

People were staring at her. It had not yet been his lot to be in the company of a lady people stared at. He hurried her into the car. He tried hard to respect her.

There wasn't much time between the station and the house for respect, but he did try. He had thought to clear the ground for it by reassuring her during the brief drive as to Virginia's ignorance of the reasons that had led to her marriage. "Led to" was how he had intended to put it, rejecting the harsher and more exact word necessitated, for he was anxious to be as forgiving and delicate as possible, now that everybody concerned had turned the lamentable page. Besides, who was he to judge? Christ hadn't judged the other woman taken in adultery.

Delicacy, however, was as difficult as respect. She herself seemed totally without it. Also it was difficult to feel she was his mother-in-law at all. She was curiously altered. He couldn't make out in what the alteration consisted. Manifestly she was aping youth, but she was aping it, he admitted, so cleverly that if he hadn't known her he might certainly, at a casual glance, have taken her for a daughter rather than a mother, though not the sort of daughter one would wish to have.

The moment they were seated in the car she herself threw delicacy to the winds. "You know, Stephen," she said taking his hand—he didn't know whether to withdraw it or behave as if he hadn't noticed—"good does come in the strangest way out of evil."

"I am not prepared to admit that," Stephen felt bound to reply.

"Oh do let's be real friends, won't we?" she said, still smiling at him and looking like somebody's slightly undesirable daughter. "Then we can *really* talk. I wanted to thank you for my great happiness—"

He tried to withdraw his hand. "I think perhaps—" he began.

"No, no—listen," she went on, holding it tighter. "If it hadn't been for you I never would have married Christopher and never would have had an idea of what happiness is really like. So you see, your thinking those wicked things of us was what brought it all about. Just like roses, coming up and flowering divinely out of mud."

He had made the most serious resolutions to let bygones be bygones, and he shut his mouth in a thin tight line lest he should be unable not to say something Virginia would be sorry for. That his mother-in-law, who was once so dovelike, so becoming of speech and discreet of behaviour, should suddenly slough the decencies and allude in highly distasteful images to occurrences he was doing his utmost to forget and forgive, that she should use, herself having been wicked, the word wicked in connection with any thoughts of his was surely outrageous.

Yet even while he locked his mouth he remembered that it was his mother-in-law's postcard that had renewed and made more radiant his Virginia's belief in him. The service this regrettable mother-in-law had done him was great and undeniable. She had in the past, and consciously, done him very great service, and he had been grateful. She had eight weeks ago done him another. Should he, because the last service had been accidental and unconscious, not repay her? Twice over now she had helped him to his wife. The side of him that judged, disapproved, suspected, that was his early training and all the long years before Virginia, made him not able to unlock his mouth; the side of him that didn't and wasn't, that longed to justify Virginia's belief in him, made him try extraordinarily hard to unlock it. He did earnestly now desire to let mercy prevail over justice; but, when he looked at Catherine, how hard it was. This blooming gaiety—he used the adjective correctly, not as Christopher would have used it—upset his plans. He had not been prepared for it. She was not like the same person.

He sat silent, struggling within himself, and they arrived at the house holding each other's hands for the simple reason that he couldn't get his away.

There on the steps stood Virginia, as if she had never stood anywhere else since Catherine left her on them the day she departed in Christopher's side-car on the momentous journey that had changed her life; only this time Mrs. Colquhoun wasn't standing there with her, and Virginia had grown considerably rounder.

"Sweet of you to come, mother," she said, shy and flushed, when Catherine had run up to her and was folding as much of her as she could in her arms.

It had not escaped Virginia that her mother and Stephen had arrived hand in hand. She gave him a look of deep and tender gratitude when he, too, came up the steps. He wiped his forehead. He seemed to be in a constant condition of rousing Virginia's gratitude for things he hadn't done. Really, he thought, following the two into the house, he was a worm; a worm decked, by his darling wife's belief, in the bright adornments of a saint.

Virginia was much struck by her mother's appearance. She didn't remember her as so pretty. She felt oddly elderly, with her awkward heavy body, and certainly she felt completely plain beside her. Her mother looked a little fashionable perhaps, for quiet Chickover, yet why she should Virginia didn't know, for she had on the same country clothes she was wearing on her last visit and the visit before that. Her complexion was beautiful. Virginia was quite glad Mrs. Colquhoun had had to go away for the day on business and wouldn't be there to see it. She felt—she didn't know, for Mrs. Colquhoun had never mentioned such things, but she felt— that her mother-in-law thought women oughtn't to have complexions once they were—well, older.

Lunch passed off well; the talk afterwards, which included Stephen who, anxious to be good and kind, remained with them and conversed to the very best of his ability, passed off well; tea passed off well; and after tea he purposely withdrew from the terrace, where they were sitting, so as to allow mother and daughter freedom to touch on matters of intimate feminine interest.

Then Virginia, after making her mother lie down on a long cane seat near hers, so as to rest before the journey home, screwed herself up to mentioning the marriage—it hadn't yet been in any way alluded to—and said shyly, turning red as she spoke, "You know, mother, I'm really very glad about Mr.—Mr.—"

"No, not Mr. anything, darling. Call him Christopher."

"Sweet of you, mother," said Virginia, looking so much relieved that Catherine said, "What is, dearest?"

Virginia turned yet redder. "I was afraid," she said, "you might want me to call him father."

"Oh *no,* darling," said Catherine, laughing nervously. "You couldn't possibly."

And taking Virginia's hand and stroking it, looking down at it as she stroked, she said, "You don't—you don't think him too—too young, do you dearest?"

"No," said Virginia stoutly.

"Darling!" exclaimed Catherine, raising the hand she was stroking and swiftly kissing it.

"How can I, when Stephen and I—"

Dear, dear little Virginia. Catherine was so much pleased and touched that she kissed Virginia's hand over and over again. "My darling little daughter," she said, "my own darling little daughter—" and added, and really at the moment believed it, forgetting how completely she had been absorbed only in Christopher, "I have missed you so."

Virginia at once retreated into her shell. Instinctively she felt the lapse from truth. "Sweet of you, mother," she said in her usual awkward little way.

She drew her hand back. It was strange, and not quite right somehow, for her mother to be kissing it like that. It made her feel uncomfortable.

"Wouldn't you," she suggested, so as to turn the talk to practical matters, "like to wash your face, mother?"

"Wash my face?" echoed Catherine, startled and staring at her. "Why?"

"I always find cold water such a help," said Virginia, "if one is rather tired."

Catherine dropped back again on to her cushions. "Darling child," she murmured, closing her eyes a minute. Cold water —on the top of the delicate structure of Sackville Street—

No, she wouldn't wash her face; she was quite comfortable, and not a bit tired, and was so very, very happy to be with her little Virginia.

Virginia got further into her shell. There was a something about her mother that she wasn't accustomed to. She had always been a loving mother, but not quite—not exuberant like this. Something had gone. Was it—Virginia searched laboriously round in her scrupulous mind—dignity?

"I mustn't miss my train," said Catherine, when the church clock struck half-past six.

"There's half an hour still," said Virginia. "If you leave at seven it will be quite soon enough."

"It's the last train," said Catherine. "Hadn't the car better come round a little before seven?"

"If you missed it, mother, it wouldn't matter. I could lend you everything, and Stephen and I would be very glad."

"Darling," murmured Catherine again, concealing a shudder. She pictured herself after the unavoidable washing, coming down next morning to breakfast. . . .

At a quarter to seven Stephen thought it proper to appear once more and converse during the few remaining moments of his mother-in-law's visit. He had decided he would pick and offer her a bunch of roses to take home with her; if he wasn't able to respond to hand-holding, if he wasn't able, after all, to respect her, he could at least offer her roses. Virginia would be pleased, and his own conscience slightly soothed.

Catherine began putting on her gloves.

"Plenty of time," said Stephen, seeing this. "It has occurred to me," he continued, "that you might like a few roses."

"How very nice of you, Stephen," said Catherine, who had planted every one of the roses with her own hands, "but isn't it too late?"

"Plenty of time. Smithers is most trustworthy about trains. I will gather them myself."

And he went indoors to get a knife and a basket.

"I'm sure I ought to go," said Catherine nervously to Virginia.

"The car isn't round yet, mother. Smithers is never late."

"I believe," said Stephen, coming out again, knife and basket in hand, pausing on the terrace and considering the sky, "you will have a comparatively cool journey back. I rather fancy there has been a thunderstorm over towards Salisbury, and it will have cleared the air when you arrive there."

He went down the steps on to the lawn, and began choosing roses with care and deliberation.

"Virginia darling, oughtn't I to go?" Catherine asked, fidgeting.

"It isn't seven yet, mother," said Virginia patiently, a little

218

hurt by this extreme anxiety not to be obliged to spend the night with them. Stephen on the lawn was carefully removing the thorns from the roses he had cut.

The church clock began to strike seven. Catherine started. "There," she exclaimed, getting up quickly, "I *must* go. Good-bye, darling. Never mind the roses, Stephen," she called.

"You have at least another five minutes before you need leave," he called back in his sonorous, carrying voice, still going on selecting the biggest blooms.

Kate appeared and said the car was waiting.

Catherine hurriedly bent down and kissed Virginia. "Good-bye, darling—I'll go at once. I'm sure I ought to. Don't get up—you look so comfy. It has been such a joy seeing you again. Stephen, I'm going—I shall miss the train—"

"Of course I'll get up, mother, and see you off," said Virginia, disengaging herself with difficulty from the rugs and cushions everybody was always now burying her in. "Stephen," she called, "mother won't wait."

Stephen hastily cut one more rose, a particularly fine one, and hurried, infected by Catherine's hurry, towards the terrace, stripping off the thorns as he came. His eyes being fixed on the thorns he was stripping off he didn't see he had reached the steps of the terrace, and he stumbled and fell up them, scattering the roses at Virginia's feet.

He wasn't in the least hurt, and indeed was on his legs immediately again; but Virginia, who had stared at his prostrate form a moment in silence, her hand pressed to her heart, made a queer little sound and fainted.

Both Catherine and Stephen rushed to her. By the time help had been called, and they had lifted her and carried her indoors and laid her on a sofa, Catherine had missed her train.

✂ X ✂

In this way it happened that she stayed the night after all, and came down next morning looking quite different. She had breakfasted in her room, had lingered in it till the last moment, but finally was obliged to face her relations; and they were startled.

There was neither bloom nor gaiety now. The one had vanished with the other. Virginia thought her mother must have had far more of a shock the evening before than had been supposed. The fainting had been nothing—when one was going to have a baby one did things like that, and they were of no consequence. She had soon recovered, and they had all three spent, Virginia thought, a very nice quiet evening afterwards, Stephen himself going to give the orders for her mother's room to be got ready, and expressing the most hospitable satisfaction at her further stay. Her mother had been a little silent, that was all; and it hadn't occurred to Virginia, who so soon was herself again, that she really had had a shock.

"Why, mother—" she exclaimed, when Catherine came down into the hall, ready to start.

"I didn't sleep," said Catherine, turning away her face and pretending to search for an umbrella she hadn't brought.

They stared at her. What a difference. Virginia was concerned. Her poor little mother must really have been thoroughly frightened by her fainting.

"But mother—" she began, taking a step towards her, wanting to say something to reassure and comfort.

"Oh, it's nothing," said Catherine, bending over the umbrella-stand.

She was a bundle of nerves and acute sensitiveness. She felt she couldn't bear to be touched. And why didn't they see that to stand there staring. . . .

She pulled the umbrellas in the stand about with shaking fingers, putting off the moment of turning round to say good-bye.

It wasn't only that she had had to wash off Maria Rome and hadn't slept—and indeed she hadn't slept a wink—it was also that in the watches of the night, of this her first night alone since her marriage, once more in that house of long calm memories, she had seen, as she stared into the darkness and thought of the inevitable next morning and its humiliations, that she was on the high road to becoming a fool. Yes, a fool; a silly fool; the sort of fool she had herself smiled at when she was younger, the worst sort of fool, the elderly fool.

But how could she stop? Sitting up in bed she asked herself this question. She must keep up somehow with Christopher's youth. She couldn't let herself crumble into age before his eyes. If only he hadn't begun by admiring her physically so much! If only his love hadn't been based on what, adoring her, he called her exquisiteness. How difficult it is, thought Catherine, wide awake hour after hour, to go on being exquisite when one doesn't sleep enough, and is tormented by fear of one's lover, on whom one's entire happiness depends, suddenly seeing one isn't exquisite at all, but old, old. It was like being forced to run a race that was quite beyond one's strength, and from the beginning being out of breath. And next morning— she knew that separated from Sackville Street and out of reach of Maria Rome's box she not only looked her age but much, much more now than her age, and Stephen and Virginia would be convinced the marriage was a bitter failure and punishment, and that Christopher was unkind to her. Christopher unkind to her! Christopher. . . .

She spent an extremely unpleasant night. The house, its memories, the prospect of next morning, forced her to think. Oh, it was unfair, unfair and most cruel, that at last she should have been given love only when she was too old. She ought of course never to have listened to him, to have turned the sternest, deafest ear. But—one is vain; vanity had been the beginning of it, the irresistibleness of the delicious flattery of being mistaken for young, and before she knew what she was doing she had fallen in love—fallen flop in love, like any idiot schoolgirl. And Christopher who didn't realise, who hadn't noticed yet, who loved her as if she were a girl, and by the very excess of his love burnt up what still had been left to her of youth. . . . Yes, she was a fool; but how stop, how stop? It was horrible to be ashamed, and yet to have to go on repeating the conduct that made one ashamed. Love—if only, only she didn't love!

She spent an extremely unpleasant night. No wonder she came down looking different. It wasn't just having had to wash away Maria Rome.

And then, while she was fumbling among the umbrellas, and Virginia was watching her in puzzled concern, and Stephen was endeavouring to identify the mother-in-law who had gone upstairs with the mother-in-law who had come down again, Mrs. Colquhoun came in through the drawing-room windows, arrived thus early across the park and garden to inquire how Virginia was after her mother's visit of the day before, and to gather from Stephen what she could of his state of mind after so searching an experience.

The situation was as awkward as it was unexpected. Stephen and Virginia hadn't thought she would come so early, or they would have sent round and warned. They could only look on and hope for the best. His mother, Stephen was aware, had decided that she, anyhow, was not obliged to continue to know the late Mrs. Cumfrit. If and when Mrs. Cumfrit came down to Chickover, his mother had informed him, she herself would always have urgent business somewhere else. Morals were, without any doubt whatever, morals, she had said, and if Stephen could reconcile his principles with leniency in regard to them, she herself neither could nor would.

It was therefore most unpleasant for every one that she should walk straight into Catherine's presence. Virginia and Stephen held their breath. Mrs. Colquhoun gave a visible start when she saw the figure bending over the umbrella-stand, and made as if she would go back at once into the drawing-room from whence she had emerged. But when on Catherine's turning round she saw her face, she was instantly placated. What a change. Judgment had indeed been swift. Here was nothing but a wreck. "He beats her," was Mrs. Colquhoun's immediate mental comment. After all, she thought, one could leave these matters quite safely in the hands of God.

It had not been her intention ever to speak to Catherine again, but a wreck is different; one could not but feel benevolent towards a wreck. If only people would be and stay wrecks Mrs. Colquhoun would always have been benevolent. She put out her hand. She said quite politely, "How do you do." Stephen thought, "My mother is a good woman"; Virginia gave a sigh of relief; and all Catherine had to do was to reply with equal politeness, "How do you do."

But she was in a highly abnormal condition. She was a mass of nerves and quivering intuitions. Caught, unprotected in the morning light, there she was standing exposed before these staring relations, unable to hide, obliged to show herself; and, with a feeling that nothing now mattered, she was overtaken by the reckless simplicity of the cornered. Through Mrs. Colquhoun's greeting she felt the truth: Mrs. Colquhoun was being amiable because she thought Catherine was down and out, and Mrs. Colquhoun was what she was, hard, severe, critical, grudging of happiness, kind to failure so long as it remained failure, simply because there wasn't a soul in the whole world who really loved her. A devoted husband would have done much to bring out her original goodness; a very devoted husband would have done everything.

And so, to her own astonishment, and to the frozen amazement of the others, instead of in her turn nicely murmuring, "How do you do," and smiling and going out to the car, she was impelled by what she saw in Mrs. Colquhoun's eyes as she took her extended hand, to say, "You need love."

What made her? It was the last thing she would really ever have said out loud to Mrs. Colquhoun if she had been in her senses, so that she couldn't have been in her senses. Nobody in the least knew what she meant. It sounded improper; it was most startling.

Mrs. Colquhoun withdrew the hand she ought never to have given, and Stephen said in a strained voice, "We all need that," and added with emphasis that it was high time to start unless the train was to be missed again.

Virginia could only kiss her mother a worried and bewildered good-bye. Fancy saying that to her mother-in-law. What could her mother have meant? Of course it was true of everybody that they needed love, but one didn't say so.

Mrs. Colquhoun took it, she considered, very well. Turning away out of the hall she waited in the drawing-room till the car had gone, and then when Virginia came in begged her not to give it another thought.

"Give what another thought?" Virginia asked, at once bristling, as she had lately so often bristled when with Mrs. Colquhoun, at the merest insinuation that her mother needed either explaining or excusing.

Well, well. Poor little Virginia. One had to be very patient with her just now.

↺ XI ↻

Christopher dined with Lewes the evening Catherine was at Chickover, and stayed with him till it was time to go to Waterloo to meet her train. He thoroughly enjoyed being with old Lucy again, and listening to his yarns about the imminent economic collapse of Europe. He had forgotten how interesting economics and Europe were. There were other important things in the world besides love, and it was a refreshment to get among them again for a bit.

They dined at the restaurant they used most often to go to when they lived together, and afterwards went back to Lewes's rooms and sat in great contentment with the two windows wide open to the summer night, each in his own comfortable old chair, each with his feet on the sill of a window, smoking and talking, while the pleasant London summer evening street sounds floated up into the room, and the dusk deepened in the corners.

Next door was the room Christopher used to rage up and down. He laughed to think how calm and happy he now was. No more ragings up and down for him. Marriage set one free from all that sort of torment. Old Lucy ought to marry. Not that he seemed tormented in any way, but Christopher would have liked him to know for himself what a delight life could be. The poor chap hadn't the beginning of the foggiest suspicion of it.

Lewes was very glad to see his friend looking so well and happy. Evidently the marriage was still a success. He found it impossible to believe that it would be lastingly successful. True, the lady on her wedding-day had seemed much younger than her years; but there were the years—he had himself seen them in black and white on the certificate, and they were bound sooner or later to gallop on faster and faster ahead of Christopher's. However, few marriages, he understood, were lasting successes, so that perhaps after all it didn't much matter.

The two therefore were in great harmony, each much pleased to be once more with the other.

"She's gone down for the day to her daughter," Christopher said, when Lewes, observing the laws of politeness, inquired after Catherine.

"She has a daughter?" asked Lewes surprised, for he had never heard of her.

"Certainly," said Christopher, as who should say, "Hasn't everybody?"

Lewes made no comment. He silently considered this further drawback to the marriage. And Christopher, happy and expansive, continued: "She has married a man years older than herself."

"Who has?" inquired Lewes, not quite following.

"Well, Catherine hasn't, has she."

"No. I'm obtuse. Forgive me. I think I was surprised your wife should have a daughter grown up enough to marry."

"It is absurd, isn't it," said Christopher, liking Lewes for this. "She's much too young, isn't she. He's a parson, and old enough to be her father."

"Whose father?" asked Lewes, again not quite following.

"His wife's, of course. The girl's only a girl, and he's a horny-beaked old rooster."

"Is he?" said Lewes, and thought things. Not that he, or, he admitted, anybody, could possibly have applied such epithets to Chris's wife, but still. . . . And had his friend considered that he was now the stepfather-in-law of a person he described as a horny-beaked old rooster?

"Why, he's old enough to be Catherine's father too," said Christopher.

"Is he?" said Lewes, reflecting how that could be. Wouldn't that make him old enough, then, to be his wife's grandfather? Well, best let it alone. It was a perplexing mix-up.

"I call it disgusting," said Christopher.

Lewes was silent. Long ago he had observed how people are most critical in others of that which they do and are themselves. When he spoke again it was to return to the exposition and illustration of the doctrines of Mr. Keynes, from which he had so injudiciously wandered.

"Come with me to the station," said Christopher, getting up at half-past eleven and preparing to go and meet Catherine at Waterloo.

"I think not," said Lewes.

"Come on. It'll do you good. You'll see Catherine again. It's time you did. And we'll arrange with her when you're to come to dinner."

Lewes didn't want in the least to see Catherine again, or be done good to, or go to dinner, but Christopher was determined, and he gave in and went; which was just as well, for when everybody had got out of the train and the platform was empty and it was clear she hadn't come, at least he was able to reason with Christopher and restrain him from fetching out his motor-bicycle and tearing off through the night to Chickover.

"It's that blasted son-in-law of hers," Christopher kept on repeating—showing, Lewes considered, a lamentable want of balance. *"He's* at the bottom of this—"

Lewes, applying his mind to probabilities, soon hit on the truth, and pointed out that the telegram that had certainly been sent was too late in arriving to be delivered in London that night, and he would get it the first thing in the morning.

"But suppose she's ill? Suppose—"

"Oh my dear Chris, try and not be a fool. She has simply missed the last train. You'll know all about it in the morning." And he took him by the arm and walked him home to Hertford Street.

When they got there Christopher insisted on his going up and having a drink. Lewes did his best not to, for he had no wish to behold his friend's married *milieu;* but Christopher was determined, and he gave in and went.

He felt a faint distaste at seeing his friend opening a door, his only by marriage, with a latch-key belonging really to a woman, but suppressed this as foolish. Fortunately the flat was not the thing of fal-lals he had imagined, and he was quite relieved on being taken into the drawing-room to find it so solid and so sombre.

"George," explained Christopher, seeing his friend looking round.

"George?" repeated Lewes, who had never heard of him.

"All this black stuff."

Lewes said nothing.

"Catherine's first husband," said Christopher. "He was old enough to be her father too."

"Was he?" said Lewes, groping about among these different persons old enough to be people's fathers.

He sank into a chair. He drank whisky. At intervals he tried to go, but Christopher wouldn't let him. For two hours he had to listen to talk that made him feel dimmer and dimmer of mind, more and more as if his roots were wilting; for Christopher was jerked back by Catherine's unexpected failure to come home, and his unhappiness at the prospect of the first night alone in their room, and his efforts not to be anxious and worried, into thinking and talking only of her.

"My dear chap—yes . . . ," "Old man, I'm sure of it . . . ," Lewes, as sympathetically as he could, from time to time interjected. But his head drooped; his spirit failed him. Women. What didn't they do to a sensible, intelligent man? Made him go all slushy and rotten; turned him into nothing better than a jabbering ass. Much of it was whisky, Lewes allowed, as Christopher drowned his disappointment and secret fear in more and more of the stuff, but most of it was woman.

"Look here, I must be off," he said, getting up firmly on Christopher's showing a tendency, after quite a lot of whisky, to become too intimate in his talk for comfort. "This room's pure George," he had been saying, "but Catherine's bedroom —you should see Catherine's bedroom—" Was he going to offer to show it to him?

Lewes hurriedly got up and said he must be off.

"You're not crawling back into your shell already?" cried Christopher, much flushed, and his hair, from his frequent passing his hand through it while he talked, much ruffled. "I'll tell you what you are, Lucy—you're nothing but a miserable whelk." And he laughed immoderately.

"I've some work I must get finished to-night," said Lewes, taking no notice of this.

"At two in the morning?" exclaimed Christopher, laughing louder than ever. "That's just the sort of thing you would do at two in the morning. Get married, old whelk—get married—" He clapped him on the shoulder. "You jolly well wouldn't—"

"Good night," interrupted Lewes abruptly.

But after he had gone Christopher soon recovered from the exuberance of whisky, and went very sadly to bed. He missed Catherine terribly. The flat was the loneliest place without her. And what if something had happened to her after all, in spite of Lewes's cold-blooded assurances that nearly always nothing happens to anybody? He didn't sleep much. He hated being alone in that dear room of happiness; and when at breakfast he got the telegram, as Lewes had foretold, saying she was coming by the first train, he determined to chuck the office and go and meet her.

Catherine, however, anxiously turning over every possibility, had thought that he might do this, and at Chickover station, eluding Stephen who was talking to a parishioner, sent a second telegram saying she wouldn't be back till dinner. Her one desire was to keep out of Christopher's sight till she had been to Maria Rome. Impossible to let him see her in the state she was in. Well did she know that this was being a slave, a silly slave, and that it was cruel to leave him all day wondering what was happening, but she *was* a slave, and this cruelty was nothing to the cruelty to them both of letting him meet her and see what she now looked like really. So she sent the second telegram.

Naturally, Christopher was excessively perturbed when he got in. What in damnation had happened in that beastly Chickover? Never again should she go there without him. Never again should she go a step without him. And she hadn't taken any luggage with her, and she would be worn out. Blast Stephen. Blast that girl. And probably the bird-faced mother-in-law had had a hand in all this too. If so, let her be specially and thoroughly blasted.

He looked up the trains, and found that one arrived at 5:30, and there was no other till after ten. The 5:30 must be the one, then. He told Mrs. Mitcham, who had shown every symptom of astonishment and uneasiness on getting to the flat that morning and finding her mistress hadn't returned, to have dinner ready earlier than usual, because Mrs. Monckton would be badly needing food, and then he went to his office after all, intending to go to Waterloo to meet the 5:30.

What a day it was. He couldn't do a stroke of work. He felt like nothing on earth after the whisky. His chief was sarcastic. Everything went wrong. At five he was starting for Waterloo when Mrs. Mitcham rang him up to say her mistress was safely back and resting.

Safely back? How had she managed that, with no train that he knew of?

He flew home. Catherine, her face beautifully rearranged, was lying in the shaded drawing-room.

"Why, darling—how? When—?" he cried, rushing across to her.

He didn't wait for an answer. There was no time for one before he had picked her up and locked her in his arms.

Oh, how blessed this was—oh, *oh* how blessed this was, sighed Catherine, her cheek against his, her eyes shut, safe in heaven again.

The great feature of Maria Rome's treatment was that it was husband-proof. Nothing came off.

◌ XII ◌

Catherine made much of Virginia's fainting.

"What she want to faint for?" asked Christopher sceptically. "A great girl like that."

"Well, she *did*. So of course I couldn't leave her sooner."

But when she was saying this sort of thing she felt uncomfortable. Such tiresome almost lying, such petty almost truth. She seemed now to walk continually in small deceits. It was as though her feet couldn't move a step without getting into a tangle of repulsive little cobwebs. Nothing much really; nothing more than she supposed most women, whom she began to think of as creatures necessarily on the defensive, had to wade through; but so different from the clean-swept path along which she had all her life till then proceeded. All her life? All her death. That hadn't been life. Up to her marriage with Christopher she had merely been dead. Now she was alive; and mustn't she take the stings and the pains and even the pettiness of life gladly, in return for its beatitudes?

But they worried her, the stings and the pains and the pettiness. Also, beatitudes were expensive. They forced her to go oftener to Maria Rome, and the oftener she went the more she needed her. It was like drug-taking. And suppose there should come a point—in her heart she knew it must come—when Maria's ministrations would merely accentuate what they were intended to hide? Once or twice lately she had fancied they had been less successful; or was it that there was more to do to her the deeper she sank in this business of being young and happy? She led a racked life, an uneasy mixture of fears and blisses. And the grey in her hair seemed to multiply, and it too had to be treated by Maria Rome, and she began to look more and more like somebody adventurous—she who was really the most unadventurous of perch-clinging doves.

The thought of Virginia's life—Virginia, so young, so needing to do nothing to herself, so completely at ease with her elderly husband—made her sigh as the overheated and overtired sigh at the thought of cool shadows and clear waters. There *was* a difference, and it was simply all the difference in the world, between their two cases. She had been horribly right when at the beginning she snubbed Christopher for declaring there wasn't. Stephen didn't need to watch Virginia as she watched Christopher, anxiously on the alert for the least sign of change in her, in what she did, what she said, in the very tone in which she said it. Stephen was safe, was at rest; Virginia would never, never do anything but love him. He was the father of her child, the authority she looked up to, the intelligence she adored. But Catherine—she wasn't going to be the mother of any child of Christopher's, she hadn't got any intelligence for him to adore, and wouldn't have wished to have authority, even if she could have, for him to look up to. For her there was nothing but strain and effort, with the tormenting knowledge that her very strain and effort were bound to bring about what she dreaded.

It was a terrible business, this business of bliss. She clung to him, clung to him, tighter and tighter, as if his youth must somehow get through and make her young to match.

Now nobody can be clung to tightly for any length of time without presently feeling that they would like a little air; and soon after the return from Chickover, when he had got over his anxiety at her absence and his joy at her return, Christopher began to have this feeling. It was gorgeous to love and be loved as he and Catherine loved, but it was a patent and acknowledged fact, and he gradually now began to want to talk about something else. Catherine apparently never wanted to. She loved, he couldn't but notice, anxiously. She seemed to have very little of the repose of real faith, and she needed an incredible amount of reassuring. And when he had reassured her, and got her quiet and placid as he supposed, there she was needing it all over again.

Marriage being mainly repetition, and Christopher now being a husband, he presently began to make fewer rapturous speeches. It was quite unconscious, but as the weeks passed it became natural to love with fewer preliminary cooings—to bill, as it were, without remembering first to coo.

He wouldn't have noticed it if Catherine hadn't noticed it and said something about it. Whereupon he began to meditate on this, as he recognised, undoubted fact, and came to the following conclusions:

A husband cannot go on cooing after he has ceased to thrill, but he can go on very happily billing. Only mystery thrills, and only the unknown is mysterious. It wasn't reasonable for the dear explored one to want still to be mysterious, for the so felicitously known to want still to be unknown. Catherine was the darlingest love of a wife, and every night when he went to sleep with his arms round her he thanked God he had got her, but she was no longer mysterious; his heart would never give great choking bumps again when he came near her. Yet that, it seemed, was what she wanted and expected. And she had a really remarkable love-memory, and never forgot a single love-look or love-word or love-vow or love-action of his, and had taken to comparing him with himself—which was rather awkward, for unconsciously at the beginning, it appeared, he had been creating precedents and setting a standard; and the standard, it appeared, was a very high one, and the precedents were difficult to follow in calmer blood.

What he now wanted, thought Christopher, reflecting on these things, was to lead a happy, healthy, love-making life, in which all the speeches were taken for granted. Was that out of the way at all? Didn't married people inevitably get into this condition after a bit? He supposed that the difference between himself and Catherine—he hated to admit there could be such a thing—was their several attitude towards billing and cooing. He wanted—and he imagined most husbands at last wanted—to bill without cooing, and she wasn't happy in any billing that hadn't been preceded by coos. Loud coos, too; loud and long ones.

Well, no man can coo for ever. Christopher was convinced of that. Not with spontaneity, anyhow. He tried to once or twice just to please her, but she instantly found him out and was tremendously upset. He then tried to laugh about it and tease her; but she wouldn't laugh and be teased. She took everything that had to do with love very seriously. Her view was that love was like God, and couldn't be joked about without profanity.

She told him this used to be his view too. Was it? He

couldn't remember, but didn't tell her he couldn't, for a certain amount of caution, highly unnatural to him, began to creep into what he said. The expression "used to be" seemed to recur rather a lot, he thought. He had heard tell of one's evil past dogging one's footsteps, but fancy being dogged by one's alleged satisfactory past, and having it shake its fists at one!

He told her this one morning, waking up in the jolly, careless mood when he would have tickled a tiger; but she only looked thoroughly alarmed, and said he never used to talk like that.

What a frightened, nervy little thing she was. What was she frightened of? He couldn't imagine; but he only had to look at her eyes to see she *was* frightened. She was happiest and most content when they didn't go anywhere, and didn't do anything but just sit in the flat together, she curled up close to him on the sofa, and he reading aloud. They spent evening after evening this way. About every third evening or so she would suddenly get into a panic lest he found it boring, and would start making eager plans about things they would do next week: they would go to the play, and have supper afterwards, or motor down into the country and drift round on the river and come home by moonlight.

When the time came she would cling to him and beg him to let her off. Let her off! What a funny way of putting it, he would tell her, laughing and kissing her. Was she going to have a baby, he began to wonder? And he asked her so one evening, when she was wriggling out of a plan they had made that involved exertion.

She seemed thunderstruck. "Chris!" she cried, staring at him.

Well, why not? he asked. People did. Especially women, he said, trying to make her laugh, because her face had gone so very tragic. They had babies much more often than they had husbands, anyhow. She must have noticed that.

"But not if—not if—" she stammered, her eyes full of tears.

Oh Lord—he had forgotten that age-complex of hers. He never thought of her age. She was as old to him as she looked, and she looked the same age as himself. He never could remember that she was convinced she was a little Methuselah.

"After all," he said cheerfully, still trying to make her laugh, "there was Sarah. I don't see why you—"

"Sarah!"

She stood looking at him a moment, and then ran out of the room.

Horrified, he ran after her; but she had locked herself into the bedroom, their bedroom—locked herself in, and him out.

This was their first scene. And it was peculiarly distressing, because nobody was angry, only sorry.

∾ XIII ∾

Soon after this the Fanshawes gave a dinner, and invited the Moncktons. It was, in fact, a dinner for Catherine, who hadn't enjoyed their dance very much, they felt. Dinners were perhaps pleasanter for her now, they decided. It couldn't be much fun, Ned had remarked, to sit looking on at that great red-headed lout of hers dancing with a pack of girls, just as if she were chaperoning her débutant s——

"Oh *hush,* Ned!" cried Kitty Fanshawe, stamping her foot.

For some reason, impossible Catherine considered to account for, except as one of the many off-shoots of their warmly benevolent dispositions, the Fanshawe family as one man loved her. They had known her slightly in the days of George, and with growing intimacy ever since. In those days they had deplored that she should be tied to one so old; they were now engaged in deploring that she should be tied to one so young. Fanshawe-like they wouldn't even to themselves judge any one they loved, but tacitly making the best of a bad job, set about seeing what they could do to amuse and entertain her.

They came to the conclusion that a little dinner at a restaurant would be more amusing than a dinner at home, and chose the Berkeley; and they reserved one of those tables in the window-recesses which have sofas fitted round three sides of them.

The party was eight: themselves, the Moncktons, Sir Musgrove and Lady Merriman—great friends of theirs, and both delightful, which made them conspicuous among married couples, who sometimes were, the Fanshawes were forced regretfully to admit, unequal in attractiveness, so that while one of them would make a party go the other would prevent its budging—and Duncan Amory, a rising barrister. But at the last moment Kitty Fanshawe caught a cold and couldn't come, and Mrs. Fanshawe invited Emily Wickford, an agreeable spinster, to take her place.

Five sat on the sofa, and three on chairs on the outer side of the table. Mrs. Fanshawe put Catherine in the middle of the sofa facing the room, between Ned and Sir Musgrove—Ned had invented a birthday for her, so that she should be the guest of honour and he could give her flowers, for Ned was good but tactless, and it hadn't occurred to him that birthdays were the last things Catherine wished attention drawn to—and on Ned's left sat Lady Merriman, and on her left sat Christopher, and on his left sat Miss Wickford, and on her left sat Duncan Amory, with Mrs. Fanshawe next to him on his other side, between him and Sir Musgrove.

All would have been well if it hadn't been for Miss Wickford. That exquisite spinster, who had refused so many offers that she could hardly be called a spinster at all, was still only twenty-eight, and had the most beautiful eyes in London. She had been invited merely to fill Kitty's place, and the Fanshawes had thought of her only because she was a great friend of Duncan Amory's, and he at any rate would enjoy himself if she came.

Unfortunately, Sir Musgrove and Christopher enjoyed themselves too because she came—at least, Sir Musgrove did at the beginning. Taking advantage of the table being round, he leaned over whenever he could to talk to Miss Wickford, and while he was doing that he naturally wasn't talking to Catherine, for whose entertainment he had been specially invited; and Christopher, whose duty it was to begin by talking to Lady Merriman, at once upset the balance of the party by talking to Miss Wickford instead.

This left Ned to amuse two neglected ladies, and as he wasn't amusing he didn't amuse them. It also cut off Duncan Amory from his dear Emily, for Emily liked beginnings rather than endings, and therefore preferred Christopher, whom she hadn't seen before, to Duncan whom she had seen almost too much; and, regarding him as years younger than herself, probably still at Oxford, or the other place, proceeded to give the boy a good time and see that he thoroughly enjoyed his evening.

She succeeded. Christopher did enjoy himself. Here was a girl who was clever as well as pretty, delightful to talk to as well as delightful to look at. In ten minutes he felt as if they were old friends. She asked him if he had any Scandinavian blood in him, because that was what he looked like—rather her idea of a sun-kissed young Norse god; and he retorted by asking her if she had any Greek blood in her, because that was what she looked like—rather his idea of a sun-kissed young Greek goddess; and they laughed, and were pleased with each other. Aphrodite for choice, said Christopher warming to his work, and glancing first at Emily's hair and then at her justly celebrated eyes; Aphrodite was fair too, and had eyes like the sea too, he said; all the most beautiful women were fair and had eyes like the sea, he said.

Emily was much pleased.

Sir Musgrove, catching the word Aphrodite, tried to chime in, for he was not only a well-known Greek scholar, engaged at that very moment in writing an inquiry into the mythologies, but he would have been interested to discuss the delicious goddess with Miss Wickford. Duncan Amory also tried to chime in, with a story about an American lady who by some mix-up at her baptism got christened Aphrodite, and the effect it had on her afterwards. It wasn't a bad story, and anyhow it was apt, and he felt aggrieved that nobody listened to it except the Fanshawes. The others were absorbed in watching Emily. Emily wasn't at all a good person to have at a party, thought Amory. She absorbed attention. Her proper place was a *tête-à-tête*. That was how he himself chiefly cultivated her. He shrugged his shoulders, and turned resolutely to Mrs. Fanshawe.

Lady Merriman was bored. Able and willing to talk about anything—book, play, picture or politician—she found herself, because of Miss Wickford, left with only half a man; half of Ned Fanshawe, too, who even when he was whole had more of good nature than of conversation. And she wished very much to talk to this young Mr. Monckton and find out for herself what could have induced that middle-aged woman to be so reckless as to marry him. However, he was engrossed. Natural, she supposed, at his age. What wasn't so natural was that Musgrove was engrossed too. He would talk to neither of his neighbours, and had eyes and ears only for Miss Wickford.

Lady Merriman, who was fond of Musgrove, and had been faithfully and patiently through the thick and the thin of him for twenty-five years, was a little put out; not on her own account, for nothing, she knew, could alter his complete private dependence on her, but on his. She didn't like her man, who was anything but silly, to look it. Also, she did wish he would amuse poor Mrs. Monckton, and distract her attention from what that boy of hers was saying to Miss Wickford. Marriage, thought Lady Merriman, observing the expression on Musgrove's face and observing the expression on Catherine's, was rich in humiliations. If one allowed it to be, that is; if one didn't keep them out by the only real defence—laughter.

The band began to play a fox-trot. One or two active young people got up from neighbouring tables and danced.

"Will you dance?" Christopher asked Miss Wickford.

"I'd adore to," she answered, getting up just as the waiter put a nice hot quail on her plate. "May we?" she asked, smiling at Mrs. Fanshawe, and floating off without waiting for an answer.

"Ah, youth, youth," said Sir Musgrove, shaking his head indulgently. "And we greybeards console ourselves with quails."

This was tactless of Musgrove, Mrs. Fanshawe considered, and she protested.

"There are no greybeards here," protested Mrs. Fanshawe with great vigour.

"Ah well—I speak allegorically," said Sir Musgrove, following Miss Wickford's movements as she exquisitely gyrated in Christopher's arms.

"I should eat your quail before it gets cold, Musgrove," said his wife—it was all Martha's fault for not having put such effervescent guests on the sofa, safe behind the table where they couldn't have got out. But some one ought to tell Mrs. Monckton not to look quite so. . . .

"Personally, I think it foolish to interrupt a good dinner and let it get cold," said Duncan Amory, who didn't at all like the way Emily was behaving.

"My dear friend, they are at the golden age when dinner is of no consequence," said Sir Musgrove. "A good-looking couple—a very good-looking couple," he added dreamily, his eye on Emily.

Well, really—hadn't Musgrove grasped the fact that the young man was Mrs. Monckton's husband? thought Lady Merriman, trying to catch the eye that was fixed so persistently on Miss Wickford.

The Fanshawes saw their mistake, and were repenting

bitterly. Of course Emily Wickford should have been put on the sofa. Better still, not asked at all. She was ruining the party for every one except Catherine's husband. Duncan Amory, usually such good company, was sulking; Musgrove—they couldn't have believed it of him; Lydia Merriman—naturally she was vexed; Catherine—well, they hardly liked to look at her.

The band left off playing, and the couples all came back except Christopher and Miss Wickford. They disappeared through the arch into the next room, Emily smiling back over her shoulder at her hosts, and Christopher holding up an explanatory cigarette case.

It was Emily who proposed this. She said she didn't want any more dinner, and thought it much more fun not to sit cooped up at that table, with which Christopher heartily agreed.

"They all seem so old," said Emily, bending forward for him to light her cigarette. "Don't you think so?"

"Fossils," said Christopher, forgetting in his admiration of the face being lit up by the match he was holding, that Catherine was one of them, but he did ask, after a minute, whether she didn't think the Fanshawes would mind their not going back.

"Oh, they never mind anything," said Emily easily. "They're darlings."

The Fanshawes, however, did mind this. They fumed. It was a stricken party that remained at the table. Mrs. Fanshawe was casting her mind back to whether Emily knew Christopher was Catherine's husband, and couldn't remember that she had made this clear when she introduced them. But how, after all, could one make a thing like that clear, short of taking the other person aside and explaining in a whisper? Just to say, "And this is Mr. Monckton," after having introduced somebody to Mrs. Monckton wasn't in this case, she was afraid, enough. On the other hand one couldn't introduce him as Mrs. Monckton's husband. Still, instinct ought to have told Emily. Mrs. Fanshawe, who never was unfair, was unfair now. She was angry. She was the last person in the world to grudge young people having a good time, and was of an easy-goingness that verged on laxity; but this deeply annoyed her, this carrying off of Christopher. Also, she considered that Christopher oughtn't to have let himself be carried off. He, at any rate, knew he was Catherine's husband.

It was a stricken party. Ned was furious, Sir Musgrove fidgeted, Duncan Amory sulked, and Catherine seemed to be shrivelling smaller before their very eyes. Only Lady Merriman and Mrs. Fanshawe talked—across the table to each other, gallantly, after the manner of women, trying to cover things up.

The music began again, and everybody watched the arch. It was some time before the two appeared, and when they did they were talking and laughing as happily as ever.

"Come here—you are very unkind, you two, deserting us like this," Mrs. Fanshawe called out to them as they danced past; but they didn't hear, and danced on.

At the end, when the party was breaking up, Miss Wickford, who had enjoyed her evening immensely, said to Christopher, "Come and see me on Sunday."

"No—you come to us," he answered.

She looked at him surprised. "But wouldn't that bore your mother dreadfully?" she asked.

"Bore my mother?" echoed Christopher, staring. "What mother?"

"Why, isn't—"

Miss Wickford broke off, instinctively feeling she was somehow getting into trouble. That little made-up Mrs. Monckton on the sofa—wasn't she the boy's mother?

"My mother died when I was three," said Christopher.

"Poor you," murmured Miss Wickford non-committally: something warned her to be cautious.

"But my wife will be delighted if you'll come."

There was the briefest silence. Then Emily managed to say, without, she trusted, showing her astonishment, "How perfectly sweet of her. I'll ring up and ask."

ᴈᵒ XIV ᴈᵒ

She never did. And it was just as well, thought Christopher, for
Catherine had, most astoundingly, taken it into her head to be
jealous of her. She wouldn't admit she was, and professed
immense admiration for Miss Wickford's beauty, but if the
emotion she showed after that dinner wasn't jealousy he was
blest if he knew what jealousy was.

It amazed him. She might have heard every word he said.
Miss Wickford was extremely pretty and quite clever, and why
shouldn't he like talking to her? But he was very sorry to have
made Catherine unhappy, and did all he knew to make her
forget it; only it was suffocating sort of work in hot weather,
and he felt as if he were tied up in something very sweet and
sticky, with no end to it. Rather like treacle. It was rather like
being swathed round with bands of treacle.

He came to the conclusion Catherine loved him too much.
Yes, she did. If she loved him more reasonably she would be
much happier, and so would he. It was bad for them both. The
flat seemed thick with love. One waded. He caught himself
putting up his hand to unbutton his collar. Perhaps the stuffy
weather had something to do with it. July was getting near its
end, and there was no air at all in Hertford Street. London was
a rotten place in July. He always walked to his office and back
so as to get what exercise he could, and every Saturday they
went down to his uncle for golf; but what was that? He ached
to be properly stretched, to stride about, to hit things for days
on end, and his talk became almost exclusively of holidays,
and where they should go in August when his were due.

Lewes was going to Scotland to play golf. He had gone with
Lewes last year, and had had a glorious time. What exercise!
What talk! What freedom! He longed to go again, and asked
Catherine whether she wouldn't like to; and she said, with that
hiding look of hers—there was a certain look, very frequent
on her face, he called to himself her *hiding* look—that it was
too far from Virginia.

Virginia? Christopher was much surprised. What did she

want with Virginia? Short of actually being at Chickover, she wouldn't see Virginia anyhow, he said; and she, with her arms round his neck, said that was true, but she didn't want to be out of reach of her.

This unexpected reappearance of Virginia on the scene, this sudden cropping up of her after a long spell of no mention of the girl, puzzled and irritated him. They would, apparently, have gone to Scotland if it hadn't been for Virginia. Must he then too—of course he must, seeing that he couldn't and wouldn't go away without Catherine—be kept hanging round within reach of Virginia? She was the last object he wished to be within reach of.

He was annoyed, and showed it. "Why this recrudescence," he asked, "of maternal love?"

"It isn't a recrudescence—it's always, Chris darling," she said, looking rather shamefacedly at him, he thought—anyhow queerly. "You don't suppose one ever leaves off loving somebody one really loves?"

No, he didn't suppose it. He was sure she wouldn't. But he wasn't going into that now; he wasn't going, at ten in the morning, to begin talking about love.

"It's time I was off," he said, bending down and kissing her quickly. "I'm late as it is."

He hurried out, though he wasn't late. He knew he wasn't late, only he did want to get into what air there was—into, anyhow, sunlight, out of that darkened bedroom.

She too knew he wasn't late, but she too wanted him for once to go, because she had a secret appointment for half-past ten, and it was ten already; a most important, a vital appointment, the bare thought of which thrilled her with both fear and hope.

She didn't know if anything would come of it, but she was going to try. She had written to the great man and told him her age and asked if he thought he could do anything for her, and he had sent a card back briefly indicating 10:30 on this day. Nothing more, just 10:30. How discreet. How exciting.

She had read about him in the papers. He was a Spanish doctor, come over to London for a few weeks, and he undertook to restore youth. Marvellous, blissful, if he really could! A slight operation, said the papers, and there you were. The results were most satisfactory, they affirmed, and in some cases miraculous. Suppose her case were to be one of the miraculous ones? She hadn't the least idea how she would be able to have an operation without Christopher knowing, but all that could be thought out afterwards. The first thing to do was to see the doctor and hear what he had to say. Who wouldn't do anything, take any pains, have any operation, to be helped back to youth? She, certainly, would shrink from nothing. And it sounded so genuine, so scientific, what the doctor, according to the papers, did.

The minute Christopher had gone she hurried into her clothes, refused breakfast, hadn't time to do her face—better she shouldn't that day, better she should be seen exactly as she really was—and twenty minutes after he left she was in a taxi on the way to the great man's temporary consulting rooms in Portland Place.

With what a beating heart she rang the bell. Such hopes, such fears, such determination, such shrinking, all mixed up together, as well as being ashamed, made her hardly able to speak when the nurse—she looked like a nurse—opened the door. And suppose somebody should hear her when she said who she was? And suppose somebody she knew should see her going in? If ever there was a discreet and private occasion it was this one; so that the moment the door was opened she was in such a hurry to get in out of sight of the street that she almost tumbled into the arms of the nurse.

It gave her an unpleasant shock to find herself put into a room with several other people. She hadn't thought she would have to face other seekers after youth. There ought to have been cubicles—places with screens. It didn't seem decent to expose the seekers to one another like that; and she shrank down into a chair with her back to the light, and buried her head in a newspaper.

The others were all burying their heads too in newspapers, but they saw each other nevertheless. All men, she noticed, and all so old that surely they must be past any hopes and wishes? What could they want with youth? It was a sad sight, thought Catherine, peeping round her newspaper, and she felt shocked. When presently two women came in, and after a furtive glance round dropped as she had done into chairs with their backs to the light, she considered them sad sights too and felt shocked; while for their part they were thinking just the same of her, and all the men behind their newspapers were saying to themselves, "What fools women are."

The nurse—she looked exactly like a nurse—came in after a long while and beckoned to her, not calling out her name, for which she was thankful, and she was shown into the consulting room, and found herself confronted by two men instead of one, because Dr. Sanguesa, the specialist, could only say three words in English—"We will see" were his words—so that there was another man there, dark and foreign-looking too, but voluble in English, to interpret.

He did the business part as well. "It will cost fifty pounds," he said almost immediately.

In a whole year Catherine had only ten of these for everything, but if the treatment had been going to cost all ten she would have agreed, and lived somehow in an attic, on a crust—with Christopher and youth. Indeed, she thought it very cheap. Surely fifty pounds was cheap for youth?

"Twenty-five pounds down," said the partner—she decided he was more a partner than an interpreter—"and twenty-five pounds in the middle of the treatment."

"Certainly," she murmured.

Dr. Sanguesa was observing her while the partner talked. Every now and then he said something in Spanish, and the other asked her a question. The questions were intimate and embarrassing—the kind it is more comfortable to reply to to one person rather than two. However, she was in for it; she mustn't mind; she was determined not to mind anything.

In her turn she asked some questions, forcing herself to be courageous, for she was frightened in spite of her determination and hopes. Would it hurt, she asked timidly; would it take long; when would the results begin?

"We will see," said Dr. Sanguesa, who hadn't understood a word, nodding his head gravely.

It would not hurt, said the partner, because in the case of women it was dangerous to operate, and the treatment was purely external; it would take six weeks, with two treatments a week; she would begin to see a marked difference in her appearance after the fourth treatment.

The fourth treatment? That would be in a fortnight. And no operation? How wonderful. She caught her breath with excitement. In a fortnight she would be beginning to look younger. After that, every day younger and younger. No more Maria Rome, no more painful care over her dressing, no more fear of getting tired because of how ghastly it made her look, but the real thing, the real glorious thing itself.

"Shall I *feel* young?" she asked, eagerly now.

"Of course. Everything goes together. You understand—a

woman's youth, and accordingly her looks, depends entirely on—"

The partner launched into a rapid explanation which was only saved from being excessively improper by its technical language. Dr. Sanguesa sat silent, his elbows on the arms of his revolving chair, his finger-tips together. He looked a remote, unfriended, melancholy man, rather like the pictures she had seen of Napoleon III., with dark shadows under his heavy eyes and a waxen skin. Every now and then his sad mouth opened, and he said quite automatically, "We will see," and shut it again.

She wanted to begin at once. It appeared she must be examined first, to find out if she could stand the treatment. This rather frightened her again. Why? How? Was the treatment so severe? What was it?

"We will see," said Dr. Sanguesa, nodding.

The partner became voluble, waving his hands about. Not at all—not at all severe; a matter of X-rays merely; but sometimes, if a woman's heart was weak—

Catherine said she was sure her heart wasn't weak.

"We will see," said Dr. Sanguesa, mechanically nodding.

"The examination is three guineas," said the partner.

"Three more, or three of the same ones?" asked Catherine, rather stupidly.

"We will s——"

The partner interrupted him this time with a quickly lifted hand. He seemed to think Catherine's question was below the level of both his and her dignities and intelligences, for he looked as if he were a little ashamed of her as he said stiffly, "Three more."

She bowed her head. She would have bowed her head to anything, if these men in exchange would give her youth.

The examination could be made at once, the partner said, if she was ready.

Yes, she was quite ready.

She got up instantly. They were used to eagerness, especially in the women patients, but this was a greater eagerness than usual. Dr. Sanguesa's sombre, sunken eyes observed her thoughtfully. He said something in Spanish to his partner, who shook his head. Catherine had the impression it was something he wished interpreted, and she looked inquiringly at the partner, but he said nothing, and went to the door and opened it for her.

She was taken upstairs into a sort of Rose du Barri boudoir, arranged with a dressing-table and looking-glasses, and another nurse—at least, she too looked like one—helped her to undress. Then she was wrapped in a dressing-gown—she didn't like this public dressing-gown against her skin—and led into a room fitted up with many strange machines and an operating table. What will not a woman do, she thought, eyeing these objects with misgiving, and her heart well down somewhere near her feet, for the man she loves?

Dr. Sanguesa came in, all covered up in white like an angel. The partner, she was thankful to notice, didn't appear. She was examined with great care, the nurse smiling encouragingly. It was a relief to be told by the nurse, who interpreted, that her heart was sound and her lungs perfect, even though she had never supposed they weren't. At the end the nurse told her the doctor was satisfied she could stand the treatment, and asked when she would like to begin.

Catherine said she would begin at once.

Impossible. The next day?

Oh yes, yes—the next day. And would she really—she was going to say look nice again, but said instead feel less tired?

"It's wonderful how different people feel," the nurse assured her; and Dr. Sanguesa nodded gravely, without having understood a word, and said, "We will see."

"He hasn't tried it on himself, has he?" remarked Catherine, when she was in the Rose du Barri room again, dressing.

The nurse laughed. She was a jolly-looking young woman—but perhaps she was really an old woman, who had had the treatment.

"Have *you* been done?" asked Catherine.

The nurse laughed again. "I shall be if I see I'm getting old," she said.

"It really *is* wonderful?" asked Catherine, whose hands as she fastened her hooks were trembling with excitement.

"You wouldn't believe it," said the nurse earnestly. "I've seen men of seventy looking and behaving not a day more than forty."

"That's thirty years off," said Catherine. "And supposing they were forty to begin with, would they have looked and behaved like ten?"

"Ah well, that's a little much to expect, isn't it," said the nurse, laughing again.

"I'm forty-seven. I wouldn't at all like to end by being seven."

"Your husband would pack you off to a kindergarten, wouldn't he," said the nurse, laughing more than ever.

Catherine laughed too. She was so full of hope that she already felt younger. But when she put on her hat before the glass she saw she didn't anyhow look it.

"Don't I look *too* awful," she said, turning round frankly to the friendly nurse, who, after all, was going to be the witness of her triumphant progress backwards through the years.

"We'll soon get rid of all that," said the nurse gaily.

Catherine quite loved the nurse.

∾ XV ∾

It was an exciting life during the next week—so much to plan, so much to arrange, and she herself buoyant with hope and delight. She couldn't, of course, leave London during her treatment, so to Christopher's astonishment she urged him to go to Scotland without her.

"But Catherine—"

He couldn't believe his own ears.

"Go and have a good time, Chris darling."

"Without you?"

"I must stay in London."

"In *London?*"

"Yes. Virginia may want me."

"Now what in God's name, Catherine, is all this about Virginia. The other day—"

Then she told him, secure in the knowledge that she was so soon going to be young again—she didn't in the least mind being a grandmother if she wasn't going to look like one; on the contrary, to look like a girl and yet be a grandmother struck her as to the last degree chic—that Virginia was expecting a baby in September, and as babies sometimes appeared before they ought she must be within reach.

Well, that was all right; he understood that. What he didn't understand was Catherine's detachment. Why, she seemed not to mind his leaving her. He couldn't believe it. And when it became finally evident that such was her real attitude and no pretence at all about it, he was deeply hurt. Incredibly, she genuinely wanted him to go.

"You love Virginia more than me," he said, his heart suddenly hot with jealousy.

"Oh Chris, don't be silly," said Catherine impatiently.

She had never since their marriage told him not to be silly in that sensible, matter-of-fact way. What had come over her? He, who had been feeling he couldn't breathe for all the love there was about, now found himself gasping for want of it. The atmosphere had suddenly gone clear and rarefied. Catherine seemed to be thinking of something that wasn't him, and once or twice forgot to kiss him. Forgot to kiss him! He was deeply wounded. And she was so unaccountably cheerful too. She not only seemed to be thinking of something else but seemed amused by it, hugging whatever it was with delight. She was excited. What was she excited about? Surely not because she was going to be a grandmother? Surely that would make her brood more than ever on the difference in their ages?

"She wants me to go to Scotland with you," he said, bursting in one day on Lewes. "She wants me to go away without her. Doesn't care a hang. Four solid weeks. The whole of August."

"How sensible," said Lewes, not looking up from his work.

"It's that beastly baby."

"Baby?" Lewes did look up.

"Due in September."

"What? But surely—"

"Oh, don't be a fool. Virginia's. She won't leave London. Why she can't go somewhere round near Chickover, where I could go too and be with her and get some golf as well— Lewes, old man, I believe she's fed up with me."

And he stared at Lewes with hot eyes.

In his turn Lewes told him not to be a fool; but the mere thought of Catherine, his Catherine, being fed up with him as he put it, sent him rushing back to her to see if it could possibly be true.

She was so airy, so much detached.

"Now Chris, don't be absurd. Of course you must have a good holiday and get out of London. It's lucky that you have your friend to go with—"

That was the sort of thing.

"But Catherine, how can you want me to? Don't you love me any more?"

"Of course I love you. Which is why I want you to go to Scotland."

This was true. The treatment was being gone through for love of him, and he must go to Scotland because of the treatment. She was to have as much quiet as possible during it—"No husbands," said Dr. Sanguesa—"You've got to be a grass widow for a little while," interpreted the nurse—"You must go to Scotland," still further interpreted Catherine.

But he couldn't go at once. It was still only July. The first two treatments took place while Christopher was still in London, and as it was impossible without rousing his suspicions to keep him entirely at arm's length, she wasn't surprised when the effect of them was to make her feel more tired than ever.

"It's often like that to begin with," encouraged the nurse. "Especially if you're not having complete rest from worries at home."

Did she mean husbands by worries, Catherine wondered? There certainly wasn't complete rest from that sort of worry, then, for Christopher, as Catherine apparently cooled, became more and more as he used to be, and possessed by the fear that he was somehow losing her rediscovered how much he loved her.

He had, of course, always intensely loved her, but he had felt the need of pauses. In her love there had been no pauses, and gradually the idea of suffocation had got hold of him. Now, so suddenly, so unaccountably, she seemed to be all pause. She tried to avoid him; she even suggested, on the plea that the nights were hot, that he should sleep in the dressing-room.

Whatever else he had tired of he hadn't yet tired of the sweetness, the curious comfort and reassurance, of going to sleep with his arms round her. Since their marriage there had been no interruption in his wish to cling at night; what he hadn't wanted was to be clung to in the morning. One felt so different in the morning; at least, he did. Catherine didn't; and it was this that had given him the impression of stifling in treacle. Now she not only showed no wish at all to cling in the morning, but she tried—he wouldn't and couldn't believe it, but had to—to wriggle out of being clung to at night.

"Catherine, what is it? What has come between us?" he

asked, his eyes hurt and indignant—when Catherine had asked this sort of question, as she had on first noticing a different quality in his love-making, he had been impatient and bored, and thought in his heart "How like all women," but of course he didn't remember this.

"Oh Chris, why are you so silly?" she answered, laughing and pushing him away. "Don't you feel how hot it is, and how much nicer not to be too close together? Let us be sanitary."

Sanitary? That was a pleasant way of putting it. She was going back to what she used to be at first, when he had such difficulty in getting hold of her at all—going back into just being an intelligent little stand-offish thing, independent, and determined to have nothing to do with him. How he had worshipped her in those days of her unattainableness. Her relapse now into what threatened to become unattainableness all over again didn't make him worship her, because that had been the kind of worship that never returns, but it lit his love up again, while at the same time filling him with a fury of possessiveness. A thwarted possessiveness, however; she evaded him more and more.

"I can't go to Scotland and leave you. Damn golf. I simply can't," he said at last.

And she, as cool as a little cucumber and as bright as a gay little button—the comparisons were his—told him he simply had to, and that when he came back he would find they were going to be happier than ever.

"You'll love me more than ever," she said laughing, for though the treatment was extraordinarily exhausting her spirits those days were bright with faith.

"Rot. Nobody could love you more than I do now, so what's the good of talking like that? Catherine, what has happened to you? Tell me."

And there he was, just as he used to be, on the floor at her feet, his arms clasping her knees, his head on her lap.

All this made Catherine very happy. She began to see benefits in the treatment other than the ones Dr. Sanguesa had guaranteed.

✦ XVI ✦

He went to Scotland, and she stayed in London. She was inexorable. It was as if his soft, enveloping pillow had turned into a rock. She lied at last—how avoid lying, sooner or later, when one was married?—so as to get rid of him, for he was insisting on taking rooms for them both at the sea near Chickover, where she could be within reach of Virginia and yet not away from him. Driven into this corner what could she do but lie? It is what one does in corners, she thought, excusing herself. She told him Virginia was probably coming up to London to have her baby in a nursing home, and that was why she couldn't go away.

He went off puzzled and unhappy, and his unhappiness filled her with secret joy. What balm to her spirit, which had lately been so anxious, to see all these unmistakable symptoms of devoted love in him. And she pictured his return in September, and herself at the station to meet him, changed, young, able to do everything with him, a fit mate for him at last.

"You'll never, never know how much I love you," she said, her arms round his neck when she said good-bye.

"It looks like it, doesn't it," he said gloomily.

"Exactly like it," she laughed. She was always laughing now, just as she used always to be laughing at their very first meetings.

"I can't make it out," he said, looking down at her upturned face. "You're sending me away. Suppose I meet that girl up there—Miss Wickford, or that other one who looked like a shark—I should comfort myself."

Even that only made her laugh. "Do, Chris darling," she said, patting his face. "And then come back and tell me all about it."

She *was* changed. He went away extremely miserable, and Lewes's talk—that talk he had thirsted for when he thought he wasn't going to get it—seemed like just so much gritty drivel.

Left alone in London Catherine gave herself up entirely to the treatment. Twice a week she went to Portland Place and suffered—for it hurt, though Dr. Sanguesa told her through the nurse that it didn't. They laid her on a table, and a great machine was lowered to within a hair's breadth of her bare skin, her eyes were bandaged, and crackling things—she couldn't see what, but they sounded like sparks and felt like little bright stabbing knives—were let loose on her for half an hour at a stretch, first on one side of her and then on the other. When this was over she was injected with some mysterious fluid, and then went home completely exhausted.

All day afterwards she lay on her sofa, and Mrs. Mitcham brought her trays of nourishing food. She read and slept. She went to bed at nine o'clock. She did nothing to her face after Christopher had gone, and Mrs. Mitcham, looking at her and seeing her so persistently yellow, asked her with growing concern if she felt quite well.

After the fourth treatment she was to begin and see a difference. How anxiously she scanned herself in the glass. Nothing. And her body felt exactly as her face looked—amazingly weary.

"It takes longer with some people," said the nurse, when Catherine commented on this on her fifth visit. "There was one lady came here who noticed nothing at all till just before the end, and then you should have seen her. Why, she skipped out of that door. And sixty, if a day."

"Perhaps I'm not old enough," said Catherine. "All the people you tell me about are sixty or seventy."

She was sitting on the sofa of the Rose du Barri boudoir being dressed. She was too tired to stand up. Those crackles, going on for half an hour, were a great strain on her endurance. They didn't hurt enough to make her cry out, but enough to make her need all her determination not to.

The nurse laughed. "Well, we *are* depressed to-day, aren't we," she said brightly. "People do get like that about half-way through—the slow ones, I mean, who don't react at once as some do. You'll see. Rome wasn't built in a day."

The next time she came the nurse flung up both hands on seeing her. "Why, aren't you looking well this morning!" she cried.

Catherine hurried to the glass. "Am I?" she said, staring at herself.

"Such a change," said the nurse with every sign of pleasure.

"I was sure it would begin soon. Now you'll see it going on more and more quickly every day."

"Shall I?" said Catherine, scrutinising the face in the glass.

For the life of her she could see no difference. She said so. The nurse laughed at her.

"Oh, you doubting Thomas," said the nurse, whose friendliness had flowered into a robust familiarity. "Just look at yourself now. Don't you see?" And she took her by the shoulders and twisted her round to the glass again.

No, Catherine didn't see. She saw the nurse's laughing, rosy face close to hers, and hers yellow and pale-lipped—just as it always was now when nothing out of Maria Rome's box had been put on it. Maria Rome had had a terrible effect on her. Her hair was startlingly more grey, now that the dye had had time to wear off, than it used to be before any was put on.

"It's the trained eye that can tell," said the nurse brightly. "I notice a *great* change."

"Do you?" was all Catherine could say.

That day she seemed so much more quiet and tired than usual, lying on her sofa in the flat and not even reading, that Mrs. Mitcham, who hadn't been at all happy about her since Christopher's departure, asked her if it wouldn't be a good plan to see a doctor.

Catherine couldn't help smiling at this. Why, that was what was the matter with her, that she *was* seeing a doctor.

"I shall be all right soon," she assured Mrs. Mitcham; for she still hoped.

It wasn't till after the ninth treatment that her hopes began to grow definitely pale. Nothing had happened. She was just as old as ever; older, if anything, for those stabbing sparks made her brace herself to an endurance that left her utterly exhausted. The nurse, it is true, continued stoutly to express delighted surprise each time she saw her, but this merely caused Catherine to distrust either her sincerity or her eyesight. She became more silent and less interested in the tales about other old ladies. Their alleged skipping began to leave her cold. It was possible, of course, that they had skipped, but she wasn't able to bring herself to believe in it really.

"Those other old ladies—" she said, on her eleventh visit.

The nurse interrupted her with a gay burst of laughter. "You're never going to class yourself with old ladies?" she cried. "Now, Mrs. Monckton, that's really naughty of you. I won't allow it. I shall have to scold you soon, you know."

"Well, but this is my eleventh time, and you said they were all skipping by their eleventh time—"

"Not all. Come, come now. It takes people differently, you know."

"Not that I want to skip," said Catherine, wearily pinning up a strand of hair the eye-bandage had loosened. "It's that I don't feel the least shred of the remotest desire to."

"That'll come. It'll all come in time."

"In what time?" asked Catherine. "I've only got one treatment more."

"It often happens that people feel the benefit afterwards. Weeks, perhaps, afterwards. They wake up one morning, and find themselves suddenly quite young."

Catherine said nothing to this. Her hopes had flickered very small by now.

The nurse, as jolly as ever, rallied her and laughed at her for being so ungrateful, when she only had to look at herself to see—

"I'm always looking at myself, and I never see," said Catherine.

"Oh, *aren't* you a naughty little thing!" cried the nurse. "I don't know what would become of poor Dr. Sanguesa if all his patients were as obstinately blind as you. Well, there's still Thursday. Sometimes the last treatment of all convinces the patient, and we shall have you writing us wonderful testimonials—"

There was no response to this gaiety. Catherine went away heavy-footed. She was poorer by fifty pounds, Christopher was coming home in a week, and that bright dream of meeting him at the station seemed to the last degree unlikely to be realised. Useless for the nurse to pretend there was a difference in her; there was none. Perhaps if she hadn't pretended Catherine would have been more able to believe. But the nurse treating her like a fool—well, but wasn't that precisely what she was? Wasn't any woman a fool who could suppose that she could be stirred up to youth again by showers of stabbing crackles?

She went home heavy-footed and ashamed. Trouble, expense, disappointment, an intolerable long separation from Christopher—that was all she had got out of this. Oh yes—she had got the useful knowledge that she was a fool; but she had had that before.

Still, she wouldn't quite give up hope yet. There was one

more treatment, and it might well be that she would suddenly take a turn. . . .

But she never had the final treatment, and never saw either Dr. Sanguesa or the nurse again; for when she got home that day, she found a telegram from Mrs. Colquhoun, asking her to come to Chickover at once.

৬৯ XVII ৫৩

There was a note of urgency in the telegram that made Catherine afraid. Going down in the slow afternoon train, the first she could catch, which stopped so often and so long, she had much time to think, and it seemed to her that all this she had been doing since her marriage was curiously shabby and disgraceful. What waste of emotions, what mean fears. Now came real fear, and at its touch those others shrivelled up. Virginia down there at grips with danger, being tortured—oh, she knew what torture—just this stark fact shocked her back to vision.

She sat looking out of the window at the fields monotonously passing, and many sharp-edged thoughts cut through her mind, and one of them was of the last time she had gone down to Chickover, and of her gaiety because some strange man, taken in by the cleverness with which Maria Rome had disguised her, had obviously considered her younger than she was. How pitiful, how pitiful; what a sign one was indeed old when a thing like that could excite one and make one feel pleased.

She stared at this memory a moment, before it was hustled off by other thoughts, in wonder. The stuff one filled life with! And at the faintest stirring of Death's wings, the smallest movement forward of that great figure from the dark furthermost corner of the little room called life, how instantly one's eyes were smitten open. One became real. Was one ever real till then? Had there to be that forward movement, that reminder, "I am here, you know," before one could wake from one's strange, small dreams?

She had to wait an hour at the junction. This comforted her, for if things had been serious the car would have been sent for her there.

It was past nine when she reached Chickover. The chauffeur who met her looked unhappy, but could tell her nothing except that his mistress had been ill since the morning. The avenue was dark, the great trees in solemn row shutting out what still was left of twilight, and the house at the end was dark too and very silent. The place seemed to be holding its breath, as if aware of the battle being fought on the other side in the rooms towards the garden.

Silence everywhere, complete and strange; except—

Yes—what was that?

She caught her breath and stopped; for as she was crossing the hall, past the pale maid, a slow moaning crept down the stairs like a trickle of blood—a curious slow moaning, not human at all, more like some poor animal, dying hopelessly by inches in a trap.

Virginia. . . .

Catherine stood struck with horror. That noise? Virginia? Just like an animal?

She looked round at Kate. Their white faces stared at each other. Kate's lips moved. "Since this morning," came out of them. "Since early this morning. The master—"

She broke off, her pale lips remaining open.

Catherine turned and ran upstairs. She ran as one demented towards the moaning. It must be stopped, it must be stopped. Virginia must be saved, she couldn't, she mustn't be allowed to suffer like that, nobody should be allowed to suffer like that, hours and hours. . . .

She ran along the passage to Virginia's room, the same room where nineteen years ago Virginia herself had been born, but instead of getting nearer the moaning she seemed to be going away from it.

Where was Virginia, then? Where had they put her?

She stood still to listen, and her heart beat so loud that she could hardly hear. There—to the left, where the spare-rooms were. But why? Why had they taken her there?

She ran down the passage to the left. Yes; here it was; behind this shut door. . . .

Catherine's knees seemed to be going to give way. The sound was terribly close—so hopeless, so unceasing. What were they doing in there to her child? What was God doing to let them?

Her shaking hand fumbled at the handle. She laid the other over it to steady it. She mustn't be like this, she knew; she mustn't go in there only to add to the terror that was there already.

With both hands gripping the handle she slowly turned it and went in.

Stephen.

Stephen half sitting, half lying on the floor up against a sofa. His mother standing looking at him. No one else. The room shrouded in dust-sheets, the bed piled high with spare blankets and pillows. Stephen moaning.

"Stephen!" Catherine exclaimed, so much shocked that she could only stare. Stephen—Stephen of all people—in such a state. . . .

His mother turned and came towards her.

"But—Virginia?" said Catherine, her lips trembling, for if Stephen could be reduced to this, what dreadful thing was happening to Virginia?

Mrs. Colquhoun took her face in both hands and kissed her—really kissed her. Her eyes were very bright, with red rims. She had evidently been crying, and she had the look of those who have reached the end of their tether.

"All is going well I believe now with Virginia," she said. "I tell him so, and he won't listen. Do you think you could make him listen? There was a terrible time before the second doctor came and put her under an anæsthetic, and it upset him so that he—well, you see."

And she made a gesture, half shame, half anger, and wholly unhappy, towards the figure leaning against the sofa.

Then she added, her bright, tear-stained eyes on Catherine's, "To think that my son and God's priest should go to pieces like this—should be unable in a crisis to do his duty—should lose—should lose—"

She broke off, continuing to stare at Catherine with those bright, incredulous eyes.

Catherine could only gaze at Stephen in dismay. No wonder Kate downstairs hadn't succeeded in saying what she was trying to say about the master. Stephen, the firm-lipped, the strong denouncer of weakness, the exhorting calm Christian —what a dreadful thing to happen. She didn't know husbands ever collapsed like that. George hadn't. He had been anxious and distressed, but he hadn't moaned. The moaning had been done, she remembered, exclusively by her. George had been her comfort, her rock. What comfort could Virginia have got that day out of Stephen? And it was after all Virginia who was having the baby.

"Couldn't the doctors give him something?" she asked, feeling that poor Stephen ought certainly too to be given a little chloroform to help him through his hours of misery—anything rather than that he should be left lying there suffering like that.

"I asked them to give him a soothing draught," said Mrs. Colquhoun, "and they only told me to take him away. Of course I took him away, for he was killing Virginia, and here I've been shut up with him ever since. Catherine—" it was the first time she had called her that—"I don't remember in our day—? I don't remember that my husband—?" And she broke off, and stared at her with her bright, exhausted eyes.

"George didn't," said Catherine hesitatingly, "but I think—I think Stephen loves Virginia more than perhaps—"

"A nice way of loving," remarked Mrs. Colquhoun, who had had a terrible day shut up with Stephen, and whose distress for him was by now shot with indignation.

"Oh, but he can't help it. Dear Mrs. Colquhoun—"

"Call me Milly."

Milly? These barriers tumbling down all round before the blast of a crisis bewildered Catherine. Stephen, who had been so firmly entrenched behind example and precept, lying exposed there, so helplessly and completely exposed that she hardly liked to look at him, hardly liked either him or his mother to know she was there, because of later on when he should be normal again and they both might be humiliated by the recollection, and Mrs. Colquhoun, not only turning on her adored son but flinging away her insincerities and kissing her with almost eager affection and demanding to be called Milly. Strange by-products of Virginia's suffering, thought Catherine. "I must go to her," she said, going towards the door.

"Dear Catherine," said Mrs. Colquhoun holding her back, "they won't let you in. It will soon be over now. And what will she say," she added, turning to Stephen and raising her voice, "what will she say when she asks for her husband and he is incapable of coming to her side?"

But Stephen was far beyond reacting to any twittings.

"Oh, but he will be—won't you, Stephen," said Catherine. "You're going to be so happy, you and Virginia—so, so happy, and forget all about this—"

And she ran over to him, and stooped down and kissed him. But Stephen only moaned.

"He ought to go to bed and have a doctor," Catherine said, looking round at Mrs. Colquhoun.

"He isn't having the baby," was Mrs. Colquhoun's reply.

"No—but mental agony is worse than physical," said Catherine.

"Not if it's babies," said Mrs. Colquhoun firmly.

What a strange night that was. What a night of mixed emotions—great fear, deep pity, immense surprise; and what a clearing up in Catherine's mind of nonsense, of her own private follies. None of the three in that room had yet in their lives been up against this kind of reality, this stark, ruthless reality, before. There were hours and hours to think in, hours and hours to feel in. A few yards away lay Virginia, hanging between life and death. From her room came no moans. An august silence enveloped it, as of issues too great and solemn being settled within for any crying out. It was the slowest, most difficult of births. She herself was far away, profoundly unconcerned, wrapped in the mercifulness of unconsciousness; but how long could even the youngest, strongest body stand this awful strain on it?

The two women away in that spare-room on the other side of the house didn't dare let themselves even look at this question. It lay cold and heavy on the heart of each, and they turned away their mind's eyes and busied themselves as best they could—Catherine with stroking Stephen and murmuring words of comfort in his ear, of which he took no notice, and Mrs. Colquhoun with making tea.

All night long poor Mrs. Colquhoun, herself within an ace of collapse, made fresh tea at short intervals, finding in the rattle of the cups and saucers a way of drowning some at least of her unhappy son's nerve-racking moans and her own thoughts. She couldn't and wouldn't contemplate the possibility of anything happening to Virginia; she insisted to herself that in that quarter all was well. Two doctors and a skilled nurse, two doctors and a skilled nurse, she kept on repeating in her mind, her shaking hands upsetting the cups. A difficult birth, of course, and a long one, but that was nothing unusual with the first child. Nonsense, nonsense, to let even the edge of an imagining of possible disaster slide into one's mind. One had quite enough to think of without that, with Stephen lying there disgracing himself and her, denying in effect his God, and

certainly abandoning his manhood—for Virginia's screams
before the anæsthetist arrived, those awful, awful screams
coming from his gentle wife, had sent the unhappy Stephen,
after two hours of having to listen to them, out of his mind. He
had killed her, he was her murderer, he had killed her, killed
her with his love. . . .

"Nonsense," his mother had said in her most matter-of-fact
way, on his shouting out things like this for every one to
hear—really excessively shocking things when one remembered all the young maids in the house; and then with
trembling hands she had led him into this distant room, and
he had thrown himself down where he had ever since been
lying, and had said no word more, but only ceaselessly
moaned.

And Mrs. Colquhoun, who had never in her life overwhelmingly loved, and never till that day known she possessed any
nerves, looked on at first helplessly, and then indignantly, and
the whole time uncomprehendingly. It was all very well, and
of course a husband was anxious on such occasions, and
should and was expected to show feeling, but within decent
limits. These limits were not decent. Anything but. What
would the parish say if it saw him? What did the servants say,
who could hear him?

She put aspirin into his heedless mouth, and asked him
severely if he had forgotten God. She tried to twit him into
manliness and priestliness. She actually shook him once,
believing that counter-shocks were good for the nerves. Useless, all useless; and by the time Catherine arrived she herself
was very nearly done for.

But tea, the domesticities—natural, reassuring little
activities—were, she found, the only real props. Not prayer.
Strange, not once did she wish to pray. If Stephen had prayed
it would have been a good thing, but it wouldn't have been a
good thing for her to pray. No emotions, if you please, she
admonished herself several times aloud—it froze Catherine's
blood to hear her—duty, duty, duty; the making of tea to
sustain the body, to compose the nerves by the routine of
it—this was the real anchor. She would gladly have gone
round with a duster, dusting the ornaments that collect in
spare-rooms, but to dust at night seemed too highly unnatural
to offer a hope of forgetfulness.

So she kept on ringing the bell for fresh hot water and more
cups, and just the sight of the housemaid in her cap and apron

at the door—she wasn't allowed inside, because of Stephen—seemed to hold Mrs. Colquhoun down to sanity. There were other things in the world besides suffering; there were next mornings, and the precious routine of life with its baths and breakfasts and orders to the cook—how she longed for that, how she longed to be back in her safe shell again, with everything normal about her, and Stephen in his senses, and the sickening load of fear on her heart lifted away and forgotten.

A cup was chipped. She held it to the light. Kate, of course, who really was most careless with china. At that rate Virginia would soon have none left.

She rang the bell and sent the housemaid for Kate, and when she came, her cap a little crooked and her hair a little wispy, Mrs. Colquhoun took the cup out into the passage to her and scolded her soundly, and it did them both good, and Kate was so much restored by this breath of normality that she was able to ask in a whisper how the master was, and Mrs. Colquhoun, dropping unconsciously into the very language of the occasion, replied that he was doing nicely.

And indeed Stephen's moans seemed less since Catherine had taken his head on her lap and was stroking and patting him. She stroked and patted without stopping, and every now and then bent down and murmured words of encouragement in his ear, or else, when she found no words because her own heart was so full of fear, simply bent down and kissed him. Did he hear? Did he feel? She couldn't tell; but she thought his moans grew quieter, and that he seemed dimly conscious of comfort when her hand passed softly down his sunken face.

"You'll wear yourself out," said Mrs. Colquhoun, pursing her lips to keep them from quivering.

"It comforts me," said Catherine.

"You'd much better have another cup of tea."

"How passionately he loves her. I didn't quite realise—"

"Loving passionately seems to get people into nice messes," said Mrs. Colquhoun grimly.

"I suppose one really oughtn't to love too much," said Catherine.

"I consider Stephen preached himself into it. That course of sermons last Lent—you remember? I thought at the time that he was almost too eloquent. It sometimes very nearly wasn't quite what one wishes a parish to hear. The love he talked about—well, he started with St. John's ideas, but soon got away from them into something else. People, especially the servants, listened open-mouthed. They wouldn't have done that if there hadn't been something else in it besides the Bible. And you know, Catherine, one can talk oneself into anything, and in my opinion that is what Stephen did. And he came to think so much and so often of that side of life that he forgot moderation, and here he is. This is his punishment, and my disgrace."

"No, no," said Catherine soothingly.

"It is—it is." And Mrs. Colquhoun, who had kept up so courageously till then, bowed her head over the tea-tray and wept.

It would be useless, Catherine felt, to argue with poor Mrs. Colquhoun about love, so gently laying Stephen's head on a cushion she went over to her and sat down beside her and put her arm round her and began to stroke her too, and murmur soothing words.

How strange it was, this night of fear spent stroking the Colquhouns. That queer imp that sits in a detached corner of one's mind refusing to be serious just when it most should be, actually forced her at this moment, when hope was at its faintest, to laugh inside herself at the odd turn her relationship with Stephen and his mother had taken. The collapsed Colquhouns; the towers of strength laid low; and she, the disapproved of, the sinner as Stephen thought, and perhaps he had told his mother and she thought it too, being their only support and comforter. The collapsed Colquhouns. It really was funny—very funny—very fun . . .

Why, what was this? She too crying?

Horrified she jumped up, and hurried across to the window and flung it open as far as it would go, and stood at it with her face to the damp night air and struggled with herself, squeezing back those ill-timed tears; and as she stood there the sluggish air suddenly became a draught, and turning quickly she found the door had been opened, and a strange man was framed in it, with Kate in the background ushering him in.

One of the doctors. She flew to him. He was very red, with drops of sweat on his forehead.

"Where's that husband?" he asked, looking round the room and speaking cheerfully, though his eyes were serious. "Oh—I see. Still no good to us. I never saw such a fellow. He might be having the baby himself. Well, his mother, then. Oh dear—

what's this? Tears? Come, come," he said, laying his hand on Mrs. Colquhoun's shoulder very kindly, and looking at Catherine. "Are you the other grandmother?" he asked, smiling.

"Grandmother?"

"A whacking boy. The biggest I've brought into the world for a long time."

<h1 style="text-align:center">XVIII</h1>

When Virginia recovered consciousness she lay for some time with her eyes shut, frowning. She seemed to have come back from somewhere very far away, and it had been difficult, so difficult to come back at all, and she was tired out with the effort. Where had she been? She lay trying to remember, her arms straight down by her side, the palms of her hands upturned as if some one had flung them there like that and she had been too indifferent to move them. Her hair, in two thick plaits, was neatly arranged, a plait drawn down over each shoulder, and her bed was spotless and tidy.

She opened her heavy eyes presently, and saw her mother sitting by the pillow.

Her mother. She shut her eyes again and thought this over; but it tired her to think, and she didn't bother much with it. Her mother was sitting quite still, holding a plait of some one's dark hair against her lips and kissing it. There was another person in the room, moving about without any noise, dressed in white. Who?

A glimmer of recollection stole into Virginia's mind. Without bothering to open her eyes—the exertion of doing that was so enormous—she managed to murmur, "Have I—had my baby?" And her mother took her hand and kissed it and told her she had, and that it was a boy. A beautiful boy, her mother said.

She thought this over too, frowning with the effort. A beautiful boy. That was the opposite of a beautiful girl. And the nurse—of course, that white thing was the nurse—came and held a cup to her mouth and made her drink something.

LOVE

Then she lay quiet again, with her eyes shut. She had had her baby. A beautiful boy. The news in no way stirred her; it tired her.

Presently there came another flicker of recollection. Stephen. That was her husband. Where was he?

With an effort she opened her eyes and looked languidly at her mother. How hard it was to pronounce that St. Such an exertion. But she managed it, and got out, "Stephen—?"

Her mother, kissing her hand again, said he had a little cold, and was staying in bed.

Stephen had a little cold, and was staying in bed. This news in no way stirred her either. She lay quite apathetic, her arms straight by her side, her hands palm upwards on the counterpane. Stephen; the baby; her mother; a profound indifference to them all filled her mind, still dark with the shadows of that great dim place she had clambered out of, clambered and clambered till her body was bruised and sore from head to foot, and so dead tired—so dead, dead tired.

Some one else came into the room. A man. Perhaps a doctor, for he took up her hand and held it in his for a while, and then said something to the nurse, who came and raised her head and gave her another drink—rather like what she remembered brandy used to be.

Brandy in bed. Wasn't that—what was the word?—yes, queer. Wasn't that queer, to drink brandy in bed.

But it didn't matter. Nothing mattered. It was nice when nothing mattered. So peaceful and quiet; so, so peaceful and quiet. Like floating on one's back in calm water on a summer afternoon, looking up at the blue sky, and every now and then letting one's head sink a little—just a little, so that the cool water rippled over one's ears; or letting it sink a little more—just a little more, so that the cool water rippled over one's face; and one sank and sank; gently deeper; gently deeper; till at last there was nothing but sleep.

❧ XIX ❧

When Christopher arrived in Hertford Street from Scotland a week later, Mrs. Mitcham met him in the hall of the flat. He knew nothing of what had happened at Chickover. Catherine had written him a brief scribble the day she left, telling him she was going to Virginia, and as he hadn't had a word since, and found his holiday, which he anyhow hated, completely intolerable directly she cut him off from her by silence, he decided it was no longer to be endured; and flinging his things together, and remarking to Lewes that he was fed up, he started for London, getting there hard on the heels of a telegram he had sent Mrs. Mitcham.

She came into the hall when she heard his latchkey in the door. Her face looked longer than ever, and her clothes seemed blacker.

"Oh, sir," she began at once, taking his coat from him, "isn't it dreadful."

"What is?" asked Christopher, twisting round and looking at her, quick fear in his heart.

"Miss Virginia—"

He breathed again. For a terrible moment he had thought—

"What has *she* been doing?" he asked, suddenly indifferent, for the having of babies hadn't entered his consciousness as anything dangerous; if it were, the whole place wouldn't be littered with them.

Mrs. Mitcham stared at him out of red-rimmed eyes.

"Doing, sir?" she repeated, stung by the careless way he spoke; and for the first and last time in her life sarcastic, she said with dignified rebuke, "Only dying, sir."

It was his turn to stare, his eyes very wide open, while dismay, as all that this dying meant became clear to him, stole into them. "Dying? That girl? Do you mean—"

"Dead, sir," said Mrs. Mitcham, her head well up, her gaze, full of rebuke and dignity, on his.

Too late to go down that night. No trains any more that

night. But there was the motor-bicycle. Catherine—Catherine in grief—he must get to her somehow. . . .

And once again Christopher rushed westwards to Catherine. Through the night he rushed in what seemed great jerks of speed interrupted by things going wrong, every conceivable thing going wrong, as if all hell and all its devils were in league to trip him up and force him each few miles to stand aside and look on impotently while the hours, not he, flew past.

She hadn't sent for him. She was suffering and away, and hadn't sent for him. But he knew why. It was because she couldn't bear, after all the things he had said about Virginia, to smite him with the fact of her death. Or else she herself was so violently hit that she had been stunned into that strange state people got into when death was about, and thought no longer of what was left, of all the warmth and happiness life still went on being full of, but only of what was gone.

But whatever she was feeling or not able to feel, she was his, his wife, to help and comfort; and if she was so much numbed that help and comfort couldn't reach her, he would wait by her side till she woke up again. What could it be like down there, he asked himself as the black trees and hedges streamed past him, what could it possibly be like for Catherine, shut up in that unhappy house, with young Virginia dead? That girl dead. Younger by years than himself. And her husband. . . . "Oh, Lord—my Catherine," he thought, tearing along faster and faster, "I must get her out of it—get her home—love her back to life—"

Pictures of her flashed vivid in his mind, lovely little pictures, such as had haunted him with increasing frequency the longer his holiday without her dragged on; and he saw her in them with the eye of starved passion, a most lovely little Catherine, far, far prettier than she had ever been in her prettiest days—so sweet with her soft white skin, so sweet with her soft dark hair, so sweet with her soft grey eyes, and her face lit up with love—love all and only for him. And he who had thought, those last days before Scotland, that there was too much love about! He all but swerved into a ditch when he remembered this piece of incredible folly. Well, he knew now what life was like for him away from her: it was like being lost in the frozen dark.

He got to Chickover about five in the morning, just as the grey light was beginning to creep among the trees. He couldn't go and rouse that sad house so early, so he stopped in the village and managed, after much difficulty, to induce the inn to open and let him in, and give him water and a towel and promise him tea when the hour should have become more decent; and then he lay down on the horsehair sofa in the parlour and tried to sleep.

But how sleep, when he was at last so near Catherine? Just the thought of seeing her again, of looking into her eyes after their four weeks' separation, was enough to banish sleep; and then there was the anxiety about her, the knowledge that she must be crushed with sorrow, the effort to imagine life there with that poor devil of a husband. . . .

At half-past seven he began to urge on breakfast, ringing the bell and going out into the beer-smelling passage and calling. With all his efforts, however, he couldn't get anything even started till after eight, when a sleepy girl came downstairs and put a dirty cloth on the table and a knife or two.

He went out into the road and walked up and down while the table was being laid. He wouldn't question any one there, though they all of course could have told him about Virginia's death and what was happening at the house. And they, supposing he was a stranger—as indeed he was and hoped for ever to be in regard to Chickover—did not of themselves begin to talk.

He knew nothing; neither when she died, nor when she was buried. Perhaps she hadn't been buried yet, and in that case he wouldn't be able to get Catherine away, as he had hoped, that very day. He found himself trying not to think of Virginia— he owed her so many apologies! But only because she was dead. Who could have supposed she would die, and put him, by doing that, in the wrong? One had to talk as one felt at the moment, and it wasn't possible to shape one's remarks with an eye to the possibility of their subject dying. Yet Christopher was very sorry, and also sore. He felt he had been a brute, but he also felt she had taken an unfair advantage of him.

He switched his thoughts off her as much as he could. Poor little thing. And such fine weather, too—such a good day to be alive on; for by this time the September sun was flooding Virginia's village, and the dew-drenched asters in the cottage gardens were glittering in the light. Poor little thing. And poor devil of a husband. How well he could understand *his* misery. God, if anything were to happen to Catherine!

He drank some tepid tea and ate some unpleasant bread and butter—Stephen evidently hadn't succeeded in making the village innkeeper good, anyhow—and then, feeling extraordinarily agitated, a mixture of palpitating love and excitement and reluctance and fear, and all of it shot with distress because of Virginia, he started off through the park, cutting across the grass, going round along the back of the kitchen-garden wall to the lodge gates, and walking up the avenue like any other respectful sympathetic early caller; and when he turned the bend and got to the point where one first saw the house he gave a great sigh of thankfulness, for the blinds were up. The poor little thing's funeral was over, then, and at least he wasn't going to tumble, as he had secretly feared, into the middle of that.

But if it was over, why hadn't Catherine sent for him? Or come home? Or at least written? He remembered, however, that she supposed he was in Scotland, and of course she would have written to him there; and, consoled, he went on up the avenue whose very trees seemed sad, with their yellowing leaves slowly fluttering to the ground at every little puff of wind.

The front door was open, and the drawing-room door on the other side of the hall was open too, so that while he stood waiting after ringing the bell he could see right through to the sunny terrace and garden. The house was very silent. He could hear no sounds at all, except somewhere, away round behind the stables, the quacking of a distant duck. Wasn't anybody having breakfast? Were they still asleep? If Catherine were still asleep he could go up to her—not like the last time when he came to this place to fetch her, and had to wait in the drawing-room, a stranger still, a suppliant without any rights.

Kate the parlour-maid appeared. She knew of course, directly she saw him, that this was the young gentleman Mrs. Cumfrit had married—there had been talk enough about that at the time in the servants' hall—and the ghost of a smile lifted the solemnity of her face, for an ordinary, healthy young gentleman was refreshing to eyes that for the last week had witnessed only woe.

"The ladies are not down yet, sir," she said in a subdued voice, showing him, or rather trying to show him, for he wouldn't go, into the drawing-room.

"The ladies?" repeated Christopher, not subduing his voice, and the house, for so many days hushed, quivered into life again at the vigour of it.

"Mr. Colquhoun's mother is staying here, sir," said Kate, dropping her voice to a whisper so as to damp him down to the proper key of quiet. "Mr. Colquhoun is still very ill, but the doctor thinks he'll be quite himself again when he is able to notice the baby. If you'll wait in here, sir," she continued, making another attempt to get him into the drawing-room, "I'll go and tell the ladies."

"I'm not going to wait anywhere," said Christopher. "I'm going up to my wife. Show me the way."

Yes, it was refreshing to see an alive gentleman again, and a nice change from the poor master; though the master, of course, was behaving in quite the proper way, taking his loss as a true widower should, and taking it so hard that he had to have a doctor and be kept in bed. The whole village was proud of him; yet for all that it was pleasant to hear a healthy gentleman's voice again, talking loud and masterfully, and Kate, pleased to have to obey, went up the stairs almost with her ordinary brisk tread, instead of the tiptoes she had got into the habit of.

Christopher followed, his heart beating loud. She led him down a broad passage to what appeared to be the furthermost end of the house, and as they proceeded along it a noise he had begun to hear when he turned the corner from the landing got bigger and bigger, seeming to swell at him till at last it was prodigious.

The baby. Crying. He hoped repenting of the damage it had already found time to do in its brief existence. But he had no thoughts to spare for babies at that moment, and when Kate stopped at the very door the cries were coming out of, he waved her on impatiently.

"Good God," he said, "you don't suppose I want to see the baby?"

She only smiled at him and knocked at the door. "It's a beautiful baby," she said, with that odd look of satisfied pride and satisfied hunger that women, he had noticed, when they get near very small babies seem to have.

"Hang the baby—take me to my wife," he commanded.

"She's here, sir," Kate answered, opening the door on some one's calling out, above the noise, that she was to come in.

It was Mrs. Colquhoun's voice. He recognised it, and drew back quickly.

No—he'd be hanged if he'd go in there and meet Catherine

in a nursery, with the nurse and the baby and Mrs. Colquhoun all looking on. But he didn't draw back so quickly that he hadn't caught a glimpse of the room, and seen a bath on two chairs in front of a bright fire, and three women bending over it, one in white and two in black, and all of them talking at once to that which was in the bath, while its cries rose ever louder and more piercing.

Absorbed, the women were; absorbed to the exclusion of every wish, grief, longing, or other love, he thought, swift hot jealousy flashing into his heart. He felt Catherine ought somehow to have known he was there, been at once conscious of him the minute he set foot in the house. He would have been conscious of her all right the very instant she got under the same roof; of that he was absolutely certain. Instead of that, there was that absorbed back, just as though she had never married, never passionately loved—every bit as absorbed as the other one's, as Mrs. Colquhoun's, who was an old woman with no love left in her life except what she could wring out of some baby. And whether it was because they were both in the same attitude and clothes he couldn't tell, but his impression had been the same of them both—a quick impression, before he had time to think, of a black cluster of grizzled women.

Grizzled? What an extraordinarily horrid word, he thought, to come into his mind. How had it got there?

"Shut that door!" called out Mrs. Colquhoun's voice above the baby's cries. "Don't you see you are making a draught?"

Kate looked round hesitatingly at Christopher.

"Come in and shut that door!" called out Mrs. Colquhoun still louder.

Kate went in, shutting it behind her, and Christopher waited, standing up stiff against the wall.

He hadn't expected this. No, it was the last thing he had expected. And now when Catherine came to him Kate would be there too, following on her heels; and was it to be a handshake, then, or a perfunctory marital kiss in the presence of a servant, their sacred, blessed moment of reunion?

But it was not to be quite like that, for though somebody came out and Kate came with her, somebody small who exclaimed, "Oh Chris—!" and who seemed to think she was Catherine, she wasn't Catherine, no, no—she wasn't and couldn't be. What came out was a ghost, a pale little grizzled ghost, which held out its hands and made as if to lift up its face to be kissed; and when he didn't kiss it, when he only drew back and stared at it, drew back at once itself and stood looking at him without a word.

❧ XX ☙

They stood looking at each other. Kate went away down the passage. Emptiness was round them, pierced by the baby's cries through the shut door of the nursery. Catherine didn't shrink at all, and let Christopher look at her as much as he liked, for she had done with everything now except truth.

"Catherine—" he began, in the afraid and bewildered voice of a child fumbling in the dark.

"Yes, Chris?"

She made no attempt to go close to him, he made no attempt to go close to her; and it was strange to Catherine, who couldn't continually as yet remember the difference in herself, to be alone with Christopher after separation, and not instantly be gathered to his heart.

But his face made her remember; in it she could see her own as clearly as if she were in front of a glass.

"I had no idea—no idea—" he stammered.

"That I could look like this?"

"That you've suffered so horribly, that you loved her so terribly—"

And he knew he ought to take her in his arms and comfort her, and he couldn't, because this simply wasn't Catherine.

"But it isn't that only," she said—and hesitated for an instant.

For an instant her heart failed her. Why tell him? After all, all she had done was for love of him; for a greedy, clutching love it was true, made up chiefly of vanity and possessiveness and fear, but still love. Why not forget the whole thing, and let him think she had grown old in a week from grief?

Creditable and touching explanation. And so nearly true, too, for if passion had begun the ruin, grief had completed it, and the night and day of that birth and death, of the agony of Stephen and her own long-drawn-out torment, had put the finishing touches of age beyond her age on a face and hair left defenceless to lines and greyness without Maria Rome's massage and careful dyes, and anyhow twice as worn and grey as they had been before she began the exhausting processes of Dr. Sanguesa.

But she put this aside. She had had enough of nearly truth and the wretched business of taking him in. How could she go on doing him such wrongs? She had done him the greatest of wrongs marrying him, of that she was certain, but at least she would leave off making fools of them both. Rotten, rotten way of living. Let him see her as she was; and if his love—how natural that would be at his age, how inevitable—came to an end, she would set him free.

For in those remarkable hours that followed Virginia's death, when it seemed to Catherine as if she had suddenly opened the door out of a dark passage and gone into a great light room, she saw for the first time quite plainly; and what she saw in that strange new clearness, that merciless, yet somehow curiously comforting, clearness, was that love has to learn to let go, that love if it is real always does let go, makes no claims, sets free, is content to love without being loved—and that nothing was worth while, nothing at all in the tiny moment called life except being good. Simply being good. And though people might argue as to what precisely being good meant, they knew in their hearts just as she knew in her heart; and though the young might laugh at this conviction as so much sodden sentiment, they would, each one of them who was worth anything, end by thinking exactly that. Impossible to live as she had lived the last week close up to death and not see this. For four extraordinary days she had sat in its very presence, watching by the side of its peace. She knew now. Life was a flicker; the briefest thing, blown out before one was able to turn round. There was no time in it, no time in the infinitely precious instant, for anything except just goodness.

So she said, intent on simple truth, "I did deeply love Virginia, and I have suffered, but I looked very nearly like this before."

And Christopher, who hadn't lived these days close up to death, and hadn't seen and recognised what she so clearly did, and wasn't feeling any of this, was shocked out of his bewilderment by such blasphemy, and took a quick, almost menacing step forward, as if to silence the ghost daring to profane his lovely memory.

"You didn't look like it—you didn't!" he cried. "You were my Catherine. You weren't this—this—"

He stopped, and stared close into her face. "What has become of you?" he asked, bewildered again, a dreadful sense of loss cold on his heart. "Oh, Catherine—what have you done to yourself?"

"Why, that's just it," she said, the faintest shadow of a smile trembling a moment in her eyes. "I haven't done anything to myself."

"But your hair—your lovely hair—"

He made agonised motions with his hands.

"It's all gone grey because of—of what you've been through, you poor, poor little thing—"

And again he knew he ought to take her in his arms and comfort her, and again he couldn't.

"No, it wasn't that made it go grey," she said. "It was grey before, only I used to have it dyed."

He stared at her, entirely bewildered. Catherine looking like this, and saying these things. Why did she say them? Why was she so anxious to make out that all this had nothing to do with Virginia's death? Was it some strange idea of sparing him the pain of being sorry for her? Or was she so terribly smitten that she was no longer accountable for what she said? If this was it, then all the more closely should he fold her to his heart and shield and comfort her, and what a damned scoundrel he was not to. But he couldn't. Not yet. Not that minute. Perhaps presently, when he had got more used. . . .

"You dyed it?" he repeated stupidly.

"Yes. Or rather Maria Rome did."

"Maria Rome?"

"Oh, what does it matter. It makes me sick to think of that old nonsense. She's a place in London where they do up women who've begun not to keep. She did me up wonderfully, and at first it very nearly looked real. But it was such a business, and I was so frightened always, living like that on the brink of its not being a success, and you suddenly seeing me. I'm sick, sick just remembering it—now."

And she laid her hand on his arm, looking up at him with Catherine's eyes, Catherine's beautiful, fatigued eyes.

They were the same—beautiful as he had always known them, and fatigued as he had always known them; but how strange to see them in that little yellow face. Her eyes; all that was left of his Catherine. Yes, and the voice, the same gentle voice, except that it had a new note of—was it sensibleness? Sensibleness! Catherine sensible? She had been everything in the world but that—obstinate, weak, unaccountable, irrelevant, determined, impulsive, clinging, passionate, adorable, his own sweet love, but never sensible.

"Doesn't it seem too incredibly little and mean, that sort of lying, any sort of lying, when *this* has happened," she said, her hand still on his arm, her eyes very earnestly looking up into his. "So extraordinarily not worth while. And you mustn't think I'm out of my mind from shock, Chris," she went on, for it was plain from his expression that that was what he did think, "because I'm not. On the contrary—for the first time I'm in it."

And as he stared at her, and thought that if this was what she was like when she was in her mind then how much better and happier for them both if she had stayed out of it, the baby on the other side of the door was taken out of its bath, and that which had been cries became yells.

"For God's sake let's go somewhere where there isn't this infernal squalling," exclaimed Christopher, with a movement so sudden and exasperated that it shook her hand off his arm.

"Yes, let us," she said, moving away down the passage ahead of him; and more plainly than ever, when they got to the big windows on the stairs and she turned the bend of them before him, he could see how yellow she was, and what a quantity of grey, giving it that terrible grizzled look, there was in her hair.

Yellow; grizzled; what had she done, what had they done to her, to ruin her like this, to take his Catherine from him and give him this instead? It was awful. He was robbed. His world of happiness was smashing to bits. And he felt such a brute, the lowest of low brutes, not to be able to love her the same as before, now when she so much must need love, when she had been having what he could well imagine was a simply hellish time.

Virginia again, he thought, with a bitterness that shocked him himself. That girl, even in death spoiling things. For even if it was true what Catherine insisted on telling him about dyes and doings-up, she never would have thought it necessary to tell him, to make a clean breast, if it hadn't been for Virginia's death. No; if it hadn't been for that she would have gone on as before, doing whatever it was she did to herself, the results of which anyhow were that he and she were happy. God, how he hated clean breasts, and the turning over of some imaginary new leaf. Whenever anything happened out of the ordinary, anything that pulled women up short and made them do what they called think, they started wrecking—wrecking everything for themselves and for the people who had been loving them happily and contentedly, by their urge for the two arch-destroyers of love, those damned clean breasts and those even more damned new leaves.

He followed her like an angry, frightened child. How could he know what she knew? How could he see what she saw? He was where he had always been, while she had gone on definitely into something else. And there were no words she could have explained in. If she had tried, all she could have found to say, with perplexed brows, would have been, "But I *know*."

She took him into the garden. They passed her bedroom door on the way, and he knew it was hers for it was half open, and the room hadn't been done yet, and the little slippers he had kissed a hundred times were lying kicked off on the carpet, the slippers that had belonged to the real Catherine— or rather, as this one was now insisting, to the artificial Catherine, but anyhow to his Catherine.

For a moment he was afraid she would take him in there. Ice seemed to slide down his spine at the thought. But she walked past it as if it had nothing to do with either of them, and then he was offended.

Out in the garden it was easier to breathe. He couldn't, in that public place, with the chance of a gardener appearing at any moment, take her in his arms, so he didn't feel quite such a scoundrel for not doing it; and walking by her side and not looking at her, but just listening to her voice, he felt less lost; for the voice was the voice of Catherine, and as long as he didn't look at her he could believe she was still there. It was like, in the night, hearing the blessed reassurance of one's mother talking, when one was little, and frightened, and alone.

She took him through the garden and out by the wicket-gate into the park, where rabbits were scuttling across the dewy grass, leaving dark ribbons along its silver, and the bracken, webbed with morning gossamer, was already turning brown. And all the way she talked, and all the way he listened in silence, his eyes fixed straight in front of him.

She told him everything, from that moment of their honeymoon when, from loving, she had fallen in love, and instantly began to be terrified of looking old, and her desperate, grotesque efforts to stay young for him, and his heart, as he heard her voice talking of that time, went to wax within him, and he had to gaze very steadily at the view ahead lest, turning to throw his arms round Catherine, his sweetheart, his angel love, he should see she wasn't there, but only a ghost was there with her voice and eyes, and then he mightn't be able to help bursting out crying.

"Is this far enough away from the poor baby?" she asked, stopping at an oak-tree, whose huge exposed roots were worn with the numbers of times she had sat on them in past years during the long, undisturbed summer afternoons of her placid first marriage. "You know," she added, sitting down on the gnarled roots, "he's the most beautiful little baby, and is going to comfort all poor Stephen's despair."

"But he isn't going to comfort mine," said Christopher, standing with his eyes fixed on the distant view.

She was silent. Then she said, "Is it as bad as that, Chris?"

"No, no," he said quickly, his back to her, "I didn't mean that. You'll get well again, and then we'll—"

"I don't see how I can get well if I'm not ill," she said gently.

"Why do you want to take hope from me?" he answered.

"I only don't want any more lies. I shan't look different again from what I do now. I shan't go back, I mean, to what I was. But perhaps presently—when you've had time to get over—"

She hesitated, and then went on humbly—for she was vividly conscious of the wrong she had done him, vividly aware that she ought to have saved him from himself whatever the pressure had been that was brought to bear on her, however great his misery was at the moment—"Presently I thought perhaps I might somehow make up for what I've done. I thought perhaps I might somehow comfort you—"

She hesitated again. "I don't quite know how, though," she said, her voice more and more humble, "but I'd try." And then she said, almost in a whisper, "That is, if you will let me."

"Let you!" he exclaimed, stabbed by her humbleness.

"Yes. And if it's no good, Chris, and you'd rather not, then of course I'll—let you go."

He turned round quickly. "What, in God's name, do you mean by that?" he asked.

"Set you free," said Catherine, doing her best to look up at him unflinchingly.

He stared at her. "How?" he asked. "I don't understand. In what way, set me free?"

"Well, there's only one way, isn't there—one way really. I meant, divorce you."

He stood staring down at her. Catherine talking of divorcing him. *Catherine.*

"How can you at your age be tied up, go on being married, to some one like me?" she asked. "It isn't even decent. And besides—in that flat together—you might think I—I expected—"

She broke off with a gesture of helplessness, while he still stared at her.

"I haven't an idea how we could manage all the—the details," she said, bowing her head, for she felt she couldn't endure his stare. "It would *hurt* so," she finished in a whisper.

"And so you think the solution is to divorce me," said Christopher.

"What else is there to do? You've only got to look at me—"

"Divorce me," he said, "when we have loved each other so?"

And suddenly he began to shout at her, stamping his foot, while hot tears rushed into his eyes. "Oh you little *fool,* you little *fool!"* he shouted. "You've always been such a little *fool—"*

"But *look* at me," she said desperately, throwing back her head and flinging out her arms.

"Oh, for God's sake, don't go on like this!" he cried, dropping on the ground beside her and burying his face in her lap. Divorce him . . . condemn him again to that awful loneliness . . . where he couldn't hear her voice. . . .

"Why couldn't you go on letting me believe?" he said, his arms tightly clutching her knees while he kept his face buried. "Why couldn't you? As though I cared what you did before! It made us happy, anyhow, and I wish to God you'd go on doing it. But you've only got to get away from this infernal place to be as you used to be, and you didn't always go to that woman, and I fell in love with you just as you were, and why shouldn't I love you just as you are?"

"Because I'm old, and you're not. Because I've grown old since we married. Because I was too old to be married to some one so young. And you know I'm old. You see it now. You see it so plainly that you can't bear to look at me."

"Oh, my God—the stuff, the stuff. I'm your husband, and I'm going to take care of you. Yes, I am, Catherine—for ever and ever. Useless to argue. I can't live without the sound of your voice. I can't. And how can you live without me? You couldn't. You're the most pitiful little thing—"

"I'm not. I'm quite sensible. I haven't been, but I am now."

"Oh, damn being sensible! Be what you were before. Good God, Catherine," he went on, hiding his face, clutching her knees, "do you think a man wants his wife to scrub herself with yellow soap as if she were the kitchen table, and then come all shiny to him and say, 'See, I'm the Truth'? And she isn't the truth. She's no more the truth shiny than powdered— she's only appearance, anyway, she's only a symbol—the symbol of the spirit in her which is what one is really loving the whole time—"

"What has happened is much more than that," she interrupted.

"Oh yes, yes—I know. Death. You're going to tell me that all this sort of thing seems rot to you now that you've been with death—"

"So it does. And I've finished with it."

"Oh Lord—women," he groaned, burying his face deeper, as if he could hide from his unhappiness. "Do you suppose I haven't been with death too, and seen it dozens of times? What do you think I was doing in the War? But women can't take the simplest things naturally—and they can't take the natural things simply, either. What can be more simple and natural than death? *I* didn't throw away my silk handkerchiefs and leave off shaving because my friends died—"

"Chris," she interrupted again, "you simply don't understand. You don't—know."

"I do—I know and understand everything. Why should the ones who didn't die behave as though they had? Why should you send our happy life together to blazes because Virginia is dead? Isn't that all the more reason for us who're still alive to stick firmer than ever to each other? And instead you talk of divorce. Divorce? Because there's been one tragedy there's to be another? Catherine, don't you, won't you, *can't* you see?"

And he lifted his head from her lap and looked at her, tears of anger, and fear, and love driven back on itself burning in his eyes; and he caught her crying.

How long had she been crying? Her face was pitiful, all wet with tears, in its frame of grizzled hair. How long had she been crying quietly up there, while he was raving, and she at intervals said sensible calm things?

At the sight of her wet face the anger and the fear died out of him, and only love was left. She couldn't do without him. She was a poor, broken-up little thing, for all her big words about divorce and setting free. She was his wife, who couldn't do without him—a poor, broken-up little thing. . . .

"I've cried so much," she said, quickly wiping her eyes, "that I believe I've got into the habit of it. I'm ashamed. I hate whimpering. But—Virginia—"

He got up on to his knees, and at last put his arms round her. "Oh my Catherine," he murmured, drawing her head on to his breast and holding it there. "Oh my Catherine—"

An immense desire for self-sacrifice, to fling his life at her feet, rushed upon Christopher, a passion of longing to give, give everything and ask nothing in return, to protect, to keep all that could hurt her away from her for ever.

"Don't cry," he whispered. "Don't cry. It's going to be all right. We're going to be happy. And if you can't see that we are, I'll see for you till your own eyes are opened again—"

"But I do see—every time I look in the glass," she answered, instinctively understanding the feeling that was sweeping over him, and shrinking away from exploiting this that was being thrust upon her of the quick, uncounting generosity of youth. How would she be able to make it up to him? She couldn't, except by loving him with utter selflessness, and then, when he found out for himself how impossible the situation was, setting him free. It was the only thing she could do. Some day he would see himself that it was the only thing.

"Obstinate, aren't you," he murmured, holding her face close against his breast, for when he was doing that it was hidden, and it hurt him too desperately as yet to look at it, it made him too desperately want to cry himself. Of course presently . . . when he had got more used. . . .

"You'll have to grow out of that," he went on, "because we can't both be obstinate, and have deadlocks."

"No, no—we won't have deadlocks," said Catherine. "We'll just—"

LOVE

She was going to say, "love each other very much," but thought that might sound like making a claim, and stopped.

They were silent for a while, and so motionless that the rabbits began to think they weren't there after all, and came lolloping up quite close.

Then he said very gently, "I'm going to take care of you, Catherine."

And she said, her voice trembling a little, "Are you, Chris? I was thinking that that's what I'm going to do to you."

"All right. We'll do it to each other, then."

And they both tried to laugh, but it was a shaky, uncertain laughter, for they were both afraid.

THE END

✑ **Afterword** ✑

When Michael Frere came to see Elizabeth about her autobiography *All the Dogs of My Life* she found him "such a boring little man. But it is because we are all growing old, and the bones of our inadequate minds come through the flesh that hid them." She hadn't always found him boring, and *Love,* one of her best novels, is largely based on their romance. In the novel Catherine is forty-seven and Christopher twenty-five. In life, when Elizabeth first met Frere in May 1920, she was fifty-four and he was twenty-four. This is important because *Love* is really a book about age. Frere's early promise was showing itself in the publishing field. He was with Heinemann, and would become managing director. The only link with Elizabeth now was her books, and she was godmother to one of his children. Their liaison had been formally dead for four years, and had been ailing since long before that.

Elizabeth heard about Frere in the first place from his mother, and was intrigued by her account of having had a child by a sporting gentleman called Colonel Reeves. Mary Frere put the baby in an orphanage and forgot about him until rumour reached her that he had fought gallantly in the Royal Flying Corps in the still recent war and was now an undergraduate at Cambridge. Did Elizabeth smell the plot for a novel? She asked Arnold Bennett to fix a meeting over lunch. He obliged, and Elizabeth and Frere became at once "tremendous friends." Elizabeth invited him to come to her Swiss chalet in August and settle her library. He accepted delightedly if, nearer the time, he felt nervous at the thought of the distinguished guests. But he endeared himself to all at once by appointing himself major-domo. *Lieber Gott* Elizabeth called him. She never allowed guests to interfere with her working hours, but she always took a walk before lunch, and *Lieber Gott* was frequently her companion. He fell head over heels in love with her.

He had come at a time when she was in need of tenderness. Her marriage to Francis Earl Russell had finally collapsed, and he was busy blackguarding her to anyone who would listen. There had always been some man in her life, and as well as the few who played significant parts, there were usually young men about whose company she enjoyed as well as pale followers who lingered on, enjoying a meagre diet of attention.

After he went back to England, Frere deluged Elizabeth with adoring letters. She was flattered and fascinated, but she had obtained freedom from the domination of men at last, and so far from needing constant companionship, she was happier, and felt far more vital alone. Or so she often said, and it was true up to a point. In London she danced with Frere and enjoyed the company of his young friends, to whom he was proud to introduce her. For her part, she discreetly pushed his career. In high spirits she began *Vera,* her final stiletto-thrust in the long battle with her husband. Frere could be a sympathetic companion, but his glooms in private made him difficult. He was never as good in reality as on paper; quite early on there were rows. Frere, who had never known mother love, wanted above everything to be emotionally dependent on Elizabeth. She used to tease him, and sometimes enjoyed putting young women in his way. The novelistic possibilities of the situation did not escape her.

Michael Frere, when he met Elizabeth, like Christopher in *Love* "didn't know much about women. Up to this he had had only highly unsatisfactory, rough and tumble, relations with them." He wrote to her like a boy for the first time in love. "I find myself pinned down by dreams, dreams of the unattainable." Those close to her remarked how young and well Elizabeth was looking. Getting rid of Francis Russell was not enough to account for it. Michael and she became lovers, in fact, in 1921 on his second visit to the chalet. In *Love* Catherine, though worldly wise, is strictly proper. But in life, by this time, Elizabeth allowed herself some latitude. Even when her marriage to Russell was breaking up she was dining in London regularly with his brother Bertrand. True to form, she was also trying to persuade him to collaborate with her in an epistolary novel. But what else went on? Whatever it was, Bertrand Russell advised her not to be indiscreet when writing to Francis. Given Russell's reputation, Frere suspected the worst, and may not have been wholly satisfied by her reassurance that the laughing philosopher "smelt like a bear garden." However tiresome his moods, Elizabeth did not want to lose Frere; whenever she told him to go, she inevitably whistled him back.

1922 was a bad year for Elizabeth. She was disappointed by some of the reviews of *The Enchanted April* although it was to prove the most popular—excepting the first—of all her novels. She suffered from depressions that she couldn't throw off. Her doctor diagnosed menopausal symptoms. If Frere wanted her to marry him she couldn't because she was still married to Russell and took precautions against his discovering any evidence that might incite him to sue her for adultery. When, for example, friends let her use their house on the Isle of Wight that Christmas, Elizabeth invited Michael to join her, but found him separate lodgings. An incident during the holiday humiliated her. A casual friendship struck up with a father and daughter in a pub led to remarks, made in all innocence by the newcomers on the assumption that Elizabeth was Frere's aunt. She put this episode into *Love.* It may well have been what sparked off this novel. There were probably other incidents of a similar nature. "But wouldn't that bore your mother dreadfully?" a pretty girl at a party says in *Love* when Christopher counters an invitation to him with: "No. You come to us."

Love is a knowing novel even though the facts of life are laid on in water colour. It was a happy idea to begin the story at *The Immortal Hour,* the musical drama which was drawing a small but enraptured audience to the Regent Theatre in the Spring of 1923. Celtic themes were in fashion just then, and Elizabeth went again and again. She made a stage door call on the leading actor, and he came to tea on a few occasions. It was all very much in keeping with the beginning of *Love,* to which, no doubt, Elizabeth and Frere went often together.

She was at pains in the description of Christopher in the novel to make him as unlike Frere as possible. We are never told much more about his background than that he has expectations from an uncle with whom he plays golf, that he shares rooms with a misogynistic friend, and works in an "office." If his background is bare, his physical appearance is detailed: great height and flame-coloured hair. Frere was dark and only a few inches taller than Elizabeth's five foot. In contrast, Elizabeth emphasises Catherine's resemblance to herself. Christopher thought that he had never heard "such a funny little coo of a voice." Elizabeth had lent that voice to other heroines. Jane Wells said she could make even German sound pretty. Swinnerton, the novelist, compared her voice to "a choir-boy with a sore throat." Her smallness is stressed. Santayana, the philosopher, on first meeting Elizabeth, the mother of grown-up children, was astonished to find that she looked like a child. Her acquaintances must have recognised her before they came to the end of *Love*'s second page. Wells had advised her that when the younger lover started to cool it was the time for the older to make the break. Had that point been reached in this affair when *Love* was being written? (*I Never Should Have Done It* was considered as a subtitle.) Two years after it was published Frere confessed that he was living with a young woman who was forcing him into marrying her. This took Elizabeth by surprise, and she was miserable about it. A year later the marriage took place. Elizabeth told Frere that she never wanted to see him again even though he said that he had been frog-marched to the ceremony. But very soon they were corresponding again. Going through drawers when she was leaving Switzerland in 1929 for a villa on the French Riviera, Elizabeth came across Frere's letters. ("Some of them very sweet. That had been a funny business. And a sweet one.") But it was still unfinished. In 1931 Francis Russell died, leaving Elizabeth free to marry again. Frere recalled her at this time, her face scarred by lifting, extremely thin, stockings wound round her legs, her face powdered white, wearing enormous hats. "Nevertheless she was still beautiful." He was full, as usual, of his own troubles, and thought he was going to die. "If he dies the light of my life goes out, and I start dying myself," she wrote in her diary. But their romance plummeted when Frere's wife turned up at a Heinemann party and made a scene in Elizabeth's presence. Elizabeth returned to France the next day and changed her will. Frere was no longer her literary executor. (His unsuitable wife ran away with a taxi driver eventually and he was expecting his divorce decree when Elizabeth met him out walking with a blonde to whom he introduced her as the girl he was about to marry. She was a daughter of Edgar Wallace, the crime writer. When Elizabeth got home she wrote in her diary: "I am so glad it is she and not I. What perfect grammar.") Her last diary entry that year was: "So ends 1932. In it, in March, I shed L.G. after nearly twelve years of him. It was high time." That was seven years after the publication of *Love*.

Love gave Elizabeth more trouble than most of her novels. For every page she wrote, she tore up six, and she was never satisfied with the inconclusive ending. She spelled out Catherine's position at the beginning of Part Two. Catherine thinks she has been ostracised by her family—really only by her preposterous son-in-law, the Reverend Stephen Colquhoun, who discovers that Catherine and Christopher took all night to return to London after a visit to his rectory. They were on Christopher's motor-bike. The bike had itself become a cause of scandal before it became a supposititious occasion of sin. Stephen found it excruciating to see his mother-in-law in the side-car, dashing round his parish, scattering his flock. But he is even more concerned to anticipate scandal and expiate sin by the speedy marriage of the errant couple. Not that the idea of a wife so much older than her husband causes him anything but disgust. His hurt is almost lethal when he hears from the pure lips of his adored child-wife (from whom he kept as much of the story as possible) that she sees no difference between her own marriage and theirs.

> "Do you not see it is terrible to marry someone young enough to be your son?" he had asked sternly—he couldn't have believed he would ever have to be stern with his own love in such a place, at such an hour.
> And she had answered: "But is it any more terrible than marrying someone young enough to be your daughter?"
> Virginia had answered that. His Virginia. In bed. In his very arms.

For so much of the novel, Stephen is the character who dictates the action and his moral collapse is an extraordinary development of the plot. Elizabeth's authorial difficulties may well have arisen from finding that she had taken aboard a heavier cargo than her delicate vessel was constructed to carry. Catherine says as much: "The stuff one filled life with! And at the faintest stirring of Death's wings, the smallest movement forward of that great figure from the dark furthermost corner of the little room called life, how instantly one's eyes were smitten open."

Agonising about wrinkles round the eyes has no place in the death chamber, but until then Catherine's predicament had agonised the reader. Part Two spells it out. Catherine enjoyed an enchanted time when bus conductors and taxi drivers called her Miss. She loved Christopher, but she was not in love with him—a very different thing. "Her vanity was fed to the point of beatitude." Her image in the glass was "radiant with the cool happiness of not being in love." But when at last she agrees to marry Christopher that Indian summer is brought to an end. She falls in love with "hopeless completeness." In doing so, she loses her beauty. Christopher "burnt up what had still been left of her youth." As Mrs. Micham, Catherine's housekeeper, said to herself: "It's them honeymoons."

It might seem that Catherine's dramatically sudden ageing is allowed to get out of hand to match the graver development of the plot. She is pictured as if she were one of Macbeth's witches when Christopher opens the nursery door and sees three "grizzled" women standing round a cot. The account of the face treatment that Catherine had undergone at the hands of a quack was taken from a description given to Elizabeth by Katherine Mansfield, her New Zealand cousin, of her own experience in Paris when she was searching for a cure for consumption. This may have been too tragic a source. If Elizabeth needed copy she had, if Frere is to be believed, her own experience to draw on.

These are questions of tone values. Elizabeth was a tragi-comedienne, and happiest when describing the human situation. It was not only with Frere she discovered that "Marriage being mainly repetition, and Christopher now being a husband, he presently began to make fewer rapturous speeches. It was quite unconscious, but as the weeks passed it became natural to love with fewer preliminary cooings—to bill, as it were, without remembering first to coo."

Terence de Vere White, London 1987